DEADLY RECIPE

Books by Randy Shamlian

Murder in the Kitchen *series*
Deadly Recipe
Deadly Essence
Deadly Pairing

For more information
visit: www.SpeakingVolumes.us

DEADLY RECIPE

Randy Shamlian

BEELINE PRESS
NAPLES, FLORIDA
2019

Deadly Recipe

ISBN 978-1-62815-990-5

"Food is theater." —James Beard

Deadly

adjective

- likely to cause death

(plus)

Recipe

noun

- a list of materials and directions for
preparing a dish or drink

—Collins Dictionary

Prologue

One foggy fall afternoon, a young girl and her thirty-year-old mother were swiftly moving along, on the fly as it were, on a rural highway in western Oregon. In a flash, their large blue sedan clipped a cow that had inexplicably wandered off from a nearby farm. The cow then catapulted fifty yards into the air, tumbled end over end a few times and landed right on top of a farmer who was in the midst of taking a break from his plowing, killing him almost instantly. The clipped cow, which was unscathed, trotted back towards a pasture with some other cows as the car blew a tire, swerved from side to side and then came to a sudden halt, causing the child to smack her head against the dashboard. Both the mother and child got out of the car in utter disbelief at what had just occurred and looked at the large dent in the front end. The mother, as she tried to call emergency services for help, went into hysterics upon seeing the farmer, whom she presumed dead. Meanwhile, the daughter was in an excited state with the scene of the flying cow repeating in her head as she looked dazedly through the rails of the wooden fence to the motionless man.

What made it doubly shocking for both the mother and daughter was that they were coming back from a birthday party for one of the daughter's second-grade schoolmates at a miniature pony ranch where they had had a barbecue, pony rides and cake and ice cream. And as the events of the day sadly turned out, the father of one of the schoolmates, an excessively large man, inhaled six hot dogs in a row. As he began to gorge on his seventh, he saw his daughter get socked in the eye by the birthday girl, who tried to take away his daughter's door gift, and he started to choke to death. As chance would have it, no one could perform the Heimlich maneuver on him since he was so profoundly rotund. He died of asphyxiation. The party was curtailed, to the great displeasure of several of the children and a few adults, but especially the birthday girl, who cried in self-pity as she left the pony ranch.

But it was as if the devil was seeking some further malice. It appeared that he had hitched a ride from the birthday party, as all was afoul. Later that evening at their home, the mother had to be sedated to calm her frayed nerves. The daughter and her grandmother watched a nature show on television as the girl rested her head on her grandmother's lap. It was an episode about a pride of lions in the Serengeti, with one segment showing an obviously hungry female chasing down a gazelle after the female and few others had spent a lazy afternoon in the shade. When the lioness caught up to the fleeing animal, it latched onto its anus with its teeth and ferociously tore it right out of its insides. The grandmother gently stroked her granddaughter's arm as the two watched quietly, fixated. And as the nature show progressed into the next segment, the male leader of the pride took one of the females from behind, gritting its teeth and roaring. The young girl smirked mischievously, a glint in her eyes, which gave the impression she was fine after all the day's activities, yet something was brewing in that young impressionable mind.

Chapter One

Eighteen years after that most peculiar day, the young girl, Martha Kittering, had not quite recovered. And although it couldn't be said that it was the defining moment in her life or her psyche, bearing in mind her genetics played a large part in both, it was an absolute certainty that her general perspective was altered ever so slightly. She wound up with a unique sense of humor that bordered on the twisted. She had turned out to be a sexy woman standing about five foot six, lean and powerful as a Tuscan sculpture. Her disposition ranged dramatically from a persistent languor to a sporadic exuberance that belonged in a fashion magazine to a misery that made her wish to be hidden in a dark cave somewhere. She could be high one minute and considerably down the next, due to her very intense bipolar condition. She was nonetheless gorgeous, blessed with an amazing pair of cobalt-blue eyes that sparkled with silver and black garnet-like flecks.

Martha—actually Marty, her name of choice—was in the process of packing away her belongings in a suitcase that lay on her stripped bare bed. She found herself in a situation that was about as peculiar as that day eighteen years earlier. You see, Marty was leaving town for good and for good reason since she had just recently done away with one of her culinary professors. She was compelled to kill, partly out of anger, partly for a bit of a thrill. It had not been the first time for her. Eight years prior, spurred on by lust that resulted in antagonism and rage, she had caused the death of an unsuspecting first-time female lover. She had enjoyed the sensation; it felt so erotically pleasing. Like getting that first waft on the nose and then the taste of cherry on the tongue from a luscious Russian River Valley Pinot Noir. As with any superb vintage, it is hard to resist not wanting more.

Her shimmering hair, the color of coal, framed her fine facial features, dangled over her tender neck and soft shoulders and lifted into the air as she moved anxiously about in her small, furnished apartment. And although she seemed distracted, she was thorough in packing her clothing, a few personal items and cleaning up her apartment. She was meticulously dressed in a pair of black linen shorts that were cut tight and a black spandex halter-top that exposed her flat belly. Encased in her navel was an almond-sized emerald, giving her the look of an exotic Indian princess. On her right wrist was a delicate white gold bracelet with alternating small rubies, sapphires, and emeralds, which paired beautifully with her stunning eyes. On her left was a white gold Pearlmaster Rolex that she affectionately called her Pearl. The few silver rings that embellished her hands were essential tools to fidget away her nervous energy.

Described as a neatnik and a clean freak by those who knew her best, she had spent two hours laboriously scouring the bathroom tile with a toothbrush and about the same amount of time on the shower, not that the bathroom was in need of a cleanse by any means. She had wiped down the shower stall, the entire tile, the cabinets, and mirror and countertop before she took a shower, only to wipe it down all over again. "So I like things clean," she would say. And then gave a sniff here and a sniff there to make sure the apartment had a fresh herbal smell to it, using only botanical cleansers, never any chlorine bleach or chemical solvents.

She paused for a moment and surveyed her bedroom like a cagey leopard through her wet bangs, glanced at a chip on the white tip of her right index fingernail and rubbed it on the side of her shorts. She looked at it again while rubbing it with the adjacent thumb for smoothness. And then she glanced down at her finely manicured scarlet toenails showcased in a pair of jeweled black sandals and wiggled her toes.

"Damn, can I ever get out of here?" poured from her lips with a voice that was reminiscent of Grand Marnier—silky, sweet and a touch husky.

She sounded as if she were blaming someone other than herself, but it was that little extra condition she had that seemed to distract her from time to time. And she dealt with it like her other maladies, in the best way she could. But, oh, how she longed to be just like the other girls—simple, not as dramatic and maybe even less attractive. But she was not nor could she be some plain Jane. And no matter how she pined or attempted to be like them, she couldn't conceal her incredible looks nor quiet her over-active intelligent mind. Like a leopard, she could not change her spots. And yet she would get these uncontrollable urges from time to time. Urges that were not as simple to satisfy as baking a batch of chocolate-chip cookies.

As if murdering her professor and all her little distractions weren't enough, she was also on her cycle and needed chocolate for the loving comforting feeling it gave her. In this, she was like so many others who require a particular indulgence to keep them whole. Prepared, she grabbed a ganache-coated cake bon bon from a box of a half dozen on the top of her bureau and popped it in her mouth. If she could eat chocolate and drink Pinot all day, she would have, but she knew better. It was her figure.

But doing away with her professor could not have been timed any better, like a blood-rare ribeye steak that is pulled from the grill so it is served perfectly at 115 degrees Fahrenheit, charred on the outside and practically mooing on the inside, exactly as the customer requested. Marty relished the way she was able to execute a killing in a precise and timely manner like a line cook who takes in hundreds of tickets for grilled cuts of beef ranging from black and blue to English-style, twice murdered that is, and not one return from a dissatisfied customer. She was quite cunning. But then again, there are those moments when a piece of meat falls from the grill and one picks it up hoping no one is looking as it is thrown back into the mix.

Marty slipped back into the bathroom and gathered all her essential oils, herbal elixirs, and other toiletries and swept them into a leather Armand tote bag. She stopped for a moment to look at herself in the mirror, still chewing on the bonbon. The prominent blue veins in her chest like rivers on a map were jagged and ran deep with neurotic currents. And her normal creamy complexion was peaked from anxiety, making her glossed lips look darker than usual.

She took notice of the port-colored rings underneath her eyes and rubbed them quickly but gently as if they would magically disappear. She was not particularly fond of facial makeup and would rather go without, except, of course, some gloss to add an accent of sensuality to her look. She quickly checked to see if her diamond earrings were intact as she gave a glance at her high cheekbones for any signs of aging. She was youthful looking, despite her weary eyes.

She casually unbuttoned her shorts, slipped them down to her knees and took a pinch of her flabless stomach. She paused for a second to peer at her flawless body that was lightly dotted with beauty marks of varying sizes. When she was a child, she would ask her mother what the marks were. Her mother would respond, "When you were born the angels came and visited you because you were so special. And the beauty marks, as well as your beauty, were their gifts to you." As Marty got older, she would add to her mother's cute little story, "And they also made me neurotic, or did I get that from you?" She peeled forward the top of her cream-colored lace panties and looked. She then stuck her hand down to her pubis to check her growth, removed the hand, pulled up her shorts and buttoned them up again.

Marty cut the light, stepped back into the bedroom with the Armand bag, grabbed her suitcases and her box of bonbons and made her way through the living room. She stepped out the front door and then locked it. A few seconds later, the door was unlocked again. Marty unhooked the apartment key from her key ring and tossed it toward a coffee table. It slid along the table straight onto the floor. She muttered, "Shit!" And then tutted as she stepped back inside the apartment to pick up the key and placed it back on the table. Mad at herself, she shook her head. She then shut the door, and in a flash, she was gone.

Chapter Two

A half an hour later, Marty was heading southbound in her metallic coal-gray super-charged car from a small town outside of Walla Walla, Washington, where she attended Chapman Culinary Academy. A very private, pricey and prestigious institution, Chapman accepts only fifty students a semester and is difficult to get in. Chapman is to the culinary world what a Harvard or a Wharton is to the business world. High-pedigree recommendations are a must to even get a whiff at the CCA. Hers was from the chef she worked for in Portland, Oregon, who had been a Bernard Jameson recipient for top new restaurant and top new chef of the year. Although the chef was apathetic to Marty's passionless cooking abilities, he did appreciate the wealthy clientele and friends her father brought in.

Marty worked in the pantry prepping all the *mise en place* for the salads and desserts she served at dinner time. She prepared a variety of onions that were either grilled or fried in some manner, shaved or crumbled assorted cheeses, and of course there were the finely julienned carrots, beets and the like that had to be planed on the mandoline. Surprisingly though, she did make a reasonably good caramel sauce. Perhaps it came from her chemistry education while she was at Golden State University in Los Feliz. Boiling the sugar to the right temperature and adding the cream so not to create an explosion so hot that it could sizzle the hair off of a woolly mammoth was a particular skill of hers.

It wasn't her lack of intelligence or beauty that was at issue for the chef; it was her grueling pace and her inability to make the plates come to life with excitement. It was that flair that for the truly talented comes naturally and one that Marty would have to work extremely hard at. The chef was taken aback once she began working for him after an evening tryout that was quite amazing for an inexperienced person. But that was an anomaly for her, as rare as unearthing white truffles long after the Italian Piedmont fall is over. Perhaps it was her temperament combined with her chemistry education that was more inclined to a slower and methodical pace as opposed to the rapid-fire drill that is not only required but essential in a restaurant kitchen.

The chef would tip his hat at times and offer her some waiting shifts. She just didn't seem to get it, opting to stay in the back of the house. Luckily, a reprieve did arrive in the form of her acceptance letter to Chapman. The chef shared his true feelings about her with his sous chef on her last day and remarked, "Nice ass, but she'll never make it." Marty overheard while she was passing by the chef's office coming from the dry storage. Her face turned a dark shade of crimson, as she sensed the comment was about her. Later that evening, after closing hours, the chef gave her a peck on the cheek and a conciliatory "best of luck," for he was glad that it wasn't his hundred and fifty grand that was going to be tossed away like some deflated soufflé.

Chapter Three

Marty had to settle her nerves. She fished out a vial of Valerian from the Armand bag, unscrewed it, and squeezed the nipple with one hand while the other held onto the steering wheel. She squirted the contents underneath her tongue and then repeated the process. She held the pool of nerve calmer for a moment and then swallowed. Some might have lit a cigarette instead, particularly those in the restaurant biz, but Marty was more of a naturalist, so much so that she brewed her own herbal elixirs. Moments later, she downed the remaining Valerian as she mulled over what had occurred at Chapman.

For her final grade in her Advanced Practical Application Baking Course, she had to prepare and bake peach scones. She would be evaluated on the recipe she created, and on the color, texture, crumb effect, flavor and overall quality of the baked scones. If she didn't pass the test, she would essentially flunk out of school. It was a summer course, so peaches were at the peak season. There was a farm stand just down the road from the academy, so Marty picked up a small basket of fresh peaches that were plump, sweet, juicy, and tremendously aromatic. Yet she wanted to utilize her herbal skills and apply it to the scones by adding some of the peach pit kernels. In small amounts, the kernels added an almond-like flavor and texture and had some anticancer properties.

Although the kernels contain trace amounts of cyanide, the handful that she used would, at most, have caused some intestinal discomfort— that is, if the professor ate the dozen or so scones she made in one sitting. She racked her brain. Extra arsenic was what they needed. What he needed, she conceded.

In a delayed reaction to her murderous actions, she said while half smiling, "Did I...? I did, didn't I?" And then she quickly interrupted herself in a slightly twisted voice: "He was always hovering and sniffing around incessantly, poking his hairy snout in my face. And then he made that sophomoric comment about how he couldn't wait to eat my scone. Fucking pervert!" Marty glanced in the rearview mirror and blurted, "Damn, I could use a cigarette," as she blew out the anxiety that lay heavy on her chest.

The professor had reminded her of her Uncle Brad and the scarred memories that she had of him vaulted away in the deep recesses of her mind. When she was seven years old, she had gone hunting with her father and her Uncle Brad. The professor had the same hairy nose Uncle Brad had. Although her father believed in the importance of teaching independence and a sense of confidence at a young age, he never expected that a family member would violate his precious princess. Yet he also did not want Marty turning out to be like her mother, an over-catered-to neurotic who was afraid to lift a finger for anything.

While her father went chasing after a deer of his own after Uncle Brad had dropped one—shot it dead, that is—Marty stayed behind with Uncle Brad as he gutted the deer. Marty looked on with amusement while bending over next to him, looking at the gushy innards while Uncle Brad decided to help himself to a cookie. What she could remember was Uncle Brad's bloody hand reaching down into her pants. She could feel him feeling her behind. There was an acrid smell in the air, and at that exact moment her father came running back to where they were and saw Uncle Brad quickly pull his hand out of her pants, shouting, "I got 'em."

Things got awfully quiet well into the two-hour trip back home. That night her father wanted to make sure Marty was okay. She just kept looking at her blood-smirched little pair of underwear that lay in the corner of her bedroom. He comforted her but did not want to spook her in any way. She was his little princess. He told her he would take care of everything and make it all better one day. He then kissed her forehead, and they gave each other their "I love you's" and "goodnight's." He picked up the underwear, went outside and lit a match to them, watching them burn to ashes as Marty quietly peered from her bedroom window two floors up. Her mother was fast asleep in a haze of barbiturates.

The following hunting season, her father and Uncle Brad took a trip to their usual spot. Marty stayed home. The following day the phone rang with the news; Uncle Brad was accidentally killed by a thirty-ought-six bullet that went clear through his temple and right out the other end. Marty's mother, Uncle Brad's sister, had her first nervous breakdown. Her father was fined and slapped with an injunction of a year of non-hunting for taking the fatal shot. It was deemed an accident.

Chapter Four

Two days prior at the end of the semester, with not a student in sight, a knock came at the office door of the baking professor, William Johnson, who was a tall, husky man with a horse nose, light blue eyes and brown wavy hair with graying temples. He was sitting at his desk wearing a white chef coat with bluish black trim with the school's scripted monogram in gold lettering on the upper left side of the chest and "Chef Johnson" in block bluish-black letters. Black chef pants and black Coraframe shoes completed his outfit. He was going over the results from the finals and logging them into his computer. In a French accent, the professor spit out, *"Entre vous,"* although he was as American as apple pie.

The professor peered up from his desk as Marty entered. He eyed her as if he were a sex-starved Go-Go club patron with lust on his breath. She was looking quite tantalizing in a pair of short jean cutoffs and a red halter-top over a black lace bra. He salivated. She reminded him just then of Marilyn Monroe in *Some Like It Hot*. She was so damn gorgeous. He quickly fantasized as he had numerous times before about drizzling champagne over her pert breasts, licking up every droplet. He especially loved the pronounced crook of her nose, the slight cleft in her chin and her tender full lips that were moist with clear gloss. She was carrying a platter of freshly baked peach scones dusted with a blend of powdered sugar and arsenic trioxide dust, your garden-variety rat poison, for good measure.

"Yes, Marty?" he asked dismissively while feeling extra aroused since they were virtually the only two on campus, especially in the baking department. It was near dark outside.

In a low, almost demure, yet sexy voice she responded, "I know I didn't do well on the final yesterday. I was having it bad. You know, my monthly thing." She paused slightly and took a step forward. "I was hoping you could grade these scones instead?"

"Funny, I was just going over your score," he retorted with some condescension. "This isn't normally how the baking finals work, Marty, let alone the real world. Imagine saying to a disgruntled customer, 'sorry that the scones suck, but I'm having my period.'"

Marty innocently raised her eyebrows and shrugged her shoulders and then caught a scent of sandalwood and citrus coming from the professor. She immediately knew it was *Agua* by Armand and got a little jingle in her clitoris. She shook it off, remembering her angst towards Professor Johnson. *Who knew he had a little class in him?*

"So who's to say you actually had a hand in making these?" the professor asked. She got that he was toying with her. Coquettishly, she stuck out her right hand and twirled it around.

Half-smiling, he said somewhat obligingly, "Let's look, then?"

She paused and then stepped hesitantly towards the desk, pulled the platter out of the canvas tote bag it was in and gently placed it down. The professor's eyes skimmed Marty's sensual bodice and her raven-like hair. He then peeled back the plastic wrap that covered the scones, picked one out, looked at it closely and broke a piece off. He then took a whiff—more for Marty's luscious aroma than that of the scone—and said, "Do I dare eat the scone?" He then chewed on it, wishing it were her warm pussy. Marty felt a little repelled, sensing his groping mind, but she was on a mission and let that feeling go for the moment. He smiled in delight as a surge of blood from his brain cavity rushed to his already hard member. Powdered sugar dusted the side of his mouth.

"So, do I pass, then?" Marty eagerly asked.

The professor got up from his chair and said, "Excuse me for a second; I need to use the john."

Marty noticed the bulge in his pants as he stepped into the bathroom. He had to relieve himself. Marty surveyed the room. On top of a three-drawer file cabinet were several bottles of Tahitian vanilla extract, a vial of peppermint oil, an opened bottle of Grand Marnier and an uncorked bottle of Piper Jouet champagne. She then gingerly walked across the room and unlatched a window that opened to the courtyard outside. She heard the toilet flush and quickly stepped back to where she had been standing a second ago.

Coming out of the bathroom, the professor wiped his hands off, tossed a damp and crumpled paper towel in a wastebasket next to his desk and stood next to Marty. She immediately caught that he was breathing heavily. She did not care to know why, or what he might have been doing in there. All she knew was the trap was baited, and the rat took it. The dust had been wiped from his mouth.

"You know, the final is over, and I was about to log in your grade." He let the moment hang for a brief second to bait the hook with Marty. "But maybe you'd like to meet for some coffee later this evening?" He stared into her eyes.

She paused for a second or two. "Tea, and it will have to be tomorrow," she said, knowing that the grades would have to be posted by that night and she could slip out of town before then, avoiding any compromising positions with the professor. Not that it would matter anyway; hopefully, he would be dead by then. "Oh, poor Professor Johnson, you just weren't conscientious of your thing, were you?"

"The Black Cow tomorrow at six," he stated clearly, holding back his excitement.

Marty responded with a curt smile and said, "See you then," while snidely laughing to herself, "No, you won't." She was savvier than the average nineteen-year-old female student who was naïve enough to fall for bullshit like that. She was no hussy. She was assured that she'd gotten the grade she needed, knowing that the way to truly satisfy a man was not through his stomach but through his cock, and that she had the goods to do just that. Making a man lust and lose control of his senses, at least long enough to change her grade to a passing one, was worthy of an "A-plus." Besides, she didn't mind giving a dying man—or at least a soon-to-be dead man—one last little visual pleasure as she had just then.

Marty was aware of her ability to provide visual stimuli to many, but what confounded her and was largely a paradox was that she was not able herself to experience pleasure on a regular basis, but only for brief moments at a time. She knew the cause of her problem, yet she could not truly accept it. But maybe she was lucky, she thought, because the intensity of pleasure she experienced was tenfold that of an average person when she did have those moments. This was a result of her bipolar condition.

As she was leaving the office, the professor glanced at her shoulders that cut into a V-shape. He took a long, hard look at Marty's pear-shaped ass that was exposed slightly by the bottom of her cutoffs. It had a certain heft that jiggled some when she walked. It made him want to roar. And then he trailed his gaze down the backs of her firm thighs. But what got him the most and secured Marty a passing grade were the gold Roman sandals she had on that laced halfway up her sleek, powerful calves. For some inexplicable reason, they triggered every erogenous zone in his body. She closed the door, and he took a full whiff of the White Jasmine scent she left behind. He reached over and grabbed another scone, began to eat it and continued grading the finals, then let out a huge moan from the throbbing ache at the base of his scrotum.

Chapter Five

That night, just after eleven-thirty, the professor's outside window crept opened. Marty, wearing black sweats with the hood over her head and black leather gloves, slipped in over the windowsill and shimmied her way into the office. She turned on a small flashlight and shined it on top of the desk. The platter of scones was gone. Like a cop looking for a prowler in an alley with his strobe light, she searched all through the office, even in the wastepaper basket and inside the bathroom, and no platter or scones were in sight. The arsenic-laced scones she made were intended for the professor and no one else. What she did not know is that the professor had brought them home for his wife to try, but she immediately tossed them away after she took a small bite of one and then spit it out. Apparently, she thought they were awful.

Marty pulled out a folded letter inside a plastic bag from underneath her sweatshirt, took it out of the plastic bag and unfolded the note, flashed the light on it to read it once more to herself. *To all, especially the female students I made sexual advances to. My actions were inappropriate, and I apologize to every one of you. Mostly, I apologize to my wife Dottie, who I have loved dearly, and the academy for behavior that has been reprehensible. I will miss you all. Lovingly, Chef William Johnson.* Not bad, she thought.

She was confident that as long as he ate just one scone, which he did, it would have done the trick, given her pharmaceutical education and knowledge of the notorious murders by arsenic poisoning over the centuries. She placed the suicide note on the desk. She then stepped into the professor's bathroom. Marty pulled a small box of arsenic trioxide dust from one of her pockets and placed it top of the vanity and then went back inside the office.

As Marty stepped towards the window and began shimmying her way over the windowsill, she thought how much of a fucking pig the professor was and how he deserved what was coming to him. Especially, how a formal complaint of sexual harassment by eight former female students and three presently had been filed against him through the academy. Marty had found this out through a gal that she became friendly with who worked in the academy's administration office. He was going to be let go at the end of the semester. Suicide would have been the perfect out for him because he should have had remorse for his actions, Marty felt. If he had, he would have put a leash on his penis by then. *So I helped him a little. Well, maybe a lot. He certainly ingested enough arsenic to have killed a horse.*

Like an alley cat, Marty slipped her way through the courtyard and then suddenly stopped and whispered, "The letter!"

She turned around and retraced her tracks to the professor's window. She popped her head up and was about to open the window when she saw a flashlight passing underneath the professor's office door. She knelt back down, waited a second and then opened the window and slipped back in. She shined a light on the desk at some letters that were leaning against a pencil holder, went through them and found the one she was looking for. The one from the personnel office. It hadn't been opened. She tried to tear it with her gloved finger but could not get underneath the sealed flap. She plucked her glove off with her teeth and then slipped her finger under the flap and pushed sideways. She felt a sharp flap slash along her finger. Marty stammered, "Shit."

She shined the light on her finger. A trickle of blood appeared. She wiped it on her sweat pant leg and then replaced her glove. She slipped the letter out of the envelope and began reading the professor's dismissal notice asking him not to return next semester for breach of contract, behavior that was reprehensible and contrary to the standards of the academy—that is, making unwanted sexual advances to students. The letter was Chapman's first step in the dismissal process, yet they wanted to end the semester cleanly by not having to bring in a new professor. They would sit down with Johnson in the following days. Marty placed the letter underneath the suicide note, and as she did, she heard the night watchmen make his way down the hall. She didn't have time to slip back outside and so crouched down on the side of the desk. The door opened and the night watchmen flashed his light around the office and the desk. He stepped towards the desk and flashed the light on the suicide note. As he was about to read it, Marty, on the opposite side of the desk, grabbed the bottle of Grand Marnier and cracked him over the head. He fell on the desk and then rolled over onto the floor, unconscious.

She flashed the light on his face. His eyes were shut. She had to move fast. She ran outside the office and a minute later returned with a low platform cart for boxes and wheeled it into the office next to the watchmen. Marty leveraged him onto the cart while pushing him into a crouched position. She grabbed the Grand Marnier bottle and wheeled the cart out into the hallway and down towards a break room, then inside next to a leather couch. She rolled him off the cart and eased him onto the couch, propping him in a slouched position, poured some Grand Marnier on his lips, drizzling some on his uniform and then placed the bottle upright on his belly, leaning it against his chest. She grabbed his walkie-talkie, hit the speak button, cast her voice to a lower register and sung in a slurred manner, "When Irish eyes are smiling…"

She dropped the walkie-talkie on the couch and whispered to the night watchman, "Sorry, Sloppy Joe, but at least I didn't kill you."

Joe Straub, dubbed Sloppy Joe for his habit of sloppy drunkenness, knew Marty. "She was the hottest thing to ever walk these halls," he would muse obsessively to his fellow watchmen. Marty knew of him because he would occasionally see her and give her the "hey baby" routine in his smoker's voice when he'd pass by her as she went to one of her early morning classes. Sloppy Joe was just another horny guy whom she ignored. If he knew that it was Marty who had knocked him out, he would most certainly let her do it all over again because that's the closest she would ever get to him.

She quickly wheeled the cart from the breakroom to make her getaway. As she did, she could hear on the walkie-talkie, "Joe, is that you?"

On the way out of the professor's office, she took the bottle of Piper Jouet with her—a little graduating gift from the professor. She smiled as she snuck out his window.

Chapter Six

The following morning, with Marty long gone, Sloppy Joe the watchmen was found, immediately fired and escorted off the campus. He tried to explain his story, but no one minded him since that was his third and final warning for drinking on the job. It was too late, anyway.

That same morning the professor was in his bathroom at home preparing for a shower and having intense stomach cramps. He rubbed the side of his belly and grimaced from the pain and his pounding headache. He turned on the shower and then decided to relieve himself. He pulled his underwear off, took a seat on the toilet and let out a loud moan. He quickly turned around and heaved his stomach contents into the toilet. A second later he felt a sharp stinging pain in his chest, and foam came out his mouth like bubbles from a corked bottle of champagne. He fell clasping his chest and, after convulsing for about a minute, was dead as a steer's guts on a slaughterhouse floor.

Fifteen minutes later, his wife knocked on the door.

"Honey, are you okay?" she asked. Apparently, she wasn't aware of the problems he faced at work.

Later that evening an announcement of the death of Professor William Johnson, including his memorial service time and place, was texted to all the Chapman students. It was the least they could do considering the circumstances. As soon as Marty read the text, she had become flush with anxiety and knew she had to get out of town sooner than she had planned. An impromptu murder can do that—change things unexpectedly. Although in the back of her mind she had started to conjure up something that was not going to be pretty, it had festered. Her decision to take advantage of the situation was made abruptly, perhaps even unwisely, and no sooner did she conceive it than the professor was dead.

"Yeah, don't eat the scones," she said sarcastically aloud and then thought, *I just hope they were tossed.* Not that they could be traced back to her, but still, no reason to kill the innocent.

Chapman had been almost a complete failure, she thought, maybe even a waste of time. *I didn't have the finesse to make a simple scone, which turned out flat, rubbery and tasteless,* Marty fretted. Her grades were appalling, and she questioned why she did not try harder. Yet she knew that it was partly due to her affliction—that dreaded bipolar disorder that screwed with the dopamine levels in her brain. She was also certain that her all male professors at Chapman were consumed with her gorgeous looks and were indifferent when it came to her grading because they all wanted her, and she just wasn't interested in being a fuck toy, not at any price.

But in truth, it was her depressed look and that unfriendly feeling she projected that made them think she was just plain stuck on herself. She didn't realize that a smile from time to time would have changed her position for the better. She just couldn't muster up any happiness—that outward glow that can make a plain woman pretty or in the case of Marty, a gorgeous woman approachable for whatever reason. Professor Johnson was the exception; with his straight-up boner for her, he didn't care if she looked stuck-up or morose.

She had tried traditional pharmaceuticals but rejected them as she rejected her chemistry education, opting for a more homeopathic way, but the supplements she tried just weren't strong enough. All in all, her ability to experience pleasure was squelched, outside of a few days every month or so when she would peak, as she called it, and then it would be maddening. Like a cocaine user who just scored an eight ball, she would go on a heightened thrill ride, only to come crashing down in dramatic fashion.

"Damn fucking scones!" she yelled.

Chapter Seven

While rolling along the Pacific coastline at good speed, Marty received a text. She picked up her cell phone. It was from Chapman. It was her final grades. Nervously, she scrolled down to the Advanced Practical Application Baking Course and saw that she had received a B-. She looked at it again and was suddenly thrilled. That meant she was able to graduate as a chef. She felt a tinge of sexual arousal in her groin, then looked in the rearview mirror at herself and puckered a sexy smile. She was enamored at her triumph and accomplishment, although she was used to receiving straight A's all through high school and college. She'd accepted her less-than-average scores at Chapman—not so bad considering her bipolar condition, she rationalized.

Marty immediately texted Roy, her longtime high school sweetheart, with the good news. As she drove into the late afternoon, she heard a rolling thunder, and then the skies opened up to a heavy downpour. It reminded her of her days in Portland and of Roy, who was in so many ways her soulmate. They were inseparable; whenever their high school friends spoke of either of them, the other was immediately included. They were practically like twins. Roy was just a little taller, with blue-green eyes. They both had the same lean body and the same length dark hair. Marty and Roy were the quintessential young Portland couple, sort of like a modern-day John and Yoko with a heavy dose of moodiness. They were the hip couple in both style and dress, both exotically pretty and looking as if they had stepped off the pages of *Vogue*.

Vanity ran deep in both of them; it came naturally with their youth and striking good looks. Aesthetically, they saw in each other their own selves. Roy also had a flamboyance that he had not yet cultivated, and a sensitivity such that even when they had sex together, Roy would pout afterwards, attributing it to his feelings towards Marty.

Marty and Roy would skip school from time to time to just be together and have fun. She wished things could be different for them but realized one must be true to one's own nature. On a Halloween weekend trip to San Francisco in their senior year of high school, they were invited to a seven deadly sins party. Before the party, they went out into town to hunt for costumes. Roy decided on being Dorian Gray complete with a picture frame for around his head, and Marty a dominatrix. While trying on costumes, Roy picked up a fake mustache and playfully put it on Marty's upper lip. He then kissed her. Marty went along, but something clicked in the back of her mind.

Later that evening at the party, at some point Marty lost sight of Roy. She waited awhile and then texted him to no response. A half an hour passed, and she decided to leave and go back to the hotel. She went into one of the bedrooms where the partygoers' coats were placed and searched for hers on the bed. She then heard a noise from the closet and out of curiosity opened the sliding door ever so slightly, only to find Roy and another man dressed as the devil lying on the floor of the closet, clutched in each other's arms in a full-on make-out session. The picture frame was around both necks. Neither man even looked up at her. She didn't say a thing except "hum" and slid the door closed. Roy and the devil continued with their debauchery, as Roy called it later, recounting the story of how he met his—as he called him—"first lover." He came out of the closet because the devil made him do it.

A moment later, Marty left the house where this new revelation had forever changed the relationship between her and Roy. It was a little chilly, and she buttoned up her coat. Marty made her way down California Street, shaking her head. She had known something was up with Roy. The sex between them was infrequent. And, much to her chagrin, it had always been missing something, lackluster. And then he started flirting with every guy he ran into. She thought it strange at that moment that she wasn't angry with him, although she'd have bouts of jealousy from time to time. And they did love each other, so much so that they would have killed for one another, just to prove their undying love. But that was just fanciful words between them. Things were different, or so it seemed.

Chapter Eight

As Marty made her way down the block and around the corner onto California Street, she slipped her hand into her coat pockets. She lifted her right hand out, holding a business card that was given to her as she and Roy entered the party. She had originally laughed when she first looked at it at the party, then a spark of interest lit her curiosity as she read it again. She pulled out her cell phone and plugged in the address on the card, and then hopped a cable car and was off on an adventure as bizarre as the Halloween party had turned out.

A little later she was walking down a side street off of Van Ness. It was dimly lit, and a light fog had rolled in from off the bay. Marty peered at her phone that gave the GPS heading and then put it back in her coat pocket. She looked at the business card and stepped towards the door of a two-story brick building. The shingle on the side of the door read: Dominika the Dominatrix ~ tel. 333-6969. She looked at the card again, slipped it into her pocket and tried to turn the doorknob. It was locked, so she rang the buzzer. A moment later a sultry female voice with a Czechoslovakian accent came through a small speaker, "Yes?"

Marty put her face near the speaker and said, "I'm looking for Dominika."

Dominika responded, "I am she. What can I do for you?"

A little nervous, Marty cleared her throat and said, "I think you gave me your card at the seven deadly sins party earlier this evening? And I was interested in what you do."

"Yes, I normally work by appointment, but I have a little free time at the moment. Would you like to come in?" Dominika replied.

"Sure," she replied as her heart began to race with excitement.

The door buzzer rang, and Marty entered the building into a long hallway. She stepped towards a lit room at the end of the hall where Dominika appeared. She was tall, very tall, strong and attractive—a provocative woman of thirty with blonde hair and full brown eyebrows, greenish hazel eyes and thin lips that were painted scarlet. She was wearing a black lambskin robe that covered her dominatrix outfit and a pair of ruby-red leather stiletto boots. She stuck her hand out to Marty as she neared. Marty was overwhelmed. She dwarfed Dominika by eight inches or more.

"Hello, I remember you. The pretty couple. You were dressed like you were a professional," Dominika said.

They both shook hands, and Marty replied, "Not me. I'm just a plain old girl from Portland."

Dominika raised her eyebrows and laughed slightly and asked, "What are you looking for?"

"I'm not sure. Maybe something new? Different?" Marty asked inquisitively.

"I think you'll be pleasantly surprised. You know we play rough and hard. You think you can handle that?"

"If you're talking about a little pain, then yes, I can certainly deal with that."

"I'm not sure you realize the extent of the pain, but I guarantee you one thing, you will experience pleasure as you have never before, so much so that you may become addicted to it."

Marty felt a twinge in her clitoris and softly said, "I'm ready if you are."

Dominika gently stroked Marty's cheek and said, "All right, my princess, just follow me and you will have your wish. But once you enter my lair, you cannot leave until I say so."

Dominika put her hand over Marty's and led her down a flight of stairs to the cavernous labyrinth below.

The stairs went along a brick wall that opened to the basement of the building. It was if they had entered a fifteenth-century dungeon. There were candles that lit the stairway about head high and several large wrought iron candle chandeliers that were drawn by ropes hung from the ceiling. The candlelight almost gave a warm gothic feel, Marty thought. She was intrigued, thrilled but nervously apprehensive about what lay ahead.

Chapter Nine

The main part of the dungeon had a large, round wooden table that was on a gyro and could be positioned at any angle. The table also spun around. It had four sets of pegs that could be positioned anywhere on the table with leather straps hanging from them along the edge of the table in a crisscross pattern. A black metal chair with red leather padding hung on a wall with a set of heavy link chains on either side of the chair. A cage-like metal table stood perched on the floor waiting for a shackled prisoner seeking something that they would never receive at home from a loving mate. There was also a stand that held a half-dozen whips of various sizes and colors.

And on the far side of the main room was a replica of a stretching rack used during the Inquisition, which Marty assumed was for those experienced customers of Dominika, something she wasn't quite ready for. Little did Marty realize the rack was tame compared to some of the other devices that were at Dominika's disposal, let alone the skill and deftness that the dominatrix possessed. Centuries earlier, Dominika could have easily been at the side of Torquemada in the wicked pursuit of compelling non-believers into converts. In a room adjoining the main dungeon, the lucky prisoner could get all the electrical impulses he or she could handle.

Dominika had a variety of nipple and clitoris clips and anal prodders that gave out electrical stimuli. There were also numerous electronic vibrators of all shapes and sizes. Inside a wrought iron armoire, hanging from its doors, were a host of handcuffs, some steel, some barbed leather and some rope. On the shelves were plenty of nooses and lubricants of all kinds, both commercial brands and staples like Vaseline and vegetable oil. There were also bottles of tomato juice. In the drawers further down were dildos and rubbers of all sizes including full body ones and plenty of rubber and latex gloves.

Further into the basement at a half level below was the water irrigation room where Dominika's clientele could indulge in douching of all sorts. She had these special douche bags that she liked filling with tomato juice and then heating in the microwave before she gave her "little princes and princesses," as she referred to her clients, the bloody Mary. She occasionally offered up her slash and salts. This was a procedure where delicate little slashes were made into the skin on various parts of the body, and granulated kosher salt was sprinkled upon them.

And then there was the tar and feather treatment she offered. Instead of tar, she used lard. It was heated to the point where it could be slathered on and then goose down feathers were blown on with a fan. This treatment did not come cheap; it was usually the out-of-town Asians who chose it. Had to do with cultural humility of some sort. They would tremble under the feathers as Dominika threatened to cut their heads off with a butcher knife. But that was all for show.

When they reached the bottom of the stairs, Dominika took her robe off, which exposed her cupless ruby-red leather bustier that matched her boots. Her breasts protruded outward in a pointed fashion. They were plump and luscious, and her nipples were fully erect. She wore a matching crotchless thong that exposed her hairless pussy.

As Marty looked around the room and avoided gazing upon Dominika, she asked, "What is your fee for all this?"

Dominika, in a demonstrative and firm voice, said, "Since this is your first time, you can decide upon a tip you'd like to leave. But we can deal with that later. Now, if you please, take all your clothes off, including your undergarments." She pointed towards a small drawing room to the side of the dungeon. "You can undress in there."

Marty obliged while Dominika prepared the platform where she was going to begin the session, one that she felt that was going to be a little more exciting than usual. Perhaps it was Marty's beauty and sultriness, perhaps her youth. Marty reappeared fully naked. Her heart was pounding. Dominika took a quick glance at her and felt the same sensation. Dominika wanted to do something special for Marty, but that would come later. She gently grabbed Marty's wrist, and they stepped towards the platform.

"Now, I want you to stand up on the platform. I'm going to tie your feet and your hands with these," Dominika said, grabbing one of the nooses that hung from the ceiling.

"By the way, what were you doing at the party?" Marty asked as she stepped onto the platform.

"Networking. Now please be quiet," Dominika demanded.

Marty became virtually still while Dominika slipped Marty's left hand through one noose, strung it tight, pulled on the rope and tied it on a post, then repeated the process with the other hand. She tied each of Marty's feet on the platform. She then readjusted the tautness of the ropes that stretched out Marty's arms in a Y-pattern.

Dominika whispered in Marty's ear, "Now if I hear you cry or moan excessively, you will feel my wrath. Okay, little princess, do you understand?" She then kissed Marty's ear tenderly.

Marty softly responded, "Yes."

"Yes, what?" Dominika suddenly sounded like a drill sergeant.

Marty, giggling at this point at the situation, said, "Yes, Dominika?" Dominika grabbed one of her whips and quickly cracked one alongside Marty's right buttock. It was a warning shot. Marty let out a scream and then began to moan extremely hard. Dominika shook her head, stepped towards Marty and stuck the butt end of the whip in Marty's mouth.

Marty began to choke. Dominika pulled out the butt from her mouth and began poking Marty's face with it.

"*Yes, Mistress,*"she instructed. "Now listen, my little princess, if you giggle again, lip off or act up like some little bitch, I will whip you so hard, you will pee your pants and then pass out from excruciating pain."

Marty bit down on her lip while Dominika stepped back and re-cocked her whip and let it rip on Marty's left calf. Gritting her teeth, Marty grimaced in pain and let out a whimper. Dominika shook her head again and just let her fly, continuing her assault on Marty's rear end. Marty's head bobbed back and forth in pain, yelling "ouch" at every strike.

Dominika stopped, stepped towards Marty and then stuck her hand underneath Marty's crotch, softly caressing her moist labia and clitoris. She then stroked Marty's glowing red buttocks and planted a kiss upon them. She wanted to hold back her sexual desire for Marty, but it was overwhelming her. She stepped in front of Marty, gazed into her shining eyes and kissed her tenderly on the lips. She then caressed Marty's breasts and nibbled on her areolas. Marty softly moaned. Slowly, Dominika worked her lips down Marty's belly towards her coiffed pubis that was black, fine and splayed slightly upward.

Dominika savored the moment with her tongue, but only briefly. Marty relaxed the tautness in her muscles and then felt more aroused than she had never been before. Without a touch, Marty shuddered, and then her body went into a slow rhythmic convulsion. Whimpering, Marty let out a succession of "oohs" while she climaxed to multiple orgasms. Dominika watched in delight.

Chapter Ten

Not a word was spoken as Dominika untied Marty. They paused for a moment, gazed into each other's eyes and then kissed. A second later Dominika led Marty up the stairs to her private bedroom, bathed in a blue glow from the mica lampshades that were spread in various locations. There were also several wrought iron candelabras lit with glowing candles. A large hand-carved French armoire stood tall on one side of the room. Covering most of the floor was a Persian rug in deep blues and crimson. A queen-sized bed sat in the middle of the room, topped with a canopy with a sheer white draping. The room had an ethereal feel to it. Marty sensed that she was going to be lifted into the heavens in utter elation and pleasure, again. Dominika had Marty loosen the drawstrings of her bustier. And then Dominika took a seat in a Queen Anne chair, undid her boots and peeled off her stockings while Marty watched in reverie and excitement.

Marty stepped towards the bed and sat up on it. Her eyes glowed lust-fully, flickering in the candlelight as she eagerly anticipated her new lover. Dominika took her panties off, stepped towards the bed and stopped. Marty caressed Dominika's body with her hands and then held onto her lover's rear as she kissed her belly and then nuzzled Dominika's naked vulva. Marty picked up a scent of tangerine and honeysuckle as she licked Dominika's smooth crotch.

At that moment, an out-of-town regular who had an appointment rang Dominika's doorbell. Dominika suddenly spurted out, "Damn, I completely forgot. My appointment. Sorry, princess, but I must go. You can stay if you like."

"It's Marty," Marty said and then hesitated. She eagerly wanted to stay and experience this new forbidden pleasure that Dominika had exposed to her. She was so young in so many ways, though. The reality of the situation shot through her. "I better get going."

Dominika was hoping to get to see Marty again to continue what had been sadly interrupted. "You come back soon." She was staring into Marty's eyes with great intensity. "Soon?"

"Yes, but I live in Portland," Marty said and curtly smiled. But Dominika got the impression she wouldn't see Marty again, at least for a while, leaving her to yearn in desire.

"Okay, Marty, you can leave after I bring my customer downstairs." Marty nodded.

And then Dominika kissed Marty on the cheek.

"I think I need my clothes first," Marty said.

"That would help. It's a little cold out there," Dominika wryly responded.

Marty chuckled and then admiringly watched Dominika put on a studded black leather robe as she left the room to go downstairs.

Chapter Eleven

It seemed as if every bit of dopamine in Marty's brain had been released like a dam opening its floodgates to a rush of raging waters. The surge was so tremendous. She had never felt so aroused, but then again, her only lover up to that point had been Roy, a latent homosexual. And it wasn't just Dominika's tenderness; it was the pain she gave that Marty suddenly craved.

She slowly sauntered down Van Ness puffing on a cigarette. She looked as if she were Marlene Dietrich in some noir film. Marty needed something strong to bring her down to earth. Her body was buzzing, and her mind was lit up like a case of fireworks on the 4th[th] of July. A double dose of chamomile tea came to mind, and so she flagged a cab to transport her to her favorite place that offered herbal beverages and finely made sweet delectables.

Crème de la Crème was a nouvelle pastry shop that was a California French fusion of sorts. A husband and wife team owned the place. The wife was from Mill Valley, a pastry chef who trained at Lenotre' in France where she met her husband, a Tunisian Frenchman who had been in Paris on a textile business trip. He loved her cream puffs; the rest was history.

The shop had a North African feel to it. It was light and airy. There was a bit of white about and sky-blue walls with silhouettes of palm trees and reeds painted on them. One wall had a large Persian rug hanging on it. There were several live palm trees scattered about the place, and it was furnished with both booths and freestanding tables. The chairs and booths were cushioned to make you feel relaxed and comfortable while indulging in the sweet fare, and plenty of Edith Piaf and the Gypsy Kings were piped through the pastry shop speakers.

Marty stepped inside the patisserie and was greeted and then escorted to a table by the husband-owner who acted as the *maître d'*. The place seated about forty and it was three-quarters full. Half of the customers were dressed in Halloween garb. A few stares came Marty's way, particularly by three rotund women who were dressed like gypsies and sitting in a booth that normally seated five comfortably. They occupied the whole booth and then some, encroaching upon the tables around them.

Marty took her seat at a small table for two not far away, was handed a menu and given a nod by the owner, who stepped away towards the kitchen. Marty briefly looked at the menu but was distracted by the rotund gypsies, especially the one in the middle, who was larger and louder than the other two and was gorging on an Opera Torte wedge. She was utterly engrossed, snorting while she devoured the delicate pastry, smacking her lips and moaning, "Oh, my God, this is so good." The others nodded agreement while noshing their own sweets.

Marty became a little agitated as she watched and listened to the three. Her thighs were still twitching from earlier. She refocused on the menu and looked at the brief note about how Crème de la Crème used only the finest ingredients such as Maui vanilla beans, free-range chicken eggs, 40 percent organic whipped cream from Napa Valley, and high-grade Montanan flour to maximize the gastronomic experience.

Marty took notice of the bavarois puffs, which she had had before and enjoyed thoroughly. They were made with a blend of pastry cream and whipped cream piped into a delicate, walnut-sized cream puff shell and topped with a thin coating of Belgian chocolate. The puffs were dipped to order so when they arrived at the table, the chocolate was semi-soft. They were creamy, decadent and full of texture. Dozens of flavors were happily consumed by the patrons, as well as boxed-up for their take-home pleasure.

The waitress stopped off at Marty's table. Marty closed her menu and gave her order of a double chamomile tea, three bavarois puffs—one vanilla, one chocolate and one Frangelico hazelnut—and a mixed-berry Napoleon. The waitress apologetically responded that raspberries and blackberries were briefly out of season, but strawberries were available. It was not a problem for Marty as she waited for her little treats and reminisced about the pleasure and pain Dominika had inflicted on her. She couldn't believe that she could experience such depths of orgasm. And the softness she felt when she and Dominika were intertwined! It was her first experience with a woman. She had kissed her third cousin twice removed once, but it never went that far. She was getting wet again just thinking about it as the creamy lubricant trickled from her vagina.

Marty was pulled away from her bliss by the waitress who put down the chamomile tea and the three bavarois puffs, which were served on a round white fine china plate. There was a ring of crème anglaise in dime-size teardrops, with alternating strawberry and mango sauce droplets in the center of the teardrops, around the border. A light dusting of powdered sugar coated the plate.

The waitress said, "I'm waiting on the Napoleon."

Marty sipped her tea, amped up from all the excitement. She indulged in one puff and then another. The blend of sweetness, endorphins, and dopamine in her brain caused a kaleidoscope of visual impulses as she looked around her. Her mind was frenetic as her motions became both animated and slow. She felt for a brief moment as if she were Alice from the Lewis Carroll *Alice in Wonderland* story, slipping down into the rabbit hole while there was also a mature little Red Riding Hood laughing as she was chased by a Big Bad Hairy Wolf. Yet she was not experiencing wonderment but only confusion. The Gypsy Queens appeared to be slobbering figures in some grotesque feast. And out of the blue, a table of several French expats started singing, *"Frère Jacques, frère Jacques,*

Dormez-vous? Dormez-vous? Sonnez les matines! Sonnez les matines! Din, dan, don. Din, dan, don."

Marty was so wound up and something stoked the fires of angst within her. She became unnerved. Perhaps it was the deep feeling of rejection that finally welled up and came to the surface. The things you want to forget, like the scene earlier with Roy and the devil. And the time when she was seven and visiting her grandparents. She had gone down to the kitchen to get a glass of goat's milk before bed. She found her grandfather humping one of the maids over the kitchen sink and couldn't get out of her head that vision of his large hairless ass swaying back and forth.

She loved her grandparents dearly. Why had her grandmother, who had known of her grandfather's trysts, just looked away? Marty felt betrayed as a granddaughter. Beads of anger dripped into her bloodstream as she peered over at the Gypsies and without thinking twice, she got up, rushed towards the Gypsy in the middle, grabbed a cream puff and smashed it on her face, yelling, "Have another, you fucking pig!"

The Gypsy cast a sharp, steely gaze upon Marty, unblinking, and then grabbed Marty across the table with one of her behemoth hands. Marty was suddenly stopped in her tracks. She had been planning on quickly running out the front door. She started to kick at the table and yelled, "Let me go, you fat cunt," as the Gypsy, hunched over the table, held on with tremendous strength. Fear surged through Marty's whole being, and then she got clubbed on the side of her face by the Gypsy's other hand.

The Gypsy spouted out, "Eat me, you skinny little bitch!"

The other women threw a cream puff each at Marty, though later regretted wasting beautiful pastry on that trollop. The Gypsy then let go and Marty fell to the floor, writhing backward to get away from the raging Cyclops. She quickly got to her feet and rushed out the door, leaving behind a melee of demolished pastries and traumatized guests.

Chapter Twelve

Shortly afterward, Marty found herself across the street in a darkened storefront across from Dominika's place. Not a person or moving car was in sight. She lit a cigarette as she waited and watched for Dominika's last customer. A half-hour later, a man in his early forties wearing a black wool coat, gray slacks, a dark fedora, and gloves stepped outside of Dominika's building and walked up the street, slowly disappearing into the night.

Marty waited about fifteen minutes and then crossed the street. Her heart was racing like mad. Her body and mind were surging. She needed to see Dominika, to feel her body, taste her breath and smell her exotic aroma. She rang the buzzer. No answer. She rang it again, thinking Dominika might be in the dungeon cleaning up. She looked up towards the second floor and saw the shadows of two figures cast by the candle-light. Not a word from Dominika. She waited, then crossed the street and then waited again for an hour or more. Numerous times she wanted to phone Dominika, but she waited.

After almost two hours, a half a pack of cigarettes smoked, and chilled to the bone, Marty started to ring Dominika on her cell phone. Just then Dominika appeared at her front door with another woman in her early twenties. She put her phone in her pocket and peered across the street. From what Marty could tell, the woman was slender, attractive and might have had auburn hair.

While Dominika held the door, the two embraced and kissed each other, for what seemed an eternity to Marty. Anger raged inside her as she peered through her steely eyes. She looked as if she were a lioness ready to pounce upon her prey. A cab pulled up to the curb, and the woman got in. As it sped away, Dominika looked down the street and in

Marty's direction. She was hidden in the darkness. Then Dominika stepped back inside the building.

Marty waited ten more minutes. She crossed the street and rang Dominika's buzzer. Two minutes later, Dominika's voice came through the speaker. "Who is it?"

Marty, with her heart and mind about to burst from rage and her clitoris buzzing with erotic excitement, finally said, "It's me, Marty."

The buzzer rang, and Marty entered the building. Marty quickly climbed the stairs and entered Dominika's bedroom. She was taking a bath. Marty poked her head inside. Dominika looked over at Marty and was shocked. Marty's hair was disheveled and covered with the splattered cream puffs, the side of her face red from the smack she took, and she looked like an alley cat that had been battered in a fight and now was coming in for more.

"Oh my God, what happened to you?" Dominika asked with concern as she started to get up from the bath.

"No, no, I'm okay. Don't get up," Marty responded.

Dominika slipped back down. Her full, round breasts shimmering from the soap bobbed in the bathwater. As she pointed to a stack of towels, she said, "Wash yourself off; there are some towels."

Marty just stood there, glaring at Dominika.

"What is it, Marty?"

Marty asked in a jealous tone, "Who was that woman you kissed before when you were standing outside?"

"A friend," Dominika genuinely said.

"She looked more like your lover." Marty was irate.

"She..." And then before Dominika could say the woman was her cleaning gal and they were just friends, she was interrupted by Marty who was raging with jealousy.

Pointing out the window, she said, "I was outside across the street. She was here more than two hours." Marty asked angrily, "Were you two making love?"

Trying to appease Marty and hoping she would calm down, Dominika said gently, "Why don't we go downstairs and have some tea and talk some, okay?"

Marty quickly responded, "I'll go make it." And started downstairs. Dominika called, "The tea is in the cupboard next to the refrigerator."

Dominika slipped out of the bath, toweled herself off, put on a robe and then put her hair up in a bun with a towel. She then grabbed a tube of lotion and applied some to her face. She hitched up a foot onto the edge of the bathtub and began applying lotion to her foot, ankle, and calf. Marty rushed in, wearing a pair of latex gloves. She pushed Dominika from her rear into the bathtub. Dominika's head hit the sidewall and then she slipped into the water—she was unconscious. Blood began to stream into the bath water from her forehead, turning it murky pink. Marty, holding an electrical stimulator, looked for an outlet. She found one by the vanity, plugged the stimulator in and turned it on. She looked once more at Dominika, whose body had sunk slightly into the bath, her smooth crotch and breasts popping through her wet robe.

Dominika was staring at Marty from the abyss. If she could have uttered some pleading words before her demise, she would have said, "Perhaps you just misunderstood the whole situation. That I was saying goodbye to a friend. Yes, we were lovers, but she is just a friend now. You know, we could have shared so much, you and me. So much pleasure. But how could I have missed seeing this with you? That you were somehow psychologically not sound? To be so jealous? I'm always safe and cautious. I should have questioned your connection with Tomas. Who are you? I would have never figured this from you. You're too gorgeous to be a murderer. And you're so young. So very young..."

"Twice tonight I was betrayed," Marty said in a sullen voice. And then tossed the stimulator into the water by Dominika's feet. The water sparked, and the stimulator flared. Dominika's body convulsed, arched, and then the lights throughout the house went out. Marty slipped out of the bathroom and slowly made her way down the stairwell. She tumbled about three-quarters of the way down, got up and then was gone in a flash.

Chapter Thirteen

The following morning, around ten, Marty was fast asleep in the hotel room, sprawled out on the bed with sheets tossed about and her head in the middle of the pillows placed on either side of her head. Roy entered the room as spry as a spring chicken and looked over at Marty, who popped her head up briefly. Roy noticed the bruise on the side of her face and stepped towards the bed. He sat next to Marty and brushed her hair back to get a better look at her face. He pulled back his hand and rubbed his fingers. They were sticky from leftover cream puffs.

Roy asked in an urgent voice, "Oh my God, what the hell happened to you?"

In a not so subtle tone with a distinct frog in her voice, "What happened to me? What happened to you?"

Really concerned, Roy asked, "I tried calling you last night. You didn't pick up or call me back. Are you okay?"

"No." And then Marty began to cry.

Roy bent his body over hers. She arched her back up to push him off. Roy stroked her hair and then got up.

He asked with true sincerity, "What happened, Marty? Tell me."

"I got into a fight with some fat chick at Crème de la Crème. She fucking pissed me off," Marty replied and covered her head with a pillow.

"She must have nailed you pretty hard to get a bruise like that."

As Roy began to pack, he said, "Would you mind driving back home alone? I'm going to hang out with Tomas and the boys for the rest of the day. I'll take the train up tomorrow."

"I need to be loved, Roy," Marty said, beckoning.

Roy got a good sense she was crashing because she always got incredibly emotional over the little things, like the time he brought her roses instead of bougainvillea for her sixteenth birthday when she had just happened to be crashing. She had ranted and cried all day. He grabbed his suitcase, stepped towards the door and turned his head towards Marty.

"You want me to stay, babe?"

Marty responded, "Just go. I'll be all right."

He opened the door and asked, "You pick me up at the station?"

Marty motioned him to go with her hand. And then Roy closed the door behind him.

Two seconds later, Marty sprang up out of bed and searched her pockets, all around the room and the bathroom for her cell phone. She was frantic and realized she must have lost it in Dominika's stairwell when she fell.

She started to panic. "Fuck!" She then put on some pink sweats and grabbed a pair of black Sunray sunglasses and the hotel keys and headed out the door.

Twenty minutes later she cautiously walked down the block across from Dominika's with the sweatshirt hood over her head, looking like a hip-hop Grim Reaper in pink. She glanced across the street at a battery of cop cars, an ambulance that had Dominika's body inside, a battery of police officers and a few plainclothesmen. The area had been cordoned off. As she made her way down the street, she crossed to the other side while continuing to glance over towards the crime scene. What she saw was fortuitous because the auburn-haired woman from the night before, Dominika's ex-lover, was in handcuffs and being escorted by a female officer into a police car. A male officer opened the back door, and then the female officer placed the presumed killer in the back seat and shut the door.

Evidence for what the police thought might have been the final act by two former lovers who had a history of domestic violence was circumstantial but nonetheless made a plausible picture of murder. As the cop car pulled away with Dominika's ex-lover, who had stopped by Dominka's because she did not hear back from her, a Detective Macklin, a late-forties full-framed five-eleven no-nonsense man with badly dyed reddish-dark hair, stepped out of the front door holding up a plastic bag with Marty's cell phone inside. His younger partner, Detective Harris, a tall precocious fellow in his mid-thirties with light brown curly hair, took a quick look at the phone, and then they both hopped into an unmarked Ford and sped away.

Marty didn't hesitate. She ran around the block back towards the hotel. She was in flight mode in concert with the ambulance siren that had just begun. As she ran, the ambulance passed her, and she could see Dominika's gray-blanketed body through the back door of the ambulance. A rush of adrenaline shot through Marty's body and then she immediately stopped, bent over and vomited into the gutter between two cars. Several people on the street looked at her as if she was some sick drug addict as they walked by. Marty wiped her mouth off with the side of her sleeve and began to slowly trot down the street.

She began to hum the song *Frère Jacques*, which she had heard the night before, in a sad melodic tone to appease her aching soul. As tears began to stream down her face, she pleadingly asked Dominika's spirit, "Please forgive me, my sweet. I lost myself in feelings of rapture for you." But what she couldn't reconcile of the previous night, when she had killed for the first time, was the guilt that she had for tasting the flesh of another woman. That was as strong if not stronger than the jealousy she felt over Dominika's friend. It was the forbidden lust that she had never experienced that wrenched her being and tore it to pieces—that lesbian lust that tasted so sweet and was as bitter as death itself.

Chapter Fourteen

A good ten hours later she pulled up the private driveway to her home, a mid-sized stone mansion on a cul-de-sac with only a few houses in Lake Oswego, Oregon, a highly prized and affluent suburb of Portland. When she had barely gotten out of her car, her father, a well-manicured man of forty-five, standing six-foot tall with black wavy hair and the same cobalt-blue eyes as Martha, appeared at the front stairway. His demeanor was serious. Martha sheepishly looked away as she stepped towards him carrying her overnight bag.

"Marty, where in the hell have you been?" he pleaded. "The Oregon State Police were here looking for you."

As Marty sighed, he could see the bruise on her face. He gently grabbed her chin with his large hand and turned her face sideways to get a better look. He then asked, "For God's sake, what happened? I've been trying to reach you, but there was a voice message saying your phone was disconnected."

Marty leaned into his chest and sobbed, "Oh, Daddy."

He hugged her hesitantly and then grabbed hold of her biceps, looked her square in the face and seriously asked, "Now, Princess, you tell me what happened last night. What were you doing with a dominatrix? The police said that she might have been killed, and the San Francisco police wanted some information regarding your whereabouts."

"I had gone to the Halloween party dressed as a dominatrix, and I was just curious about what they did. And I probably lost my phone when I was there. Dominika was killed?" She feigned shock.

"Tomorrow morning, you and me and Roy are going straight to my attorney's office because two detectives from the San Francisco police are coming up tomorrow afternoon, and they want to set up an interview. They're going to want to know everything."

"I didn't do it," Marty explained.

"This is pretty serious, so we need to get every bit of minutia and anything else that you may have forgotten on the table with my attorney before the police talk to you. Do you understand?"

"Yes, but Roy won't be able to make it, he's still down in San Francisco."

"Was he with you when you went over to this whore's place?"

"She's not a whore, but no he wasn't." A tear trickled down Marty's cheek.

"All right, this I see may require some intervention. Let's go inside," her father said, knowing his daughter's proclivity for drama.

Marty pursed her lips, and they headed towards the front door.

Two days later, after Detectives Macklin and Harris from the San Francisco Police Department Homicide Squad came and went, Marty was taken off the suspect list and put on the keep-an-eye-out list, at least for a time. Macklin and Harris' investigation on her whereabouts came up against a brick wall when they went to get the surveillance tape from the St. Francis Hotel, where Marty and Roy had stayed that weekend in San Francisco. Apparently, the surveillance equipment had malfunctioned, and they were not able to verify the times Marty was supposed to have come and gone, much less any evidence of her showing up just after the time of Dominika's murder. Roy also testified that he was with her at the hotel during said time.

Macklin, in the final summation, felt that it was the ex-lover who had murdered Dominika, but not before he pegged Marty for it. He originally thought she and Dominika got into a fight, ergo the bruise on her face, after one thing led to another following some kinky activity. Marty left and then came back, electrocuted her out of revenge for the hit she had taken and then lost her cell on the way out of the building. But after they verified the Crème de la Crème story, the revenge thing was out the window.

At first, Harris believed they had their woman in the ex-lover who had been there close to the time of the murder, but something with Marty's cell phone and the St Francis surveillance equipment malfunctioning did not sit well with him. Suicide was ruled out of the equation. Dominika had a striving business, and she was described as being a fun-loving, happy person in the dominatrix community.

The San Francisco District Attorney's Office ultimately charged the ex-lover with the murder, clearing Marty after the interview with Macklin and Harris. Although Macklin, whether for his own personal thrill or not, asked Marty if she and Dominika had had sex that night. And had the ex showed up at that time? Marty denied any such thing happened. The DA got the ex for a good twenty years to life for the murder following a quick trial where Marty never had to testify. The jury had an easy one since the ex had a record of abuse. It was a clear-cut case of murder even though they had mostly circumstantial evidence. Marty's father wound up dropping ten grand to someone at the St. Francis for a two-dollar piece of plastic, five grand to the Fat Gypsy to avoid any assault charges and a whopping twenty grand to his attorney for his intervention in the matter. He had given a call to the San Francisco DA, a buddy of his from Golden State University Law School.

Subsequently, Marty made as few visits to San Francisco as possible, and when she did go, it was only to visit Roy who started to attend med school. And never again did she ever put on a dominatrix costume for Halloween, except for a time when she became a dominatrix herself.

Chapter Sixteen

Marty was making a little headway down the I-5 freeway, but she started to get hunger pangs. She pulled off just north of Portland, into a drive-through, and ordered a double cheeseburger with extra bacon and their house secret sauce and French fries. She'd have salad tomorrow, she rationalized, as she drove back onto the freeway, slid her hand into the bag, ate a few French fries, grabbed the burger, unwrapped it with one hand and took a big bite. She ate about half and then searched for the bottle of Piper Jouet in the back seat, peeled off the cover and eased the cork off with a napkin. The champagne fizzled over, and she sucked on the bottle. A passerby looked over and shot her a look of scorn. She just licked her lips and took another sip.

Relief settled in from the distance she traveled enhanced by the fuzziness from the champagne that she had savored along the monotonous drive. She decided to head over to the Pacific Coast Highway, somewhere north of Portland, skipping going home. After all, her mother was probably zoned out on Xanax and whiskey sours. Marty just wasn't in the mood to deal with her inebriation and the dwellings-on how Marty's father left her for that little slut. Although, she thought, her mother was probably right about her father's wife, who was as young as Marty. Marty thought she was cute but a total bitch. She had caught herself imagining stringing her up with some rope and giving her the whip, cracking it on her tight little ass. Yes, she married Marty's father for the money, but what else is new. She would never acquiesce to calling her step-mom. But it was always a chore with her mother. Never getting any comfort from her, always having to give it.

She wondered why she had not heard back from Roy. He seemed to be distracted of late, and she felt she had to work extra hard to even get a simple hello from time to time. He had his life, yet he had always been there for her. So, people change, and maybe she wasn't as important to him anymore. He had his life mate, his friends like Tomas and their way of life. She was feeling sensitive and maybe even a little insecure.

It was getting near dark, and Marty started to feel a little drowsy. She steered her way into a lookout point just north of Golden Beach. She knew it well. It was one of her favorite places, perched high above the vast blue Pacific that was so peaceful. She had been there many times before. She wished she and Roy had made love underneath the moonlight in rhythm with the surf nearby, but for some reason, that romantic dream had never been fulfilled. One day, though, she would have a house that had a huge picture window she could look out at the serenity of the Pacific Ocean while sipping on some milky chai. She was dreaming, but one day she would have her wish come true.

Marty had parked her car and shut it off and then slipped her sandals off, put the seat back, stuck her left leg out the window and took in a deep breath of ocean air. She let out a contented "hum" and closed her eyes. In what seemed minutes, she had been asleep for hours. She woke to the gravelly noise of tires coming her way. She opened her eyes. It was dark, a blue-black darkness partially illuminated by a crescent moon that hung in the distant sky above the ocean. She looked in the rear-view mirror and saw a sheriff's car and an officer step out holding a flashlight. She pulled her leg in and composed herself, wiping the dribble from the side of her mouth with a grease-stained napkin from earlier. Her leg had fallen asleep, and it stung with pins and needles. All she could hear in her head was the sheriff saying, "Ma'am, please get out of your car with your hands up; you're under arrest for murder." Her mind started to race. Calm down, Princess, she said to herself, as if her father were speaking to her.

The sheriff, a tall, slender man in his late twenties, average looking with sandy brown hair and wearing a pair of wire-frame glasses, stepped towards her car. He took a glance inside the rear window and then walked alongside the car, flashing his light around the ground looking for anything suspicious. Marty said to herself, "Come on, let's get this over with." He stepped up to her door and flashed the light quickly at Marty's face and then inside around the passenger side. He caught a whiff of alcohol, beer or wine maybe, and charred hamburger. He flashed the light in Marty's eyes and then removed the light.

He asked, "What are you doing here?"

Her cobalt eyes that flickered like the night sky instantly mesmerized him. His heart started to race with excitement over her beauty.

"I pulled off to take a rest," Marty said, not wanting to arouse any suspicion of where she had been.

"You know it's not safe for a pretty gal like yourself to be out here all alone at night."

"I was about to get going, anyway," she said, thinking she could go on her merry way without incident.

As an impulse, the sheriff asked, "You mind if I step inside and take a seat?"

Without hesitation, Marty said, "Okay." Thinking, *whatever it takes.*

"Nice. I'll just pull my car around, so I can hear my radio."

He quickly got into his car and pulled around the front of Marty's and then lined it up along the passenger side. In his over-excitement, he stopped so quickly and shut his car off so distractedly that he thought he put the steering lever into the park position. He didn't realize that the car had stalled and was stuck in neutral. He quickly pulled down his passenger side window and got out. Marty applied some fresh lip-gloss as she regained her composure.

The sheriff stepped inside Marty's car. "I just wanted to make sure you weren't attempting something that would endanger your life," he said.

"No, I wouldn't do that. I was just tired. Besides, that's a long way down." Gesturing with her head towards the cliff.

"It would be a shame. You're such a beautiful woman," he said, chuckling and trying to ease into Marty's good graces.

"You're not a bad-looking guy, either," she said, playing him up.

With his heart running through his throat, he said, "I don't normally do this with someone I just pulled over, but you mind if I kiss you?"

She laughed slightly. "Go ahead. But you didn't pull me over."

"Right," the sheriff numbly muttered and then took his glasses off as he neared Marty.

He kissed her neck and then slipped his right hand underneath Marty's top and began rubbing her breast. Marty could not help but think that this guy worked fast. He slipped her top down towards her belly, exposing her breasts, and then he rubbed her left breast, inadvertently flicking his wedding band on her nipple while kissing her right breast. Marty became instantly grossed out at the noises the horny sheriff was making. It sounded like a suckling marmot with half groans and moans while he slobbered all over her breast with his spit.

Marty freaked out. "What the fuck?!" she screamed to herself. Then, as the sheriff was thoroughly engrossed with her breasts and his lust, Marty watched in amusement as his car rolled backward along a slight decline towards the edge of the cliff. As the car reached the edge and began teetering over the cliff, Marty tapped the sheriff on the shoulder. He looked up at her as she pointed at his car. Startled, he jumped out of the car and watched his transportation and likely his job, tumble down the cliff.

Marty got out of the car, chuckling to herself. The sheriff had his hand on his head looking at the destruction. And then shook his head saying, "Oh shit" over and over again.

Marty quipped, "Oops" while pulling up her top.

He then said, "You better get going," realizing the seriousness of the situation.

As she got in her car, the sheriff asked, "You think I could call you sometime?"

She shook her head and said, "I don't think so." And then drove away, tossing the empty bottle of Piper Jouet out the window as she sped from the lookout point back towards the Pacific Coast Highway.

The sheriff searched for his cell phone in his pockets. It was in his car. All he could say was, "Fuck!" Marty was gone. He didn't even catch her name and had been careless in his actions, not even running her plates before he stepped into some vortex from hell. Good thing. But he knew he couldn't or wouldn't explain that one, except to his buddies over JD shots and beers at some local sports bar. "She was so fuckin' hot," he'd go on.

And they'd ask, "Did you fuck her?"

He'd say with utter shamelessness, "Oh yeah, she was great!"

"What was her name?" Getting into his story and the chick who was as elusive as a phantom.

"Sheila," he'd say.

They'd all repeat her name sequentially in a variety of inflections and with grins on their face, "Sheila, Sheila, Sheila," with the sheriff smiling harder at every pronouncement of "Sheila." This was all before he went home to his pregnant wife who would ask him how the game was. He'd respond, "Good." And then she'd ask, "Who won?" And so the story goes.

Chapter Seventeen

Sometime in the early morning hours, Marty drove over the Golden Gate Bridge, and since it was a little too early for Roy to be awake, she meandered into downtown San Francisco and slowly drove by Dominika's old place. The night that changed her life forever seemed like almost a century ago. What was it that still brought her back here, searching deep inside herself? What if Dominika had just passed her by at the party? She would have never been given Dominika's business card, and that night would not have turned out the way it did. But it was like a dog who gets to taste the flesh and blood of a live clucking chicken for the first time; he gets a bloodlust that he can't shake, and he keeps hopping a fence or digging a hole underneath the fence to get at more of the fresh poultry. *Is that why I'm here? I don't know.*

All she knew was that Dominika's place was now a children's day-care center. If the families only knew. But it's funny, she thought, how she tried to become a dominatrix in her last year at Golden State. How she became so enraged with her father, who sold his pharmaceutical company without even telling her after she spent four years of her life in school, thinking that one day she could take over the company. That was the plan anyway. She vented her angst on the clientele she tried to cultivate, but they thought she was too merciless. Her last customer wound up rushed to the hospital because he passed out and suffered a mild stroke after she whipped him ferociously. Fortunately for her, she had her few, yet dwindling clients sign a disclaimer waiver. She just did not have it in her, especially after the rage wore off over her father. It was basically a break-even proposition after renting a mini-warehouse, which she had converted into a dungeon. She also had a bag of tricks, which she sold most of, though she kept a whip or two.

Shortly after, Marty was fast asleep in her car in front of Roy's Nob Hill apartment. Roy and his life-mate, Enrique Flambé, a Latin-American male of twenty-three, who stood five foot eight with dark curly hair and brown eyes, got up to have breakfast, not knowing Marty was outside. But they did expect her at some point during the day. Fresh from a weekend trip to a gay dude ranch in Cheyenne, Wyoming, they wore a matching pair of bucking bronco robes and pajama sets—Roy in red and Enrique in blue—while they drank fresh-brewed double French roast coffee and ate day-old croissants from the Oh La La Bakery with soft Irish butter and homemade blood orange marmalade made by either Roy or Enrique. They were both heavily active homemakers. Roy was more into cooking, though, while home decorating was Enrique's forte.

"What do you think she's going to say when we tell her I quit med school to go to culinary school," Roy said reluctantly.

"Maybe she'll want to come work for us when we open our bistro?" Enrique said.

"You know how sensitive she can be; she'll wind up turning into a drama queen and storming out of here. You know how that is? We're going to be living her dream," Roy sadly said.

"You don't have to tell her," Enrique suggested.

"Of course, we do, but when is the question. Better to get it over with. She'll be here soon. I'll let her know," Roy said just as a knock came at the door.

Roy opened the door. Roy and Enrique glanced at each other, silently commenting on Marty's appearance. She looked like a wreck. "Hey, baby," Roy said, hugging Marty. Enrique said, *"Ola Amiga,"* and waited his turn to hug.

While having coffee, Roy and Enrique gave minute details of their dude ranch weekend getaway where they were served crème de menthe frappes upon arrival and some lovely chardonnay-grape hard candies to suck on their way to the airport. They had their showers, and then the trio went to breakfast at the local grill.

As they waited for their meals, Enrique asked, "Okay, after we have our yummy food, we should go to the de Young. What do you say?"

Roy said, "No, the Legion of Honor. Much more interesting artwork."

Marty sensed an argument was about to ensue, and she was right.

Enrique said, "We always go there. How many times can you look at Mon blah and De gagh?"

"How many times can you look at boring landscapes?" Roy shrilled.

"The de Young has it going on, and you know it. It's modern." Enrique was getting louder.

The restaurant patrons got a little impatient with the shouting.

"Legion of Honor," Roy shouted.

"De Young," Enrique shouted even louder.

"Boys, boys! Enough already. We'll flip a coin and settle this." Marty was a bit frustrated with the situation.

"Okay," Enrique said angrily.

Marty pulled a quarter out from her purse and set it on top off her thumb and her index finger.

"I'm taking heads," Roy said furiously.

"Then I'm taking tails." Enrique was practically in tears.

Marty flipped the quarter, and it flew over to the next table. She got up, excused herself to the couple sitting there, went under the table and searched for the quarter. It went underneath the table stand, and she was unable to reach it.

"Sorry," she excused herself and grabbed another quarter from her purse. She flipped it again, and it flew into the water glass of the same table where she'd lost the previous quarter.

"Oops, I'm sorry," she said to the couple.

"All right, Enrique, I'm the tie-breaker. I'd say we go to the Legion of Honor," she said.

Almost immediately Enrique angrily said, "Roy and I are opening up our own bistro after he goes to culinary school." He then got up and stormed out the restaurant.

Marty looked at Roy very confused by the whole mess. Roy feebly screamed out, "Enrique, where are you going?" At that point, the waiter came back with the manager, and they asked Marty and Roy to leave because they were bothering the other customers.

Chapter Eighteen

Roy and Marty left the restaurant, a bit dejected, had a quick breakfast burrito in a hole-in-the-wall joint, and then took public transportation to the Legion of Honor. Roy explained to her on the ride that he didn't want to be a doctor and was going to go to the Cordon Bleu in the fall. Marty quietly listened to him and said, "That's nice." She was mostly quiet the whole way as Roy babbled on about how he found his true passion in cooking and briefly apologized for Enrique's behavior. Marty wasn't sure, though, what was more abhorrent: Enrique's childish rant or Roy's dismissing what had happened at the restaurant.

When they got to the Legion of Honor, Marty's emotions were flat, and she was sullen, partly due to her tiredness and coming off her peak, but also because Roy had not told her before about his plans. She felt betrayed. She thought they were close enough that he would have told her sooner. She could only rationalize that people are just funny sometimes in how they can be. "So, he's going to be a chef, huh."

Inside the museum was a Hieronymus Bosch exhibition that Marty took a slight fancy to. It perked up her excitement a little, but she was still feeling her drab and languid usual self. Roy stood in front of Bosch's painting "Seven Deadly Sins and Four Last Things" with bemusement and excitedly said to Marty, "Babe, remember the Seven Deadly Sins Party that we went to in high school? There's a painting of the same name. How funny is that?"

Marty was at the point of being annoyed with Roy and especially at being called "babe." She did not care for that. And where did that come from anyway? Was he being affectionate and had Enrique sensed it and gotten jealous somehow? Well, she and Roy romantically ended the day she found him in the closet. There was no going back in time with him.

Besides, he just seemed so self-absorbed, much more than he had ever been.

"How could I ever forget," Marty said sarcastically, stepping over to Roy as they both viewed the very vivid and detailed oil-on-wood painting of circled images with an obvious religious connotation. There was no precise date on the painting since Bosch never dated his works, but it was from the early fifteen hundreds. It had four small circles in each corner respectively detailing the death of the sinner, judgment, hell, and glory. These surrounded a larger circle in which the seven deadly sins were depicted, starting with wrath at the bottom, then, moving clockwise, envy, greed, gluttony, sloth, lust, and pride. At the center of the seven deadly sins circle was another circle with a figure, presumably Jesus Christ, rising from a tomb. Below that image, a Latin inscription read: Beware, Beware, God Sees.

Marty asked Roy, "Would you ever have this hanging in your apartment?"

Roy played along with Marty, "You mean like steal it?"

Marty said, "No. Let's say you could borrow it. Could you see yourself with it?"

"First of all, it's better to steal than borrow, because when you borrow you're obligated to give it back. But why? I don't need a reminder of how I live," Roy said smartly.

Marty responded, "Touché."

They continued with the exhibition and viewed Bosch's other paintings including "The Ship of Fools," "The Cure of Folly," "The Conjurer," "The Temptation of St. Anthony" and "The Owl." But when they reached "The Garden of Earthly Delights," Marty was bedazzled.

"Wow," she said. "I love it; it's so brilliant and inventive," as she stared at the incredibly detailed three-paneled painting. What captured her full attention was the wild orgy of the center panel, not the less mesmerizing depictions of The Garden of Eden flanking on the left and Hell on the right.

Roy rhetorically said, "It's all about lust, isn't it?" He was well aware of Marty's sexual proclivities.

"It's the only force that keeps me motivated," she said almost defiantly.

"Oh yeah, how bad have you been lately, you sinner?" Roy asked.

"I let a cop suck on my tits, so he would leave me alone," Marty said.

"You dirty whore—or was he the dirty copper?" Roy said mockingly in a voice like James Cagney.

"Nah, I've had more enjoyment flossing my teeth," she said sarcastically.

On the ride back from the museum, there was not one question of how you are doing or what are your plans. Not even a "Hey, Marty, you look great, other than the rings underneath your eyes." No, it was all about Roy and his quest for fame and the bistro that he and Enrique were going to open. And how he was going to decorate the place. He and Enrique, he meant. "I think I'm going to call him Ricky from now on. He just seems overly sensitive about his name of late," Roy said. "That's what we should call it, Ricky and Roy's Bistro or maybe, Roy and Ricky's Bistro. No, we'll put his name first; he'll be happy when I tell him that. Looks like I'll have to get some designer chocolates and roses. You know, cheer him up, but he better be home, or else I'll have to eat the chocolates myself."

When they got back to Roy's apartment, Roy went into the bathroom. Enrique was nowhere to be found. Marty grabbed her bags and slipped out the door without a goodbye. Her emotions welled up inside her so fiercely, and she was afraid that if she stayed, something awful would happen that others would never be able to forgive her for, let alone herself. She got into her car and drove straight up to Sonoma.

Chapter Nineteen

When she arrived, she hit the first winery she could find in the Russian River Valley, which began a five-day gargle, swallow, fuck and suckfest where she did every handsome Tom, Dick, and Harriet she could find. Finally, on the last day of her marathon bacchanal, she came up for air by a kidney-shaped swimming pool at a high-end spa. She lounged on a chaise soaking up the late afternoon sun, a lot number and a little less stunned than five days prior. She tried to ponder her future in an almost semi-conscious state, just not wanting to deal. She was in a fairly good financial situation with the inheritance she received when her grandparents passed away, but she wanted to do something with her culinary education. Yet she had just come off of six straight years of pure college-level academics—and a murder—and was in need of a good rest, at least for this one afternoon.

She finally awoke and shook off the haziness in her head. Drank the last bit of Arnold Palmer she had by her side and picked up her cell phone. There were some twenty or so text messages, mostly from Roy and a few from her mother. She didn't even bother and headed back towards her room. While walking past an umbrella table, a man's hand reached out and grabbed her wrist. He was in his early forties, good-looking, with chestnut brown hair and a nice tan, wearing a cream silk short-sleeved shirt, dark tan pants, cherry loafers and a pair of sporty rose-tinted Serengeti's. Sitting next to him was a woman, a Marilyn Monroe look-alike, very attractive, in her early thirties, wearing a one-piece black bathing suit underneath a sheer white smock that accentuated her voluptuous body and a pair of round tortoiseshell sunglasses. The pair were gulping a zesty well-chilled Chardonnay that had a nice balance between oak and apricots.

Marty looked down at the man's hand, and he let go of her wrist. He said, "Excuse me, but would you like to share some wine with us?"

Marty said flatly, "No." And began to walk away.

The persistent man said, "Then, how about joining us for dinner to-night?"

"Where and when?" Marty said as she continued to walk towards her room on the other side of the pool.

"Seven at the Oak Tree Inn. You can drive over with us," he said, hoping she would return to the table and converse, so he could get a better glimpse of her toasted and oiled body that shimmered under the warm California sun.

"Meet you there," Marty said and disappeared around a corner of the spa.

Chapter Twenty

Marty arrived at the Oak Tree Inn at seven-twenty on the dot after a long nap, a massage and a shower. She felt almost like new, but she had been drained over the past few days and was starting to feel that dreariness that she always had, especially over the news about Roy going to culinary school. Oh well, I wish him all the best. It'll be a long time before I see him and Enrique again, she said apathetically to herself.

Inside the entryway of the restaurant, on either side, were glass-framed wine cellars that proudly displayed their prized and robust selection of wines. As one would imagine, there was plenty of oak wood paneling, carefully done in a modern and streamlined fashion. On the walls were Tiffany oak-leaf sconces dotted with acorns that acted as bookends for a substantial collection of early California plein air paintings, remnants from the restaurant's previous decorations before they remodeled a few years prior. And a golden-crazed orb and hammered copper candleholders that emanated a rich glow were atop the white-linen-draped tables.

She was escorted to the table where the spa couple awaited her. This time, Marty noticed the blonde was sporting a bronze wig, a black evening dress, a string of white pearls and no sunglasses. She looked extremely familiar, but Marty could not get a bead on it. The gentlemen wore a navy blazer, a raspberry linen shirt with a cream-colored scarf, olive drab slacks, and sunglasses. He stood up and admired Marty as she arrived wearing a grayish-blue silk strapless dress with a Cézanne-like peach and floral print and dark gray pumps. He sat back down as Marty took her seat.

He said, "Looking ravishing. We weren't sure if you were serious about coming."

Marty nodded and curtly smiled. And then the gentleman gestured to the woman and said, "This is Angela Jordan."

The woman put out her hand to Marty and then shook her hand. "I thought that was you," Marty said with a slight chuckle. Angela coyly smiled back.

"And I'm Stan Kravitz," the gentleman said as he shook Marty's hand. As he did, Marty's dress slipped down some off her breasts, and Stan caught a glimpse of her two-tone skin color. He envisioned himself massaging her supple tits that looked like they would welcome some cool, creamy lotion.

Angela said, "Kravitz Films."

"Okay. I didn't quite place you two at first, but now I know. Nice to meet you both. I'm Martha Kittering. You can call me Marty," Marty said.

Stan asked, "Up here for the wine, Marty?"

Marty responded warmly, "What else? For the Pinot. I just finished culinary school and was long overdue for a break."

Stan asked, knowing the answer, but he just wanted to be assured, "Are you lodging at the spa by yourself?"

"Yes, I am alone," Marty said.

"Now you're not, but how wonderful, though. What school did you go to?" Angela asked.

"Chapman," Marty said

The waiter came by and gave them their food menus that offered an eclectic array of California fare. Stan already had a wine menu and ordered a bottle of '07 William Heymus Pinot Noir. The waiter sped away.

"Wow. Maybe you can cook for us some time?" Angela said.

"Sure. You both live in Los Feliz?" Marty asked.

"He does. I mostly live at my home in Santa Barbara when I'm not filming," Angela offered.

"Not sure where I'm going next, but I would gladly prepare a dinner for you two."

"I was thinking maybe a party of fifty or more." Angela was working Marty at this point.

Marty raised her eyebrows with a look of surprise and thought, just like that?

The waiter brought the wine, opened it up and gave a splash to Stan. He gave it a whirl, a sniff, a gargle and a swallow and then nodded. The waiter poured the wine, and they raised their glasses for a toast.

"Here's to an endless night of pleasure, girls," Stan said without hesitation.

The women both smiled and pursed their lips, and then Angela let out a giggle. Marty smiled, knowing that the two she was sitting opposite were up to no good. They drank the velvety Pinot Noir wine that sung on their tongues with wild cherry opulence and seductive feminine notes. They all gave their approval with vocal gestures of delight and then opened their menus.

Without looking up from his, Stan said, "You know, Marty, I know some folks over at The Food Channel if you were looking for some work."

Marty peered over her menu and with all her might held her excitement back, but her voice crackled as she said, "Really?"

Stan put his menu to the side and said, "Really."

Marty's eyes welled up as she said, "I love The Food Channel. That's why I went to culinary school."

Angela looked bemused because she'd seen this over and over again—the magic that is Hollywood and how things can happen in a flash or just a phone call.

With a curt smile, Stan said, "I'll arrange it then."

"Stan the man," Angela said with an air of adulation.

Marty got up from her chair, stepped towards Stan and kissed him on the cheek. Stan blushed only slightly, but how he wanted to ask for the check right then and there and take Angela and Marty back to his room at the spa. But culinary pleasure before carnal pleasure, he laughed to himself, knowing he would need his strength for those two felines. Even though Marty had this melancholic sedateness, he sensed she could be a tiger in bed and, of course, Angela, when she wasn't acting, as now, had pent-up energies that turned her into a ferocious, hungry lioness.

Angela was aroused at the response from Marty. As Marty sat back down, she asked, "Okay, so what are we having?" She wanted to get the show on the road for the final course of the evening.

"Angela, your usual?" Stan asked.

"Umm, the lobster and pimento Newberg chimichanga looks scrumptious, but I think I'm in the mood for the Sonoma oysters bathed in sparkling chardonnay and toasted shallots as my appetizer and the grilled petite filet with the beurre rouge sauce as my entree," Angela said.

"Okay. Marty?" Stan asked.

"The Mediterranean fire-roasted quail cacciatore with capers and niçoise olives and the pan-seared red snapper with the nectarine salsa and lime cilantro gastrique," Marty said.

"Interesting combo. Stan, what are you having?" Angela asked.

"The gorgonzola and oyster mushroom mille-feuille and the shrimp scampi over heirloom tomato macadamia pilaf, less the shrimp. And a mache salad with a Chenin Blanc balsamic vinaigrette. We can all share." Stan always knew what he wanted.

"Stan's a veggie head," Angela said to Marty and smirked. "But he has a hearty appetite," as she winked at Stan.

Stan then blew Angela a kiss while Marty caught a scent of Angela's perfume. She knew it since she had tried a sample recently. It was fairly new on the market and not only that, it was organic. French Vanilla Umbree or something. Vanille Ambree, that's it. How seductive it was! It could not have been more perfectly matched with a woman. Marty had seen Angela half naked in several movies; what a pair of beautiful breasts she had. That was no body double on the screen.

Marty assumed that she and Stan probably made these trips from time to time to relatively discreet locations to do their thing. After all, as far as Marty knew from the celebrity gossip magazines at supermarket checkout stands, Angela was happily married to a well-known actor and they had a couple of children. She remembered seeing Angela and Brent Painesly, an attractive (though not to Marty), hugely successful actor-husband, frolicking on the beach of St. Tropez with their two adolescent girls on the cover of *Nyk, Now You Know Magazine.*

Back in the day during the 30s, 40s and well into the 50s, Nyk was called Nick the Dick, as in Nick the celebrity detective who would get the inside skinny on all the juicy goings-on in Hollywoodland. But a married actor having an affair with a film producer was just one of those social mores of Hollywood or for that matter the whole society of the rich who indulged themselves in one predilection or another just as Marty did. *I guess I'm no different than anyone else who has lust in their heart and wine in their veins,* she thought, justifying her actions. So, all is delicious and beautiful and scintillating and most seductive. And not a Nyk camera in sight. If they only knew!

After another bottle of William Heymus Pinot over a very satisfying delightful dinner, a dessert of fresh raspberries and honey-sweetened double cream and a bottle of Schramsberg sparkling wine, which they all shared, Stan got up, stepped towards Marty, flipped his sunglasses off and whispered in her ear, "I'm ready for a wine and pussy tasting. How about you?" Marty gazed for a moment into his yearning eyes and then they all got up for that evening cap.

Chapter Twenty-One

Feeling a little tipsy, Marty left her car behind and drove back to the spa with Angela and Stan in his S65 AMG Mercedes-Benz white sedan. Elvis played on the Sirius radio station. Marty sat in the back seat with her dress slightly hiked up, so she could feel the plush covers on her bare behind. "Ooh, that feels nice, hmm," she said to herself, grinning. She wondered how many little nymphs sat in this seat in anticipation of a *ménage a trois*. Who was going to make that first move, Angela or Stan—or would they both go in for the kill at the spa? *Oh my God, I've had so much sex in the last week, but this is so damned exciting. Whew! I've never felt so alive and so fucking horny for this long.*

Angela reached underneath her seat and pulled up a small wooden hinged rosewood box with an ivory inlay design on top and opened it up. "Take a whiff of that," Angela said in her sultry voice as she turned towards the back seat. Marty sat forward to catch the sweet, pungent aroma of the *cannabis sativa*. Marty got the feeling they were all in a movie. "Russian River Valley Red. Umm, one of my favorites," Angela purred like a cat.

Angela pulled out a rolled joint, closed the lid, and placed the box back underneath the seat. Stan flicked open a Sterling silver lighter and lit the joint while Angela took a slow and easy drag. She held it for a second and then handed it to Marty, who was reluctant at first.

"Go ahead, it makes you real horny. Right, Stan?" Angela said while slowly blowing out the smoke towards Marty.

"Smells great. But I'm already horny if you want to know," Marty said coyly.

Angela gingerly bit down on her lip, and Stan raised his eyebrows. And then Marty took a soft drag. It had been a while. She pulled in the smoke. Her lungs expanded, and then her mind eased into a delicate elation. She passed the joint to Stan who took in a nice healthy puff as Angela turned up the CD player. "Can't Help Falling in Love" played.

"You like it, Marty?" Angela asked and then hummed along to the lyrics, "For I can't help falling in love with you."

"Oh, yeah," Marty said. She was already starting to feel the doubling effects from the wine and pot. "Feeling no pain."

"This is one of the reasons why we come up here," Stan chuckled as he took another long, wet drag off the joint.

Angela began to sing in a Western twang, "Don't bogart that joint, my friend, pass it over to me." And then said, "Stan, just don't mop it like a cigar if you're going to bogart it, okay."

Stan took another hit, a long, wet hit.

Marty started to feel goosey with Angela's fun banter. Her focal point centered on one thing and that was her clitoris. Her thighs began to twitch. She could not wait to get to the spa. Angela placed her hand on Marty's thigh and slowly moved it up towards Marty's crotch. She was wearing no panties, of course. Marty cooed as Angela's warm caressing hand brushed up against her pubis.

"Oh, you naughty girl," Angela said softly to Marty as they tenderly kissed.

Angela grabbed Stan's hand and placed it underneath Marty's dress. Marty's vagina was extra-warm and slippery moist. The aroma in the car was intoxicatingly wonderful. And no sooner had they pulled up to the parking lot at the spa than they all got out. Stan grabbed a stainless-steel suitcase from his trunk, and they headed to his suite.

Chapter Twenty-Two

Inside the suite, Angela excused herself to change into something more fitting for the occasion. Stan placed the suitcase on their large bed and opened it up to expose a dozen premium high-priced bottles of wine and liqueurs, all encased in foam rubber padding.

"I gather this is the other reason why you come up here?" Marty said smartly as Stan kissed the glistening nape of Marty's neck.

Stan then pulled out a bottle of '06 Roaring Bear Cabernet Sauvignon and held it up to Marty. "This is a $2500 bottle. A rare and incredible vintage. Marty, I know how you like your Pinot, but I think you'll appreciate this baby."

Marty got a tingle in her vagina, kissed Stan on the lips and rubbed his groin. As she did, Angela appeared, wearing only her sheer smock from earlier by the pool, a pair of white lace panties and a pair of low-heeled bedroom slippers with white rabbit fur. She had taken her wig off, and that is how Marty remembered seeing Angela Jordan. She was as dazzling and beautiful as on screen with her golden chestnut hair, her vivacious body, and gorgeous breasts.

Stan closed the suitcase and placed it underneath the bed, looked at Angela with glowing admiration and said, "Ms. Jordan has arrived for her performance." Angela took a bow.

She then saw the bottle Stan was in the process of opening and said, "That's because he likes you, darling. Normally, he'd save that bottle for some overseas distributor he'd want to impress. Stan, why don't you text your friend at the Food Channel about Marty?"

Stan handed Angela the bottle and got out his Blackberry. He asked Marty, "How do you spell your last name. And is that your real name, Marty?"

"It's Martha, and it's Kittering, K, I, T, T, E, R, I, N, G. Kittering," Marty said.

Stan then sang from the R.P. Weston tune, "Second verse, same as the first. Henry the eighth, I am, I am." Marty looked over at him very oddly. He then said, "Never mind" and laughed at himself.

Angela coyly mimicked her name and said, "Here, kitty, kitty, kitty, kitty," as she poured the wine.

Marty looked at Angela with her tongue in her cheek, thinking, *I'm going to lick your pussy like a cat* and then meowed.

"Ang, let it breathe a little, okay," Stan said as he fingered the text on the Blackberry and sent it off. He wrote a name and number on a piece of paper and handed it to Marty, saying, "Marty, make sure you call this fellow no later than tomorrow or the next day at the latest. His name is Elliot Hyde. He's one of the big execs over there."

"Thank you, Stan," Marty said sincerely.

"No, thank you. But call him right away. He can set you up with something you can sink your teeth into," Stan said as he eyed Marty's seductive body. He then slipped his hand underneath Marty's dress and got a good feel of that fleshy part of the gluteal cleft that extends down from the anus to the vagina. It's one of those strategic locations that stimulates arousal in both the giver who strokes it with their thumb and index finger, as Stan was doing, and the receiver whose sensation is felt through the whole vaginal-anal zone, as was the case with Marty. Stan then sunk his face right in Marty's backend and helped himself to her salad as she backed her way to straddle the chair. Stan hitched forward to get the leverage he needed. Angela stepped up in front of Marty, slipped Marty's dress off her breasts and lipped her erect nipples. Marty's eyelids were half-shut, and her eyes rolled upward from the intensity of pleasure she was experiencing. She moaned heavily and sighed "Oh" as she began to orgasm.

Amused, aroused and delighted, Stan, half-laughing, said, "Oh my goodness." And then started to sing the classic by Ella Fitzgerald, "Come to Me, My Melancholy Baby."

Angela poured some wine in a glass and stepped towards the bed, flipped off her slippers, so they flew up in the air, and hopped on the bed while Stan unzipped Marty's dress and kissed the back of her neck.

Angela began to entertain the two by continuing to sing while gyrating her hips, "Come to me, my melancholy baby/ Cuddle up and don't be blue/ All your fears are foolish fancy, maybe/ You know, dear, that I'm in love with you/ Every cloud must have a silver lining/Wait until the sun shines through." And then Marty stepped towards the bed where Angela eagerly welcomed her by slipping off her panties. The two kissed and then positioned themselves to make love to each other's vagina with their mouths and tongues. Stan watched intently as he poured a glass of his very expensive and worthwhile wine.

Chapter Twenty-Three

The following late morning was a little cloudy as they all met for breakfast on the café patio after Stan and Angela had packed their luggage in Stan's car. This way, after breakfast they could head straight back to Santa Barbara and Los Feliz, respectively, after their morning meal. Stan ordered his usual of Irish oatmeal with fresh raspberries, blueberries and blackberries, toasted almond slivers and soy milk drizzled with local clover honey, and a glass of fresh greens juice loaded with kale, kelp and plenty of spinach.

Angela had an egg white omelet with Fontina cheese and chives, toasted multi-grain bread with fresh Napa creamery butter, a piece of turkey breakfast sausage, fresh squeezed orange juice with a splash of vodka, and a cup of Moroccan coffee. And Marty had the chorizo tofu scramble with whole-wheat homemade Indian bread, two pieces of the applewood and rosemary smoked bacon, a small bowl of mixed melon and berries, and an Arnold Palmer. On the table was a selection of lemon-lavender marmalade, red raspberry-jalapeno jam and fresh strawberry preserves, a jar of the local clover honey, and the spa's own chipotle red chili sauce.

After breakfast, Marty paid the bill in appreciation, and they all exchanged phone numbers while Angela gave an affectionate stroke on Marty's arm, expressing her contentment. She said, "Marty, you're a very special woman. I'm glad we met."

They all got up, and as Marty and Angela hugged, Marty said, "Me too."

And then Marty and Stan hugged, and he said to her, "You call me when you get to town and let me know what happened with Elliot."

"You got it, Stan, and thank you again," Marty remarked.

He winked at her, and Stan and Angela exited the spa. Marty went inside the spa for a quick facial as it began to drizzle outside.

As Stan and Angela drove out of town onto the rural highway after stopping to replace the bottle of '06 Roaring Bear, Angela said, "Wow, is she something else?"

Stan said, "She ought to be in pictures with her looks and those gorgeous eyes. We're going to have to do that again."

Angela gave an affirmative hum and asked, "What am I forgetting, Stan?"

"I don't know. Did you forget something?" Stan said. "Ang, can you give me my vitamins?"

She grabbed a leather bag from the back seat and pulled out a few vitamin bottles and a bottle of water. She opened up the vitamins and gave a handful to Stan, opened the water and placed it the cup holder between them. As he went to pop the vitamins in his mouth, one fell on the mat in front of him. He bent over and fished around for it. Looking up, he noticed the car had steered into the other lane as they came into a curve in the road. Meanwhile, Angela had rolled her window down and put her arm out to feel the drizzling rain and daydream about the previous night.

And as Stan tried to readjust the wheel, he lost control and the car skidded into the other lane with a semi-truck heading their way. He swung the steering wheel way to the right, but he could not gain control and made a beeline straight off the road and into an oak tree. When the car, which was going well over fifty miles an hour, hit the tree from the left, Angela was immediately tossed from the car some twenty yards. When she landed, her head hit a small boulder, crushing her skull. She died instantaneously. She had forgotten to put her seatbelt on. Stan's airbag blew, but he suffered severe trauma to his body and head and died en route to the hospital via airlift. Stan's wine and liqueur suitcase survived without a scratch or broken bottle.

After Marty's facial, she stepped outside the spa to go back to her room and saw in the distance a billow of smoke, thought nothing of it and went back to her room to change into her swimsuit. She sat on a chaise and pondered Stan and Angela. She shook her head in disbelief at how the evening turned out from a chance meeting. She put on her MP3 and listened to Elvis, "Can't Help Falling in Love." Angela let her download it earlier. She sat back in the chaise and then an attendant brought Marty an Arnold Palmer and her car keys. She had had him drive her car back from the Oak Tree Inn for a gratuity of forty bucks. As she handed him the tip, the attendant, in a grieving yet excited tone, said to Marty, "Did you hear…" and then Marty pulled the earplugs out of her ears and heard "…that Ms. Jordan and Mr. Kravitz died in a car crash?"

Marty, not quite sure of not wanting to hear what she just heard, in a shrill voice let out a, "What!?"

The attendant repeated, "Ms. Jordan and Mr. Kravitz died in a car crash only a few miles from here."

Marty dropped her drink, which crashed, broke and splashed all over the ground, and then she ran to her room. For three days she was an emotional wreck, and if any guests had been staying near her room, they would have heard her at times in heavy laughter followed by bouts of rage mixed in with bellowing crying jags. Her depression ran deep, partly due to not eating, except for a few chocolate wafer candy bars and half-dozen or so pitchers of Arnold Palmers and some sesame melba toast crackers that were tossed about the room with the box shredded and torn. She could not remember or tell you what day it was or how long she had been in the room. She was like a junky that had all her drugs hidden and needed a fix so badly, she went into maniacal withdrawal. After the third day, she cleaned the room up herself, showered, packed and left the spa as calm and sedate as she had ever been.

Chapter Twenty-Four

From that day forward, she could never watch an Angela Jordan movie again. Marty would never admit it, but she had fallen madly in love with Angela. Part of it was that Angela was so beautiful and seductive, but it was that quality that she had that made her larger than life. International stardom can do that and completely affect the perceptions of the masses, including Marty. Whether Angela Jordan felt the same about Marty would never be known. Whether all that had occurred and all the lovemaking and even Angela whispering "I think I'm falling in love with you" in Marty's ear had been alcohol-induced sweet-nothings or not, that love could never be actualized since Angela Jordan was dead. But would that love have been real or just forgotten like a passing storm in the night, some lustful fancy? But why Marty felt perversely responsible for the death of both Angela and Stan, she'd never know.

Before she left the spa, she put a call into Elliot Hyde's office. She had set up an appointment with his secretary for two days hence. The ride to Los Feliz would do her good and clear her mind, she felt. As Marty drove past the accident scene, she could see the oak tree had some black charring on it but was relatively unscathed. She tried to avoid it but was compelled to look. Marty reached in her Armand toiletry bag and pulled out Angela's panties that Marty had taken as a memento. She wanted to put them up to her face and breathe in, but the pain was too sharp. She tossed the panties, as well as the memories of Angela, out the window. After flying off into the sky, the panties settled into a brook that ran along the road and got lodged behind some rocks. A moment later, Marty was sick to her stomach from the sadness and grief and lack of quality food. She pulled off the side of the road, opened her door and vomited. She then wiped her mouth off, sat there for a minute to compose herself, took a swig from a bottle of water, shook her head and drove off with a look of intent and determination.

Upon arriving in Los Feliz, she had three things in mind: get a new outfit for the meeting at the Food Channel, get a good jog and a workout in and prepare for an interview, considering potential questions she might be asked. But what she did not know is that she could have worn clothes from a secondhand store, not showered for a week, eaten a can of anchovies, and she would still land a decent position because she just had that allure—the look and natural scent that seduces people.

When she arrived at the Food Network Studios in Culver City, just outside of Los Feliz, Marty was dressed in a lightweight Greg Armand gray pinstriped pantsuit, black-heeled Timmy Shoos, a touch of lip gloss and her own blended perfume of tangerine and honeysuckle. She had on her usual jewelry adornments and carried a black Ferris Nano briefcase, which might have been unnecessary, but why not gild the lily, she said to herself with an air of confidence. She waited just briefly for her appointment with Mr. Hyde in the secretarial area, and then his secretary escorted her into his office. He was standing at his desk, roughly five foot ten with sandy graying hair and blue eyes. He wore a dark blue suit. He had a conservative, polite nature. There was a photo of him, his wife and three teenage boys on a side bureau next to an image of Jesus.

He greeted her by shaking Marty's hand and had her take her seat. Marty was used to people she met for the first time being taken aback by her gorgeous looks, but Elliot Hyde didn't even flinch—not even a one-eyed stroll down the vegetable aisle, yet he was courteous.

"A terrible thing, what happened to Stan Kravitz," he said sympathetically. Marty noticed that he did not mention Angela. Perhaps he did not approve of their clandestine relationship.

Marty shook her head and said, "It's very sad."

"How did you two know each other?" Elliot asked.

Knowing that any information she gave about Stan could not be verified, she said, "From the wine country. Shared a common interest." Or at least we did, she said in the back of her mind.

"Well, he highly recommended you, and that is good enough for me. So what are you looking to do?" he asked.

"Well, I attended Chapman Culinary Academy," Marty responded.

Elliot nodded his head and raised his eyebrows, impressed.

"And I love the World Chef Cook Off Show and was hoping to find something here at the network," she said, thinking *I could have given a better answer.*

"Well, Martha," he said, and Marty interrupted him.

"Marty," she said almost apologetically.

"Marty, this, as they say, may be your lucky day because the WCCOC show was just purchased by a new producer, and the fellow in charge is looking for a personal assistant. I'm not sure if that is something you are interested in, but, it could be a worthwhile situation."

Marty said without hesitation, "Why certainly. Sounds like a perfect fit." *How nice would that be*, she thought.

"Then, let's go over and see this gentleman. His name is John Abruzzo, of Abruzzo Peppers," Elliot said and got up from his chair.

"Oh, okay," Marty said, slightly surprised since she had not heard or read anything in any of the trade magazines that mentioned that new scenario with Abruzzo Peppers and the show.

Chapter Twenty-Five

They walked down one corridor and then another in an L-shaped path to the opposite end of the building, passing several Food Channel personnel who either nodded or said hello to Elliot. When they reached John Abruzzo's office, his secretary was at lunch. The door to his office was slightly ajar, and Elliot took a peek in. John was on the phone. He saw Elliot and waved him in. Elliot and Marty stepped inside the office while John was occupied with the conversation he was having in Italian. He was a bit animated, especially when he said, "Mama, please," as he turned sideways in his chair almost in embarrassment. Marty had heard Italian spoken before, but he was using a unique dialect. She caught only the side profile of his face and his hair. He had a full black mane. From what she could see of him, he looked very handsome.

She noticed an array of products from the Abruzzo Pepper Company that included giardeneria, peppercinis, yellow wax peppers and roasted red peppers, jarred, canned, marinated and stuffed, in a cabinet off to the side of John's desk. She easily recognized the brand that was a staple in many gourmet stores she frequented in Portland, San Francisco, and Los Feliz. Besides being the main sponsor of the World Chef Cook Off Show, everyone or at least anyone in the food industry knew Abruzzo peppers. They were as familiar as Barilla pasta or Pellegrino sparkling water. She used Abruzzo peppers at Chapman in several preparations, especially in her homemade formaggio tortelloni with a roasted red pepper sauce and on the vegetable panini with grilled zucchini and yellow squash with Havarti cheese, the peppers and an herbed aioli, although a few slices of Proscuitto de Parma would have done the trick.

Marty and Elliot stood there, and Marty could sense the emotion coming from him. This was all new to her. Such passion he had! And what she surmised, he was only speaking to his mother. And then when he said the word *madone,* he put the tips of his fingers together, held them up and was shaking them, as if he was ringing someone's neck. Marty was incredibly excited about this new prospect. John tried to get off the phone with his mother as he held the speaker and whispered, "I'm sorry" to Marty and Elliot. As he did, he got a good look at Marty. He immediately said into the speaker as he batted his big black eyes that were the size of a horse's at Marty, "Okay, Mama, I gotta' go. I love you. Ciao." And then he hung up the phone.

John immediately stood up, faced Marty and Elliot and apologetically said, "My mother, always worried about her son."

"John, I wanted you to meet Martha Clittering. You were looking for a personal assistant?"

John suddenly busted out laughing. Elliot got red in the face, and Marty held her tongue because she wanted to laugh also at what Elliot had said. Whether it had been a Freudian slip or a faux pas by Stan when he texted Elliot about Marty, it was no doubt a slip of the tongue.

John tried to excuse himself and said, "I'm sorry, something my mother said. Delayed reaction," but Elliot was not buying it.

Elliot said, "I'll let you two be then." And left the office.

John stepped around from his desk and stuck his hand out towards Marty. She finally got a good look at him. Not only was he tall, six foot one or two with broad shoulders, he was very good-looking with high cheekbones. This guy's one hot pepper, she said to herself. She shook his large strong hand that was gentle to her touch. She felt immediate chemistry between them. Not sure if he had heard correctly, John said, "What is your name?" And then laughed again.

"It's Kittering," Marty said, emphasizing the first syllable.

John said, "I'm sorry, I thought…" as Marty interrupted him.

"I know, he said Clittering."

"How come you didn't say anything?" John asked while admiring Marty.

"I have more important things on my mind, like interviewing for this job without causing a man I want to work for to feel guilty," she said unashamedly.

"Okay, so it's Martha?" John asked.

"Everybody calls me Marty, even my gynecologist," Marty offered up smartly.

"You're funny," John said, chuckling, and continued, "how about I ask you a few questions?"

"Please do," she said almost smirking and thinking that making someone laugh is a great way to start any relationship, especially a working one. Her father taught her that, and it tickled her to know that was what had occurred, not by the telling of some joke, but by this kind of serendipitous humor. And if you can't laugh at yourself, who then can you laugh at? It *was* funny how Elliot flubbed her name. Perhaps her father wanted people to look at his daughter in a different light since she had a gloominess that tended to have a negative effect on others. Since a smile didn't happen too often with her, humor would be the ideal foil to counter any ill-at-ease feelings that might rear their heads, especially in those who did not know Marty well. "Just a fraction more," her father would say to her about her smile, but to his dismay, that perfect smile never occurred, and so he humbly acquiesced to the humor strategy. And to his chagrin, it had worked for Marty.

"So, tell me, Marty, what are you doing here?" John asked while composing himself and wondering why such a gorgeous babe as this was not sailing on some forty-footer in the Bermudas or the South Pacific eating lobster tail and drinking Dom.

"Funny as it may sound, it's this show. Your show is why I went to culinary school to be a chef," she said.

"Really? So what's the first thing you think about when you wake up?" he asked.

Marty wondered where he was taking this interview.

"Besides the usual routine of brushing my teeth and putting on the tea, I think about recipes and how to formulate flavors and particularly scents. Interesting that you ask," Marty said.

"Why I ask is that most people couldn't tell you what makes them tick because they're most often not passionate about anything. I mean really passionate to the point where it will keep them awake at night. So when did you last ponder?" John said.

"Last night, but mostly about today," she said.

"For over fifteen years, the only thing that has been on my mind has been peppers, if you can appreciate that. Now that we have the show, my focus is to revamp it, bring some life into it. Otherwise, they might cancel it, as they were planning to. If it weren't for the Abruzzo Pepper Company, this show would most likely be history. The ratings have been down, so I'm not only going to have to do a bit of creative development, we're going to have to work fast and hard to turn this ship around. It's a gamble, but one we are willing to take. Give me a quick scenario about how you would change the show," John said.

Marty thought only a second and said, "First, change the name of the show to The Ultimate Chef Challenge. Second, make it so that teams of three with a head chef are given a list of food items that they have to actually go out and either fish, forage, gather or hunt, or a combination thereof. And they're only given forty-eight hours to find what they need. They're filmed in the process by a team of two with just a handheld. That film is streamed back to the studio and then edited, to be viewed the following day after the forty-eight-hour search on an overhead screen above the teams while they prepare the meals made from the ingredients they had collected. And then the live audience will vote as to who is their favorite team, and that will be tallied by a panel of judges who will also give points on each prepared item of the meals. Then the judges total all the points, and at the end of each show, a winning team is selected. Then they move on to the next week. Does that sound like I pondered with some conviction and passion?"

"Yes. Okay, so you brought a resume with you?" he asked.

Marty said, "I did," and went into her briefcase for her resume. As she did, she could not believe the response or actually lack of response to what she just said about her idea for the show. She was baffled. But what she did not know was that all the while he was registering what she had told him, he had come up with a plan of execution. He thought it was precisely what the show needed, a major shakeup, but he had to do it with finesse, especially with his production team. They would have to think it was his idea; otherwise, he would lose them in spirit and certainly motivation. Taking on the show was a gamble, and he did not want to lose any of the production team this early in the game.

Marty handed John her resume. He perused it for a second and then asked, "I see that you have a chemistry degree and that you did an internship with Martin Remy Pharmaceuticals in their research and development department. So what's your real passion? How come you're not working in that field with some drug company?"

Marty said with some regret in her voice, "Martin Remy was my grandfather. I practically grew up with a chemistry set in my crib. And then the company was taken over by my father since my mother was the only child and she was never involved. It seemed to be a natural fit for me to enter the business. And then like an experiment where it seems certain that it will have a specific result, something changes. It's alchemy."

"I can understand that. I was going to school to be an actor and got pulled into the family business. It's like you have to go in a different direction to your intended course to understand which way you are supposed to be headed, but then life tends to steer you in a certain path, anyway," John said philosophically.

"True. Although cooking is chemistry in large part, I suppose. Temperatures, reductions, chemical reactions. Just look at baking," Marty solicited.

"Yet it's a creative endeavor. You don't have much cooking experience, but that's not so important to me. I'm not looking for a chef. I'm looking for someone like yourself who has some fundamental culinary knowledge, who is also intelligent, who is organized, someone I can lean on, on a daily basis. I really want someone who can assist me and who won't be afraid to be up close and personal at times. So far, you've impressed me with your education, especially that you just graduated from Chapman. I certainly love your idea for improving the show. I would like to expand upon that in greater detail. So do you have any questions for me?"

"Sure. How did you wind up here as the producer of the show?" Marty asked.

"All the Abruzzo Pepper commercials you see, I'm the one that wrote and produced most of them," he said and then mimicked his own creation, "In Italy, Abruzzo is known for its peppers. So, when you think of peppers, the only name to remember is Abruzzo. Molto. Enjoy."

"Huh," Marty gestured with an impressed look.

"It may not be as clever as Peter Piper picked a pepper, but it works." He continued, "Anyway, when the show started to get in trouble, since we were the major sponsors, my family thought it would be advantageous to take it over and also be able to make our commercials here at the studio," John explained.

"Is that your role with the company, to make commercials?" Marty asked.

"I'm also in charge of the print advertising, such as in magazines like *Gourmet Today* and *Cuisinarts*. My sister handles sales and distribution, and my younger brother does the importing and packaging. The parents are semi-retired. They split their time between Florida and, of course, Brooklyn," John said.

"You're from Brooklyn, then?" Marty surmised.

"Born and raised, but spent many summers in Abruzzo, Italy with my peasant relatives tending to the pepper crops. We import most of our peppers from the family farms over there, ergo Abruzzo Peppers," John said proudly.

"Ergo, your name," Marty said.

"Ergo the name," John said. "So, Marty, you want to come work for us?"

Marty felt so at home with this handsome beast of a man with his olive skin and a voice like Michael Bubble and his charm that made her want to unzip his trousers and, well, take a bite of his hot pepper right then and there. "When can I start?" she said.

"Right now if you like," John said enthusiastically and continued, "But what I want you to do is give me a multi-page breakdown of your idea with the theme of the first three episodes: what food items and how and where the chefs can gather all the ingredients. Also, the do's and don'ts list of what they can and can't do. Then we'll have my production team put in their two cents, so they can do a cost analysis, and we take it over to Elliot to get the network's seal of approval. Simple as that, but first, how are the head chefs selected and who chooses their team members?"

"Just as it is now with a mass competition between the chefs. The top ten chefs can choose from the other contestants who didn't make the cut, and then they move against each other but modify it so it's not drawn out like it is now. I think that's why the show is losing ratings; it's not holding the audience's attention. Move it along more quickly. With the overhead screening of the teams in the field while they do their cook-offs, I think it should create more of an interest in the show," Marty said, sounding like she had put much thought into her answer.

"I see. But maybe have one episode dedicated to just selecting the top eight chefs out of the twenty-five, as is done now. And then the subsequent four episodes are a head-to-head with a two-sided bracket, then two episodes for the semi-finalists and the final episode to crown the winning chef and his team. So, that's a total of eight episodes. Run four competitions a year, that'll keep the ratings pumping along. We have a base audience already; with an improved format, I think we may just have a winner here, Marty. What do you think?" John excitedly asked.

"You said his team. Didn't you mean his or her team?" Marty was being cute and maybe even deflecting some of the onus of what she might have just created. Just like that, an interview question's answer changes a major cooking show's direction. And she's responsible? Life is sure funny how it works out, she thought. But it was time to dig a little deeper into herself and bring out what made her who she was. Opportunities like this do not come around often.

"You caught me. I'm just a sexist pig, but your top chefs are mostly, if not all, men. Don't ask me why," John said, raising his eyebrows and throwing his hands upward as if he had swallowed the canary.

"Maybe because they have bigger spatulas," Marty said jokingly while grappling with herself. Come on, Marty, stop the nonsense and get professional, she said to herself.

"Some bigger than others," John retorted. "But the heck with that, I'm excited about this concept, Marty. Where have you been hiding? So, how about you work in the office here with me until I can get you set up somewhere else. And have you had lunch? We can call out for some. There's a really good Greek place just outside the studio," he said, shuffling in his desk for the menu from the restaurant. He handed it to her.

"Sure. Umm, hummus and a Greek salad with grilled chicken. Thank you, Mr. Abruzzo," she said without looking at the menu.

"Really? Call me John, okay, Marty? And we'll take care of all the necessary paperwork later. But, welcome aboard. Yet I'm thinking it's your job now to order and pick up the food, pick up my dry cleaning, send out thank you notes to all the industry people with whom I want to maintain some rapport, assist me with the daily goings-on, know what I'm thinking at all times, be a hatchet woman if need be."

"Thank you. My pay?" she asked.

"Will eight-fifty a week work?" he said. "Consider it a way of paying you for your fantastic idea."

"A thousand would be better," Marty smiled.

John looked at her for a second. Being the gambling man that he was, he responded, "Nine and quarter."

"Sounds good, John," Marty responded very brightly, knowing she had just stepped into the hottest job she could think of and not only that, she had negotiated for more than what was offered her. You got it going on, baby, she said to herself and then asked John, "You think it will work?"

"Your show idea? We'll make it work. By all means, keep it under your hat, especially with the production crew. They get sensitive towards non-TV types if you know what I mean." He then pulled out a credit card from his wallet and handed it to her. "I'll have the stuffed grape leaves and the lamb gyros with extra yogurt sauce. Add a 15 percent gratuity to the delivery driver, okay? Thanks. You can use Ginger's phone," as he pointed towards his secretary's office out front. "Or your own."

John then picked up his office phone and dialed the studio maintenance for a desk, so Marty could work nice and close to him. He wanted her nearby at all times, so he could smell her delicious scent and peer at her even lovelier body. Ginger was blonde, young and cute, Valley-girlish, but had nothing on Marty. "California," he said to himself in delight as he watched Marty step away from his desk. He missed New York, though, his children, but certainly not his strange, albeit a bomb-shell of an ex-wife, who was frightfully intimidating. Even more so were her freak relatives from her home country of Belarus—actually, Russia, but they were kicked out of the country because they were a menace to Russian society. But they caused even more trouble in Belarus and were eventually deported for their nefariously corrupt ways. "Go to America, they'll know what to do with you," the Belarusian officials told them as they left the country, instructed in no uncertain terms to never return. "Cheap thugs," was the sentiment the officials had towards the Fukovne-yev clan.

About an hour had passed after Ginger left for the day. Marty was full swing into her report, ironing out all the details, which wound up being more than she anticipated. John was hoping he could get the breakdown, so he could go over it and make any necessary modifications. He stretched out his arms and asked, "I meant to ask, are you living in town somewhere?"

Marty looked up and responded, "I'm not. I'm actually living out of my suitcase."

"I see. How about we call it a night, and I cook us some dinner?" he asked.

Marty almost said no, but she felt a good home-cooked dinner was the ticket considering how she was feeling after the incident in Sonoma. What she needed was to be held, caressed even, by someone like John. Exactly like John. She needed to be loved in so many ways.

"Yes, that would be perfect," she said in a soft voice.

"Great. I have some *baccala* soaking," he said and grabbed a jar of roasted red peppers from his Abruzzo pepper stash.

"Dried cod, hah?" she said.

"Nice peasant food. You'll like it. So, you want to follow me? I'm only fifteen minutes away."

"Sure," Marty responded.

Chapter Twenty-Six

The two were at John's multi-level seventh floor Marina Del-Ray apartment that overlooked the marina and had a flavor of the 70s with lots of teak wood paneling and shelving. The place was stark, save for a black leather couch, a smoked glass coffee table, a teak dining room set and a stereo system that all appeared to be a little sun-bleached and aged from the salty air. John and Marty arrived just about sunset, which gave the apartment a warm orange glow. It felt inviting to Marty while offering a stronger waft of John's cologne.

"The furniture came with the apartment," John said, excusing the weathered look. "Haven't had a chance to replace it yet."

Marty replied, "Has that beach feel." She then noticed that there were several moving boxes still unpacked in the living room. John turned on the stereo to some breezy jazz station and pulled a bottle of Montepulciano and two wine glasses from the stereo cabinet. Marty admired his finesse as he knifed the foil off and placed it in a nickel-plated wine opener, with a wine grape design, on the kitchen counter. John said, "Montepulciano from the homeland. It's a red, but it works with the peppers. I have a Trebbiano in the fridge, if you prefer?"

"That's perfectly fine," Marty said.

John opened the bottle, poured the wine in the glasses and handed one to Marty. She held it to the light coming from the kitchen and licked her lips. It had a deep rich glow. She took in the waft. It hit her lips so sensually. John watched her motions and gestures as she sipped the Montepulciano. It brought back memories of his sixteenth summer in Abruzzo and the beautiful fourteen-year-old Regina whom he fell madly in love with. Marty had that same primitive sultriness.

He remembered he had almost lost his life to Regina because of her over-protective father who liked to carry a Benelli shotgun and had a very happy trigger finger. Luckily, yet sadly, she was sent way to an undisclosed convent nearby. He didn't see her again that long and unforgettable summer, nor the following summers either, as she was always sent away upon his arrival until she got married at seventeen to a local boy. Ironically, Regina and her husband were growers who supplied the Abruzzo Pepper Company with their crops. After all, she was a cousin three times removed.

Marty raised her glass and said, "*Molto bene.*"

John said, "*La mia ragazza, hai così ragione.*"

"Sorry, my Italian actually sucks," Marty chuckled with a little embarrassment.

"That's okay. I said, 'my girl, you are so right,'" John said.

"I was just in Sonoma before I came down here. A mini-vacation," Marty said and thought about what John called her, my girl. Was it wishful thinking? In any event, she didn't mind.

"Life is good. I'm sure the wine was too. You want to help me cook dinner?" John said.

"Sure," Marty responded. "What do you want me to do?"

"How about rinsing the spinach and then we'll toss a little chiffonade of *porchetta* and some shaved Pecorino-Romano on top and whatever dressing you like. And there's some fresh mint if want to use that. And the oil and vinegars are in that cabinet," he said as he pointed.

"Wow, look who's in charge of the kitchen," Marty said in a sarcastic but reverent tone.

"It's in the blood. After all, I am in charge of what I hope is the soon-to-be most popular chef show on TV," he said.

Marty raised her glass. John poured her some more wine, and they toasted. John then went into the refrigerator and grabbed the *baccala* that was soaking in milk and drained it in the sink in a colander. As they worked together, simpatico, they were like long-time lovers brushing up against one another with familiar affection. Not a trace of clumsiness, especially for two people who had just met that day. They had instant chemistry.

John sautéed a few thinly sliced garlic cloves in some extra-virgin olive oil while Marty prepared the salad. He sliced the roasted peppers in strips after pat-drying them and then placed them in the pan with the garlic. He grabbed a bag of frozen cubes of court bullion out of the freezer and added a handful to the peppers and garlic. He let them slowly melt and added the reconstituted cod to the pan and let it slowly simmer.

Marty watched John as he took a taste of the broth and asked, "Where did you go to school, John?"

"I went to City College for my undergrad. Then I got my MBA at Trenton," he responded.

"A real Renaissance man. Where did you get your acting training?"

"Hudson Valley," John said. "I dropped out after a year, though," he said and then spooned some broth. "Come here, you want to taste something good?"

Marty stepped towards him, and he placed the spoon up to her mouth. She batted her eyes and then closed them as he eased the spoon into her mouth. She swooshed it around and then let out an umm and said, "Succulent."

"You think it needs some wine?" he asked, liking the word 'succulent.' *Not only is she sexy, she's mouthing words that are sexy. Did I do the right thing by inviting her over here? This could be an invitation for trouble. But why hold back? Why not go for it? Life was meant to be enjoyed, and I deserve that, especially after the torturous marriage to Raveneiztkya. That's right, she'll be here in two days to haunt me,* John emphatically reminded himself. *God, how I'd love to devour Marty and taste her succulence. Madone.*

"It could, but it's great the way it is," she said while getting a good scent of him. She thought about it and concluded from an earlier summation that it was Lacoste Essentials. She recognized bergamot, sandalwood, tangerine and a touch of patchouli. It was nice, but she preferred Acqua di Gio. She also felt that she could blend a fragrance that would be better suited to his more natural scent. She was confident of that.

Chapter Twenty-Seven

Over dinner, John asked Marty, "If you had a dying wish for your last meal, what would you have to eat?"

"Helluva' of way to put it, John, but I would have my grandmother's *poulet aux quarante gousses d'ail*, roasted capon with forty cloves of garlic with roasted root vegetables like parsnips and rutabagas and carrots and gold Yukon potatoes," she said romantically.

"Look who can speak *au francais*?" John said jokingly.

"I should know more, having French blood in me. But I guess I do okay with the cooking terms," Marty said, a little humble.

"I think you might have to make that dish for me," John said.

"It's best in the fall and winter. It tastes better then for some reason. But I suppose I owe you, John. The Rémys were from Provence. Even though they had a cook, my grandmother roasted chicken like no one else. She stuffed the garlic underneath the skin with some fresh sage and chervil. It was phenomenal," Marty said. "And of course, eggplant parmigiana made with real Italian bread crumbs, not panko, and a grilled ribeye with summer greens tossed with a twenty-five-year-old balsamic vinegar. And a large bowl of *mousse au chocolat* and ladyfingers. And you?"

"Okay, I'm starting to understand you a little. I have to say, you're a woman after my own heart. My favorite dish besides veal and peppers is lamb *vinnochio*. Pan-seared lamb chops with fennel, potatoes and green olives. Maybe some homemade gnocchi with butter, fresh thyme and Parmigiano-Reggiano. And fava bean soup with a roasted chestnut puree, spring peas, artichokes and flecks of sun-dried tomatoes. And can't forget the cannolis with citron, pistachio and chocolate bits, of course," he said lavishly.

"I can appreciate that," Marty smirked.

"I'm in heaven is what you will say after an Abruzzo meal," John said.

"Confident, hah? I've heard that a few times before," Marty said jokingly, yet in a flirtatious way.

"I'm sure you have," he said in a more serious tone and got up from the table and started to remove the plates. Marty wanted to help, and he said, "No, that's okay. Why don't you take your shoes off and relax on the couch and I'll make a little dessert?"

Marty went into the living room, stepped out onto the balcony and looked out towards the marina. She thought, *this is nice*, as she took in the briny air. A few seagulls flew about, making their shrill cries, and a lone pelican was perched on top of a light pole gazing towards the ocean. She could hear the soft chug of a motorized sailboat entering the marina, apparently with a recreator or two who had returned from a day's worth of leisure activity on the water. She pondered where she would live as she fell dazedly into the marina's goings-on. Certainly, something like John's apartment would be ideal but might be a little too pricey. She could not have been more pleased by how the day had turned out. It was quite okay that she wasn't cooking somewhere because she was working at the Food Network on her favorite show. How lucky was that? And she smiled brightly.

Marty went back inside and asked John, "You ever eat seagull before?"

"Yeah, you poach it with a rock. After about two hours, you toss the seagull away and eat the rock," he said sarcastically and thought, she's a little kooky, but is she friggin' sexy? He'd dated some hot babes in the past, and of course, the lunatic wife, who was the most stunning statuesque broad he had ever laid eyes upon with her long strawberry blond hair, but Marty was so intoxicatingly beautiful. He asked himself, "Am I setting myself up?"

"That bad, huh?" Marty said.

"Well, I think if seagull were any good, you probably wouldn't see as many around," John said. "It's not like squab, you know, your garden variety pigeon, which isn't so bad tasting."

"I guess it would be easier to buy chicken at the store than try to catch a few seagulls," Marty said.

"In Abruzzo, we'd chase after the chickens that were in front of the house, and when we'd get one, we'd break its neck and then pluck the feathers," he said with gusto.

In an Italian accent and practically to herself, Marty said mockingly, "Sounds-a like you had a good time," as she looked at a photo on a shelf, featuring John in a gray suit, with a very large and rotund boy of possibly ten with short, straight, cherry-red hair, wearing an oversized navy blue suit standing on his right, and a pretty young teenage girl with curly black hair in a blue dress standing on his left. They were in front of a Catholic church.

"Are these children yours, John?" she asked.

"What's that?" he said, not hearing her.

"The boy and girl in the photo with you, are they yours?" she asked louder.

"Yeah, that's my little princess, Christina, and Fat Freddie at his Catechism," he said.

"Why do you call him Fat Freddie? Isn't that mean?" she asked.

"That's 'cause he is. Every time you see him, he's either sucking on a lollipop or chewing on a chocolate chewy roll. That's why he's so fat. We've tried everything for him to stop bingeing on junk food, but he can't or won't. At some point, you have to be able to help yourself." John sounded frustrated. "But then again, the mother makes it worse by buying those jumbo bags of crap. It's an impossible situation. Poor kid."

She understood not being able to help yourself, especially with the dark urges she got, but she thought, I hope he is not malicious to her. She sat down on the couch and slipped off her Timmy Shoos. He didn't seem like he was that way, but calling your son Fat Freddie was harsh. Still, it was really funny. She was never one to make fun of other people's maladies, but the way John put it, you couldn't help but laugh. He was comical in a sardonic way. Yet people who were overly coarse, excessively rude or downright mean did not last very long around Marty, with very few exceptions.

As she was thinking about that, John's cell phone rang. It had been quiet for several hours. He picked it up and then disappeared into the bedroom.

She wanted to ask him if he was married, although she did not see a ring. There was the greater likelihood that he was not married because the kids and wife were nowhere to be found unless they had not arrived in Los Feliz yet, but the apartment was too small for a family of four. Certainly, there was enough room for two people, though. And then she asked herself, "Where am I going with this?"

Chapter Twenty-Eight

As she sat there on the couch, she went through a short stack of magazines on the coffee table. They were your standard Hollywood trade magazines and a recent copy of *Gourmet Today*, a traditional high-end foodie publication that offered lots of recipes, articles and exotic photos from places like Milan, Malaysia, and Santa Fe. And there was an almost year-old October issue of *Cuisinarts*. She remembered seeing some recent issues back at John's office. On the cover was a caricature of the Garden of Eden, with semi-nude figures representing Adam and Eve picking apples off a serpent-looking apple tree with a bushel full of the forbidden fruit next to them on the ground.

Marty positioned a pillow behind her and rested her head on it while she stretched out on the couch. She went through the *Cuisinarts* magazine. It was primarily a food arts photographic publication with a few articles and plenty of advertising. Having a copy of *Cuisinarts* displayed in your restaurant, salon or home was considered hip, cool and almost necessary if you wanted to be taken seriously as a restaurateur or gourmand.

This issue was dedicated to apples, with a centerfold of a darkened bare room with a tall, thin male completely covered in gold leaf foil standing with his feet spread apart while crouched over slightly holding a woman covered in silver leaf foil horizontal to the floor biting on a golden delicious apple. The positions of the two bodies formed the letter A, for apple. And in the center of the floor sat a fedora covered with gold leaf foil with every variety of apple imaginable inside the hat and all over the floor, as if the apples were flowing out of the hat. The variety of apples included your more commonly known Granny Smiths, McIntosh, Red and Golden Delicious to the Braeburn, Jonagold, Pink Lady to the more obscure varietals like Champagne Gold, Hannas and Arkansas Blacks.

On the following two pages were photos of a completely white background with a male, a talented, young world-renowned chef working in Chicago somewhere, and a female, the pastry chef from the Islandia Hotel in San Diego. They had been voted top chef and top pastry chef respectively. They were both naked except for sliced fanned McIntosh apples covering their pubic area and the female's nipples. This particular spread had created a huge buzz in the culinary world, prompting requests for more like it featuring the hottest male and female chefs exposing themselves, but to no avail. The editors of *Cuisinarts* were thankful for the greater interest in their publication but privately were appalled at such requests. "We're not pornography, we're culinary art," was the emphatic response from the editor-in-chief.

Marty thought it cute how *Cuisinarts* did their clever, artsy pages filled with essentially non-useful photos and images. Amusing to look at, but what real function did it serve? The editors of the magazine would beg to differ, especially Condo something or other, the magazine's owners who shared in the revenue that it produced, yet Marty felt that if they were trying to create this image of Adam and Eve, male and female, Ying and Yang so to speak, why not juxtapose the apple with the pear? That was more like opposites. Certainly, the apple was indicative of the male: masculine, strong and sturdy, much like an apple tree or for that matter, not unlike a Granny Smith apple that was solid and firm.

And yes, a very good variety of apple like an Arkansas Black can often be very crisp, a cross between tart and sweet and juicy, whereas the pear was more feminine and delicate, and when you bit into a fully ripened pear, such as a Jade-Green Asian, it exuded succulence and spice and an aroma that was perfume-like. Even the pear tree as it stands and grows is more feminine and ornamental than the apple tree that can turn gnarly over time. The apple may have its wisdom and knowledge, but the pear had its exotic seduction, and that was quintessential to Marty. Seduce the world, and it was your Garden of Eden, your oyster in which beautiful pearls are produced.

Marty quickly fell into a deep slumber with the magazine falling to the floor and her breathing similar to a bear with snarls and sniffles. She was fucking tired, and even if El Johnny Macho with the garlic on his breath and olive oil on his lips ripped her suit and panties off and took her to his bed, all she'd want to do is sleep. Yet as she dozed off into her dream world, she could see herself naked as a blue jay in an apple orchard being chased by El Johnny wearing nothing but a cowboy hat and a bolo, riding an apple tree branch like a horse and scooping her up to save the day, eventually making wild passionate love to her underneath an apple tree, no less.

Chapter Twenty-Nine

She woke the following morning with a light blanket over her and caught the wafts from frying peppers and eggs and fresh-brewed Italian espresso. She was certain of that because it was her favorite coffee.

John saw Marty slowly awake and said, "Good morning, sunshine."

She looked over at him. He wore a pair of black silk shorts and an aqua marine silk short-sleeve shirt that was opened to his belly. Around his neck, he wore a gold chain with a gold pepper pendant, similar in looks to a golden horn, a common feature of Italian culture. She thought she was in a Chippendale's nightclub for a second as she stretched her arms and legs and realized her suit was off. She had on only her bra and panties. Marty wrapped the blanket around her, stepped towards the kitchen and sat at the bar that overlooked it. John poured her some espresso. She took a sip and thanked him.

With her eyes barely open, a bit groggy, she asked, "Ah, what happened?"

"You, my girl, were out like a light. I played the valet. Your clothes are in the bedroom," he said.

"Merci, John," she said. "I didn't mean to fall asleep."

"That was my production crew I was talking to on a conference call about the plan for the new format for the show. For two hours, so it was my fault," he said.

Marty humbly smiled and asked, "Are we going in today?"

"Well, it's Saturday. But I thought we could get at least a half day in and maybe go out for a late lunch, early dinner and relax," John said.

"Is this personal?" she said inquisitively.

"Well, you are my personal assistant. Besides, we have a big new show to produce," he said, smiling.

"Are you serious?" she said. "What about the breakdown and the network?"

"Still going to need the breakdown. That's what we can do today. And tomorrow?" he said.

"Not a problem, I'm here. And the network?"

"Elliot's in my pocket, in a manner of speaking. They'll agree to the new format because if the show goes, so goes the sponsorship. Anyway, they're still making money, regardless of their threats," he said.

"Okay. What are we having, so we can get this show on the road?" she asked.

"It's called egg in a basket. An egg dropped in a piece of hollowed-out Italian bread with roasted red peppers and mozzarella cheese," John said.

"Are you trying to impress me or get me fat?" Marty asked sarcastically.

"Need your nourishment, right?"

"We jog later, okay," Marty said.

John plated up the eggs in the basket and served the dish to Marty and himself. He sat down next to her and poured her some orange juice. Marty cut into the egg with her fork. The golden yolk oozed out of the toasted Italian bread and glowed brightly on the white porcelain plate, like a California sunrise. She bit into the rich breakfast. It not only lit up her taste buds in a delightful way, it had a variety of textures that contrasted the creaminess of the eggs and cheese, the velvety red pepper and the crunch of the bread. She was enjoying it tremendously and dreamily said, "It's really good."

She wanted to ask him about his wife—ex-wife, she wasn't sure—but she didn't want to disrupt the moment. And then John's cell phone rang to the Mexican Ranchera song *Cielito Lindo*.

John said, "There goes my breakfast." He hit the send button on the cell and said, "Yeah?"

From the other end came a sultry and husky female voice with a Russian accent, "Johnny, it's Raveneitzkya."

"Oh, really?" John said sarcastically.

"I want to come to California with the kids," she said.

"Not a good time," he said.

"You fly us first class. It's Christina. She's crying all the time," she said.

"What's the matter with her?" John asked with pure suspicion.

"It's the boys, always the boys."

"You have her call me, then," he said.

"We want to come to California tomorrow," she whined.

"No, Raveneitzkya," he said.

"Excuse me, did you say fucking no?" she said forcefully.

"I said no, but now I am saying fucking no. Don't start in with me, Raveneitzkya!" he practically yelled.

"Oh, okay, so you want your daughter to be raped like you raped me and that cousin of yours," she said.

"There you go with your fucking bullshit. Always twisting something good into a black lie." John was furious with her. "Christina texted me last night and not a hint of trouble. So what's your angle?"

"Johnny, Johnny, you always deny us the good life," she said.

"That's right. You have the house in Brooklyn and the summerhouse in the Hamptons and the monthly nut I give you besides the allowance Christina and Fat Freddie get and all private schooling and all the private lessons and the vacations I pay for. And what, you're looking for more? Go get a friggin' job," he said remonstratively.

"I work. I'm a mother. You know the kids need to see their daddy," she said pleadingly.

"I was just there two weeks ago. No, Raveneitzkya," he said.

"Okay, we come anyway," she said.

"No. End of story. Goodbye," John said.

"I have your credit card. See you in a few days. Bye-bye, Johnny," she said and hung up.

"You fucking crazy bitch," he yelled into his Cranberry and tossed it on the counter.

Marty said, "Are you okay?"

"No. She's a lunatic. She's going to fly out here with the kids when I told her not to," he said, brushing his hair back with his hand in disgust.

"You're divorced, right?" Marty asked.

"Of course, but she squeezes me worse than if I was in hock for ten grand to a bookie," he said. "I can't get rid of her. She's a leech."

"How long have you been divorced?" Marty asked.

"Not long enough. About a year and a half," he said.

"Who divorced whom?" she asked.

"Well, she divorced me," he said almost reluctantly.

"Can I ask why or is that getting too personal?"

"I had an affair, but—" he said.

"Yes. So was she justified?" Marty asked.

"It's not as simple as you think. It was a gal I knew back in the old country and…Raveneitzkya, she's so diabolical. You don't know what it was like. She doesn't know what love is. She's ruthless and mean," he said.

"Why didn't you divorce her in the first place?" Marty asked.

"Excuse the expression, but if I had, she would have cut my nuts off, literally. She's that crazy," he said.

"How did she find out you were having an affair?" Marty said.

John paused and then said, "The husband flew over from Abruzzo and told my wife."

106

"And then what happened?" Marty said.

"She cut my nuts off. She practically took everything I had, except she couldn't touch the company. Thank God for that," he said and blew out his frustration.

"Do you regret your actions with this married woman?" Marty asked with a disapproving tone.

"Hell, no. I'd do it all over again," he said.

"You would? You still love her, this Abruzzo gal?" Marty asked.

"Her husband killed her with a shotgun. But, no," he said.

"My goodness, that's ruthless," she responded, yet she also knew that you just don't forget the love you have in your heart for someone that easily, even if they are dead.

"That's it, we're going sailing," he said.

"We are?" Marty asked. "You have a boat?"

"Why do you think I live by the marina? Can you meet back here in an hour?"

"An hour and a half," she said. She dropped the blanket, stepped towards the balcony and asked, "Which one's yours?"

John took a glance at her tanned sexy body as he stepped closer to her. He wanted so desperately to slip her panties off and take a bite of her ass. It had been awhile since he had been with a woman. The divorce had really toyed with his mind. He had thought about asking Ginger out, but she wasn't his type, and besides, he didn't want to get things messy at work, especially over a secretary. And then there was Janet from production. She was attractive, but she was too uptight. Marty was intentionally getting him lathered up, as the saying goes, and it worked. John pointed to a twenty-five-footer with a dark cherry-red hull.

Marty said, "She's pretty. What's her name?"

"My Cherry," he said glowingly.

"Is that a Catalina 250?" she asked.

"Holy shit, you know what it is," John said in almost disbelief.

"My dad's an avid sailor. We used to go out on the water all the time," she said.

"So, do you know how to sail?" he asked.

"Better as a mate, but yes, I can handle one," she said.

"How come you didn't mention it earlier?" he asked.

"Some girls need to keep a few secrets. Can't give everything away in one fell swoop. It's like gulping down a nice vintage. You want to savor the nuances," she said and motioned towards the other room. "Clothes in the bedroom, right?"

John, in a bit of a daze of disbelief, said, "Yes," as he looked at Marty step away. *Check her out*, he thought, *Raveneitzkya was a cunning and provocative cookie, but Marty is one of those special type gals that are rare and intriguing as hell and that you don't get to see too often.*

"And, by the way, you better tie up your dinghy, it just might sail away," she said, grinning.

John stopped and thought for a second and then looked down at his very hard erect penis. He laughed at himself and said, "Need to hoist out the anchor." He then looked out towards the marina again and said, "Funny girl," while shaking his head.

Chapter Thirty

They slipped out of the marina in the Catalina 250 with stores of the chilled Trebbiano, a lunch of cold cuts that included hard salami, capicola, dried ham, provolone cheese, some fresh basil, a small red onion, a jar of Abruzzo giardeneria, a small jar of mayonnaise, extra-virgin olive oil, red wine vinegar, a freshly baked loaf of French bread purchased at the Le Cote d'Azur Bakery right around the block from John's, plenty of bottled water and a ripe Casaba melon for dessert.

Marty was dressed in a pair of navy blue linen shorts, a white cotton shirt tied up at the belly with her bathing suit underneath, and a pair of sunglasses she had just bought before they hoisted off for an afternoon of sun, sailing, and relaxation. John wore a royal blue Body Armor top, white shorts, white topsider rubber shoes and sunglasses.

As John maneuvered *My Cherry* out of the marina, he watched Marty apply sunscreen to her face, arms and legs. She had no apprehension and no airs about her, yet there was a mystery about her that triggered a deep curiosity to get to know her completely and fully. She was no ordinary girl, certainly, not in her looks or the way she carried herself. Even though John felt that he might have been a little whimsical by hiring Marty on the spot, he always felt a certainty in his professional decision-making process.

Academically, she had the necessary tools, but maybe she could have used a little more business management in her arsenal. She did have a business minor from Golden State, but she had also grown up in a highly entrepreneurial family. At some point, a little business savvy would have rubbed off on her. And of course, although not specific to television production, she had taken food service management courses that dealt with labor and food cost analysis. In addition, John remembered from her resume that she had a course in restaurant start-up costs and development. And her idea for the new concept had hands-down won him over. Besides, if he had a choice of a pretty, let alone gorgeous, woman and one not so, he would choose pretty any day of the week. That was his prerogative as a business owner, and he had no qualms about it.

Once they got out of the marina, they caught a good headwind and swiftly sailed out towards the open sea. The wind that blew briskly put an enchanted smile on Marty. She stepped towards the keel and then looked back at John standing stoically and firm as he manned the wheel. She got a tingle throughout her body. She wanted to kiss him so badly and thank him for the opportunity he was giving her but held her excitement and asked him, "That ringtone, your ex-wife? What was that?"

John said underneath his breath, "That fucking bitch." And then said, "That's the Frito Bandito song. You're probably too young to remember."

"It sounded like *Cielito Lindo*, the Mexican ranchera song," she said.

"That's because it is." And then sang, "*Ay, ay, ay, ay! Oh, I am dee Frito Bandito. I like Frito's Corn Chips. I love them, I do. I want Frito's corn chips. I'll take them, from you.* Sound familiar?"

"*Ay, ay, ay.* You're too funny, John," Marty said, amused.

"The song reminds me that every time she calls, she wants something from me. Like a bandit holding you up at gunpoint for your money," he said.

"*La bandita*," Marty quipped.

"Exactly. It's always by hook or by crook with her. That's just her style. And I knew this even before we got married," John pined. "Sometimes we do the right thing for all the wrong reasons."

Marty knew what that felt like and asked, "What's her name?"

"Raveneitzkya," he said.

"That's a lot of syllables," she said.

"Yeah, she's long and twisted like her name. It's perfect for her. Named after the bird of death. The raven," he said smartly.

"She's a handful, I gather?"

"You don't know the half of it. Her whole family I have to deal with. They're all demented. I think they have a long line of gypsies in their pedigree because they don't think like normal people. She handed me the divorce papers at some Chinese restaurant between the pork fried rice and the egg foo young while her nimrod cousins sat outside in their car waiting for trouble. I almost choked to death. They had to give me the Heimlich, and I wound up with egg all over my face," he said in a frustrated manner.

Marty shook her head and grinned.

"Marty, I think she wanted me to die that day, and now she's just slowly killing me for that one little mistake. But I'm what they call her gravy train, her sweet and sour sauce because she gets to live the life of leisure, yet she's pissed off because she has to share the kids. She's such a whack job. She keeps saying that I raped her, referring to the time we met in a Manhattan nightclub and I took her to The Plaza to impress her. Trust me, Marty, I'm not some misogynist. You'll see when she gets here what a floozy nut she is," he continued.

Marty saw that John was troubled. She stepped towards him and rubbed his shoulder. He looked at her for a second and lifted her sunglasses to her forehead. He then pulled his sunglasses off and planted a gentle kiss on Marty's lips. It felt good and satisfying, but she felt that dullness inside her. Where was that tiger when she needed it, she pined?

He hugged her and got a feel of her hip with his hand. She whispered in his ear, "Don't worry, John. I'm here for you."

That's all he needed to hear. She unbuttoned his shorts, slipped them down with his underwear, kissed his penis and proceeded to orally pleasure him as no other woman had. He moaned, "Oh, my God," as she worked her lips and tongue with magical precision.

She then took off her bottoms and slipped up between John and the wheel. She kissed his neck while he inserted himself into her vagina with a gentle ease. They were breathing a bit heavier as John slowly thrust himself towards Marty's body. A motorboat passed by in the opposite direction with a few onlookers who hooted and then blew their horn. John barely noticed while holding onto the wheel. He thought he was pleasuring Marty, but she had this look as if she were not present in the moment. John slowly stopped and asked, "What is it, Marty?"

Reluctantly, she said, "I'm sorry, John. It's not you. Trust me. I just get these flat feelings. It's the chemical makeup of my brain."

"It's okay. Maybe we shouldn't have gone this far?" he said sympathetically.

"No, you excite me, and I wouldn't want to be any other place than right here with you. It's that I have difficulty in feeling pleasure sometimes," she said sadly.

"I'm sorry," he said. She then slipped from underneath him and pulled up her shorts. "Why don't you open up the Trebbiano? Maybe that will cheer us both up. The wine glasses are over the sink," he said as Marty stepped down into the cabin while John zipped up his shorts. "I hope I'm not fucking things up with her," he said to himself. "Take it slower, cowboy; you don't want to lose out on something special."

Marty returned up top with two glasses of the wine that had flavors of almond and citrus like a Southern California day. She handed a glass to John and asked, "How is it that you're still not unpacked and you have My Cherry?"

"It came with the apartment," he said and sipped his wine.

"I can help you get your place straightened out if you like," she said wanting to put him at ease and let him know that he hadn't lost her.

"Yes, that would be helpful," he said and smiled.

"John, you like to read food-related books?" she asked.

"Sure," he said.

"Who's your favorite author?"

He had to think about for a second or two. "Well, I certainly like Luca Tangello's *The Uncompromising Gourmand* and Apricot Porter's café cookbook. It's like an old school-new school meets new school-old school philosophy," he said.

"What do you mean by that?" she asked with a furrowed brow but with an inkling of what he was talking about.

"Tangello said that the true essence of life is not only in how you live but in how you eat. He was into cooking from the home garden. We grew up that way, especially my parents being from the old country. People had these micro-gardens, these little plots of land where they grew beautiful tomatoes, zucchini, and squash, cucumbers, and peppers. Tangello even made his own wine, like a lot the old-time Italians in the neighborhood. And then this whole modernization came along and destroyed everything." John spoke with sentiment in his voice and continued, "My father used to get worked up over all the fast-food joints that kept popping up everywhere. He'd say, 'It started when they began to put a cheese in a can,' referring to the change in how we eat as a society. 'Who eatsa' cheese in a can?' he used to say all the time in his broken accent. People still had gardens here and there, but then Apricot Porter with a few others re-invented that process that had been there before. It was back to these micro-gardens where it all started," he said with keen enthusiasm. "Now slow cookery is a movement. Like it was something new."

"I see. What was an old way became new and what became new was just the old way. Like a recipe that gets passed down through the generations without alteration, but look at all your high-end health food stores," she said and asked, "So you ever get to the growers' markets?"

"Not yet, not out here. Back home I did. And you, who is it you like to read?" he asked.

"*The Cook's Friend* by Alex Stephens. It's a good comprehensive book on ingredients and cooking. And of course, there's *Leroy's Gastronomic* and the *Escoffier* books that are interesting to look at. But I like this amusing short story by Jelly Black. It's called *Cat Nip*. It's about this café owner who gets visited by a restaurant guide inspector and the most terrible things happen to the food by folly—on a Friday the 13th, no less. It's very cute," she said.

"What happens?" he asked.

"I'll have to get you a copy," she said.

"You tease. But didn't Jelly Black write *Bombes Away*?" John asked.

"I hope that's not an omen and we're going to sink?" Marty said, smiling. And out of nowhere, heavy clouds started to roll in from the west. They didn't notice, as they were absorbed in each other's company.

"That's all right; I'll save you," he said.

"You my Prince Charming?" she asked and then kissed John on the cheek.

John smirked and then said, "In the flesh, baby. So, how about movies? What's your favorite food film?"

"Well, since I'm a pinot freak it has to be *Up, Down and Flat Out* with Paulie Prime. I love it when he explains to the waitress why he's so into pinot noirs and says something like, 'It takes finesse to grow the grape and lure it into its fullest potential.' How true is that, not just in growing pinot grapes, but in relationships between two people who care about each other," she said.

"You think you need to lure me in?" he said rhetorically. "I don't. It's about bringing out the best in each other, especially when you have the right chemistry. Like a beautiful recipe that produces something delicious," he continued.

"I like that analogy, John. You can be a tender man, but I wasn't sure when you called your son Fat Freddie," she said.

"I'm not trying to be mean. He knows I love him. I just wish he didn't eat that shit all the time," John said empathetically.

"Maybe when he gets older, he'll lose the weight. So what's your favorite movie?" She asked.

"*Bonaparte and the Chef's Wife* with Reginald LeMayle and Antoinette Palmier," John said.

"I don't think I've seen it," Marty exclaimed.

"It's a French film where Napoleon has an affair with his chef's wife who's this gorgeous young tartlet, and Verrat, her husband, makes the most extraordinary civet of wild boar. Napoleon boasts about it to his worldly guests, telling them how it's marinated in Bordeaux and blood pressed from the carcass, but they never get to eat the dish. He insists that it's not the same if it's made any other way. There are these seductive scenes where Napoleon hand feeds this mistress strawberry cream cake while they have their sexual liaisons. And then *voila*, one day the chef's wife falls in love with the pastry chef and they run away together. Napoleon feels wronged and believes that Verrat is at fault for his wife leaving so he has him sentenced to death using the same press that he, Verrat, used to make the civet of wild boar. It's sort of a romantic black comedy," John said.

"Sounds tragic, but maybe I'll make strawberry cream cake one day, and we'll have to watch it," Marty mused.

John smiled and raised his brow. And then suddenly, the wind started to pick up, and the skies opened up with a heavy summer storm. "Okay, let's head this baby back in," John said. He turned the wheel and told Marty to get the life preservers from inside the cabin.

Chapter Thirty-One

They made it back to the marina and docked *My Cherry*, moored her and headed back to the apartment building soaking wet. They stopped underneath an awning and looked out towards the heavy storm and the huge swells.

"Holy shit," John said. "That was close."

Marty wiped a bead of rain off John's face. He gazed into her eyes, feeling a powerful attraction towards Marty. And Marty felt a storm rising within her that she could not resist. He then kissed her tenderly, and as he did a bolt of lightning struck *My Cherry* and practically split her in two. They watched in utter disbelief. What if they had been still in the water when that happened? they both thought simultaneously.

John wanted to check the damage. Marty held him back, saying, "No, John, wait till the storm is over. Nothing you can do now."

"What if it sinks?"

"It's destroyed, forget it. Won't your insurance cover it?"

"Yeah, maybe," he said.

"Let's go upstairs," Marty said. And they did and headed straight into the bedroom where they took off their clothes, toweled each other's heads off, slipped into bed and made passionate love for the rest of the afternoon as the storm raged outside.

Afterwards, as they lay in bed, John said, "That was a close one. You might have been right about that omen."

"You know what they're going to call that storm?" she said.

"What?" John asked.

"Raveneitzkya," Marty said almost reluctantly. She watched John's reaction; he laughed almost uncontrollably. Marty busted up herself, as John's laughter was so infectious.

"You're a funny girl," he said, still laughing.

"Just don't tell her. I wouldn't want to be on her blacklist," she said.

"I don't blame you; she's as belligerent as they come. That reminds me. She'll probably be here in a day or two. You need to be careful at work, okay, Marty? Especially if she shows up at the studio," he said.

"Mum's the word, darling," she said.

"Besides work, which we should probably get rolling on, I wanted to ask you something. I want to offer you something," he said.

"What's that?" Marty asked.

"I have an extra room here. So if you're interested in moving in, I'd like to offer it to you," he said.

"Is this a personal thing?" Marty was intrigued by his offer.

"I know. What, we have known each other, two days? You do need a place to live, and we're going to be together quite a bit. And we are lovers. Unless I'm lying next to some other hot babe?"

Marty shot him a quick smile, "That's an offer that's hard to resist. Can we sleep on it?"

"Sure, Marty. I know it's sudden and I don't want to pressure you. So, what do you say we have a little surf and turf for dinner? I'm starving. We missed out on lunch," he said.

"Steak and lobster?" she said.

"Sort of. Sklirts and sclams," he said, smiling.

"What's that? Are you tongue-tied?" she asked.

Laughing, he said, "I meant to say, skirts and clams."

"Sounds sexual," Marty mused.

"Everything seems to be with you. But who am I to say? It's grilled skirt steaks and steamed clams, Brooklyn-style."

"I think that might do," she said. "So, who showers first?"

"Why first, let's both hop in together," he said, and Marty blew him a kiss. They got out of bed, and Marty noticed a small pepper tattoo on John's right buttock.

"Look at that. You have a pepper on your ass. When did you get it?" She asked as they walked into the bathroom and John turned on the shower.

"They used to call me Johnny Peppers. Well, some people still do. It's from when I made a couple of porno movies," he said frankly as they stepped into the shower.

Marty stood there for a brief second and stared off and then said, "Imagine that."

"That was my brief acting career, besides a few very Off-Broadway plays," he said.

"So, what did you play in?" she asked.

"Not that you would probably know, but one film I was in is called *The Temptress*. It's a very loose adaptation of Shakespeare's *The Tempest* about this beautiful witch who stirs up storms out at sea, so she can cause ships to wreck on her deserted island. And then she seduces the sailors one by one. It's a classic," John said with his tongue in his cheek.

Marty grabbed the soap and lathered John's penis. She said mockingly, "Johnny Peppers, in the flesh."

John spoke as if he were a player on stage, "Show us thine bush for thy come yearning."

"Bravo," Marty said as John stroked her vagina.

John said, "Marty, just keep that between you, me and the soap, okay?"

"Wonders never cease to amaze," she said.

Shortly after their showers inside the bedroom, as John was putting on his underwear, Marty snapped his buttocks with his towel. John yelped and said, "You brat."

"Oh, by the way, I have a little secret too. I was a dominatrix for a short period," she said.

"Really?" John inquired with a sudden burst of admiration and intrigue.

Chapter Thirty-Two

John and Marty stepped out the marina side entrance of the apartments. The rain had stopped, and they headed down to take a look at *My Cherry*. She was still afloat, and there was a fair amount of damage to her, but it looked like it could be repaired without having to salvage the whole boat. John was pleased. They made their way to Marty's car in the parking garage underneath the apartments and drove off to a local gourmet store where they picked up two dozen fresh pisser clams, a pound and a half of skirts steak, some more wine including a new Brenny Walsh 2008 Pinot Noir Ridgefield Vineyard Marty wanted to try and a few other supplies. On the way back, John stopped off at a convenience store to purchase some lottery tickets while Marty stayed in the car. When he got back in, he checked his numbers on an older ticket and said, "I hit a tree at least."

Marty said, "For a guy that went to Trenton, you sure talk funny."

"I get this way when I'm excited, like I am now when I'm with you. Besides, you can take the boy out of Brooklyn, but you can't take the Brooklyn out of the boy," he said.

In a Brooklyn-like accent, Marty said, "Yeah, I know wha' ya' talkin' about."

Marty started the car. John lightly pinched Marty's cheek and kissed her on the shoulder. He then handed Marty a lottery ticket. "This is for you," he said.

Marty took it from him, curiously looked at it for a second and then slipped it above her head on top of the visor and said, "That's very romantic of you, John." And then she drove off.

"If you hit, I get a third, okay?" he said matter-of-factly.

Marty thought that he must take his gambling seriously. *He's already brought up a bookie and then he buys me a lottery ticket and gives it to me like it was some rose. It's interesting as you get to know someone. I wonder what other surprises he might have in store for me, but then again, if he knew who I really was... Not that I'm a terrible person. I just happen to have killed some people who, for the most part, deserved it. That's justifiable in my book. Maybe he would understand if I explained it to him. Love conquers all, right? Am I falling in love already? Jeez, Marty, you're such a silly girl.*

Back at the apartment, Marty sliced up the leftover French bread from lunch and to go with the cold cuts prepared an antipasto salad of chopped radicchio and romaine lettuce, micro sprouts, pea shoots, julienned carrots and radishes, capers, olives, and pepperoncini and dressed it with a creamy vinaigrette. She cut up the Casaba melon. John sautéed some diced shallots, added some of his frozen bouillon cubes and let them melt, then added some Trebbiano and the clams and let them steam. After about four minutes, he added the concasse tomatoes and chopped Italian parsley and let it all steam for a few minutes while he grilled the lightly seasoned skirt steaks on the stove grill. Marty set the table, lit some candles and poured red wine. John finished off the clams with fresh creamery butter and just a splash of heavy cream. In a flash, the clams and meat were done, and they sat down together. John dished out the clams in a soup bowl and topped it with the broth as Marty served the salad.

John paused for a moment, lifted his wine glass and said, "I just wanted to thank you for being here, Marty. You're going to make this surf and turf more enjoyable."

"Thank you for having me, John. I just wanted to say I've done some impetuous things in my life, but I never thought I'd move in with a man I'd just met," she said.

"So, does that mean you are?" he asked.

"Yes," she said and smiled, and then they both toasted their new arrangement.

"Let's dig in then," he said with enthusiasm.

As they indulged, John said, "I was thinking about food films, and I almost forgot about *Opening Night* with Danny Menute and Jerry Shallot."

"That's a great little movie," she said.

"Certainly. It was ironic that they were pinning their hopes and success of the restaurant on Tony Prosecco, the Italian crooner, showing up on their opening night, and he never did, and the restaurant eventually failed anyway." He continued, "Food service is such a precarious industry."

"Isn't it? Don't some ninety percent of restaurants fail within the first year or two?" she stated.

"Even with a well thought-out plan, great ideas and a good location, you aren't guaranteed success. Some things just don't fly," he said.

"You're not having second thoughts about The Ultimate Chef Challenge?"

"No, not at all," he said.

Chapter Thirty-Three

After dinner, John and Marty made their way into the bedroom where they slowly undressed each other and then caressed each other's bodies tenderly and affectionately before making love.

Afterwards, Marty lay there distantly. John said, "I enjoyed that."

Marty responded with a half smile, but then her lips dropped back down to a partial frown. John inquisitively asked, "What's this sadness inside you?"

Marty said, "It's something I have to live with. The way my brain works."

"Is it depression?" John asked reluctantly.

"Not really. I have a wacky bipolar disorder," Marty responded.

"What do you do for it?" he asked.

"Some herbal concoction I make."

"I think they have meds for that, don't they?" John said.

"Gave them up a long time ago. They make me feel like I'm not me."

"Not you? Don't you like to be happy?"

"Oh, when I'm happy, I'm really happy," Marty said.

"But when you're not, you're really not. True?" John stated.

"Yeah, but it's like cheating. Taking something artificial."

"You take herbs, right? Don't pharmaceuticals have their basis in herbs?" John asked.

"Not the same, though. It's natural versus synthetic," she said.

"Life is fleeting. Why wait? Isn't it easier to pop a pill?" John asked somewhat rhetorically.

"I'm perfecting an elixir I've been working on. Then I think I'll have this thing really under control. Until then, you'll have to deal with my unhappy face," Marty said, almost feeling like she shouldn't have said that.

John sang in a crooner's voice, "My funny valentine, sweet comic valentine/ You make me smile with my heart. Your looks are laughable/ Unphotographable/ Yet you're my favorite work of art./ Is your figure less than Greek?/ Is your mouth a little weak?" John touched the end of Marty's mouth with his index finger.

Marty asked, "Who's that?"

John responded, "The one and only, the incomparable Frank Sinatra." And then continued the song, "When you open it to speak/ Are you smart?"

Marty smirked and sarcastically said, "Cute."

After they had sex, John lay in an elongated position with his body stretched out, and one arm stretched back. He was deep in thought. Marty lay sideways, her body up against his with her crotch rubbing next to his thigh and one knee half bent draped over his belly.

"I have to be honest with you. Not that I lied, but Elliot is putting a lot of pressure to increase the ratings. The network is on the fence with the show, so we have to do something fast because we just might not get into a new season," John said in bemoaning voice.

"We just start getting rid of some of these chefs," Marty said.

"What is that going to do?" John asked with some hesitation. "And who do we replace them with? We've had a call out, and all we get are loons. Untalented crazies who want to become stars overnight just because they think that they make the best Denver omelet in town."

"John, you don't see it. I don't propose we just give some of these chefs the pink slip. What I'm saying is, we kill them. Do away with them. Most of these chefs are so uninteresting and unattractive. They lack, you know, presence."

John sprang up and squinted his eyes and said, "Are you fucking crazy? That's absurd. Who do you think we are, the mob, the Corleones?"

Marty sat up too. Trying to sound convincing, she said, "The ratings will shoot through the roof. We'll have so much attention from the culinary world with chefs wanting to be on the show, they'll be on a two-year waiting list."

John said in a shocked tone, "That's coldblooded murder. Marty, no way, I can't be a part of that. It's delusional."

"It's as simple as filleting a fish or butchering a venison carcass. You just have to be a little creative."

"Oh, my God, it's murder, Marty," John said in an emphatic tone.

Marty, still caught up in her idea, said in a singsong way, "It's only murder if we get caught."

"I'm not having blood on my hands," John shrilled.

Marty began to slowly massage John's flaccid penis and said, "What, you want to go back home to Brooklyn holding your dick in your hand or you want to be a success?" She then squeezed down on his penis to get the message across. "Are you going to let this thing fail? I don't know about you, but I love this show."

Pausing a second to ponder, John responded, "Hypothetically, who's going to do it? What, do we hire someone?"

"No, I'll do it," Marty said with chilling confidence.

"You have to be fucking joking?" John said in disbelief and then laughed.

"Since you won't do it, and hiring someone to do it would be opening a can of worms, who else?" Marty declared.

"I can see you now trying to wrestle Chef Bubba to the ground with a knife in your hand," John said, trying to get a grasp on what she was saying.

In a serious tone, Marty said, "Just leave it to me. But first, there's the issue of equity sharing we need to discuss."

John shook his head and in a half-agreeing voice said, "And I thought you liked me for my Italian charm. You're one crazy broad."

"If you only knew," Marty said, smirking.

John rolled over towards Marty, kissed her breast and then rubbed her crotch. He just figured she was just pulling his chain, so he played into her game.

After they had sex for the third time that night, John got up to urinate and imagined a baked Alaska exploding on set and killing a few chefs. He laughed it off. He stepped back into the bedroom. Wanting to move on from the conversation earlier about killing off the chefs, he said, "So what happened with your chemistry education? How come you didn't go to work with your father?"

"Sore subject. He sold the company. Part of the reason why I didn't go work with him," Marty said.

"Yeah, what's the other part?" John was more than a little curious.

"He left my mother for a younger woman and started another family," Marty said.

"You were angry at him?" John said, knowing that was the case, and slipped back into bed.

"I was furious," Marty energetically bemoaned.

"You two talk at all?" John was concerned.

"Rarely. The holidays sometimes," Marty felt a little uncomfortable and wanted not to talk about it.

"How did your mother handle it?" he asked.

"Well, she's been in and out of the mental wards for treatment," she said.

"She has what you have?" John was digging deeper.

"Yeah, but worse. Much worse."

"So how do I know you won't try to kill me?" John was sensing her tension with the conversation and hoping to lighten it with a joke.

"You're too important to the show. Which reminds me, the equity sharing. More like a bonus," Marty said with focus.

"Yeah?" John wondered why he always attracted women who had financial gain in mind.

"I'm thinking we double our ratings, I'm guaranteed fifty thousand," Marty said confidently.

John laughed to himself and then smirked, thinking her idea about killing off the chefs had to be a joke and said, "Okay, you're on."

But what he didn't know is that she had already been devising her grand scheme. She still had that bloodlust. And this time it was for profit.

"Then tomorrow you draft the contract, and I do what needs to be done," Marty said.

John started to kiss her belly, going in for the fourth time. Marty slipped out of bed and said, "First things first."

John sung with a groan, "Stay, little valentine." Marty then stepped towards the bedroom balcony as John admired the silhouette of her naked body illuminated by the silvery glow of the moon. Each curve of her body highlighted her seductiveness, and he realized that he could not get enough of her. Heaven and earth could not shake his undying lust for her and this feeling of love that began to flourish inside him in a strange and curious way. No woman had ever made him feel like she did, sexually, emotionally, psychologically or otherwise. Marty had seduced him from the moment he met her at his office, faster than a shooting star flashing across the night sky. And that silly little smile or lack of one was not going to get in his way with someone whom he felt would forever change his life.

As Marty continued to look out towards the moon she recited, "Deep into that darkness peering, long I stood there, wondering, fearing/ Doubting, dreaming dreams no mortal ever dared to dream before."

John asked, "Who's that?"

Marty responded, "Edgar Allan Poe."

"He's a little dark, isn't he?"

"I can be a little dark. Besides, my moon's in Pisces," Marty said. She slipped into the bathroom and shut the door.

Chapter Thirty-Four

The following Monday morning the Food Network studios were abuzz with activity. While the World Chef Cook Off Competition prepared for a Friday taping of their next show with a live audience, John introduced Marty to Jim, the lead manager of the production team, who was in his mid-thirties, five ten or so, with mild brown hair and blue eyes. Jim was overly confident, with a large dose of pomposity. He shook Marty's hand, said his hello and went on with the production. Social etiquette was not at the forefront of his mind. It was partly that he was a bit arrogant, but largely that he was trying to keep a show moving along that might be on the chopping block.

John then shifted his attention to Janet, Jim's assistant. She was in her late twenties, tall, athletic, slender and pretty with green hazel eyes and dirty-blond hair that was tied up in a bun. She wore a pair of black rectangular-framed glasses, a dark gray skirt, a white silk button blouse that showed off her small but pert breasts, and black pumps. She was half on the phone and half up Jim's ass. Jim and Janet could have been Siamese twins; their personalities were that alike. Janet curtly smiled at Marty when introduced and virtually fluffed her off. John excused Janet's attitude as her just being busy, which was certainly the case, yet being rude was not in the job description. Marty had no room for that. If she had her way, which she fully intended to happen, she would change their attitudes by acquiescence or by the axe—a cleaver would do. She might not have been the most cheerful person going but being rude to the point of obnoxiousness was inexcusable.

Jim was going over the production schedule with Chef Bubba Arnet, a large imposing African American man of fifty-five who had a barrel-shaped body and stood about six foot. Chef Bubba owned one of the more popular restaurants in Los Feliz, Bubba's Barbecue Place. His appetite not only included his owned Carolina-style brisket that was sweet, spicy and mustard-tangy; he also had a hankering for white women, especially young and pretty ones. "I like my women tender and moist like my brisket. And lily white," he'd say privately. Chef Bubba was a bit preoccupied, but as he caught an eyeful of Marty, he gave her a snaring smile that exposed a gold tooth that complemented his diamond-studded gold pinky ring and the gold rope around his neck.

Marty nodded as John and she walked past the WCCOC stage. As they did, a side door to the studio opened, and who should appear but a very tall, buxom strawberry blonde in a very tight-fitting stretch blouse and knee-high skirt with black stilettos and round black sunglasses. A security guard, escorting her, pointed towards John. She came through the door as if she were some 50s movie starlet with an entourage of a Slavic-looking male, buffed and handsome, with dark wavy hair, dark eyes and a goatee, and a female who was just as tall as he, around six foot, gaunt and lanky with stringy dark hair. On closer inspection, she had a glass eye that was as black in color as her good one. Their clothing was also black. Marty was taken aback when she caught a glance of this provocative towering woman who for an instant reminded her of Dominika, a ghost from the distant past.

John looked over at his ex-wife. Anxiety ran through him, and he said to Marty, "Here she is, Raveneitzkya Fukov, and the freaks, her cousins."

Marty shot him a look as if he were making a joke but was amused because they were just as advertised.

"That's her real name if you can believe it," John said with a straight face.

"Fukov?" Marty questioned, still not believing it. John nodded his head, but she just took it as him joking. But Fukov ran through her head a few more times until she resigned by chuckling "No way" to herself.

Following the adults was Christina, a thin, pretty sixteen-year-old girl wearing white and orange clothing, and Fat Freddie, a very rotund boy of thirteen with cherry-red hair, his blue shorts and a white-and-blue striped shirt making him look even rounder.

John raised his hand and gave a, "Hey, guys," directing his attention towards Christina and Fat Freddie.

Christina quickened her pace and ran up to her father, and they hugged. John said, "There's my little princess."

Christina said, "Hi, Daddy."

Marty welled up, thinking about her relationship with her own father and how he would call her his little princess.

John introduced Marty to Christina. There was an instantaneous liking and bond between them as they both said hello and smiled at each other. Christina had the same big brown eyes and high cheekbones and smile as John. Fat Freddie and Raveneitzkya and her cousins—who looked like they played on some European basketball team, they were so tall and so distinctive, Marty thought—made their way towards them but kept their distance from John. Fat Freddie hugged John half-heartedly as John rubbed his head and said, "There's my guy. How are you doing, Freddie?"

"Oh, okay, Dad," Fat Freddie said while the murder of ravens stood more towards the stage with an air of absolute disdain. Raveneitzkya was more interested in what was going on on the stage with Chef Bubba and the production crew. She showed no interest in the relationship between John and their kids.

John reluctantly waved his hand at Raveneitzkya to say hello. As for the cousins, he could give a shit.

She, in turn, barely even looked at John as she curtly nodded back at him.

John then introduced Marty. "This is Marty, my new personal assistant."

Raveneitzkya, making it sound like it was meant to be under her breath, quite audibly and contemptuously said, "Another one of John's floozies?" And then she walked closer towards the stage followed by her cousins, who looked like gangsters, Marty thought as she seethed.

"John was right; she is a fucking bitch. Where does she get off, being that way?" Marty's mind tightened as vinegar ravaged her veins.

Trying to offset Raveneitzkya's negative energy, John asked Christina, "Where you guys staying?"

Christina responded, "The Pampered Inn."

John, sounding frustrated at how much it was going to cost him, said, "Great."

"Yeah, Dad, they have this awesome pool slide," Fat Freddie said excitedly.

"Okay, guys, what do you say we go to Magic City?" John said to Christina and Fat Freddie.

Christina responded, "I'd prefer we go shopping in Beverly Hills."

"You sound like your mother, Christina," John said, being a little more serious as he watched Raveneitzkya work the crowd. Chef Bubba who looked like he was getting that hankering for the Raven. "Let's go to Magic City and then we'll go to Beverly Hills afterward, okay, Christina? Marty, you want to join us?"

"Thank you, but I think it best I work on the new show," Marty responded. That was the first and foremost on her mind, focusing her angst. Not only was Chef Bubba uninteresting to Marty, he was an ardent pig who didn't deserve the limelight, which was going to make her job of getting rid of him that much easier. She couldn't believe he had grabbed her butt earlier in the office with Ginger, Jim, and Janet there. She played it cool because she didn't want to raise any suspicions once the police started their investigation, which they most certainly would once they found his body.

And that reminded her, she needed to do a search on Chef Johnson's suicide and make sure no incriminations had been aired against any Chapman students, specifically her. There had been no calls from the parents, Chapman or the Sourton Police, so hopefully, all was clear with Chef Johnson's death being a suicide. And as far as she could remember, the San Francisco police sealed her file regarding any connection to Dominika. She had been assured of that by the DA. She had to be discreet and use an untraceable computer. No need to leave clues anywhere. It was time to roll up her sleeves and tighten up her thinking process. It was showtime.

"You're right. Maybe we all can meet later for dinner?" John said.

Marty said, "Okay," and then offered, "Nice meeting you two," directed at Christina and Fat Freddie.

"It was nice to have met you too, Marty," Christina said as Marty smiled at the three.

As she stepped away, John said to Marty, knowing that Raveneitzkya had done her wrong, "I'll give you a call later." Marty walked past the stage, glancing at Raveneitzkya, letting her ferocity linger as she devised her next move to make The Ultimate Chef Challenge a reality.

Knowing that he didn't have the energy to tangle with the ex-wife, John said to Christina, "Go tell your mother we're going to Magic City, and you'll meet up with her later tonight. Okay, Christina?" She obliged and stepped towards the stage. John said to Fat Freddie, "What do you think of my new assistant?"

While unwrapping a very large chocolate chewy roll, Fat Freddie said, "She's sweet, Dad." And then he bit off a big hunk of the chewy roll.

"She is, isn't she?" John said with a smirk, looking at Marty walk towards the stage exit that led to the offices.

All of sudden, after Christina told Raveneitzkya what her father had told her to say, Raveneitzkya yelled at John, "Already, you start trouble! I was getting in the mood for piña coladas at the beach with nice fresh pineapple, but no you have to steal Christina and Freddie from me!"

John yelled back, "So, what, you came out here to have fun on my dime?"

There was dead silence from everyone as all eyes were glued to Raveneitzkya and John. Marty also stopped in her tracks at the other end of the stage area to observe the commotion.

"Okay, Johnny, you really want trouble? I will give you trouble!" Raveneitzkya got even louder while pointing her finger. "I wanted to go to that Snott's Berry Farm for the fried chicken dinner with the fucking blackberry jam, so Freddie can try. And you know how he likes his fried food! Now we have to change our plans. Always have to do what Johnny wants!" And then she cursed at her cousins, using Russian expletives, in her anger towards John.

At that point, several other people, including Elliot Hyde, popped their heads in the stage area. Everybody loves a good fight, as much as they hate to admit it, and the one brewing between John and Raveneitzkya made for good office chatter and excitement. Yet Elliot was not one of those everybodys.

"End of story, we're going to Magic City. And the kids will see you later," John said, keeping his distance because he knew if she were close to him, she would start poking him with her index finger.

But to no avail. Raveneitzkya made a beeline straight for him. John was not having any of it and headed toward the door Raveneitzkya had entered through. She chased after him and yelled out, "You pussy! Johnny, you've always been a pussy. You fucking pussy!" And then she waved at her cousins to follow her and then wallowed her way to the door chasing after John.

Chapter Thirty-Five

Marty pulled out of the studio parking lot and drove to a local costume store. Twenty minutes later she left with a shopping bag. She then headed to the mall and purchased a pair of men's slacks, a polo shirt and shoes. She went back to the hotel where she was staying. She had made the commitment to move in with John but had not done so yet since his children would be in town, and she didn't want to impose upon their privacy as a family, especially if they wanted to stay at his apartment overnight.

She showered, toweled herself off and put on a very tight spandex top. Then wrapped her chest with electrical tape to flatten her breasts. She dressed in the men's clothing and slipped her hand into the costume bag and pulled out a bluish-black beard and some cosmetic glue. She applied the glue to the beard and then applied it to her face. She glanced in the mirror at herself and said in a husky voice, "Hello, Marty."

Fifteen minutes later she pulled up near the Pampered Inn by the front entrance wearing a pair of black men's sunglasses. She shut the car off and waited. About an hour later, near dusk, the murder of ravens left the Pampered Inn, hopped in a white SUV, and drove off. Marty followed them into Los Feliz to Chef Bubba's barbecue restaurant. It was a stand-alone structure that was covered with thatched wood and had once been a seafood joint called the Anchor Inn complete with a giant anchor used as a flagpole out front by the entrance and porthole windows that went all the way around the building.

Marty waited about an hour and a half, listening to the musings of Nabokov on audiotape until Raveneitzkya and her two cousins, the female of which Marty affectionately called Dead Eye for her one glass eye, exited. She followed them to an underground club in downtown Los

Feliz where they disappeared out of sight down a flight of stairs. She waited five minutes and then made her way down into the club after slipping the doorman, a burly muscular dude with numerous tattoos, twenty bucks. She entered a dark, dank and nondescript basement with plenty of blue lighting, lots of tattoos and leather. There were lots of freakish people hanging out. Marty eyed the place and saw the murder of ravens at a table with another man, wearing leather, who looked like the male version of Dead Eye but with long sideburns. They were all drinking shots of Swedish vodka with the bottle sitting between them on the table.

Marty stood at the bar nearby, thought about getting a glass of red wine but bought a beer instead and sipped it as she listened in on the conversation the murder of ravens were having. They reminisced about their time in Belarus when they were all involved in human trafficking. They were comrades in the trade, even Raveneiztkya before she moved to America and met John. Dead Eye looked over at Marty, who walked back to the bar some ten feet away and looked into her beer. Marty's heart pounded with excitement as she listened intently to the conversations at the table with the earplug.

Dead Eye spoke in Russian and said, "I miss those old days when you could make a quick ruble on a pretty blond or two."

The long side-burned Russian jokingly said in English, "I bet you don't miss that pretty blond who poked your eye out with a nail?"

"That fucking whore. If I ever find her, I will kill her with my bare hands," Dead Eye said in English, as her feathers were ruffled, and then poured herself a shot and slammed it down. She wiped her mouth with the back of her hand.

Raveneitzkaya said, "If any of you had any balls, you would start grabbing little girls here in America. There's lots of them and lots of cold hard cash to be made." She got up from her chair and said, "I hate to spoil the fun, kiddies, but I need to take care of business." Raveneitzkya tossed some money on the table and said, "For a cab if you need it." And then she made her way towards the door.

Dead Eye immediately got up. Just as Marty was about to leave, she pushed herself onto Marty and planted a kiss on her lips. She said, "Come with me, and I will fuck your eyes out."

Marty said into Dead Eye's ear in a softer voice, "Sorry, I don't think so" and sped out of the club.

Dead Eye went back to the table, grabbed the bottle of vodka, took a long swig and angrily yelled out, "Wussy!"

Chapter Thirty-Six

Marty followed Raveneitzkya back to Bubba's Barbecue Place. She watched her get out of the SUV where she spritzed some perfume on herself and sauntered up to the entrance. Marty thought she was a very seductive woman, but she had this pit in her stomach over the hatred that had built inside of her just in the brief ride from downtown. She wanted to take Raveneitzkya out in the worst way from what she had grasped of the conversation among the murder of ravens. How despicable were they to traffic in human beings? Those poor defenseless girls who had no chance of a real life, let alone the moral indignity they, whoever they were, must have suffered. Every person she did away with deserved what they got, Marty rationalized. Raveneitzkya would get hers, but not tonight. *Tonight is for me, for John and The Ultimate Chef Challenge,* she said to herself, but she had not expected Raveneitzkya to go back to the restaurant. Why?

Marty knew that the Raven was up to no good. She wanted something to pin on her for John, and this might be one such opportunity. She owed him for the dream job he had given her. And she was falling in love with him and would do whatever to protect his interests against any indifference, intrusion or difficulty. Besides, wasn't that her job as a personal assistant, she thought, to protect his interests? This witch was stealing a good part of his livelihood. His children deserved more of that, not Raveneitzkya because of being their mother or through some divorce. She was taking advantage of John's goodness. *It's time I put a stop to it.* She took the beard off, peeled off the glue from her face and changed into a tight-fitting dress inside her car. And then she applied some lip gloss and covered her upper chest area with glittery lotion.

Inside the restaurant, Raveneitzkya took a seat at the bar. The last customers left, and the bartender said, "We're about to close. Won't be able to serve you."

Just then, Chef Bubba stepped into the bar area and said, "That's all right. Give her what she wants."

Raveneitzkya said, "Thank you," to Chef Bubba while she grabbed a pack of cigarettes out of her purse and said, "I'll take a vodka. The good kind."

The bartender said, "No smoking." He poured Raveneitzkya a shot of the house vodka. Not what she expected.

Chef Bubba said to the bartender, "You can head out. I'll take care of the rest."

The bartender said, "Okay." He shot a look of curiosity at Chef Bubba and Raveneitzkya, clocked out on the computer screen, grabbed his tips, said, "Goodnight," and left.

Chef Bubba fired up his lighter and put it in front of Raveneitzkya. "Go ahead." He lit her cigarette.

"They're making it so a girl can't even have a puff in her own house," Raveneitzkya said and offered one to Chef Bubba.

"I get enough smoke," he said jokingly. He went behind the bar and poured himself a whiskey. All the while he had a La Glorita torpedo waiting for him to indulge. "You mind if I join you?"

"Please do, my dark handsome man," she said seductively. He stayed behind the bar and leaned towards her.

Feeling a little looser from the whiskey, he said, "You sure are one sweet potato."

"You know I am, darling. You like vanilla pudding?" she said, working up to her next move.

"I prefer a nice rump roast before I have my pudding," he said.

"You do, hah?" she said and stood up. All the while Marty was peering at them from outside the restaurant through one of the portholes while taking photos with her cell phone.

"Oh, I most certainly do," Chef Bubba said.

Raveneitzkya waved her hand up and down her torso and said in the manner of a game show hostess previewing a winning prize, "I was voted hottest MILF in Brooklyn. I even beat out those guido chicks with their big tits and their shaved pussies." Raveneitzkya knew a word like "pussies" would trigger excitement in Chef Bubba. She was right. He stepped from behind the bar and headed her way, taking his apron off.

"You want to go somewhere, or you want to do it here?" he asked in a low husky voice.

"Not so quickly. It's going to cost you a little more than just the brisket dinner you comped us earlier," she said.

"Oh, yeah?" Chef Bubba questioned her with furrowing eyes.

"Oh, yeah. For the vanilla pudding, that's three hundred. For the rump roast is six hundred. And to take my clothes off is an extra one hundred. That makes a nice clean one thousand for this lovely body you see in front of you," Raveneitzkya said and smiled.

"Your husband know you do this?" he asked.

"If you are referring to Johnny, he is not my husband. Besides, I do what I want. And if you want, you pay, okay?"

"All right. And we do it here. I'm not paying extra for a hotel," he said.

"You won't regret it. Be the best thousand dollars you ever spent," she said, softening her tone.

"It better be the best fuck I ever had. Never paid that much before for a piece of ass," he said sarcastically as they stepped back towards the kitchen.

141

As Raveneitzkya was taking her clothes off, she said, "You like hairy pussy? Because I have one. It's not like these American girls who look like bald eagles. What the fuck? God gave them hair down there, and they love to torture themselves with wax jobs. I don't get it."

Chef Bubba was thinking that he hoped she shut the fuck up because if she didn't, he would ask for a refund.

"Oh, I forget. The money?" Raveneitzkya demanded as she peeled off a chef knife from a magnetic rack and then pointed the tip at Chef Bubba's neck and then went around his back and stuck the knife towards his belly from behind.

Marty clicked a string of photos. *Perfect.*

Chef Bubba got the point and yelled out, "Take it easy with that. It has an edge, you know." He got a feel of her strong thigh and rubbed it. "Umm, umm, umm, feel those ham hocks," Chef Bubba said with Southern gusto. He couldn't wait for what was to come. Raveneitzkya gave him another jab with the knife, caught by Marty, and then he slipped away from her. Chef Bubba stepped into his office and returned with the cash. He laid it on a workbench. Raveneitzkya counted the money and then undressed fully, except for her shoes. Marty could not believe what she was witnessing. Raveneitzkya had so much growth down below that it practically went down to the middle of her thighs. Marty got the willies over Raveneitzkya's wooliness. She could mop the floor with that, Marty joked and then turned her head away. *I can't look anymore.*

While Chef Bubba stripped down, he looked at Raveneitzkya's pussy and raised his eyebrows, thinking he had some twine that she could use to braid it. He then took hold of Raveneitzkya and tossed her around, bent her over and inserted himself in her rear. Meanwhile, Marty continued to take photos with her cell through a strategic porthole that opened up to a side view of the two in action.

Raveneitzkya moaned, "Oh, your brisket is so big and warm," while Chef Bubba made the best of his thousand dollars by grabbing hold of Raveneitzkya's fleshy breasts and humping away for twenty minutes. Both of them were sweating profusely. Marty could not believe it.

"Okay, tick-tock, time's up," Raveneitzkya said in a pant.

Chef Bubba huffed, "I'm almost there, sweetheart."

"Two more minutes," she said. He continued to hump Raveneitzkya for ten more minutes but to no avail.

"Sorry, Mr. Bubba, but I have to go," she said and pushed him off her and got dressed. "I can come back another day if you like? I give you a discount."

Chef Bubba was trying to catch his breath. He raised his hand and waved to say see you later—maybe much later—as Raveneitzkya left out the kitchen. Marty quickly hid behind some bushes, so the Raven wouldn't notice her.

Five minutes later Marty saw the lights going out all through the restaurant. She quickly made her way towards the back of the restaurant and rang the delivery doorbell. A minute later she could hear Chef Bubba moving through the kitchen. He said, "Are coming back for more, you hot hairy Russian, you?" He then opened the door with a surprised look and said, "Miss Kittering, what are you doing here?"

"I got hungry," she said.

"I'm about to close up and was ready to leave."

"No, I'm hungry for a big black man," she said.

"Well, why don't you come right on in," he said with exuberance and excitement in his voice. Marty stepped inside the restaurant. Chef Bubba took a quick look outside and then locked the back door. "So, you have a taste for dark meat?" he continued as he stepped towards the workbench that was still warm from his activity only minutes ago. Marty followed him and then grabbed his large round ass. "Well, I guess you are hungry, aren't you?" He eyed Marty's glistening body. She had lotioned-up to capture his attention, not that she really needed it because he wanted some of that. Marty was the exact type of woman he favored.

"When you grabbed my butt in the office today, I said 'Marty, now there's a man that knows what he wants and is not afraid to go after it,'" she said.

"Damn right, darling," he said as he moved his crotch towards Marty, wanting to kiss her lips. Marty slipped to the side of him as he missed his target. "I see you like to play games," he grinned.

Marty said, "I do. What I want is for you to strip down. Then I'm going to tie you up, and then I'm gonna' give you what you been desirin' because I can tell you're a lustful man, Bubba."

"You're a take-charge woman. Tie me up, hah?" he said. "I don't know if I like that," he continued.

"That's the way I work," she said.

"You're not going to charge me, are you?" he asked.

"Hell, no. I'm just going to show you a hot time," Marty said and then rubbed her pussy.

"Alright," he said, licking his lips. He began to undress.

Marty put on some rubber gloves.

Chef Bubba looked at her peculiarly and said, "What the hell you doin'?"

"Don't worry," she said and grabbed some butcher's twine off a nearby shelf and placed it on the workbench. And then grabbed some vegetable oil as Chef Bubba got completely naked.

He said, "You going to undress?"

"In time. Now get up on the bench. And lie on your back," she commanded like old times, drawing from her experience as a dominatrix.

"Okay," he said and did.

Marty then cut four long strands of twine, grabbed one of Chef Bubba's hands and wrapped his wrist with the twine and then pulled his arm back towards the leg of the bench and tied the wrist to the bench leg. She repeated the process with the other hand and then his legs, tying his ankles to the legs at the other end of the bench.

"You are one kinky bitch," Chef Bubba said.

"I've been wanting to do this ever since I saw you the first time on TV," Marty said to give him one last erotic morsel to chew before she took care of him for good.

"Motherfucker, I'm horny," he blurted out.

She doubled up the twine around his wrists and ankles for good measure. She then unscrewed the top of the jar of oil and poured some on top of Chef Bubba's belly, arms and legs. She then rubbed the oil all over his body, intentionally missing his fully erect penis, which had been inflated by some male enhancement pill he took right before he did Raveneitzkya.

Chef Bubba said, "You going to take care of business?"

"In a minute," she said. She grabbed a plastic garbage bag, slipped off her gloves and tossed them into the bag. She stepped out of his view and took out some electrical tape from her purse. She pulled off an eight-inch piece and quickly placed it over Chef Bubba's mouth. He squirmed his head and body while trying to speak through the tape. Marty gave him a shush and then his eyes got buggy. He knew something wasn't quite right. Marty put on another pair of rubber gloves, grabbed a bottle of Manzano sauce from her purse, took the top off and smiled as she doused Chef Bubba's penis, which was sore from the earlier humping. If he could have screamed, he would have been heard throughout Los Feliz. He squirmed and writhed and then passed out from the excruciating pain.

Marty then went into the smokehouse that was connected to the kitchen. She opened the door to the smoker, which had a rotating rack system. She opened the feeder door and tossed some split applewood onto the embers that were still aglow. She went back into the kitchen and grabbed a bucket of the pre-mixed dry rub Chef Bubba used for his brisket, which included kosher salt, coarse ground black pepper, brown sugar, sweet paprika, mild chili powder, onion powder, dried oregano, garlic powder, dry mustard and cayenne pepper. She then sprinkled the dry rub all over his body, released the wheel locks on the workbench and rolled it into the smokehouse, lining the workbench up to the smoker. She cut the twine on his wrists and ankles. She then opened the smoker door and shimmied Chef Bubba's legs onto the smoker shelf and then his upper body. She rolled the workbench back in the kitchen. Went back in the smokehouse, closed the door to the smoker, turned on the rotating rack and then checked the fire down below. She stoked the embers and cleaned up her mess in the kitchen.

She then cut all the lights in the kitchen. Her cell phone rang a few times. She checked; it was John. He texted her, wondering where she was. She let it be for the moment. And then she heard a cell phone ring in Chef Bubba's office. It had to be his wife, she surmised. And then the restaurant phone rang several times. Chef Bubba needed at least three more hours to get that nice crispy bark going. She stoked the embers again and then added some more applewood to get the fire roasting. She knew that wasn't how you barbecue, but she had to move the process along.

She went back in the kitchen and saw car lights outside through one of the portholes. She slithered her way into the restaurant dining room, hiding in the shadows, and saw through the large picture window that it was a security guard who must have been checking the restaurant. The alarm? Chef Bubba hadn't set the alarm. After a certain hour, they probably checked to see if he was still here. His car was out back, so maybe they'd just move along. She hoped so.

The security guard made his way around the back towards the kitchen and keyed the door. Marty ran back into the dining room and hid behind the bar. The security guard, who had a flashlight, entered the kitchen area and made a quick run through the restaurant, the restrooms, and storage rooms and said, "Hello, Chef Bubba. Anybody here?" He then stepped back into the kitchen and checked the walk-ins, freezer, dry storage, and Chef Bubba's office. And then he took a few sniffs, stopped and stepped towards the smokehouse. Sniffed again and made an odd face as if he smelled something strange. He then set the alarm by the kitchen door, went out the door, locked it and drove away. Marty watched the security guard drive away through the parking lot and down the street. She blew out her anxiety, grabbed an open bottle of pinot, pulled the cork and took a swig and then another one.

She sat down behind the bar and fell asleep shortly after. She woke to smoke billowing out from the kitchen and into the restaurant. She had forgotten to open the flume to the smoker. She quickly ran into the kitchen and turned on the exhaust fan to the Ansul system. It was slow to draw up the smoke, so she grabbed a towel, wet it underneath the sink, put the wet towel over her mouth and ran into the smokehouse. She could barely see as she coughed heavily. She found the flume control and turned it to full exhaust and then ran back into the kitchen. The smoke started to slowly dissipate. She waited another five minutes, rolled the workbench back into the smokehouse, grabbed a pair of insulated gloves hanging by the smoker and opened the door. As the rack came up to the opening, Marty shut off the rotating rack.

Chef Bubba was done to perfection. She slowly shimmied him onto the workbench and rolled him straight through the kitchen and into the dining area right up to a large rectangular table, shimmied him onto the table and rolled the workbench back into the kitchen. Marty took off the gloves and tossed them into the garbage bag, ran back into the bar and grabbed the open wine and a sawed-off shotgun Chef Bubba had for protection. She glanced over at Chef Bubba's barbecued body illuminated by the parking lot lamps, sorry for a moment that she couldn't risk taking a picture, then went back into the kitchen, grabbed her purse and the garbage bag and headed towards the back door. She tried to open it, but it was locked. "Chef Bubba's keys," she said and went into his office, grabbed a towel and picked the keys up off his desk with the towel. She keyed the lock with the towel and opened the lock, returned the keys, grabbed the garbage bag and her purse and ran out the back door. The alarm was immediately triggered.

Chapter Thirty-Seven

There was an emerging sunrise and not a cloud in the sky except for the murky haze that highlighted the Pacific Ocean as Los Feliz' palm-tree-lined coastline swayed quietly in rhythm with the heartbeat of Los Feliz' early morning hour. A gray-smirched yellow Volkswagen Thing drove past the pier, made a couple of left turns and then pulled up to the parking lot of Bubba's Barbecue Place. Paul Cooz, a tall, lanky forty-year-old man with chestnut brown hair and a pair of eyes the color of the Pacific Ocean, stepped out of the vehicle. A battery of police vehicles, the Los Feliz County Coroner's van, the security service vehicle and a few other vehicles of various makes and models were parked randomly outside the restaurant.

Cooz, a fifteen-year veteran of the Los Feliz Police Department, had been on the homicide squad most of his career. He was quick-witted, sharper than most and had a predilection for the culinary. He wore a good pair of well-fitting Wallabies on his feet that matched his tan trench coat. He flipped off his Wayfarers and rubbed the corner of his windswept wet eye and securely hung the sunglasses on his neck-slung detective's badge. He paused for a moment at the car door to let out his four-legged companion, a spotted cream-colored American Yorkshire pet pig named Boo. Leashless, Boo followed in stride next to her master, who was more like her contemporary. They were in a sense, partners in crime.

As they were about to enter the front door of Bubba's Barbecue Place, Boo urinated. A cop in blues opened the front door, nodded his head hello and said "Detective." Cooz responded with a morning saluta-tion and quickly sensed something peculiar with his prominent snout as the two cohorts entered the restaurant. The cop shook his head in amuse-ment at Boo as the door closed behind them.

Randy Shamlian

Boo and Cooz made their way towards a crowd of Los Feliz' finest who surrounded the table where the charred human carcass of Chef Bubba lay. The usual crowd of crime scene investigators sifted through what evidence they could gather, mostly in the kitchen and few items around the body. One of the detectives stepped aside as she saw Cooz coming her way. Cooz was a little taken aback by the barbecued body that was sprawled out on the table. He had seen charred remains before as a result of some type of home or vehicle fire, and of course he'd eaten plenty of barbecued brisket, even Chef Bubba's, which he thought was plenty good, exceptional even, but he had never seen a barbecued person before. This was all new territory for him. In his line of work, he'd seen a lot of crazy shit, but this had to be the top of his list.

Boo circled the table in excited anticipation. "Boo, be careful, you know how you are with cayenne pepper," Cooz commanded. Boo took a quick lick of the body and then let out a "snort."

Jonesy, one of the seasoned veteran detectives, who was about fifty, average height and build with reddish blond hair, responded in a sarcastic tone, "And how do you know that the vic was basted in cayenne pepper?" He turned to Fajida, a detective in her early thirties, with long dark hair, black eyes and a touch of hardness in her pretty Spanish face, and proudly said, "See, Fajida, I know a thing or two about cooking."

Cooz shot back, "Well, first of all, Jonesy, Chef Bubba wasn't basted, he was dry rubbed with not only cayenne pepper, but kosher salt, chili powder, dry mustard, brown sugar and a few other spices."

"How do you know that? And how do you know that it's the chef?" Jonesy sounded annoyed that Cooz could be so sure.

"Bubba's Place has some of the best barbecue this side of the Appalachian Trail. Everybody knows Chef Bubba was from North Carolina. It even says it on his signage. And they use lots of cayenne pepper. Very distinct," Cooz said slyly.

"It's a theory. Where's the real proof, besides some ingredients? This could be anybody," Jonesy said.

"He wore a diamond ring on his right pinky. That was his signature," Cooz responded.

One of the crime scene investigators started to rub the vic's pinky. As he did, the hand snapped off from the wrist.

"Whoops, just a little too done," Fajida quipped.

"Be careful," Cooz yelped.

The crime scene investigators began to squabble amongst themselves. Boo took a chomp of the barbecued hand and managed to get a chunk of the thumb and index finger.

"Boo," Cooz pointed out, "don't come squealing to me about an upset stomach."

As chaos ensued, the Homicide Captain and another rushed through the front door directly towards the scene. Upon seeing the melee, the Captain stammered, "All right, what the hell is this?" And as he got a clear view of the body, he gave out a, "Jesus!"

"It's the owner of the restaurant," Jonesy declared.

"An accident? A murder? What do we have here?" the Captain asked.

"He was killed," Cooz commented. "Somehow, I don't think he could have barbecued himself and then made it onto this table."

Irritated, the Captain asked, "How come you're not a chef somewhere?"

Cooz smiled, "I am. Certified even."

"Yeah, we know," the Captain said, wanting to respond by saying "certified nut" but held back lest he'd face some disciplinary tribunal, although he knew Cooz could easily handle a ribbing. "Okay, Cooz, you take the lead on this since it's your forte." The Captain peered at Boo who was licking her chops. "Is he eating the evidence?"

"Boo's a she," Cooz said.

The Captain looked Cooz in the eyes and remarked, "You're one nutty dude! I don't know why we let you run with this pig?"

Boo let out a "SQUEAL!"

"She has a sensitive nose," Cooz said.

The Captain gave a quick gander at Cooz's nose and remarked, "Right. So where are we at with the Ramsey case?"

"Dead end?" Jonesy said.

"Let's wrap it up then and get working on this case," the Captain said, and he and his assistant exited the restaurant.

Fajida asked Cooz, "You want us to interview the restaurant staff?"

"Who the hell would do something like this?" Jonesy asked with absolute uncertainty.

"Pissed-off ex. I wanted to fry my last boyfriend's nuts," Fajida casually stated.

"Whoever it was knows a thing or two about barbecue," Cooz commented. "Fajida, start with the kitchen crew and whoever closed up last night. Jonesy, check out if our chef was in with any of the loan sharks." Cooz looked at the body and then cupped his hand close to Bubba's crotch and moved it towards his nose to get a whiff. "Hmm...?"

Fajida looked over at the troubled Cooz and with curiosity asked, "What is it, Cooz?"

"Manzano. He never used it in his preparation," Cooz said.

"What does that mean?" Jonesy responded.

"I don't know yet, but it could exclude anyone that works here," Cooz said. "That's a start."

Another detective stepped up to the table with the security guard who looked a little shaken, like he needed a drink, and said, "This is Bill McCoy. He's the one that found the vic. Said he responded to a call that the alarm was not set. Came into the restaurant, saw no one around.

Smelled something funny. Didn't think too much of it, set the alarm and left. Came back later when the alarm was triggered and found the body."

Cooz asked, "Bill, are you alright? You look a little peaked."

Bill looked away from the body and said, "Yeah, I'm alright. Fucking scary shit. I was in here when he was roasting away. I smelled it. It was nasty."

Cooz asked, "It's a smell you'll never forget. So you think the killer was in here when you came through the first time?"

Bill said, "Must have because the alarm was triggered afterward. They must have been hiding. Shit, I could have been killed. I could have been barbecued."

The detective who interviewed Bill said, "There was no forced entry."

Cooz shot the detective a look and said, "Maybe, but most likely not barbecued." He pointed to Chef Bubba and said, "This was very specific, not some random act. Did you see anything out of the ordinary, like a car or a stranger or anything that looked out of place last night?"

"Besides the smell, of course, and Chef Bubba's car being out back. But that happens in restaurants. Maybe he got loaded and took a cab or got a ride from someone and left his car behind and forgot to set the alarm," he said. "But I didn't see anything else that looked odd or suspicious."

"He ever do that before, forget to set the alarm?" Cooz asked.

"Yeah," Bill shook his head.

"Okay, Bill, we'll contact you if we need you. Thanks," Cooz said. Bill nodded and then made his way out the front door.

Fajida said after Bill exited, "It wasn't him, he was too spooked."

"I know what I'm not having tonight for dinner," Jonesy said smartly.

"Let me guess," Fajida said sarcastically. "A frozen dinner and a donut for dessert."

"I had the donut before I got here," Jonesy said with a smirk.

Cooz then bellowed out as if he were an actor on stage, "Food is theatre."

Jonesy turned towards Cooz and said, "What?"

Cooz repeated his words in a less dramatic fashion, "Food is theatre."

Fajida started to laugh and asked, "So, what are you trying to say, Cooz?"

Cooz emphatically responded, "This was all done for a spectacle. It's somebody on or connected to that chef show."

Chapter Thirty-Eight

News spread quickly through the Food Channel offices of the gruesome death of Chef Bubba. Janet, upon hearing the news, vomited all over Jim and then he vomited because she vomited all over him. It was the most grotesque thing they had ever heard of. "How could that happen," Janet said in horror and disbelief. Jim felt the same way, but only in that she vomited on him. Jim didn't particularly care about Chef Bubba, nor did he care about any of the other quasi-celebrity chefs on the show.

"Good riddance," he said to himself. They were just cogs in the wheel. If there were replacements, the wheel could keep turning, although Chef Bubba was their biggest attraction. They had the next two episodes in the can, so they would have to pull some wannabe someone or another chef off the shelf to replace Chef Bubba. They would have to re-shoot the ending of the second episode to name a different winner, though. Easy to do, he thought. They had a few replacement choices, but it was slim at best. Jim was getting anxious and needed to talk to the boss. John was spending the morning with Christina and Fat Freddie and was nowhere to be found since he had shut off his cell. Family came first.

And as soon as the news media picked up on the event, they were all over the story like bees on honey. News crews quickly started to line up outside the studio, putting their own spin on how Chef Bubba was killed. One channel illustrated the story with a clip from a Bubba's Barbecue Place TV commercial showing Chef Bubba slicing up some of his well-charred brisket, dipping it into his mustard-based barbecue sauce and then chewing on it in his snarling way. Then the chef forked a slice of his homemade sweet potato pie with a good heaping of maple-syrup-infused whipped cream, pointed it towards the camera and put it in his mouth while gesturing, "Umm, umm, good." The news reporter said, "It was not a good ending for Chef Bubba Arnet. This is Jennifer Sanchez for Live Action News at The Food Channel Studios."

"Such a macabre act could only be performed by the obstinacy of the devil," Elliot said in private to his secretary. "And I have an uneasy feeling who it just might be. I need to talk to John Abruzzo. See if you can get a hold of him. I've tried a few times, and he hasn't returned my call." The secretary did not say a word. She picked up her phone with urgency as if the world was going to end.

Elliot said, "Never mind. I'll just go over there now."

As Elliot walked down the L-shaped corridor, there was a low murmur of chatter, and he could not help but think of the Tower of Babel and the hellishness that had occurred in the last couple of days since Raveneitzkya arrived. Such behavior was reprehensible for any woman, let alone a mother of two teenaged children. Elliot was having second thoughts about the WCCOC show but was under contract for one more season. Canceling it before then could be messy and costly.

Elliot arrived at John's office. Ginger got up from her desk as she greeted Elliot and said, "Mr. Abruzzo hasn't arrived yet, but Ms. Kittering is here." Elliot was a little confused about Marty sharing John's office after the less than a week she'd been employed. He saw how attractive she was and had noticed the instant chemistry between John and her. Romance and business were not a good combination to his mind. Never in his twenty-five years as an executive had he dated or entertained the idea of dating office personnel. Ginger knocked on John's door and then opened the door and let Elliot in.

Marty got up from her desk just off the side of John's and said, "Mr. Hyde."

"Ms. Clittering, have you heard from Mr. Abruzzo?" he asked, looking harried and upset.

"Not yet, but I assume he'll be here shortly," she said.

"Where could he be?" Elliot blurted out.

And then Marty stepped to his side and said in her most sincere and heartfelt voice while raising her sparkling cobalt-blue eyes to his, "Are you okay?"

Elliot's eyes got weepy, and he bent his head down slightly and moaned, "No, I'm not. She's a harlot, the devil's daughter." He cupped his hand underneath the side of Marty's breast. Marty didn't flinch and held her tongue. She had to play naïve, yet concerned about Chef Bubba's death, she thought.

"I hate to trouble you at such a bad time, but it's my wife. She's having an affair," he said and rubbed the side of Marty's breast.

Marty slowly stepped away and said, "Why don't you have a seat and I'll get you some water," as she assisted him into a chair, thinking, *all I need is another horny guy getting a boner for me, but maybe that's a good thing right now. Keep him off the scent.* But then there was John. She'd been dreading it all morning. *Once he finds out, I'm going to have to put on my best acting performance of the year. It was a gamble telling him my thoughts, but I figured maybe he would understand. Just a tad too much for him to handle. I can pull it off; I'm sure I can.*

As soon as Marty brought Elliot a glass of water, John hurriedly stepped inside the office. His eyes beamed on Marty. She, in turn, gave him a look saying with all the body language she could conjure up that it wasn't her. Elliot stood up.

"I just heard the news," John said, greeting Elliot. "This is not good." He returned his gaze to Marty, directing the comment and his extreme disapproval at her.

"Can we have a moment in private?" Elliot requested.

"Sure," John said. Marty got the message and closed the door behind her as she left.

"John, this is awful. We're going to get some bad publicity. And that incident yesterday with your wife was not conducive to good business practices," Elliot said, concerned. "You two look like you have a bit of animus between you. And the couple that was with her, they didn't look too sociable. It appears that she may have had some type of motivation to kill Chef Bubba Arnet."

"I know what you're thinking, but it certainly wasn't them. Whoever it was, we can handle this," he said. "Maybe, a little publicity is what the show needs?" John speculated.

"There may not be a show," Elliot said, funneling part of his frustration over his wife, wanting a taste of John's lovely new assistant and fighting the devil within into this new twist of events.

"You think this is a good time to talk this way? We do have a contract for another season, and we also have this new concept to improve the show. It's a winner," John said.

Elliot backed off a little. "Okay, let's get a meeting pulled together with some of your people and my people, and we'll come up with a plan to deal with all the backlash."

"Have the police been here?" John asked.

"Not yet," Elliot said and left the office.

Marty gingerly stepped back into the office. She intentionally left the door open. Ginger had her ears glued to the office. John shut the door and then grabbed Marty's arm and pulled her away from the door. In a low voice, he said, "Don't tell me that was you who did that?"

"John, I swear to you on my hands and knees, that was not me. What I told you two nights ago was a joke. I was trying to get a rise out of you. You know, I was playing with you," she said in her most sincere voice.

"Then where the hell were you? I tried all night. Doesn't that look suspicious?" John was trying to restrain himself.

"Honestly, I got a massage, some garam masala and nan, a bottle of pinot and watched a movie. I shut my phone off because I wanted to relax, and I knew you were with Christina and Freddie. I wanted to give you your space. I swear to you," she said.

"Please, please tell me it wasn't you, Marty?" John pleaded.

She put her arms around John, but he was limp. She nudged up against him and spoke softly in his ear. "I think I'm falling in love with you. I wouldn't ever do anything to hurt you. Do you think it may have been Raveneitztkya?"

"Marty, I have feelings too, but…I don't know. She's crazy. I never knew her to be that vicious as to barbecue a person. That's some sick shit. You have to be twisted beyond belief to do something like that," he said in a crazed way.

Marty stroked John's face and kissed his cheek, "It's all right, John. Don't worry. We can manage this." She put her hand on his hip and kissed him on the lips. John got lost in the moment with her and then his office phone rang.

Chapter Thirty-Nine

The day drew nearer to darkness as Cooz pulled into a parking lot. He walked towards the entrance of Assagio's Gourmet Pizza and Deli. Once inside, he veered towards the prepared meat section. He took a gander at a variety of homemade sausages, kielbasas, and hot dogs and then picked up a package of sausage and stepped toward the order counter. A young man tattooed from head to toe, wearing a white apron, greeted Cooz at the counter and asked, "What can I get you?"

Cooz handed him the package of sausage and looked up at a menu placard. "Let me get a medium pie with white sauce, roasted garlic, heirloom tomatoes, Napa Valley smoked Gouda and some of this sausage."

The tattooed young man grabbed hold of the sausage. "Chardonnay basil. Sounds like a winner. Give us twenty minutes."

Cooz made his way down the front counter towards a pizza cook who he had been eyeing for a couple of months now. He had been attracted to the way her curly blond hair flowed out from underneath the pink skullcap she wore. Occasionally, he'd catch a smile from her, and when she was not looking, he got a glimpse of her tight-fitting chef's pants that accentuated her bulbous behind. It was the added treat that brought him into Assagio's at least three times a week. Cooz smiled at the little chefette, as he referred to her in his own mind, and quipped, "Love your pie."

"I'm sure you do. I see you here often. My name is Evie Ann."

"Hi, Evie Ann, I'm Paul Cooz. But call me Cooz."

"Hey," she said with a twinkle in her eye.

He then surveyed the wine section while he waited for the conversation to take shape.

"You a cop?" she asked.

"Only when I'm working," he said.

"Are you working now?" she continued.

"If flirting is working, then I guess I am," he said.

Evie Ann smirked and finished making his pizza. Cooz selected a bottle of Gerkin Hills Chardonnay while eyeing the cutie pie from the corner of his eye. She was a foodie; that was good. She was interested. He knew that he could finesse her if he made one of specialties, but he'd have to work his way into it. Maybe pan-seared sea scallops over a black-truffle-infused risotto or a grilled monster T-bone topped with his homemade steak sauce and garlic bread. The salad was always an afterthought. Maybe she was a vegan? But then, would she show the interest she had if she knew that he indulged in animal flesh?

Lorna, his last girlfriend, was uninterested in the culinary arts but had a rack that wouldn't quit and was great in the sack. He still found himself daydreaming about her tight pussy…a habit that required occasional cold showers. She opted to spend much of her time running along the beach for hours at a clip. Great for the onlookers, and certainly it did wonders for the sex life. The lack of gastronomic intrigue didn't do much for the conversation, though, as it dulled the motivation towards intimacy and ultimately falling in love. She walked out on him with a last comment that he was just too much into food. And as if that was some consolation, she remarked, "I just don't have time for that in my life right now."

Chapter Forty

Armed with a pile of files under his arm, the pizza and the bottle of wine, Cooz slipped through the front door of his ranch house deep in Laurel Canyon. He had inherited the piece of property from his dear old granddad, Pierre Cooz, several years back. Pierre had been a chef at the Brown Derby during its heyday and acquired the ranch from Clark Gable as a gratuity for the special meals he prepared for Clark and Carole Lombard. The ranch gave Boo some sprawl space and her own private domain connected to the house, which allowed her to come and go as she pleased. She was like a roommate, less the makeup and bras hanging from the shower curtain rod, Cooz quipped from time to time about his living arrangements.

Cooz tossed the pizza on the kitchen counter, pulled out a plate, served himself a slice and headed to the living room with his evening meal and homework. He set himself up on the couch and turned on the television. He remoted it to the Food Channel and then opened the bottle of Gerkin, indulged himself in a small snort, filled the glass full and then opened the new case file. A photo of the barbecued remains of Chef Bubba set his mind back to when he was last in the kitchen of Bubba's Barbecue Place, with Chef Bubba applying the cayenne-spiked dry rub on half a dozen beef briskets.

He pondered the motive of the killer. Why would they go to such lengths to get rid of a chef of a barbecue joint? Could it have been a competitor? Unlikely. Angry wife or lover? He'd been divorced for five years. Wife got half and left happily. Besides, if he had scorned a lover along the way, she would have needed help in moving a 275-pound body. It wasn't the mob. He owned the restaurant free and clear and had no other real debts, and he wasn't a serious gambler. His gut told him that it was someone with a fetish, someone with the fundamentals of food cookery know-how. The Manzano was the key since they didn't have any other tangible evidence.

Cooz grabbed another slice. Boo entered the living room carrying a little rubber doll in her mouth and hopped on the couch next to her roommate. Cooz gave her quick rub on the head and fed her the crust from the pizza. He glanced at the television and caught the news broadcast on the Food Channel. A photo of Chef Bubba appeared on the screen. He turned the volume up and put down the file.

The newscaster reported, "Bubba Arnet, the chef and owner of the Bubba's Barbecue Place in Los Feliz, California, was found dead today in what appears to be a possible murder. Details from the Los Feliz Police Department indicate that he was gruesomely barbecued. This is certainly a horrific story, which we are sad to report since Chef Bubba was one of the top contestants on the World Chef Cook Off Show that airs on this network. In a related story, Franz Kilmer, a noted sausage maker from the hamlet of Wurstburg, Germany, was arrested only days ago for using human body parts in his bratwurst sausage. Apparently, numerous townspeople have gone missing and are feared to have been eaten by the patrons of Kilmer's sausage shop." An image on the television screen showed a man next to the shop doubled over and holding his mouth in disgust.

Boo "SQUEALED!"

"I agree with you, Boo. The world's gone looney." Cooz looked down at the half-eaten slice of pizza. "I just might have to hold off on ordering the sausage for a while. What do you say we go over to the set of this cooking show tomorrow?" But Boo was fast asleep. "Long day on the job?" Cooz draped a small blanket over Boo. She let out a long sigh. Cooz laughed. "Sweet dreams, sweetheart." He pulled out a small piece of paper from his pocket and made a call on his cell.

Chapter Forty-One

Cooz savored a glass of ginger green iced tea at a window booth at the Duxelle Café. He waited for Evie Ann, his breakfast guest. He regretted not asking her out sooner, but he was still licking his wounds from Lorna. Funny how that is; you know that the relationship is going nowhere, but you hang on for self-serving purposes. But wasn't that the case with most relationships, sexual or otherwise? Evie Ann walked into the café. He looked up and did a double take. She was sexier than he first thought, wearing rose-tinted Serengeti shades, a pink tank top and well-worn cutoff denim jeans that were almost white. Golden locks flowing down to her mid-back set the frame of this sexy beauty. She stepped towards the table, and Cooz almost stumbled on his words but knocked over his iced tea instead as he stood up. It spilled all over his trench coat. He brushed the tea off his coat and stuck his hand out to shake. It was wet.

Evie Ann took a seat and said, "Did I startle you, Cooz?"

"I'd be lying if I said no. Who knew you looked so good underneath your chef's clothes?" he said.

"I look better underneath these clothes," she said without blinking.

"Really? Because there's not much left to the imagination," Cooz said.

"If I could work in the nude, I would," Evie Ann said coyly.

"I would say that that might cause a spectacle," Cooz responded.

Evie Ann grabbed a menu. "So what looks good?"

The waiter stopped by and asked, "What can I get you two?"

"The acai granola bowl is worthy," he said, testing her culinary interests.

"Hum, something a little heartier, like the venison hash with jalapenos and a stack of mango buckwheat pancakes and whatever he's drinking," she said.

Cooz smirked that she wasn't a vegan. Not that that would hinder the relationship, but her carnivorous tastes made cooking meals a bit more exciting. "Now that's more like it," Cooz said to himself.

"What are you having, sir?" The waiter asked Cooz snidely since he felt that Cooz was taking his sweet time.

"The house omelet and a side of red chili honey bacon," Cooz said sarcastically while waving his head side to side. The waiter headed off to put in their orders. Cooz hoped that the waiter wouldn't spit in his omelet. The two people you don't want to piss off—your barber because he might cut your ears off and your waiter. His grandfather taught him that, but it was too late, Cooz knew.

"Cooz?"

"Yes, Evie Ann?"

"Is the trench coat meant to mean something? You don't secretly like to flash people?" she asked.

Cooz laughed, "Do you remember that detective show, *Colombo*?"

"No," she said.

"I guess you were a little young. He was the detective that wore a trench coat and smoked a cigar. It took place in Los Feliz. It might have been what motivated me to become a detective," he said aloofly.

"When in Los Feliz, right? You're not going to flash me, are you?"

"I'm perversely adverse to such behavior," he said as he winked and continued, "So, when did you realize you wanted to cook?"

"When I was in the crib, and my mother fed me jarred food. That was some awful shit," Evie Ann said.

"You had a burgeoning palate as a toddler?" Cooz asked.

"That was the worst thing I can remember growing up. So when I got out of high school, I attended chef school."

"You want to have your own restaurant someday?"

The waiter brought Evie Ann's iced tea.

"Well, to answer your question, I'd like to be a celebrity chef," she said.

"Isn't that interesting. How are you going to achieve that?" Cooz asked.

"On the World Chef Cook Off Show. They have a casting call going on," she said.

"You heard about Chef Bubba Arnet?" Cooz asked as the waiter walked past the table.

"No, what happened to him?"

"He was murdered, or at least we believe he was," Cooz said almost reluctantly.

"That's awful. He was one of the top chefs on the show," she said with surprise.

"I'm investigating the case," Cooz said.

With a curious look, Evie Ann responded, "Really? Do you have any idea who might have killed him?"

"Can't really say, but whoever did it has some wicked sense of humor," Cooz responded.

"What happened to him?"

"He was found barbecued."

"Holy shit! Who and how?" she asked.

"That is the million-dollar question or questions," Cooz said.

"Well, I hope they get what's coming to them," she said, shaking her head. "Wow. So tell me, do you ever go hunting for truffles with Boo?" She was trying to change the subject before she got grossed out at the thought of a barbecued body.

166

"I haven't heard of a whole lot of truffles being found in Los Feliz. But, ya' know, I do like to go collecting wild mushrooms up in the San Gabriels," he said.

"Yeah?" Evie Ann said with eyes wide open. "I love chanterelles. Any kind of wild ones. With all this rain we've been having lately, there should be some up there. You want to go sometime?"

"Certainly. How about this weekend?" Cooz was not wasting any time.

The waiter served the food. Evie Ann asked the waiter, "You have Manzano sauce?" Cooz glanced over at Evie Ann and for a brief second pondered her with a bottle of Manzano and the nude Chef Bubba. He quickly put it out of his head. It wasn't her.

"Yes, anything else I can get you both?" the waiter asked.

"More iced tea, thanks," Cooz responded.

The waiter grabbed a bottle of Manzano from the next booth over. Evie Ann poured some syrup on her pancakes and then doused the pancakes with Manzano sauce. Cooz was stunned.

"I like the sweet against the salt and heat," Evie Ann remarked.

"Real scientific," Cooz managed as the waiter poured him more iced tea.

"It's all about the contrast," Evie Ann commented with a smile.

The waiter stopped by their table and said, "Didn't mean to listen in on your conversation, but our chef just got a gig on that chef show."

"What's his name?" Evie Ann asked.

"Matt Comatus, Chef Matt," he said.

"I wish him well, then," Evie Ann responded with a tinge of jealousy.

"Thank you, I'll let him know," he said and left.

Chapter Forty-Two

Cooz pulled his Thing into the Food Channel Studio parking lot and stepped out of the vehicle with Boo following him. There were chefs of all sorts lined up around the building where he was going. Upon closer inspection, he was amused at the peculiar clothing and get-ups most of these so-called culinary professionals had dressed up in. He laughed to himself and thought, *What people will do to get fame and fortune.* He walked by a man who was dressed in Spanish Matador clothing equipped with a sequined suit, a montera on his head and a red cape-like apron. He wondered what his specialty of the house might be. Skewered beef, maybe?

There were sushi chefs, traditionally garbed cooks in whites and in chili-pepper-printed black chefs clothing. Being a chef is one thing, being a celebrity chef required some intrinsic attributes, like charm and finesse. Chef Bubba had a bold personality with a bit of a Southern twang, which gave him character. Certainly, he 'cued his brisket to perfection, just enough fat so it was always moist with a slightly sweet-twangy heat that lingered on your lips and made you want more. The brisket, with his celery-seed-flecked creamy coleslaw and fluffy buttermilk biscuits, was second to none.

How were they going to replace a persona like Chef Bubba? That was what people tune in for. They want someone that they either want to be like or who will provide entertainment as well as be able to cook the pants off of anyone. Whoever the producer was, he had a task in front of them. But Cooz's job was to find the killer of Bubba Arnet, not to ponder the success of the World Chef Cook Off Show. But it was hard not to keep from being entertained in the entertainment capital of the world. In some perverse way, that's why Cooz enjoyed being a homicide detective. The thrill of solving a case kept him intrigued.

As Boo and Cooz got closer to the entrance, one of the chefs spat out, "I bet that pig of yours has some tasty chops."

Cooz stopped dead in his tracks. Boo was a bit frantic and headed straight towards the chef who spoke out. Boo "snorted" at his feet. Cooz pulled out his badge and softly spoke to the chef, "She likes knuckles. Human knuckles."

The chef cowered. "Sorry, man!"

"Not to me," Cooz said, his narrow eyes trained on the man. "Say sorry to her."

"I'm sorry, little piggy," the chef mumbled.

"Her name is Boo, not 'little piggy.' Now, say 'sorry, Boo,'" Cooz said.

"Sorry, Boo," the chef repeated.

Boo "SQUEALED" and walked towards the entrance with Cooz. There was an uproar of chatter from the line of chefs. Cooz was greeted by a security officer, flashed his badge and entered the building. The line of chefs continued and ran down a corridor towards the film stage. He spotted Evie Ann, who was dressed in pastel pink chef clothes, and walked past her. She was engaged in conversation with a couple. Cooz waved at her as he neared the stage. She smiled back at him. There was some fascination about Boo. Cooz slipped onto the film stage as he was directed by one of the production crew towards Jim, who was in the middle of casting.

Jim was a bit neurotic at the loss of Chef Bubba, which was putting pressure on with further possible sliding of ratings. Finding and then fostering new talent is time-consuming and could prove costly since The World Chef Cook Off Show competes with a couple of other chef shows for ratings. Talent was out there, but like diamonds in the rough, they must be dug out and polished. How can you prepare for unforeseen accidents, or in the case of Chef Bubba, murder by barbecue?

Cooz was met by Janet. She told him, "You can't have that thing in here. We cook food."

Cooz responded, "If you're referring to Boo, she has a badge."

The assistant tutted and responded, "Well, just keep it away from the stage, then. Mr. Green will be with you in a moment. You may want to take a seat."

"Is he in charge? I just need to ask him some questions about Bubba Arnet," Cooz said.

"Mr. Green is in charge of production. I guess that's good enough. It's tragic. Everyone is frightened at what happened to him. I hope you find that animal," she said. In fact, Janet could not have been any happier with Bubba Arnet gone. As creepy as his death was, she almost savored it. We could use some fresh faces on the show, she thought, and hopefully, with the casting call, they can get a few new ones. It's such a pain in the ass, she thought; you have to sift through tons of applications and resumes, look at head shots, see if they have screen presence, see if they have some talent, some personality, maybe even some charm, and hopefully draw audience attention so the show could get better ratings. But the new show idea John had in mind could be the silver lining. Otherwise, she'd be like all these other hopefuls, needing work because the show was canceled.

A chef wearing a cowboy hat and boots stepped up on the stage carrying a guitar. Jim looked at him oddly. The cowboy chef introduced himself, "I'm George from Amarillo, Texas, and I'm going to sing you a ditty." Jim rolled his eyes. The cowboy chef strummed his guitar and started to play a ballad. "If you make it to Amarillo by morning, I'll make ya' some huevos rancheros. And when the sun is high in the sky you can try my biscuits and gravy…So when you make it to Amarillo by morning, I'll make you my chicken fried steak or chili con carneee!"

Jim yelled out in frustration, "George, George…kill it!" George stopped his playing and looked dumbfounded. "This is a cooking show, George. We'll give you a shout if we decide to use you, okay."

George tipped his hat and thanked Jim politely.

Jim stepped towards Janet. "What does he think this is, the idol show?"

"Hope his food is better than his singing," she responded. "A Detective Kook is here to see you."

Jim looked over at Cooz. "What can I do for you? Please make it quick; my time is limited."

"It's Detective Cooz. Like couscous, but with a 'z' at the end. What do you know about Chef Bubba? Was he threatened by anyone? Anyone here have a beef with him?" Cooz asked.

Janet shot Jim a look, which Cooz happened to catch.

"Besides being a pompous ass, he drew the ratings. I couldn't say he was threatened. When any of the chefs get bumped off the show, they never have complaints because it brings them immediate recognition," he said.

"So, since he drew ratings, you kept him on the show? It's like professional wrestling, you already know the outcome?" Cooz said.

"We do have a panel of judges," Jim said.

"So they're influenced to some degree?" Cooz continued his questioning.

"What do you think?" Jim said sarcastically.

"Anybody here use Manzano?" Cooz asked.

"Why?" Jim asked abruptly.

"Pertains to the case," Cooz said.

"Manzano and hot sauce are always available. This is a cooking show," Jim said snidely.

"Looks more like a talent show. If you can recollect anything that's important, give me a call," Cooz said and handed Jim his business card.

"Nice pig. Does it sniff out truffles?" Jim asked.

"We haven't gone truffle hunting lately," Cooz said. Boo then took a "snort" of Jim's rear end. Jim reacted by scooting forward. Cooz laughed. "Thanks, Jim."

Cooz headed back down the corridor and walked passed Evie Ann. She was wearing pink chef clothes. She even had a pair of pink leather clogs and a pink skullcap on her head. Cooz and Evie Ann exchanged smiles. Cooz stopped for a brief second to say hello. "Evie Ann." He quickly looked at all the contestants and said, "Long line."

"Hey. Yeah, I guess I'm not the only one that wants to be a celebrity," she said.

Chuck Chlodnik, the chef standing next to Evie Ann, was a little bit frumpy and roundish with wiry brown hair, slate gray eyes, and gold-rimmed wire glasses. He asked, "Does she help you solve cases?"

"Yes, she can take one whiff and tell if you're lying," Cooz said.

"Come on?" Chuck laughed.

"She's that good," Cooz said confidently.

"I'll remember to always tell you the truth, Cooz," Evie Ann declared.

"Don't worry, Boo and I are like twins in some respects," Cooz said and then thought of what he said. He didn't want to give the impression he was a pig.

Evie Ann smiled and mocked Cooz in her mind. "If he starts sniffing my ass, I'll know what he's talking about."

"Good luck to you all," Cooz said as he and Boo headed back down the corridor. He ran into Janet and pulled her aside. He said, "Excuse me,

Janet is it? Can you tell me if you have seen or heard anything off-color that may have any pertinence to what happened to Chef Bubba?"

She paused and said softly, "There was an incident yesterday with the producer's ex-wife. She was here yelling at John Abruzzo, our producer. She was threatening him that she was going to cause him trouble. She was loud and obnoxious. A little crazed, I'd say."

"Did she make any threats against his life?" Cooz asked.

"No, but she chased after him and then they went outside. That was the last I saw of her and her cousins, who were with her. And then John took his kids to Disneyland," she said.

"I see. What's her name?" Cooz asked.

"Raveny something or other. Raveneiztkya," she said.

"She lives here in town?" Cooz asked.

"They're on vacation. I believe she lives in New York," she said.

"And where can I find the producer?" Cooz asked.

"Should be in his office," she said, pointing, "Just around the corner."

"That was helpful. Thank you. Oh, and by the way, you might want to look at…" Cooz pointed towards Evie Ann and continued, "…the gal in the pink. She's really talented." He then looked down at Boo and said, "Come on, Boo."

"Not a problem. And by the way, if you ever need to get in touch with me," Janet said as she handed him her business card. She continued towards the stage and then stopped and looked back at Cooz and said, "I don't know if this is important or not. But something did happen with Chef Bubba the other day. He grabbed John's new assistant on her behind. She didn't do or say anything, but it was certainly an uncomfortable situation. I thought you might find that interesting."

Janet didn't like Marty from the very moment she met her. It was the competitive element in her personality, and perhaps it was also that Marty was going to be working intimately with the boss, and that didn't sit well with her. She wanted to be the one who was confided in. That's how it was when John took over the show. She felt that she could be relied upon, especially if John wanted something more. Maybe even her body. *I'm sexier than her,* she thought. *I'm blond and athletic and very pretty. Maybe I should show him more attention. Ha ha, I hope Marty gets in trouble with the police. Maybe even gets kicked out of the studio. Bye-bye, little girl.*

Cooz nodded and then Boo and he headed towards the exit while he looked at her card. Her name was Janet Fink. He thought the giving of her card had been personal because Janet had shifted her tone from when he had first met her. Or else she had some other motive related to tipping her hand about the producer's assistant. Not a bad-looking babe. A little snooty, though.

Janet yelled back at Cooz and pointed at the offices, "It's that way," as she smiled.

Cooz just waved his hand behind him. He pulled out his cell phone and hit Fajida's number while he walked out the exit and down the line of exotically dressed chefs.

Fajida picked up, "Cooz?"

Cooz spoke into the cell as he walked back to his car, "What did you get on any of the restaurant staff?"

"The bartender who was on last night said this tall strawberry blond, with two others who looked like her bodyguards, was in for dinner, left and then came back alone at closing time. Thought she possibly sounded Russian," Fajida said.

"Yeah, I think that's our girl. She sounds like the ex-wife of the producer of the Cook Off show where I'm at right now. Let's bring her in before she leaves town," he said. He then put Boo in the Thing, told her he'd be right back and then headed back towards the studio. Something Janet had said.

174

Chapter Forty-Three

Cooz went back inside and made his way to the World Chef Cook Off offices. He was directed to John's office and was greeted by Ginger who told him that Mr. Abruzzo was in a meeting, but his assistant was available. Ginger buzzed Marty since Marty had told her after Mr. Hyde left that she couldn't just knock and walk in the office. Marty's anxiety level had begun to climb, and she needed to have a little more control over the situation, especially if Ginger caught Mr. Hyde sneaking a rub or two. Although she was not fond of the unsolicited affection, better that than rumors and conjectures, which could instigate suspicion. "Yes, please send him in," Marty's voice came over Ginger's phone speaker. "All right, Marty," Marty said to herself, "Take a deep breath and be as natural and calm as can be."

Cooz entered the office, and Ginger closed the door behind him. Marty met him at the door and said, "Hi, I'm Marty Kittering, Mr. Abruzzo's assistant," and stuck out her hand for Cooz to shake.

"Hello, I'm Detective Paul Cooz with the LFPD. I'm investigating Bubba Arnet's death," Cooz said as he shook her hand.

"We expected to see the police at some point, but Mr. Abruzzo is in a meeting and will be tied up most of the morning," Marty said. "Can I help you with anything?"

Cooz responded, "Actually, you can. Did Bubba Arnet make any advances towards you, grab your behind or were you two involved in any way?"

Marty was taken aback. "What? Where did you get that idea?" And then she remembered Bubba had grabbed her ass, and it was that fucking bitch Janet who had told the detective. She was the only one who saw him do it. Jim was drooling over Ginger.

He asked, "So he didn't grab your behind?"

"He may have accidentally brushed up against my ass," she said.

"There was no relationship other than that during production?"

"I just started working here, and I came from out of town. I didn't know him," she said.

"How did you get the job?"

"A referral," she said.

Detective Cooz, "From whom?"

"Stan Kravitz."

Cooz furrowed his brow and asked, "Didn't he just die?"

"Yeah," Marty said with a tinge of sadness.

"You ever go to Bubba's Barbecue Place?"

"No," she said.

"You ever use Manzano?" Cooz asked.

"Aw, no," she said and almost bit her tongue when she responded.

He persisted, "Never?"

Marty sighed and said in a frustrated tone, "Yes, a few times in my life. I'm not really fond of it."

As Cooz handed her his card, he said, "Okay Ms. Kittering, if you can have your boss give me a shout, I'd appreciate it."

Marty said, "Certainly," and Cooz exited the office. Her mind raced, yet she sensed her crotch had gotten moist and her heartbeat was elevated from the grilling by Cooz. She looked at his name on the card and wondered if he was related to Pierre Cooz, the famous chef who began the Cooz d'Or, The World Cooking Competition that's held every four years.

Chapter Forty-Four

Cooz asked Ginger on the way out, "Where's she from?"

"You mean Marty? I think, um, the Portland area," she said as Marty had an ear on the conversation behind the door of John's office.

He asked, "By the way, is anyone in charge of your food supplies?"

"Yes, Javier."

"Where can I find him?"

"On the other end of the studio by the stage. He's usually working on the cooking equipment," she said.

"Thanks," he said and proceeded to hunt down Javier.

Cooz made his way back to the stage area. The line of potential contestants seemed to get longer as he stepped up to Janet, who was in the middle of questioning a short man in his twenties with bushy brown hair wearing all green chef clothes complete with green rubber clogs. Janet began the interview with, "What is your name?"

In a heavy Irish brogue, he said, "Sean O'Shamus." Janet wrote his name on a legal pad.

"And what is your specialty?"

"I'm a potato chef," he responded.

"Okay," she said, unimpressed.

Cooz interrupted. "Excuse me, where can I find Javier?"

"He's taking in a delivery, I think. Out back," she said and pointed towards the back of the stage. Then she handed a form to the chef in green and said, "Fill this out and wait till we call you."

Cooz walked towards the back of the stage area and found Javier, a Mexican American man of forty, medium build and height with dark hair and medium brown eyes. He was going over the delivery of goods from a high-end gourmet food supplier. The delivery driver waited as he checked off each item on the invoice. Cooz asked, "Are you Javier?"

"Yeah, what can I do for you?" Javier asked as he handed the delivery driver his pen back and said to the driver, "See you next week."

"Detective Cooz, L.F.P.D. I'm investigating the death of Bubba Arnet," Cooz said. "I need to know if anyone in the last day or so took some Manzano sauce."

"Manzano sauce? He didn't drown in it, did he? Oh, yeah, he was barbecued," Javier said with his tongue in his cheek. "Not that I know of."

Cooz smirked. "Can you check?"

Javier responded by keying the door to the storage room. He opened the door to a long narrow room with shelving that went up to the ceiling on either side of a center aisle. There were plenty of Abruzzo peppers, jarred olives, jarred baby corn, jarred grape leaves and other items, as well as a variety of Asian sauces that included hoisin sauce, soy sauce and plum sauce. Next to the Asian sauces were the pepper sauces including four bottles of Manzano sauce still in their boxes. Javier picked up a clipboard and ran his finger down it and saw that no one signed for Manzano in the last two weeks and gesticulated a "Hum?"

"So?"

"So, it looks like someone took a bottle between now and three days ago because the par is five," Javier said.

"So, if it goes to four, you order more?"

"Correct," Javier said.

"No idea who took the sauce?"

"Nope," Javier said.

This frustrated Cooz, but he knew he was onto something. "How come you guys don't have cameras?"

"This show costs three-quarters of a million dollars an episode. I don't think a two-dollar bottle of hot sauce is going to bust the budget," Javier said.

Cooz, a bit impressed, said, "I didn't know a cooking show cost that much."

"Not cheap, but that's cheap compared to the other chef shows. If you ask me, I think whoever killed Chef Bubba is one crazy nut or some real smart cookie," Javier said.

"Probably both, but I couldn't agree with you more," Cooz said. He thanked Javier for his time and exited the studio.

Chapter Forty-Five

Jonesy escorted Raveneitzkya inside a Los Feliz Police Department interrogation room. She was given a chair next to an empty table, and then Jonesy left. Raveneitzkya was her irreverent self, in no mood for nonsense since she was pulled from poolside. She was dressed in a yellow sundress with a two-piece pink polka-dotted swimsuit underneath. A pair of large, round yellow sunglasses were perched on her head. She chewed on a piece of bubble gum in lieu of a cigarette to distract herself from her annoyance. She realized that what she was up against was serious. But, like a pimple on your ass, it goes away eventually, as she would say when things got rough. Cooz and Fajida entered the room. Fajida leaned up against the wall while Cooz sized up Raveneitzkya and contemplated his angle of approach. Jonesy and another detective were in the next room peering into the interrogation room through a one-way glass window.

"I'm Detective Cooz, and that's Detective Torres," Cooz said, pointing towards Fajida.

"What, no coffee?" Raveneiztkya was a bit smug.

Fajida had no room for attitude and asked, "You think this is the Pampered Inn? I can get you a bottled water if you like."

"No, thank you," Raveneitzkya responded with more attitude.

Cooz directed his question at Raveneitzkya. "So, how do you say your name?"

"Raveneitzkya Fukovneyev," she said.

"You didn't take your husband's name?" Cooz asked.

"Fuck, no. I am Russian. Besides, who wants an Italian name?"

"As far as we know, you're an American citizen," Fajida said.

"As far as I know, I was born in Russia. Thank you," Raveneitzkya said.

"We have some witnesses that say you threatened your ex-husband," Cooz said.

"That's right. He's a son-of-a-bitch. He said, 'come to California with the kids' and then he steals Christina and Freddie from me to go to Dismal land," she said.

Fajida rolled her eyes and mockingly repeated, "Steal."

Raveneitzkya stared at Fajida. "What, are you ashamed of my manner of speaking? That's 'cause you are Americans. You're actually afraid to speak your mind."

Fajida shot back, "No, it's called tact. Which is something that you lack."

Cooz said, "Okay," trying to cut off any potential confrontation because he knew Fajida would take on most challenges. He continued with the interrogation. "So, what were you doing at Chef Bubba's place at closing time?"

"I was waiting to have sex with him," she said.

"And then you killed him right after the sex?" Cooz asked.

"Are you crazy? You really want to know the truth, Detective Ex-Cooz Me? Because that's what you're looking for, right? He took me up the ass with his big hard penis," she said and watched Cooz's and Fajida's eyes widen. "You like that? You want to hear more?" Raveneitzkya prompted.

"Yeah, we want to know how you did it. How you killed him. Did you knock him out? Threaten him with a gun or knife and then stick him in the smoker?" Cooz probed.

"What, you have camera pictures to show I did this thing to him? No, you don't, because if you did, you would see him giving it to me hard.

And nothing else. And did he give me a pounding. My fucking ass still hurts," she said.

"Jesus, you are vulgar!" Fajida said. "Can you tone it down?"

Raveneitzkya threw Fajida an insolent look.

"We know you were the last one to be with Bubba Arnet, and you made threats, not to him, but maybe you killed him to get even with John? You were angry with your ex," Cooz said.

"I've been angry at Johnny ever since he raped me," she said.

"He raped you?" Cooz asked.

"He took away my virginity," she said.

"Sounds like you've been waiting for the right moment, like now?" Cooz said, trying to hook her.

"Maybe you would like to get raped yourself, like when I get my lawyer after you. And he'll rape you good. I know the drill. I'm not taking this shit. You have nothing on me; otherwise, you would have arrested me by now," she said, challenging Cooz.

"Would you like to go, then?" Cooz asked.

"Yes, but, let me tell you something. I may be guilty of fornication, but I'm innocent of killing that man. That's terrible, what happened. Who the hell would do such a crazy thing like that?" she asked in a more toned-down, sympathetic voice.

"Okay, Raveneitzkya, you can go, but stay in town until we clear you," Cooz said.

"Are you kidding? I go when I go," she said and got up from her chair and gave a snide look at Fajida, who held the door for her. Then Raveneitzkya sang, "Say goodbye to Hollywood, say goodbye my baby," as she exited, taunting Fajida who was about to go after her. Cooz held her back.

"Did she just sing Billy Joel?" Fajida asked angrily with a furrowed brow.

Jonesy and the other detective entered the interrogation room. Jonesy said, "Holy shit, is she brazen. You could have put an electric prod on her, and she still wouldn't have flipped."

Fajida said, "I think this Russian did it with her dirty cousins. A little revenge."

"She didn't do it. Having sex between two consenting adults is not a crime," Cooz said.

"Even if it's deviant?" Fajida interrupted him.

"She's unbelievable, that one. If we had some evidence, like her fingerprints on the smoker or maybe even the back door, but we don't, so we need to go back to that Food Channel and work some other leads. I say we follow up on the producer's assistant. She looks like she has motive, since Bubba grabbed her ass and she basically denied it. Maybe he was pursuing her hard, and she didn't like it and got angry enough to kill him," Cooz said.

"What's her name?" Jonesy asked.

"Martha Kittering. Goes by Marty," Cooz said and continued, "Let's get some background on her."

Chapter Forty-Six

Marty had moved in with John after Raveneitzkya and the kids went back home to New York. Ironically, John had to go to New York himself to present his ideas for a new ad campaign to Conde-Ment, the editors of *Gourmet Today*. Although with the recent events with Chef Bubba, he wanted to delay the trip, really what could be done about it, except handle the media? But even a shocking celebrity murder is quickly forgotten in a day or two. How long can they stretch a story? Marty insisted he go. She would update him with any pertinent details. John always felt that trouble followed Raveneitzkya. He was glad Raveneitzkya was cleared of the murder. Even though he deplored her, it was best the kids have some stability while he was living in California. He would always miss Christina and Fat Freddie when they were not around and had planned to secretly meet with Christina when he was in the city. Freddie tended to open his mouth and repeat anything John said to his mother, whereupon the mother would show up and stir up trouble. So, best to keep it quiet with Fat Freddie that he would be in town, he thought.

Marty decided she wanted to take care of some business of her own while John was gone. Besides a couple of chefs she was preoccupied with, she had her eye on an attractive young gal from the audition. Her interest was in Evie Ann. She had a look and presence that Marty thought would be a ratings-getter on the new show. So she became a little friendly with Evie Ann, and in the process, Evie Ann told her about Cooz, which made Marty feel that they—she and Evie Ann—should meet for lunch and talk about the upcoming show. Evie Ann could not have been more enthused since this was her dream. Whatever the producers of the show, ergo Marty since she was an agent of the show, wanted, Evie Ann was more than willing to give. Marty had her undivided attention.

They met at Le Cote d'Azur Bakery just around the corner from John's place. Marty and Evie Ann had a lunch of a quiche Lorraine that was made with lardons, rosemary ham, Gruyere cheese, a creamy fresh herb custard, which was in a light and delicate pâte brisée, a flaky pie-like crust that almost resembled strudel dough, it was so tender and airy. The chef/owner of Le Côte d'Azur Bakery was from Nice and made plenty of his hometown favorites like Niçoise salad, which Marty and Evie Ann split with their tasty quiche and a couple of Perriers.

Their conversation over lunch consisted of mainly small talk about where they grew up, food, of course, and culinary school. Marty observed Evie Ann in action and knew right away she possessed the qualities that would create interest in the new show. Marty had watched the taped interview of Evie Ann from the studio, and she had camera presence. Jim and Janet both agreed. Evie Ann also had charm and she looked awfully cute in her pink chef clothing. Marty knew she would attract a lot of young men, which the show did anyway, but a foxy little babe like Evie Ann was what the show needed. Yet she would be just one piece of the puzzle to making it successful.

Afterwards, for dessert, they shared a mixed fruit tart that was dotted with raspberries, blackberries, strawberries, kiwi and orange wedges filled with kirschvasser-laced pastry cream and brushed with an apricot glaze. Evie Ann picked up a fresh baked Johnson, a palmier, and a couple of apple frangipane tarts for the hike she and Cooz had planned for the following day.

They headed towards the Los Feliz pier, partly out of Evie Ann's curiosity about Bubba's Barbecue Place, which was on the drive over. The other reason was to visit Rosa the gypsy fortune teller. Marty was reluctant to go back to the scene of the crime, let alone to go to see some phony gypsy fortune teller. She had distrusted fortune tellers since her childhood. Her mother would occasionally take her to one by the wharf in

Portland, and she got the creeps because the gypsy would always stare at her with her robins-egg shaded eyes that seem to peer through Marty's soul in a way that made her feel unguarded. Marty didn't like people who tried to gain greater awareness about her, particularly if they cast an evil gaze upon her. But she figured it best to placate Evie Ann's whimsical nature. Maybe she could get some secondhand information from Cooz, whom she had to be concerned with since he was a serious detective and posed a threat to her existence and prospects of achieving success and certainly happiness.

Marty drove her car past Chef Bubba's restaurant, which had been temporarily closed for renovation. Evie Ann got the willies and said, "Oof, how could that happen? I hope he wasn't alive when they stuck him in the barbecuer?"

"It's actually called a smoker, but does your new friend think it was more than one person?" Marty asked. Marty knew that it was a smoker from her Uncle Brad. He had one at his house that was not quite as elaborate as Bubba's. It only had one rack that was long enough to smoke a side of elk, which he did one time to everybody's enjoyment. Before his sudden departure, the family would occasionally go over to his place to have gatherings and eat barbecued pig, game birds and sometimes turkey. Marty didn't care much for barbecue, which probably made it easier for her to do away with Chef Bubba.

"I'm not supposed to talk about it," Evie Ann said while ingratiating herself with Marty, "…but, yeah, because Chef Bubba was such a big man, Cooz figured it had to be at least two people."

"Makes sense. Did he say anything else?" Marty asked.

"He mentioned Manzano sauce, as if who killed him had this thing for it. He even looked at me strangely when I used some at the Duxelle Café. Oh, yeah, I just heard the chef over there is going to be on the show. Is that right?" Evie Ann said.

"Matt Cumatos. He's talented, but uninspiring. I have to tell you, Evie Ann, you are going to be the new star of the show," Marty said and then for emphasis continued, "Turn you into a celebrity chef."

Evie Ann's eyes grew wider. She stood quiet, waiting for Marty's next words.

"Even though the show looks like a competition, it's really not. We want to draw ratings and make the show a success. We're working on a new format for next season, and we can sway the judges to whatever outcome we want. And as far as I'm concerned, you have the whole package," Marty said while pulling up to the pier and parking. They both got out of the car and headed towards Rosa, the Gypsy fortune teller.

Evie Ann could hardly contain her excitement and asked as if she couldn't believe it, "Really, they want me to be the new star chef?"

"It's not set in stone, but I have a lot of pull with the producer, John Abruzzo. We're seeing each other. Actually, we're living together," Marty said.

"No shit, you can do this for me, Marty?" she asked.

Marty nodded, agreeing, and then Evie Ann hugged Marty, and out of reflex Marty kissed Evie Ann on the lips. It was one of those moments where everything was silent for a second for both of them to absorb, and then Marty said, "Yes, I can. It will take me a little time to finagle, but please keep it to yourself."

"I don't know what to say," Evie Ann responded as they stood in front of the fortuneteller's, about halfway down the pier. They went inside.

"Let's see what happens," Marty said. They were greeted by Rosa, whose face was indeed rosy, enhanced by rouge. She had travel lines and creases on a face that had seen many far-off places and a hunch as if she had worked as many years carrying loads of wood on her back. She had several layers of dark clothing on, the final layer a trailing shawl, which seemed excessively warm yet gave her an air of authenticity. The foyer was dark and draped with ruby velvet curtains. It was warm inside, and the air was stifling, which didn't make Marty's apprehension any easier.

Rosa spoke in a voice that was dank from years of cheap cigarettes and cheap brandy. "Hello, I'm Rosa the Gypsy. You come for your fortunes to be told? That's twenty dollars. For twenty-five, I tell you two secrets to behold. Hmm, what do you say?" She lifted the curtain to the fortune room for Marty and Evie Ann to enter. They took a seat on either side of a round table covered with a crimson cloth topped with all the tricks of the trade including tarot cards and a crystal ball as a centerpiece. There was a life-sized statue of Merlin the magician in the corner of the room and a photo of Tsar Alexander and his family seated on a couch with the pretty yet troubling Anastasia. Red fluted glass sconces accented the room and gave off a somber glow, Marty felt, as if there was much sadness in Rosa and in the many who passed through that room looking for quick answers for their unfulfilled lives. The room seemed to embody desperation and longing.

Marty and Evie Ann handed Rosa a twenty-dollar bill each. "Okay, what do you prefer? Tarot cards? I can look into the crystal ball, read your palm or numerology. Whichever you prefer." Rosa spoke in a mesmerizing tone.

Evie Ann shrugged her shoulders and looked at Marty for her answer and then said, "You can read my palm." She stuck her palm out across the table towards Rosa.

Rosa took Evie Ann's hand and held it and then rubbed her other hand over the hand, getting a feel of the contours and lines of her life and its maps of longevity, luck, and fortune. She then eased Evie Ann's hand under a lamp nearby and studied the lines. She said, "I see much happiness in the future with your career and love. Good things are upon the horizon, yet I see trouble spots with new acquaintances and your naivety.

You must use caution and trepidation; otherwise, you will fall prey to wantonness. You will have two happy and healthy children and live a long and prosperous life. But love is never what it appears." She then gently let go of Evie Ann's hand and looked at Marty. When their eyes met, Marty looked away, and yet Rosa saw something. "And, you my dear. What would you like?" Rosa asked.

"Show me what you can do with your crystal ball," Marty said with an undertone of irreverence.

Rosa removed a light cotton kerchief from the crystal ball that was illuminated from within by a kaleidoscope of multi-colored lights for effect. And then she slowly threw out her hands over the ball and gyrated her fingers like an octopus' tentacles to summon the vision she sought. The insight came to her as she peered into the ball and, in a dramatic fashion, she flinched back and then cocked her head, peering at Marty. She spoke in an eerie voice, "I see sensitivity, maybe from being born while the moon was rising in Pisces, but perhaps it's in your family lineage. I also see trouble all around you brought on by deception and deceit. This is by your own doing. You seek an untruth that will create tremendous unhappiness. Like polar opposites tugging at your mind and your soul at the same time. And your restlessness will eventually cause you to run to a faraway place where you may find your ideal dream, like a treasure that is buried in the unlikeliest place. But until then, I see much death and destruction. Beware of the deadliness that lurks within..."

Right then and there Evie Ann grabbed Marty's arm as she got up from her chair, and they both fled the fortune room and then exited the door that led to the boardwalk.

Rosa yelled out, "Beware of the deadliness!"

Marty and Evie Ann didn't stop running until they got to Marty's car while Rosa stared at them from the doorway of her store. When they got to the car, they were huffing, trying to catch their breath. Evie Ann said, "Oh my God, that was freaky!"

Marty was bent over in exasperation. "I wonder if she was picking up the vibe about Chef Bubba. Maybe she was just weirded out because of what happened to him? I'm sure everybody around here heard the news."

"Wow, sorry, Marty. I didn't expect that. If anything, she usually adds a little fun to your life, sort of like some pricey fortune cookie," Evie Ann said apologetically. "I'm sorry."

"Don't worry about it. I'm ready for a drink. How about you?" Marty said, opening her car door. Evie Ann nodded her head and got in the passenger side. Marty sped off while they both busted up in laughter. And then Marty probed Evie Ann about going up to the San Gabriels with Cooz.

"Yeah, I think we're leaving around eight. Get a good start. Hopefully, the weather holds up," Evie Ann said.

"Wish I could go with you. John's still in New York," Marty said.

"You want to come? I'm sure Cooz won't mind," Evie Ann responded enthusiastically.

"Thanks for asking. That's sweet, Evie Ann, but I really need to work on the new show. Especially after what happened to Chef Bubba, it's been crazy with all these chefs knocking on the door. We're getting calls from around the world," Marty said.

"Maybe, some other time. I can imagine, though," Evie Ann said, thinking that this renewed interest in the show, although morbid, would not hinder her opportunity of making it big.

Chapter Forty-Seven

Early morning dew clung to the forest fauna as a layering of clouds slowly dissipated in the Southern California sun. Cooz, Evie Ann, and Boo hiked deep into the San Gabriel Mountains. The three enjoyed the quiet solitude around them as they briskly trekked up a trail along a ridge.

Evie Ann called out, "Let's look in here," as they suddenly came upon a thicket of trees. Their pace slowed as they headed off the trail with eyes to the ground. Little did they know Marty shadowed them, dressed in mountain hiking wear and her blue-black beard, undetectable as the buzz of freeway commuters far off in the distance.

The grasses and foliage were lush from the unseasonably wet and cool summer, ideal for wild mushroom growth, which is usually somewhat dormant till the early winter. Cooz spotted some lion's mane. They dug up the mushrooms and corralled them in a small basket. They continue to forage and found some morels and a stray oyster mushroom. Evie Ann smiled broadly. The base of the basket slowly began to fill, not only with the exotic fungi but a variety of shoots and a few, sparse wildflowers. Evie Ann spotted some blue-streaked mushrooms. She excitedly said, "Cooz, I think I found something that might make our day a little interesting."

"What's that?"

Tickled, she said, "Magic mushrooms."

"I can't do them," Cooz said.

"Cooz, they're perfectly harmless. This is the perfect place, on a perfect day with a perfect woman to enjoy these mind-altering edibles," Evie Ann seductively spoke.

"No chance," Cooz said with a hint of interest.

"I bet I can get you to," Evie Ann said while she slowly took her top off, unhooked her bra and exposed her full rounded breasts. Cooz was intrigued and stepped towards her. She took off running through the thicket. He began to chase her. She turned around and then held up her breasts and said, "You can have them if you take some of these with me." He caught up to her, and Evie Ann handed him one of the psilocybin mushrooms. He popped it into his mouth. She followed suit and they slowly chewed and then each swallowed the hallucinogenic forest candy in anticipated wonderment.

"You're a bad influence, Evie Ann," Cooz said.

"I'm just a girl who likes to enjoy the natural things in life," she said and planted a kiss on Cooz's lips. He cupped his hand on one of her warm fleshy breasts while Boo strode away and sniffed through the brush.

Cooz gently peeled down her black lace panties to expose a splay of pubis furred with fine blond hair. He brushed his hand down her belly, down over her pubis towards a small raspberry-shaped clitoris that was mounted high between her cabernet-shaded labia. He took in a slow, easy sniff of her scent and caught a slight waft of orange blossom that triggered his senses. He dropped to his knees then tenderly kissed her labia and drew in her succulent juices. Marty watched from about a hundred yards away through binoculars. She blushed as she became aroused and let out an "umm" while crossing her legs. And then shook it off, realizing Cooz was her foe. Cooz and Evie Ann's kissing quickly turned into removal of all their clothing, which turned into lovemaking. Boo had seen it before and politely kept herself occupied.

Cooz and Evie Ann were coupled together, flesh against flesh. Evie Ann began to chuckle. Like an infection, Cooz burst out in giddy laughter as he looked up into the sky and saw a spectrum of colors and let out a 'I.'

"See, I told you," Evie Ann said, and began to laugh and then licked Cooz's face like a dog.

"What was that?" he asked.

"You had some icing on your face," she said, giggling.

Cooz asked, "So who was that guy you were next to in line at the studio?"

Evie Ann said, "Oh, um, his name is Chuck Chlodnik. He's a chef at the Glendale Assisted Living Facility. Knows his stuff."

Cooz said, "Chlodnik. Isn't that some type of borscht?"

Evie Ann said, "Not sure."

Cooz said, "Let me have a bowl of chlodnik." Evie Ann laughed at his joke.

Suddenly, Boo got spooked. A thunder of noise headed their way. Cooz and Evie Ann reacted quickly and noticed a wild boar coming in their direction. "Run!" Cooz yelled. They ran through the thicket away from the charging boar.

"Oh my God!" Evie Ann cried out as fear and amazement at the situation stunned her mind.

They jumped over some logs and came upon an accessible tree. "Get up," Cooz commanded. Evie Ann jumped onto to the tree and scurried her way upward.

Boo "SQUEALED" and then took a flying leap into Cooz's arms. He then handed Boo to Evie Ann. As Cooz began to climb, the boar got a hold of his boot and started to gnaw away as Cooz tried to shake it off. Cooz's boot slipped off his foot, and he continued up the tree with the boar snorting and stomping.

Then out of the blue, a hunter with a rifle appeared. He yelled, "Don't move" while he aimed his rifle and shot the boar dead at the base of the tree trunk. The boar bled from the back of its skull, gave a few twitches and died quickly where it lay. The hunter stepped towards the boar and then looked up at the naked couple. "Well, thanks folks, I've been after this sow for two hours. It escaped from the trap I had set up."

"I think the next time I come up here, I'll bring my gun," Cooz blurted out.

The hunter said, "Not a bad idea. So you two want to come down now?"

Cooz asked, "Can you throw us our clothes?"

"Oh, sure," said the hunter with a smirk and then gathered up the clothing and handed them up the tree to Cooz. The hunter continued to look on.

"You mind turning in the other direction?" Cooz asserted.

"Sure thing," he responded. Amused by the situation, he turned away.

Cooz and Evie Ann climbed down the tree and gave the boar a good stare. Boo sniffed it and snorted. They quickly got dressed. "Thank you," Evie Ann told the hunter.

"Not a problem. You helped me out. Heck of a way to ruin your afternoon, though," the hunter replied.

"It got the blood flowing," Cooz candidly laughed.

"I'll bet!" The hunter pointed at Boo, who was shivering with fear. "So, that your pet pig? What's its name?" The hunter asked.

"Boo," Cooz replied.

"Funny," the hunter said.

"Why's that?" Cooz asked.

"Boo being scared," the hunter continued.

Evie Ann laughed, "Funny!"

"So, how about you guys join me for lunch of sage-roasted wild boar with a Manzanita berry and choke cherry glaze and a salad of miner's lettuce and cat-tail shoots with a Roquefort buttermilk dressing?" The hunter said.

Cooz and Evie Ann looked at each other. They both smiled and said, "Sure."

Evie Ann added, "We have some exotic mushrooms and garlic ramps."

"Sounds righteous," the hunter said.

Cooz and Evie Ann gathered their belongings while the hunter tied up the feet of the boar and slipped a branch between the legs. Cooz got the idea and grabbed the back end of the branch while the hunter grabbed the front end. They headed towards the hunter's camp. Evie Ann and Boo merrily followed along. Marty was thoroughly amazed as she watched. Although her view was spotty at times, she could not help but to chuckle as she made her way back towards her car, but not before she foraged for some wild mushrooms herself.

"So, where you from?" Cooz asked.

"Just down the road in Hemet," the hunter replied.

Evie Ann thought the hunter sounded and looked familiar, but then again, she was starting to feel the effects of the psilocybin. Although the amount they took was roughly a gram and half each, which by street standards wasn't a whole lot, it would ultimately provide short-term euphoric sensations and some bouts of laughter. Evie Ann tapped the hunter on the shoulder and said, "Hey, you remind me of someone."

The shooter chuckled a little and said, "My wife tells me that but says it ain't the man I married."

She kind of laughed a little and got a closer look at the shooter. She had recognized him for his pudgy nose and big ears and said, "I know who you are…"

And then the hunter interrupted her and said, "I'm Larry Fritzsimmons. I was on the World Chef Cook Off Show. That's my one claim to fame."

Evie Ann excitedly said, "That's right. What a freakin' small world." And then said, "Yeah, you heard about Bubba Arnet?"

"That was some strange shit. But the universe works in peculiar ways. The producers called me back in. I guess they want to re-shoot the last show I was on to look like I won instead of Bubba," the shooter said.

"No kidding," Evie Ann said. "So, what's your name again?"

"Larry Fritzsimmons," he said. And then Evie Ann texted Marty about what happened with the wild boar and being rescued by Larry Fritzsimmons. She wanted to tell her about the mushrooms but held off, not knowing what Marty would think. "It was freakin' wild," she ended the text. They were in a no- service zone and the text would have to wait 'til later to be sent.

"Sorry, we ate some funny mushrooms," she said and then continued, "You know I'm going to be on the show next season. They want to make me a celebrity chef on the new format," Evie Ann said, sounding like she was drunk. Cooz had been listening in and was curious to know how that all came about. And when did it happen?

Larry Fritzsimmons responded, "No shit?"

Evie Ann said, "Got it straight from the producer's personal assistant."

Cooz almost stopped dead in his tracks and asked Evie Ann, "When did she tell you this?"

"I had lunch with her yesterday," Evie Ann said.

"Her meaning Marty, the dark-haired girl with the blue eyes?" Cooz asked.

Cooz wanted to tell her about Marty being a suspect, but with this Larry Fritzsimmons there, he couldn't say anything. He had to wait, but he knew once he said something to Evie Ann about Marty, she would probably think that he was jealous. *How do I approach her without scaring her off?* he thought. This was a new relationship, and he didn't want to blow it.

"Yeah. We had lunch at this French bakery and then we went to see a Gypsy fortune teller on the Los Feliz pier. It was wild," Evie Ann said.

The killer returned to the scene of the crime. Cooz's mind started to race. He wanted to bolt out of there with Evie Ann right then, but he started to feel a burst of psilocybin in his brain and let out a laugh.

Larry smiled and asked Cooz, "Feeling good?"

But Cooz wasn't feeling good because he was starting to get out of his comfort zone between the trippy feeling in his head and getting deeper into the woods while wanting to get back to town to start prying into this Marty Kittering without painting himself in the corner with Evie Ann.

And then Larry Fritzimmons said something very strange. "It's really easy for someone to get lost up here, especially if you're all alone."

"You know people that have?" Cooz asked with a dose of law enforcement attitude. It was in the tone with which Larry said, "It's really easy," that didn't sit well with Cooz.

"Just saying," Larry Fritzimmons said, getting his own ire tweaked some.

"Just saying, what? Don't try to spook us, especially with the girl here," Cooz said, pissed off.

"Dude, man, you don't know what being scared is all about," Larry Fritzimmons said exaggeratedly.

Meanwhile, Evie Ann was hanging on every word. She was starting to feel uncomfortable with the animosity brewing between Cooz and Fritzsimmons. Evie Ann had just realized that Fritzimmons looked like a pig with his pointed, hairy ears and snouty nose.

Cooz started to think that maybe this freak barbecued Bubba Arnet to get back on the show and said, "I hate to cut this field trip short, but I just got a text that they need me down at the station. We have an ongoing investigation into the killing of Chef Bubba."

"Okay, you got me," Fritzimmons said smartly, knowing that there was no cell phone service and Cooz was bullshitting, probably about being a cop or whatever he was. "If you can just help me get this boar to my camp."

"Not far, I hope?" Cooz asked.

"Almost there," Fritzimmons said. "So, you a cop?"

"Yup, a detective," Cooz said with clarity.

"Right, man. I got ya," Fritzimmons said in an almost infantile way. "You can let her go," he said and then stopped.

"Good," Cooz said and continued, "Take 'er easy."

"Good luck, Larry," Evie Ann said and then Cooz and she turned the other way and headed back towards their car with Boo following along.

"Yeah, you too," Fritzimmons said and laughed underneath his breath.

As soon as they got far enough away, Cooz said, "What an asshole. He's probably the one that killed Chef Bubba." And then he realized he shouldn't have said that.

"Yeah, I was starting to get uncomfortable. You got a text?" Evie Ann asked.

"No, I just wanted to get the hell out of there," Cooz said. "Why say shit like that?"

"For his own fucking entertainment," Evie Ann said.

"If I weren't a cop, I would have knocked him out," Cooz said angrily.

"I hope he loses to David Peel, you know, Stoner," she said.

"There's another winner," Cooz said sarcastically.

Chapter Forty-Eight

As soon as Cooz and Evie Ann got to her hybrid sedan, Cooz asked, "Are you all right to drive?"

Evie Ann handed Cooz her keys, they both hopped in the car and then drove off back towards Los Feliz. About a mile down the road both of their cell phones started to ring. Evie Ann quickly updated Marty on the events that took place and wrote, "What a creep that Fritzimmons is. And he looks like some wild boar up close. I didn't know he was so ugly."

Cooz received a text from Fajida. It had to do with Martha Kittering. Give me a call when you can, she requested. But he couldn't, not while he was in the car with Evie Ann.

Evie Ann commented, "You know, texting while driving is not advisable. It's also illegal in the State of California."

Cooz said, "I'm a cop." And then put his cell phone down.

Meanwhile, Marty had got a jump back to Marina Del Rey with a nice little assortment of wild mushrooms of her own and was near the Five freeway when she turned on her cell phone. She was cautious about that, especially how her location could be traced through her cell these days. Best to be safe, she figured. She received the two texts from Evie Ann. She quickly read them and then turned off her phone, pulled off the exit and made a U-turn to go back the way she came. Going back up towards the mountain she may have passed Evie Ann and Cooz driving in the opposite direction. Evian Ann thought she saw Marty's car, but it was some bearded guy. She felt a little trippy still. Then she got all goosey suddenly, while she let out a silly shrill of a laugh. She had a new bud who just happened to be on the inside of where she wanted to be.

"What was that?" Cooz quickly shot at her.

"Just thought of a new name for Fritzimmons. Fritzy the Pig," she said while texting Marty back the same thing she just told Cooz.

Cooz rolled his eyes and said, "Sounds about right."

Chapter Forty-Nine

Chuck Chlodnik, at first glance, wasn't someone you could picture as a celebrity chef. He was frumpy and had a permanent look of gloom on his face. And he didn't exude utter confidence either, but his skill as a culinarian was quite deft. He headed up the kitchen at The Glendale Senior Assisted Living Residence where he took care of the dietary needs of twenty residents or so. He prepared them breakfast, lunch, and dinner, including dessert of their choice, as well as snacks.

Chuck had a cushy job, demanding at times, and almost predictable outside of the daily antics of the residents. He was well taken care of by the corporate owners of the facility. He was highly unfulfilled, though, perhaps missing the buzz of the restaurant life or more specifically, the limelight that comes with being a celebrity chef. His heart's desire was to become one of the main attractions on the World Chef Cook Off Show.

Instead of being read Dr. Seuss as a child by his mother, he was groomed by her to become a master chef from early on by the likes of Julie Chen's *Mastering French Cooking*, the *Bernard Jameson Cookbook*, *Leroy's Gastronomic*, *The Happy Cook* and *Benny Cocker's Cookbook*. He welcomed his mother's obsession and took full advantage of every opportunity available to learn something new about the culinary arts. In his teenage years, Chuck could always be seen reading magazines like *Gourmet Today*, *Bon Bon* and *Fine Food and Spirits* with an occasional *Young and Dumb* stuffed between articles on fish tacos and beurre blanc.

Interning in the kitchen at the Ritz Carlton for one summer, he continued at Johnston and Wells to receive a degree in the culinary arts. After graduating, he toured extensively through Italy and France, tasting everything he could in villages and towns from Tuscany, Milan, and

Sicily to Paris, Strasbourg and Marseille. He would stop along the way for several weeks at a clip to offer his assistance in any restaurant kitchen that would take him in. Upon returning to the States, he attended Purdue University to get his undergraduate degree in Hotel and Restaurant Management. He went on to cook in several restaurants and hotels as a sous chef and then as an executive chef. An eventual opportunity arose while at The Glendale where his grandmother was residing. Two weeks after he landed the job, his dear grandmother departed.

If ever a morning is to be guaranteed chaotic at The Glendale, it's Monday morning, no matter how well-prepared Chuck was for a new week.

"You call this food," Mrs. Haggert screeched. Chuck had had it. As she bent down to pick up her mail, he grabbed Mr. Haggert's Arnold Palmer PHD Tour driver.

Chuck, with a maniacal look on his face, set himself for a tee off as he addressed Mrs. Haggert, "That's the last food you'll ever eat." And he swung, nailing Mrs. Haggert on the side of her face and knocking out her false teeth, which went flying across the room. She fell, her knees hitting the floor first, and then she rolled over. She was dazed but still had fight in her. Chuck took one look at her and went berserk. He took all his clothes off, except his shoes and underwear, and ran through the halls of The Glendale hooting and hollering and singing, "I knocked her out, I knocked her out." No sooner did some large female orderly see him than he was restrained until the police could take him away. Several days later Mrs. Haggert, albeit with a bandaged face, was terrorizing the new chef, saying, "You call this food?" although she was barely audible with her broken jaw and cheekbone. Meanwhile, Chuck sat solitary in a mental hospital ward sedately oblivious and being fed institutional swill by some overgrown orderly that smelled like hamburgers and french fries, the fast food he just ate before assisting Chuck.

Deadly Recipe

Chuck never made it on the World Chef Cook Off Show.

Chapter Fifty

At the Duxelle Café, Chef Cumatos, who was in his early thirties, tall and sinewy but strong, with light brown curly hair and watery blue eyes, cooked up the house specialty omelet, a preparation of exotic mushrooms that included morels, porcini and chanterelles sautéed with shallots, butter, a touch of white wine and *fines herbes* and the right amount of Brie cheese. It was the early morning hours, and he was alone at the restaurant performing a quick food inventory before he made his way to the markets. In a Teflon pan, the chef slowly cooked the base of the omelet mostly through with a bit of the egg mixture still undone on top. He then added the essential fillings and was about to fold over the omelet when the restaurant phone rang. He quickly turned the flame off and darted into his office.

He picked up the phone and said, "Chef Cumatos."

On the other end was a manly voice that said, "Your sink in the ladies' room is running."

The chef said as he slightly chuckled, "Who the hell is this?" And then he hung up and headed straight towards the women's restroom in the dining area.

A shadowy figure appeared in the kitchen. It was Marty, wearing her beard, and garbed in a linen supply uniform holding a disposable cell phone. She made her way to the stove and sprinkled some sautéed mushrooms onto the open omelet. She quickly exited the rear kitchen door from where she entered. The chef returned to the kitchen almost immediately after Marty exited and glanced over at the back door thinking he heard something and then flipped over the omelet, plated it up, grabbed a slice of bread, dabbed it with some soft butter and began to indulge in his meal as he filled out his inventory sheet.

Marty walked to a side street where her car was parked, hopped in and drove away, saying to herself *that was easy enough*. Although she wouldn't have minded the omelet Chef Cumatos made for himself, less the mushrooms she added, of course. But as for Matt Cumatos, he was talented, but he wasn't what the new show needed. When she watched the dailies of him being interviewed, he just appeared flat, unenthusiastic and quite boring. She didn't know why Jim and Janet would even select him as a contending chef, although he was highly skilled, trained at Duluth, one of the top culinary schools in the country next to Chapman, and ran a nice restaurant. She didn't mind that he was going to suffer, especially after the conversation she had with Javier when she was watching the dailies of Matt Cumatos.

Javier said, "He's a dirty guy."

Marty said, "What do you mean?"

"He hires these illegal girls. Screws most of them and then gets rid of them. There was this pretty Dominican he got pregnant and then called immigration on after she told him she was having a baby. He's a *puto*," Javier said.

"How do you know this?" Marty asked.

"The taco shops. You want to know anything about what's going on with the *mojados*, just hang out at the taco shops. Sooner or later, you hear things," he said.

Days later Chef Cumatos was rushed to the hospital with what appeared to be a severe case of food poisoning. He died almost instantaneously. A later autopsy revealed that liver and kidney failure occurred due to poisoning by consumption of the *Amanita phalloides,* commonly known as the "death cap" mushroom.

The same day, the Duxelle Café was shut down for business indefinitely by the Health Department until an investigation into to the origins of the potential lethal toxins could be found. Fear ran rampant amongst the mushroom industry and the general public. It had a major impact on mushroom sales across the board from the basic white button to the exotic.

The homicide squad room at the police station was bustling. Cooz, Fajida and Jonesy, the Captain and his assistant all converged into the squad room. "Okay, you three," the Captain asserted. "One chef who is murdered is an incident. Two dead chefs who are connected to a popular national chef show is more than alarming. It's going to put a lot of heat on this department. This latest victim, Matt Cumatos, died of mushroom poisoning. We need to find out if that was an intentional act of murder or if he just fucked up and ate the wrong mushroom."

"The type of mushroom he ate resembles the straw mushroom, which is perfectly edible. According to their mushroom supplier, they didn't sell straw mushrooms to the restaurant," Cooz stated.

"Did he happen to eat some other mushrooms elsewhere?" the Captain asked.

"From what they gathered when he was at the hospital, he hadn't had any other food other than the restaurant's house omelet two days prior. The Health Department is still trying to confirm if all the restaurant's mushrooms, prepared or otherwise, are clean," Fajida remarked.

"Whoever this killer or killers may be, it tends to lead to the cooking show. That is what we have. But, we do have one suspect," Cooz said.

"Who is this?" the Captain demanded.

"A Martha 'Marty' Kittering. She's the producer's assistant. Twenty-five, dark hair, a real knockout. She went to Chapman Culinary Academy. Some pricey school up in Washington. Apparently, one of her professors committed suicide while she was there. By arsenic," Cooz said.

"You have to be kidding me. Who the fuck kills themselves with arsenic? If you're going to kill yourself, you get it over quickly, like a thirty-two through the brain or some sleeping pills and a bottle of whiskey," the Captain said fervently. "I wouldn't wish that on my worst enemy."

"When she was around eighteen, she was connected to a murder of a dominatrix in San Francisco, but part of the case was sealed. Don't know all the details," Fajida said while reading off the information from a notepad.

"Cooz, I want you to get your tail up to that Chapman school, find out all you can from their administration and also from the local police and the coroner. And then I want you to make it down to San Francisco. See if you can find the lead detective on that dominatrix murder. Make sure it's by the book, Cooz. And no personal trips to the Fisherman's Wharf for crab Louie," the Captain said.

"I prefer sushi," Cooz said casually.

The Captain quickly shot back angrily, "Would you feel better if I sent Jonesy?" And then looking at Jonesy and Fajida, the Captain continued in a little softer tone, "I want you two to keep an eye on this Krittering gal. See if she makes any unsuspecting moves. If she is as sharp as she thinks she is, she'll certainly be expecting us. So be tactful."

"Captain, are we putting her on twenty-four-hour surveillance?" Fajida asked.

"Not yet, not until Cooz gets back. For now, just keep a watch of her whereabouts during her after hours from work. I'll give you some extra manpower, okay?" the Captain said.

"Got it," Fajida said.

And then Cooz's cell rang. He said, "Let me take this real fast?" He stepped aside. He flipped open his phone and said, "Hello." He waited and listened in and then said, "Okay. Thanks, Janet," and hung up his phone. Cooz went almost as white as cold beef fat. He directed his attention towards the Captain and said hesitantly, "Umm, that was the chef show. Looks like we might have another dead chef. Larry Fritzimmons. He was camped up in the San Gabriels, and the Forest Rangers think they found his tibia with a foot attached. The rest of him they haven't found yet."

The Captain looked at him and then said, "Jesus, this is starting to turn into an epidemic. Jonesy, why don't you get up there and find out what happened?"

"Right," Jonesy said and then remarked, "This could turn out to be a federal case if it's their land and all."

"Might be better off, but what the hell's the matter with you, Cooz?" The Captain asked.

"We were just up there yesterday. We ran into him. I can't believe it's him," Cooz in utter disbelief. And then he thought to himself, how the hell could this Marty chick do something like possibly chop him up? Did she go up there? But how would she know where to go? He racked his brain.

"You think he might have been eaten by some bear?" Fajida queried.

"What were you doing up there?" the Captain asked

"On a hike with this gal that I've been seeing," Cooz said.

Fajida let out a long "Oh," while smiling at Cooz, responding to the revelation of his new girlfriend.

"We have some murders to solve," the Captain said, shooting a disapproving look at Fajida.

"Not two days ago," Cooz quipped. "We just only had one."

"What the fuck is this shit? It's like the goddamn Twilight Zone. Chefs getting cooked, poisoned and eaten. What next, exploding pizzas? All right, you three, get me some answers. Better yet, find me a perp," the Captain said disgustedly. And as they all exited the squad room, the Captain said, "Could this Marty Chitterling have done this, killed these three chefs? The work of one person?"

"Her name is Kittering," Cooz said as they all walked down a corridor.

"Thank you for clarifying that. And don't wait till you get back to let me know what happened up there. Have a nice flight," said the Captain, a bit frustrated. He and assistant then stepped into his office.

Cooz, Fajida and Jonesy made their way out towards the precinct's front entrance.

Cooz started to think. Evie Ann had texted Kittering on the way down from their trip. She certainly had to have mentioned Fritzimmons. And had Kittering texted her back? Did she follow them into the woods? And why? For the poisonous mushrooms, that's why. But why go through the trouble? She could have gathered them somewhere else. Could forensics tell if the mushrooms were from the San Gabriels? Yet, to implicate Kittering, they would need a warrant for the text messages, he realized.

So what do I really have here? A missing bottle of Manzano, three dead chefs, a gnawed leg and foot, poisonous stomach contents, possible text messages between Evie Ann and Kittering, who may be the perp based upon her *modus operandi* and a coincidental scenario where Bubba Arnet may or may not have groped her giving her probable motive. Evie Ann's text messages were the key. Or not. This Marty could have been sitting at home painting her toenails as far as he knew. It was all speculation, even to try to get a clue as to her M.O.

When they all got outside in the parking lot, Jonesy said, "Catch you guys later." Fajida waved, and Cooz nodded at Jonesy as he headed towards his car.

Cooz pulled Fajida to the side and said, "I got a fucked-up situation."

"Yeah?" Fatija questioned, really wanting to know.

Cooz went on, "I was up there with this Evie Ann. I mean, what if Marty Kittering and she are in bed together? Ya' know, partners in crime. It's all kind of tying in. Evie Ann could have picked up some of those poisonous caps when we were foraging and met up with Marty later that night after we got back and schemed the two killings with her."

"Then they both went back up to the mountains and killed Fritzimmons and then somehow poisoned Cumatos the next day? You think that's what happened?" she asked. "I think that's pretty farfetched," Fajida said, peering at Cooz as if he'd lost his marbles.

"Evie Ann texted Marty on the drive back down. What did Sancho Panza say to Don Quixote? The proof is in the pudding. If I can get a hold of those text messages and prove that they conspired, then we got them," Cooz said.

"Are you sure? But, suppose—and that's a heavy supposition—how the hell are you going to get a warrant? The judge'll laugh you right out of the courthouse," Fajida said, shaking her head. "What do you have as evidence? A bowl of pudding, your honor," she replied as she laughed at Cooz.

"You don't have faith in the law, Fajida. We start pressing them hard until they give us what we need then. We can be bad guys when we need to. Sooner or later, one of them will lose their cool. And we'll be there when it happens. Trust me," Cooz said.

"They, meaning Kittering and Evie Ann? Ha, ha, ha, you're ready to give her up over some text messages you don't even know what they're about?" Fajida asked. "Because that's what will happen. Goodbye girlfriend or take yourself off the case. Either way, goodbye girlfriend."

"She's not my girlfriend, but we're dealing with three potential killings, and they sure seem to have a motive. They've been hanging out together, and Kittering has been pumping up Evie Ann with these fantasies about becoming the new star on the show. You know how people get when they're promised a little bit of fame?" Cooz said. "And when it's that close, you can almost taste it. And you'll do almost anything to get it, including murder anyone that gets in your way."

"You're jealous, aren't you? I still think the Russian did Bubba Arnet. And who's to say Cumatos didn't die by accident? And we really don't know what happened with Fritzimmons. Maybe it was a bear or a mountain lion? Do we know that for sure?" Fajida said persuasively.

"It's weird. You know how when you're with someone, and they're texting back and forth with some friend or whoever? It's like they detach themselves from the moment, and you seem to lose them to this thing that is inanimate."

"Yeah, it happens all the time when I'm with my kids. Welcome to the new world," Fajida said.

"Well, anyway, Kittering is connected to four deaths that we know of. Besides, you haven't seen this woman. She could seduce the pants off the devil if she wanted to. Do me a favor? And I don't care what the Captain said. Go over to the studio and hit this Kittering up. Find out where she was this past Sunday and Monday morning. And then go over to Assagio's and question Evie Ann about the text messages but go gently with her. Her last name is Pierce. Evie Ann Pierce. You can't miss her. She has blond curly hair and wears pink. And she's real cute," Cooz said.

Fajida said coyly, "Yeah, let me play the heavy while you're on vacation. But I still think you're jealous."

"What am I jealous about? But give me a call later, okay? See you in a couple of days," Cooz said, and then he hopped in his Thing and drove off.

"Don't eat any oysters," Fajida said as she got in her car. "You just might not have a girlfriend to come home to."

Chapter Fifty-One

Fajida drove over to the Food Channel Studios and made her way to John Abruzzo's office. Ginger greeted her, whereupon she asked to see Marty. Ginger said, "They're all in a meeting. I don't know how long Ms. Kittering will be. If you want to wait?"

Fajida said rhetorically, "It's pretty serious, I bet," as she took a seat and picked up a *Cuisinarts* magazine off a coffee table.

"The show's dead in the water. Doesn't look good," Ginger said reluctantly and then added, "Maybe I shouldn't have said that."

Fajida nodded with pursed lips, knowing that it certainly was.

Meanwhile, John, Marty, Jim, Janet, a host of production and camera crew, Javier and several others were in a closed-door meeting sitting around a large oval table. The room was somber as everyone was privy to the recent death of Matt Cumatos and the missing Larry Fritzimmons, who was supposed to be there that morning to do a re-shoot and who was probably dead based on the information from his wife, who had confirmed Fritzimmon's abandoned camp, and the foot and tibia from the Forest Service.

John spoke with solemnity but with an air of confidence. "You all know that our show was hit hard with the death of Chef Bubba, and worse yet, there's good indication that Larry Fritzimmons is missing, to put it delicately. This means that the show, as it is, cannot proceed. I spoke with Elliot Hyde this morning, and we came to a collective decision to cancel the show indefinitely."

There were several sighs from the production crew, thinking that the word "indefinitely" usually implies a kiss of death, but John continued, "All is not lost, though. As absurd as it may be, the ratings on the last show shot through the roof, and we are planning to go into production with the new show, The Ultimate Chef Challenge, which most of you all know about."

Jim interrupted and asked, "John, when do you think we'll be on air with the Chef Challenge?"

"Ten weeks. I know that might be pushing it, so I'm bringing in some folks from Treasure Chase to help with the in-field shooting. In any event, we need to ramp up casting. Sadly, we lost one potential chef in Matt Cumatos. Let's hope that was an unfortunate mishap. Besides our production concerns, the Food Channel wants to do a revised background check on all personnel affiliated with our show and the others. And I guess they're going to beef up security with extra camera surveillance. I'm sorry to say, but I don't have much choice in the matter. So if anyone here has anything to hide, best to leave now." Not one person got up. John's cell phone rang. It was a text from Ginger. She let him know that the Los Feliz P.D. were in the office to speak with Marty. He inched over to Marty and whispered in her ear. She looked him in the eyes for a brief second to let him know that it was all right while she got up from the chair. John ever so slightly gave her a confident brush on the wrist as she stepped from the table and exited the office.

Marty closed the door behind her and stepped through Ginger's office area, expecting Detective Cooz. Fajida stood up and stuck out her hand. "I'm Detective Sanchez. I just have a few questions."

Marty and Fajida quickly shook hands, and then Marty led her into John's office and closed the door behind them. Marty played it cool and said, "What can I do for you?" Marty remembered she had to pick up lunch for John and the crew since they'd be in meetings all day.

"Ms. Kittering, can you tell me where you were on Sunday? Did you go up to the San Gabriel Mountains?" Fajida asked.

"No. Sunday morning, I got up, went for a jog and then had breakfast. Later in the afternoon, I took a drive," she said.

"Where did you go?" Fajida asked.

"Over to Covina and then back home," Marty said.

"You stop for gas or buy anything along the way?" Fajida probed.

"No," Marty quickly shot.

"Were you alone?" Fajida asked.

"Most of the day. I picked up John from LAX around nine-thirty. And then we went home. It was closing in on eleven by the time we got in," Marty said.

"How about Monday morning?" Fajida dug a little more.

"I was at home until we went to work," Marty said. She had her alibi because John was out like a light until she returned from the Duxelle Café when she woke him up with fresh coffee and almond granola she had made after she got back from taking care of business up in the San Gabriels. She had been so pumped up she needed to work out her nervous energy.

"You two live together? You and the producer?" Fajida asked.

"Yes," Marty said.

"What's your relationship with Evie Ann Pierce?" Fajida asked.

"What do you mean?" Marty responded a little more defensively.

"Are you friendly? You hang out together?" Fajida asked.

"Yes. I took an interest in her because of the show. She has potential," Marty said.

"Excuse me for asking, but are you two secretly lovers?" Fajida asked.

"No, but why would you ask that?" Marty chuckled.

"Why then would you promise Evie Ann that she would become a star on this new show you're working on? You have some ulterior motives? Maybe you fancy her?"

Marty's face flushed while becoming slightly obstinate, and she said, "No. But, are we done because I need to get lunch for everybody?"

"Yes, but how is it that you play the gopher and also make big decisions on a successful show?" Fajida asked.

"For your information, I'm the one that came up with the idea for the new show we're producing. But it just happens to be my day to get the food," Marty said.

"Okay, we'll be in touch," Fajida said and exited the office.

Marty let out a heavy sigh of relief and then said, "Dammit, Evie Ann, you shouldn't have opened your mouth."

Chapter Fifty-Two

Marty walked to her car at the Food Network Studios parking lot. She got in the car and drove away. A moment later Fajida pulled out of the lot and followed Marty towards Assagio's. Marty looked in her rear-view mirror and, as expected, saw Fajida following her. Marty arrived at Assagio's, parked her car, grabbed her purse and went inside. Evie Ann was busy making pizzas. Marty handed the tattooed attendant the list of lunch items, and he told her it would be about twenty minutes. Marty then stepped over towards Evie Ann. She looked up at Marty and, surprised, said, "Hey, Marty, how are you?"

Marty shot her a smile. "I'm okay. Come to pick up lunch."

"You get my text messages the other day?" Evie Ann asked.

"Yeah, I'm sorry, it's been real crazy. Weird how you ran into Fritzy," Marty said.

"Yeah, weird what happened to Matt Cumatos," Evie Ann said.

"Strange things have been happening," Marty said and then stepped towards a refrigerator case and pulled out a cranberry juice. She opened it up and drank from the bottle and intentionally spilled the drink over the front of her white suit. "Oh, shit!"

Evie Ann said, "Here you want to clean it off?" She handed Marty a wet towel. Marty tried dabbing it, but it was too late. The suit was stained.

"I can't go back to work like this and I need to get back right away," Marty said in a disgruntled voice.

"Why don't you go over my place? It's only a block away. I have a couple of suits that probably can fit you," Evie Ann said.

"Okay, thanks."

"It's the tan building, number three eighty-six with the flamingos on the lawn. Apartment C," Evie Ann said and gave Marty her keys.

"Thank you, Evie Ann," Marty said.

Evie Ann pointed towards the back door and said, "One block over. And watch out for the cat. She likes to get out when you're not looking."

Marty said, "I'll be right back." She headed out the back door, slid across the street and jogged towards the block over, found Evie Ann's building and entered her apartment. She said, "Here kitty, kitty." The cat brushed up against Marty's leg and purred as Marty closed the door. "No, you don't," and the cat scooted. She stepped towards the bedroom, went through her pocketbook and pulled out some rubber gloves and slipped them on. She then went through Evie Ann's chest of drawers. She rummaged through her bras and panties and took in the whiff of her perfume that permeated the room and let out an agreeable "Umm." She shut the drawer and unbuttoned her suit top and then lay down on her bed. She felt flushed for a moment as she moved her arms as if she were making a snow angel. She almost wanted to undress and slip naked under the covers, but time was short. She got up, straightened the bed and stepped towards the kitchen. She looked in the refrigerator for some club soda but found French sparkling mineral water instead. She took her jacket off, poured a little mineral water on a paper towel and dabbed the stain on her jacket. She repeated the process, with modest results.

She then noticed a basket she assumed that Evie Ann and Cooz had used to gather the mushrooms. Marty looked inside and saw a few wild mushrooms and wild flowers that were starting to dry out. She pulled out a small plastic bag that contained a few poisonous cap mushrooms and removed them. She placed them underneath the other mushrooms so they were in the crease of the cloth napkin that lined the basket. She looked at the basket and was satisfied that Evie Ann would not notice. She then put back on her suit jacket and buttoned it up. She stepped towards the front door and locked it behind her and then wiped the door handle with the damp paper towel. Pulled off her rubber gloves and headed back to Assagio's. When she got to the back parking lot, she tossed the paper towel and rubber gloves into a dumpster and went inside.

Marty's thoughts were that it was quite evident now that she and Evie Ann were being considered as suspects, so why not illuminate the trail a little by going over to see Evie Ann. That would look like she, Marty, was starting to panic. And if the police decided to arrest Evie Ann, they'd do a search and find the mushrooms. She would insistently deny, of course, that she had anything to do with the murder and say that it was she, Marty, who went over to her place and planted the mushrooms, which would make Evie Ann look even guiltier. John, on the other hand, would most certainly give testimony that she was at home all morning, which would give her a feasible alibi for poisoning Cumatos, clearing her of any suspicion. If the police probed why she went to Assagio's right after being questioned, she would respond by saying I was just picking up lunch. Is that a crime?

As far as Fritzimmons, they were in the woods, she was highly certain of that. There were more people buried or lost deep in wooded forests, or for that matter buried in the desert and out at sea, who will never be found. And even if they did find parts of Fritzimmons, there were no forensics that could implicate her. What did Cooz have on her? A bottle of Manzano that went missing, hah! A coincidental suicide at Chapman by a professor who by all accounts was in the shitter with his career and who had a lawsuit happening over sexual harassment. And the case with Dominika was sealed. She really liked Evie Ann and thought they could have been good friends, but this was going to spoil any chance for her to be on the Ultimate Chef Challenge.

Marty pulled Evie Ann to the side and handed her her keys, making sure no one was looking other than Evie Ann, and said softly, "Suits were too small. Thank you, though, Evie Ann. I owe you."

"No problem. I think your lunch is ready."

"I'll call you," Marty said and hugged Evie Ann, kissed her on the cheek and then stepped towards the cash register. Evie Ann blushed a little as she smiled and went back behind the counter. She gleamed inside, feeling that she and Marty were friends.

Chapter Fifty-Three

As soon as Marty left, Fajida entered Assagio's. She made like she was a customer for a moment, checking the store's inventory, as she eyed Evie Ann whom she pegged off the bat. Fajida ordered a roast beef and Swiss with horseradish mayonnaise and pickled red onions. She then stepped up towards Evie Ann and quickly flashed her badge at her. "Evie Ann Pierce? I'm Detective Sanchez. You have a moment?"

Evie Ann looked up at her and nodded, stepped around from the counter and said, "You want to go outside?"

They stepped out back, and Fajida got right to the point. "I know you're busy, but how well do you know Marty Kittering?"

"Friends from the show. Hung out once," Evie Ann said.

"You guys intimate?" Fajida asked.

"Did Cooz put you up to this? Is he kinky?" Evie Ann nervously smirked.

"Can't say, but Matt Cumatos is dead from poisonous mushrooms, and they think they found Larry Fritzimmons' remains up in the San Gabriels. This is serious, my little girl," Fajida said.

"Oh, my God," Evie Ann blurted.

"You and your chummy new friend texted each other on Sunday. You want to know something? I think you two conspired together to kill Matt Cumatos and Larry Fritzimmons, so you could have an edge on that new show," Fajida said, thinking that was gentle enough, like a rock through a plate of glass.

"No!" Evie Ann cried. "Where's Cooz?"

"Don't worry about Cooz. You just might think about getting yourself a lawyer and maybe even giving up your lover, so they'll go easy on you. Have a nice day," Fajida said as she went back inside Assagio's.

Evie Ann's eyes got red as tears leaked from her eyes. She then bent over in fear and anxiety and threw up next to the dumpster.

Chapter Fifty-Four

A Forest Ranger truck pulled up to the taped-off camp area of Larry Fritzimmons. Jonesy stepped out of the passenger side of the truck. The Ranger, a tall and burly man of forty-five, with rusty steel hair and green-black eyes, stepped out of the driver's side and tossed on his ranger hat. They were the only two there since it was a low-priority case.

"Chances are he got caught in his own trap and was attacked by a boar or a mountain lion or even a bear," the Ranger said and continued, "Then some coyotes or a wolf came along and gorged on his body. That's a highly probable scenario."

Jonesy looked around the camp and stuck his head in a small one-man tent. He saw nothing but a rolled-up sleeping bag and asked, "Did he have any weapons?"

"I found a .45 pistol and a thirty-ought by his traps that the sheriffs took," the Ranger said.

"They were just lying there on the ground?" Jonesy asked.

"The rifle was leaning up against a tree, and the pistol was nearby. My best guess is when he got strung up the pistol slipped out of his holster; otherwise, he might have been able to shoot the rope to set himself free," the Ranger said.

"Assuming that he was a seasoned hunter, I just can't see it. No disrespect intended, but then again, this is not my territory," Jonesy said as he picked up a stick and sifted through a makeshift campfire made from surrounding stones. Nothing but ashes and a few charred pieces of logs. Then he noticed a large brass jean pant button. He picked it up and rubbed the soot off it. It had a large letter J embossed on it. He handed it to the Ranger, and Jonesy asked, "Did you find any articles of clothing, shredded or otherwise?"

"Not one stitch," the Ranger said, holding up the brass button. "This is from a pair of Johnson jeans."

"Ran out of firewood?" Jonesy said sort of smartly, but he was respectful of the Ranger.

"Couldn't say. All his other personal belongings, including his truck, the sheriffs took. We left everything else here because we knew you were coming up. The family asked us if we could lug all the rest of his belongings back to our office. Nothing much left other than this stuff and the traps he had set up. It's a good two miles in if you want to hike half the distance?"

Jonesy knitted his brow and said, "Not really."

"Looks like there was a wild boar in one of the cage traps. It dragged it about twenty yards before it got itself free."

"Find any blood trails?" Jonesy asked.

"We had a heavy downpour the night before we found his camp abandoned," the Ranger said.

"You think someone could have come up here and done him in? And then chopped his body up and tossed it about for the animals to scavenge?"

The Ranger looked at him oddly and said, "That's some morbid shit. But it doesn't look like that. Besides, the sheriffs are deeming this an accident since the foot and femur we found have markings of being chewed on by a wild animal. There was no saw or hatchet type activity if that's what you're asking. Like I said, wolves especially love to chew on human bones. And this isn't the first time I've found human remains up here, especially in the last several years."

"Certainly. But this fellow Fritzimmons and Bubba Arnet, the barbecued chef we're investigating, were on that same chef show," Jonesy said. "We think these two deaths might be perpetrated by the same person. For whatever motive."

"Unless we find the rest of his body or some witness that pops out of a tree somewhere, I don't see much that is going to say that it was murder. But then again, I'm not in the forensic business. Only going off of what the medical examiner said and what I've seen in the past, this looks like an accident," the Ranger said.

"Well, I appreciate your time," Jonesy said. "But one other thing? If he had trapped one boar, would he have left?"

"There's no catch limits on wild boar. He could have trapped until the cows came home. Why the question?" the Ranger asked.

"One of our detectives was up here and happened to run into him when he shot a boar," Jonesy said.

"Hum. Maybe you should have this detective call the sheriffs and offer up that bit of information. But I'll let you know if I hear of anything," the Ranger said.

"Good enough, but you said that there was a rope noosed to the foot and femur and that's how you found it. How would that happen?" Jonesy asked.

"One type of trap he used. Got caught in his own snare and maybe that's how he got mauled dangling from a tree," the Ranger said.

"He had traps, and he had a rifle. Why use some primitive method like that?" Jonesy asked.

"Maybe he got drunk and started to fuck around with the rope and got slung up. We can take a look, but it's going to be dark by the time we get out of here," the Ranger said.

Jonesy looked deep into the woods and paused for a moment and then said, "That's all right, I took enough of your time." They both hopped in the truck and drove off.

The Ranger was partially right. Marty had made her way back up to the trail Cooz and Evie Ann were on later that Sunday afternoon. She had the sawed-off shotgun she took from Bubba's Barbecue Place stashed in her knapsack. She headed south by southeast along the trail. There was not a soul in sight, not even a Ranger. And when she caught a faint smell of a burning fire, she veered off the trail and stealthily made her way closer to the campsite, stopped, pulled out a pair of binoculars and scoped out the campsite. All was clear. Marty inched her way on the ground and came upon a truck with duelies on the back end and a shell on top of the bed. She peeked in the window of the shell and saw a wild boar on top of a tarpaulin that was on top of a plastic cement-mixing bin filled with ice. There was another bin filled with ice and a tarpaulin on top, obviously awaiting another wild boar. She knew, if this were Fritzimmons' truck, which was highly likely, he would be back soon because the scent of the carcass would attract a lot of vermin including bear and mountain lion. She was aware of that because she spent most of her childhood hunting with her father.

She found a spot behind a boulder just behind the tent, put on a pair of rubber gloves and then a pair of leather gloves over the rubber gloves. An hour later, she heard someone making his way towards the camp. She peeked out over the boulder and saw Fritzimmons. He was carrying a rifle and had a .45 in his holster. She slowly grabbed the rifle, loaded it with two cartridges and gingerly snapped it in the armed position. Fritzimmons entered his campsite, stepped towards his cooler, grabbed a beer, opened it and took a long swig. He then sat down at a small table and laid his rifle on the table. She would have to wait until he moved away from the table. If she could get him with just his side arm, she had a better shot at taking advantage of him. He quickly finished the beer, grabbed another and sat back down as he picked up a book and started to read.

After the third and then fourth beer, he finally got up to take a leak. He stepped towards a tree, unzipped his trousers and proceeded to pee. In a flash, Marty had the gun against the base of his head and said in a manly voice, "Don't make a move." Fritzimmons flinched as he went to grab his side arm. Marty quickly jabbed the back of his neck with the shotgun and said, "Uh, uh. Hands up." Fritzimmons turned quickly, trying to grab the shotgun, and Marty whacked him on the head with the shotgun. He stumbled to the ground and then slowly got up. There was blood on the side of his face. He was grimacing.

Fritzimmons pleaded slightly, "What do you want, man?"

Marty said, "I want you to slowly take out your gun with your fingers and toss it my way."

"I don't have much to offer, but you can have whatever you want," he said and then slowly pulled out his gun from the holster and tossed it towards Marty.

Marty held the shotgun on him while she rummaged through a cache box for some rope. She found a bail of rope wrapped like a figure eight and unraveled it. She made a quick slip knot, pulling one end with her teeth to make it taut, slipped the rope through the hole to make a noose and said, "Turn around and put your hands behind your back." He slowly complied. As Marty got closer, he swung around to hit Marty with his forearm, and Marty shot him in the hip, but just grazed him. He quickly stumbled back and fell to the ground. Blood appeared on his shirt, and droplets of the blood pooled on the ground. Fritzimmons passed out briefly and then awoke to pain. By then Marty had tied his arm behind his back and commanded him, "Get up."

He dabbed his torn shirt with his hand and then wiped it on his pant leg. He had a burning sensation just above his hip. He winced as he kneed himself off the ground. He gingerly stood up while Marty strung out the rope some eight feet and then took another bundle of rope and a winch out of the cache box as well as a fat pink grease pencil. She picked up his rifle off the table, grabbed her knapsack and said, "All right, start moving. Wait. Where's your cell phone?"

"In the truck," he said painfully thinking that there was no reception anyway.

"And your wallet," Marty demanded.

Frtizimmons pointed at his truck.

"All right, let's go," she said.

He asked, "Which way?"

"Towards your traps."

"I don't know what you are doing, but it's fucked up," he said, almost crying, and began to walk down the trail and then off into the woods.

"Keep quiet, Fritzimmons, I don't want to hear your voice. Besides, it's not nice to scare people," Marty said and then started to mark their path with the grease pencil along the tree barks every twenty yards or so.

"Are you that chick with that cop who had the pig?" he suspiciously asked.

"Let me clear my throat. Just shut the fuck up, or I'll shoot you right here," she said with meanness in her voice.

"My mother always said to watch out for scorned women," he said insolently.

Marty stepped closer towards him and poked him on his bloodied hip. He buckled forward and grunted and then slowed his pace. Marty said, "Did your mother also tell you not to piss off a woman with a shotgun? So, keep moving."

Chapter Fifty-Five

Marty and Fritzimmons came upon his boar traps after the two-mile hike. The traps were basically six by four by four wire cages with a front panel that had a trigger mechanism that released and then closed by the movement of the boar. The boar would be lured into the cage by fresh corn kernels that Frizimmons first placed outside the cages, so the boars would grow comfortable around them. After several feedings over a day or two, he would place the corn kernels inside the cage, usually with success. He'd trap a couple of boars, shoot them with his pistol and gut them. Then he would move the traps about twenty-five yards away, so he could repeat the corn-conditioning process. He would then cart the gutted boars in a wheelbarrow one at a time back to his truck and put them on ice until he got his fill and packed up to go home. He'd butcher the boars into the various cuts, wrap them in butcher paper and mark them with the date and cut of meat. He would keep one boar for himself and the others he would sell to friends or customers he had cultivated over the years.

"I want you to undress. Everything," Marty said as she held the shotgun on him and then released the rope around his hands. And then she stepped back as Fritzimmons flipped off his boots and then his socks. His flannel shirt he peeled off gingerly. His exposed wound was a surface scratch that had stopped bleeding. He then unbuttoned his jeans, unzipped the fly and took them off. He hesitated and then took his underwear off as Marty gestured with the rifle to keep it going. He was buck-naked at this point. Marty tossed him the noosed rope.

"Put it around your ankle," she said. He complied, and she then said, "Up against the tree like you're humping it." He stepped up to a small oak tree and stood against it. "Closer. And turn your head to the side,"

Marty said and tossed the bundle of rope to loosen it. She started to walk around the tree, wrapping the rope around it and Fritzimmons.

"You fucking bitch," he kept repeating as Marty made about eight revolutions around the tree. She then tied the end of the rope to a branch. He spat on her—hitting her beard. She jabbed him in the ribs with the butt of the shotgun. He let out a groaning "oh."

Marty then stepped away from the tree some ten feet, pulled out one of the whips from her dominatrix days out of her knapsack, gave a couple of warm-up snaps and then struck Fritzimmons on the back. Fritzimmons let out a yell that could be heard for miles along the mountain range, but no one did hear. They were deep in the forest, several miles from any trail. And the only reason why Fritzimmons' foot and femur were found is because his wife had called the Ranger station since he was supposed to return for the shooting at the studio. But Fritzimmons had never showed, for obvious reasons. The Ranger had traced back to Frizimmons' trap location by the pink markings on the trees Marty left and then found the rope stuck underneath a boulder about twenty yards away. Marty repeated the process over and over until Fritzimmons' head just wobbled to the side from the intensity. He was unconscious at this point.

Marty then surveyed the situation and tried to push the caged wild boar towards Fritzimmons. It was too heavy, and the boar wasn't having any of it. It charged at her with its tusks and teeth ready to shred her. She stopped and then looked up at a branch that was about twelve feet above her, jutting out from the tree over towards the cage. She took out another bundle of rope from her knapsack and the winch and wrapped the rope around a tree that was roughly six feet to the side of the one Frizimmons was tied to. She then hooked the winch to the rope and strung the winch strap out towards Fritzimmons and then untied him, unraveling the rope from around the tree. He fell to the ground. Marty took the rope that was attached to Fritzimmons' leg, gathered it up and tossed it over the jutting branch. The rope unraveled as it came over the other side of the branch. Marty grabbed the one end and pulled it taut as far as she could until Fritzimmons' leg started to pull up. Then she tied the rope to the winch strap while holding the rope taut.

She was getting anxious because she felt she had spent enough time already and needed to get back to town to pick up John from the airport. She then slowly cranked the winch, lifting the limp Fritzimmons by his leg. He was dangling in the air now by several feet. He regained consciousness, briefly realizing his fate as his face turned flour-white with fear, and then he passed out cold. She cranked some more and just barely had him high enough. She took Fritzimmons' pair of jeans and draped it over the cage, so the boar couldn't get at her, and then she pushed the cage as hard as she could underneath Fritzimmons. She removed the pants and then unsnapped the secure clips at the top portion of the cage and lifted it up. The boar was timid at first and then charged at her, grunting and showing its teeth. She didn't know who was uglier, the boar with its hairy snout or Fritzimmons with his hairy pointed ears.

She released the winch, but it went too far, and he dropped right into the cage. The boar went into a frenzy and started to jab at him with its tusks and then it ripped at Fritzimmons' fleshy thigh and ultimately began to gorge on him with its ferocious teeth. Blood pooled on the ground. The boar reminded her of a shark when it senses blood in the water. "Are you scared now, Fritzy? Swine eat swine, you pig," Marty said as she watched, armed and ready, from behind the tree with the winch tied to it as the boar climbed up over Fitzimmons' body and up and over the cage. As it did, the cage rolled over on its side with the bloody carcass lying limp in a huddled pile.

Marty gathered up all of Fritzimmons' clothes and then untied the rope from the tree and the winch and untied it from the rope that secured him. She took out Fritzimmons' pistol and tossed it by the tree and then stuffed his boots, clothes and the winch and rope into the knapsack. She then leaned his rifle up against the tree, looked at Fritzimmons and headed back to his campsite.

When she got to his campsite, she started a fire from some glowing embers to burn his clothes. She thought maybe that was too thorough, but she didn't want to leave any trace of evidence, including his clothes, that might somehow be traced back to her. And too much forensics opened up more speculation, which can almost implicate an ant for being on the wrong hill, she felt. She'd watched those forensic cop shows from time to time and mused how outlandish some of the stories were, but why take any chances with any potential evidence. She knew that if the boar didn't finish him off, the wolves certainly would, particularly with darkness looming.

And then suddenly, the hunting trips with her dad and especially Uncle Brad, who would always try to frighten her with his howling when he told his stories of the *big bad wolf,* popped in her head. She was glad he was dead but why now? Happy thoughts, she mulled in her mind. Once the fire got going enough, she tossed in his socks and underwear and then his shirt. They burned quickly and then she threw in his jeans. She started to feel rain drops. The jeans were almost ashes when she decided to leave. She grabbed the knapsack and left as the rain started to pour heavily. Lightning struck in the mountain sky as if the heavens were raging.

When Marty got back to her car, she opened her trunk, peeled off her beard and stripped naked. It was still raining. She placed all her clothing and the beard in a black plastic bag and threw it in her trunk with the knapsack, shut it closed and hopped in her car. She threw on some fresh clothing, slipped on some clogs she had from Chapman and sped away. About five miles down the highway, when she came upon a deep ravine, she stopped her car, got out, opened the trunk, grabbed the plastic bag and tossed it over into the ravine and then drove off. Ten miles further down the road she came upon another ravine and repeated the process with the knapsack that contained the winch, rope and Fritzimmons' boots and then drove away. She just needed to get rid of the shotgun. She eventually crossed a river, stopped, looked around till she saw no head-lights coming and then tossed the shotgun in the river. She drove off. The rain slowly subsided. And then when she arrived close to Marina Del Rey, she pulled into a manual car wash and scrubbed her car inside and out and drove home.

Chapter Fifty-Six

After Marty left Assagio's with lunch for everyone, she made sure Fajida was not following her, and although it was a little bit out of her way, she drove near downtown Los Feliz to this part bodega, part head shop she had been to before and picked up a couple of packets of Spanish fly. She got back in her car and pulled out the fresh fruit bowl Janet had ordered that contained a mélange of melons, orange wedges, strawberries, blackberries, apples, pears and grapes with honey-glazed walnuts and Greek vanilla yogurt condiments on the side. She opened the packets of Spanish fly, lifted the lid to the fruit bowl and sprinkled the contents on top of the fruit. Stirred it with her finger and stuck her finger in her mouth to see if it was detectable. She was satisfied and said out loud, *"Voila"* and then closed the lid and placed it back in the box with the other lunches.

Marty thought that the Spanish fly was what the doctor ordered for Janet and the perfect revenge. In essence, it is an aphrodisiac made from the bodies of blister beetles and when ingested irritates the genitourinary tract. It is purported that the Marquis de Sade once gave aniseed-flavored pastilles that were laced with Spanish fly to prostitutes at an orgy. His act of generosity proved nearly lethal to himself; he was sentenced to death for poisoning and sodomy but was later given a reprieve. In college, Marty had carried out some experiments to try to replicate via chemical compounds the effects of *kanthans*, the Spanish fly, on her roommate with limited to no results. The commercial Spanish fly formula that you can buy over the counter or order online proved much more effective. It was the real deal.

When she got back from Assagio's, she passed out the lunches to everyone and when she gave Janet's hers, she curtly but condescendingly smiled and said to herself, "Good luck, you uptight bitch." Marty watched practically every bite she took. Janet even offered some to Jim, but he turned her down. And when she got to the last piece of fruit, she lifted the bowl to her lips and drank up the juices to the last drop. Afterwards she finished the yogurt while she sucked on the spoon. It was a working lunch after all, and they all got right back into their meeting. Marty watched from the corner of her eye the effect on Janet. She started to grind her crotch with her legs crossed and let out a sigh. Jim happened to look over at her, and she gave him a seductive glance. That was the first time she had ever given him any notice, but he ignored it, looking back at the consultant John had hired to go over details of filming in the field.

Janet couldn't take it anymore. She got up and stepped towards a food and beverage table at the back of the conference room and grabbed a banana, glanced over at John and lip-synced "bathroom" and stepped out the back door. She rushed down the hallway into the women's restroom, slipped into a stall, locked the door, ripped her panties down and rubbed her vagina as she moaned and said softly but urgently, "Oh my God, why am I so horny?" She then laid a seat cover on the toilet seat, sat down, hiked one foot against the stall door, inserted the banana into her vagina, and proceeded to stimulate herself with in and out strokes. Marty gently opened the restroom door, entered and slowly eased the door closed. She stood by the wall by the door and just smirked as Janet pleasured herself with moans and groans until she climaxed and then wiped herself clean and flushed the toilet. Marty quickly exited, thinking she got the *Rat Fink*.

Janet stepped out of the restroom as Marty walked back towards the meeting. Janet went the other way and happened to run into Elliot Hyde. Elliot gave her his speech about his wife cheating on him, and Janet smiled seductively and put a hand on his arm. She led Elliot towards the food storage room and unlocked the door. They both entered the room, faces flushed, and closed the door behind them. Marty, observing their clandestine meeting, walked to the security offices. What Janet and Elliot had not realized was that there was a surveillance camera inside the storage room now. Elliot knew of the extra security—he had put it into place with John's approval, of course—but he just plumb forgot. After all, his desires were about to come true.

Marty said to the relatively young security guards who were monitoring the studio surveillance cameras, "You guys want to see something interesting?" They nodded, and she said, "Go to the food storage room." One security officer went to his computer screen and keyed a link. The main screen displayed Elliot and Janet. "Can you get audio?" Marty asked. And then the security officer hit a link and although a little vague, they could hear shoveling noises.

They heard Janet say, "Are you a big boy? Are you big yet?" The security officers chuckled while Marty stood there with a smirk and her arms crossed thinking, *I got you, you little bitch.*

They all watched Janet and Elliot inside the storage room with eyes glued to the screen. Janet shoved Elliot against a shelf, undid his belt buckle and pants and pushed them down. She then bent down as she pulled his underpants lower, got hold of his penis and rubbed up against it while she stuck her tongue practically down his throat and began to literally devour poor Elliot. He didn't know what was coming. She sucked on his tongue and then his nose. She then had Elliot take off his pants and sit on the edge of a box of Abruzzo canned roasted red peppers with his legs spread. And then she did the most amazing thing; she went into a hand stance, inched her way towards Elliot and clamped onto his testicle sack while nestling her nose perfectly into his gluteal cleft. She sucked wildly on his one testicle like a clam that had just drawn in a sea anemone while she blew warm air through her nose. Elliot felt as if he were in heaven and began to hum his best Sunday church hymn.

Marty checked back into the meeting room where they were about to go on break and then went back to the security surveillance room and asked, "Are they still at it?"

"They're wrapping it up," one security officer said.

Marty asked, "Can you erase that?"

The bearded security officer said, "Not supposed to. Mr. Hyde's orders."

"Given the circumstances, I don't think he'll mind," Marty mused.

The security officer smiled as he hit a command. Marty then said, "Thanks, guys. This was just between us." And then she exited the room.

Chapter Fifty-Seven

Cooz walked into the administrative offices at Chapman Culinary Academy and discreetly pulled out his badge for the ready. Delilah Dish, Dee Dee for short, had been a second-year culinary student who helped out in the administrative office for extra money and such. Delilah was a spicy gal from Dauphine Street in New Orleans. She had been inspired by her uncle, who was a saucier chef, to attend Chapman. Dee Dee was in her early twenties and pretty, with long, wavy coffee-brown hair, sapphire eyes and pearly teeth that were slightly crooked. She had been friendly with Marty and was the one who told her about Chef Johnson. She looked up from her desk and said, "Can I help you?"

Cooz, "Yes, I'm Detective Cooz with the Los Feliz Police Department. I'm here to see a Mr. Turbinado."

Delilah buzzed Mr. Turbinado, paused and then spoke into the phone. "Okay." She led Cooz into a large office across the corridor. Cooz thanked her and stepped into Turbinado's office, whereupon Turbinado and Cooz shook hands.

"Have a seat," Turbinado said as he gestured at the chair in front of his desk. "What can I do for you?"

"As I said over the phone, we're investigating several homicides, and one of our suspects attended this school," Cooz said.

Turbinado questioned Cooz with a slight air of suspicion. "Yes?"

"She was here when one of your professors, a William Johnson, committed suicide. We think maybe the homicides and the suicide are related," Cooz said.

"So, you think the suicide was a murder? And who was this student?"

"Martha Kittering," Cooz said.

Turbinado was as cool as a cucumber. His main concern was preventing scandal from touching the academy. He responded, "What evidence do you have to suggest that Martha Kittering may have killed Professor Johnson? Or that it was, in fact, a murder?"

"We're trying to establish motive to connect her to Bubba Arnet, who was barbecued, a Matt Cumatos who died of mushroom poisoning and another chef who has gone missing. They're all connected to the World Chef Cook Off Show where she is currently employed," Cooz said.

Turbinado asked, "So what is it that you want to know about Martha Kittering?"

Cooz thought this guy was one hard nut to crack. "Was she a troubled student? Did she have any psychological problems?"

"No. She was a fair to average student, who came with solid credentials but didn't quite dazzle any of the professors," Turbinado said.

"When your professor committed suicide, was he involved with her romantically?"

"Not that I know of," Turbinado said, raising his eyebrows.

"Were you aware of his psychological makeup at the time, then, as to why he may have committed suicide?" Cooz asked.

"He was fired that same day. Over—" Turbinado paused and continued, "—over a sexual harassment lawsuit that was pending from several former and current female students. He had left his suicide note on his desk, which I thought was a little peculiar."

"Yes, that is a little odd. Was Martha privy to that lawsuit?" Cooz asked.

"I wouldn't know, but it was highly confidential," Turbinado said.

"You think anyone else had a beef with the professor, or was anyone fired that you might have a suspicion about?" Cooz probed.

"This is the first time I've considered that anyone might have killed William. But there was one of our security guards who was let go that same day. His name is Joe Straub. He was drinking on the job," Turbinado said.

"You have an address?" Cooz asked.

"Sure," Turbinado said, "but you didn't get it from me." And then he typed in some commands on his keyboard, wrote the address on a piece of paper and gave it to Cooz, thinking that Sloppy Joe Straub would most likely offer him nothing that could cast a disparaging light on the academy, himself or even Marty. He knew her vaguely through Delilah and was supposed to have dinner with the two one time, but it never transpired. Cause for a momentary fantasy, but he had Delilah, who provided him with plenty of excitement.

Cooz got up from his chair, thanked Turbinado, shook his hand and left.

Moments later Delilah stepped into Turbinado's office, stepped towards Turbinado and brushed up against him. He stroked her behind, and she asked, "What did he want?"

Turbinado said, "He thinks Marty Kittering might have killed Johnson and that Chef Bubba down in L.F. and who knows who else."

"No way! Little Miss Raspberry Truffle?" she said with a snarl.

"He's on a fishing expedition," Turbinado said.

Delilah asked, "So what do you want for lunch, Brandon?"

"You," he said with vigor in his voice. After all, he was her little sugar daddy and mentor at Chapman. He figured he best get his fill because it wouldn't be long before she was finished with school and long gone. Delilah locked the door, stepped towards Turbinado and slipped her breasts out of her top.

Turbinado started to kiss one of her nipples. Delilah said, "I can't believe it. Raspberry Truffle a killer?" Delilah started calling Marty Raspberry Truffle after a girls' night out that started with some fresh and succulent Pacific oysters bathed in champagne shallot gastrique that they devoured. Then the night got raucous at some country western bar where they got drunk on chocolate raspberry truffle martinis, a tasty but noxious concoction made with Stolichnaya Razberi Vodka, Bailey's Irish Cream, White and Dark Godiva Liquor and a splash of half & half, and rode a mechanical bull to the crowd's excitement. They woke up the next morning in the same bed completely naked, an Armenian cucumber between them and well hung over, but didn't remember a thing from the previous night. Or so they said.

Turbinado said, "More like a man-eater." Delilah knew that in some respects that was true.

After Turbinado and Delilah had their afternoon delight, she texted Raspberry Truffle about Cooz.

Chapter Fifty-Eight

Cooz hit up his GPS in his rental car and plugged in Sloppy Joe's address. He made his way over to his residence but had to finagle his way since the exact address went off the grid when he neared the house. It was one of those rectangular two-bedroom pre-fabricated homes that resembled a trailer on a piece of property deep in the woods. Joe just happened to be sitting outside on a lawn chair, smoking a cigarette, sipping Grand Marnier on the rocks and looking a little disheveled. A bottle sat on a small aluminum table next to him as he surfed the net on some low-end laptop that was as small as an old-time transistor radio.

Cooz got out of his rental and approached Sloppy Joe with his badge pulled out. Sloppy Joe said in his light, twangy drawn-out way, "What can I do for ya'?"

Cooz slipped his badge in his coat pocket. "Are you Joe Straub? I'm Detective Paul Cooz from the Los Feliz Police department investigating a murder. Mind if I ask you a few questions?"

"A little ways from home, huh? But go right ahead," Sloppy Joe said.

"You ever see Professor Johnson and Martha Kittering together? You know, in a friendly way?"

"Hell, no," Sloppy Joe said emphatically. He took a drag of his cigarette and then continued while blowing out the smoke from his nose. "She wouldn't have anything to do with him. Did she kill somebody?"

"Can't say. But did you ever see any of the other female students with him?"

"Not really," Sloppy Joe said.

Cooz asked, "Mind if I get personal?"

"Shoot."

"How did you get fired from Chapman?"

"They said I was drinking on the job," Sloppy Joe said, then took a gulp of his drink and continued, "But that ain't the case. Someone knocked me out when I was in Johnson's office. Got the imprint from the bottle they used on my head. It's an inversion of 750 M.I.L." And then he cocked the back of his head towards Cooz. "See."

Cooz held back a laugh and asked, "What were you doing at the time? Did they sneak up on you?"

"I was looking at some letters on his desk, being nosy and then, bam, next thing I knew I woke up in the lounge with a bottle of Grand Marnier next to me. They thought I was drunk and fired me," Sloppy Joe said.

"By 'letter,' you mean his suicide note?" Cooz asked.

"Didn't have a chance to read it. Couldn't tell you if it was the note," Sloppy Joe said.

"Who do you think may have done that to you?" Cooz probed.

"A woman because I smelt an orange or some tangerine perfume on me the next day," Sloppy Joe said.

"That's your best guess? A woman? You think it might have been Marty Kittering?"

Sloppy Joe cocked his head and furrowed his brow and said, "Shit, that bitch. What the hell would she do that for?"

"Do I have to tell you? We think she may have killed your Professor Johnson. She was probably in there dropping off the suicide note, and then you showed up. Lucky, she didn't kill you," Cooz said.

Sloppy Joe's eyes popped out, and he said in a shrill voice, "Whooee, that fucking cunt! I would have never figured her for that. She could have killed me. Imagine?"

Cooz said, knowing that it surely wasn't the case, but he wanted to further elicit Sloppy Joe's feelings about her, "You two didn't have anything going on between you?"

"I wish. Shit, she was the hottest thing going. I'd try to flirt with her in the hallway, but she just fluffed me off. Damn, I can't believe it. But, you know, come to think of it that was probably her, I bet," Sloppy Joe said although he really had no idea. But just thinking it might have been Marty would give him something to fantasize about for a few days or more.

Cooz inquired, "Listen, I have a bit of a ride back into town. You mind if I use your bathroom?"

"Sure, inside to the left," Sloppy Joe said. Cooz stepped towards his house and went inside. He looked around. There was a half-drunk bottle of generic vodka and over two dozen empty Grand Marnier bottles on shelves, the kitchen table, and on top of the refrigerator. There were even a couple in the bathroom, which was long overdue for a cleaning.

Meanwhile, Sloppy Joe was smitten over this current bit of information about Marty. He shook his head and smirked. "Can ya' believe it," he said out loud.

A few minutes later Cooz stepped back outside and said, "You have one hell of a collection of liquor bottles."

"Yeah, ever since Marty, assuming it was her, hit me over the head, I've had a thing for the 'Grand Marn Year,' and it ain't cheap," Sloppy Joe said.

"Are you working?" Cooz asked.

"Hell no, there's nothing out there but drive-thru joints," Sloppy Joe said and then continued in a mocking tone, "May I help you? Hell no!"

"Best of luck," Cooz said and shook Sloppy Joe's hand. He stepped towards his rental car.

"You see Marty, tell her I said hello and tell her I'm not mad at her," Sloppy Joe yelled out. Cooz waved and got in the car and drove away.

"Marty, Marty, Marty, mmm, mmm, mmm," Sloppy Joe mused and poured himself another Grand Marnier.

Chapter Fifty-Nine

Cooz made his way to the local coroner's facility after he had a brief chat with the sheriff, who provided him with virtually nothing but "Can't help ya'." His office was manned by four deputies and himself and not only was manpower limited, but he had no interest in starting to sniff around the only real revenue the community had—Chapman Culinary Academy. And Chapman was even thinking about moving its campus to Walla Walla, so it would be a very bad idea to incite any disharmony. The Sheriff referred Cooz to the coroner to get him off his back. He knew Willis was a codger who could outsmart any city slicker any day of the week or at least that was his thought.

Cooz was starting to feel he had very little at this point. That Sloppy Joe was sloppy at best. And how credible was he anyway? He was most likely trying to save face for things that had gone bad for him. And he really got nothing from Turbinado or the sheriff, so he was hoping for something more substantial from the coroner.

The coroner's facility, which the locals called the silo, was just that. It was actually a metal corrugated building with a silo next to it that was adjacent to Willis' farm where he mainly grew corn in the summer and pumpkins and other types of squash in the fall. Willis was the part-time coroner and a full-time farmer in his late sixties, possibly older, but he was a sturdy solid man who had a full head of gray hair and had eyes that were as blue as the sky. He wore bib overalls and a straw hat to keep the sun off his head while he ran his plough to gather the last bit of corn left on the stalks. Cooz pulled up to the silo as Willis shut off his tractor and slowly hopped out and then took his hat off and wiped his sweaty brow with a bandana handkerchief. Willis asked, "You the detective from Los

Feliz? The sheriff just phoned me," as he patted his cell phone in his pocket.

Cooz said, "Yes, sir. I'm Detective Cooz." He stuck out his hand and then shook Willis', which had amazing girth and strength but was gentle as could be.

Willis pulled out a pipe from his front pocket, stuck it in his mouth and said, "You here wanting to know if that professor was murdered?"

"We do have reason to believe that our suspect may have killed William Johnson based on her *modus operandi*," Cooz said.

Willis responded, "She's a suspect at this point, and you haven't arrested her yet because you don't have enough evidence to convict her, is that what I'm gathering? And you're here looking under rocks trying to find something you can use?"

"Didn't you suspect possible homicide? Who kills themselves with arsenic?" Cooz asked.

Willis peered up at Cooz while he struck a match, puffed on his pipe and responded, "You'd be surprised what people do out of guilt or shame. Back before I retired to farming, I was a young and spry professional like you in Seattle. I worked as a criminal psychologist but found it too disturbing because I saw the awful things what people—and I use that term loosely—what people did to others. The criminal mind can be quite perverse."

Cooz was a little frustrated at Willis's colloquial mindset. Wanting to get down to it, he said, "Didn't the sheriff investigate it as a potential murder?"

"Why should he have? There was ample evidence that the deceased was distraught over being fired and for being caught over his infidelity. I've seen people do worse things to themselves for the most insignificant reasons," Willis said.

Cooz then asked, "Did you do a toxicology scan to determine how the arsenic got into his system?"

"Why? They found the rat poisoning right on his bathroom counter-top," Willis said.

"So, what? He put it into some clam dip and had it with some crispy wafers?" Cooz said in a frustrated tone.

Willis said with a slightly raised voice, "What's the difference. He committed suicide."

Cooz responded, "Can we exhume his body to determine how he ingested the arsenic, so we can potentially get an understanding of the particulars of the killing?"

Willis chuckled, "Listen, son, what's that going to get you? Whatever he ate, he ate. It wasn't like we found him dead in some alley. He was at home. He obviously ingested the arsenic willingly."

"You don't think he may have been poisoned and then the rat poison and a suicide note were planted in his office to cover up the murder?" Cooz asked poignantly.

"It's not in my purview to ascertain that. It's the sheriff's. Besides, it's too late. The body was cremated," Willis said.

Cooz asked, "What about the note and the rat poison? Were they dusted for fingerprints?"

Willis responded, "You're asking for the impossible. The rat poison was most likely tossed out, and the note was presumably given to the wife, who as far as I know, didn't want anything to do with her husband. Which was part of the reason why she had him cremated, I suppose. Who would keep a suicide note, anyway?"

Cooz asked, "So who sells rat poison around here?"

Willis said, "Well, there's your Swanson's feed store, Heinz's hardware store and then you got your Walters in Walla Walla. And a few other places. What, you think they're going to have a tape for you of this killer buying the stuff, so you can go back home being the hero? I'd say, what's done is done."

"Either this killer is as smart as they come or just damn lucky," Cooz said.

Willis, obviously sensing Cooz's frustration, asked, "What is it that you have going on down there?"

"A murder by barbecue, a mushroom poisoning and a gnawed foot and tibia by some animal presumably after the body was dismembered in some way. All these three victims were chefs, and all were tied to this one chef show. And we think it all has to do with this gal that attended Chapman Culinary Academy at the time the professor supposedly committed suicide," Cooz said.

"Sounds like you might have some type of female Sweeny Todd on your hands, then," Willis said, changing his tune slightly on hearing of the number of murders. Cooz's theory sounded a little likelier now.

"Yup, but the problem is that we have no strong evidence to convict her. Just plausible opportunity and some type of motive, which I'm starting to think is partly thrill-killing and mostly because she has this insatiable appetite to be somebody. But she's so damn gorgeous and she comes from money. I don't get it," Cooz said.

"Maybe even a little anal-retentive personality that likes to keep a clean house. But if she's that pretty, like you're saying, there is a greater likelihood that she may have used a disguise or two, so she wouldn't be recognized. I think you're dealing with a very smart one here. Putting some thought into what she's doing. I'll give the sheriff a shout and see what he may think, but it's too late now for any evidence that we could actually use," Willis said.

"Well, I have to get on my way towards San Francisco. Apparently, she's connected to another murder down there about eight years ago,"

Cooz said and handed him his card. He nodded his head as he stepped away.

"I'll give you a shout if I hear of anything," Willis said as he looked at the card and lit his pipe.

As Cooz started to drive away, he popped his head out his window and said, "Text me. And thanks, by the way." Willis nodded.

For a moment Willis wanted to go inside his house and start researching his old psychology textbooks to put together a profile of the killer and maybe help Cooz determine whether he was chasing the right person or not in Marty, yet he knew that the L.F.P.D. had their own criminal psychologist he could consult. But these types of bizarre murders are exactly why he got out of criminal psychology. He knew when he got the call about Johnson, when he heard the word arsenic, that it wasn't some ordinary suicide. But there was something in his brain that made him sign off on the death certificate without remorse. Willis hopped back in the tractor, grabbed a bottle of coke from a small cooler, twisted the top off and drank from it. He started the tractor and headed back to his cornfield as a malaise came over him. Then he lit his pipe and felt a momentary sense of relief as he collected the last bit of corn of the season.

Chapter Sixty

Cooz had just got off the phone with Fajida and laughed at how she handled both Kittering and Evie Ann, especially how she laid into Evie Ann. He was laughing at himself because he knew if the roles were reversed with him and Fajida, she would have said to lay into Evie Ann, cute or not. Like calling the kettle black because that is the way Cooz would have played it. He had asked Fajida to go easy on Evie Ann, yet Fajida preyed on her vulnerability. She must have sensed something, but Fajida had to work it that way to flush out if Evie Ann had anything to do with the murders. Spook her a little by raising the level of anxiety. Evie Ann did call him and left several voice messages about being shanghaied by Fajida. At first, she sounded scared and then, in the later message, angry. He realized he had to distance himself from her because of the sticky situation it caused.

Kittering went to see Evie Ann. That must mean that they were running scared about being potential suspects, he speculated. And if they tried to get a warrant for both Kittering and Evie Ann's cell phone records, and the records proved his speculation wrong, the whole case would backfire on him because there wasn't really any other evidence. And once he apprised the Captain of his relationship with Evie Ann, because of her connection with Kittering, he would be excused from the case. So he hopped on a plane to Portland because he needed to find something, somewhere. He would get up early, sniff around her hometown and then get down to San Francisco and get back home by the following night and deal with the Captain when he got home. It wouldn't be the first time the Captain was pissed off at him.

When he got on the plane and took his seat, he wondered why the sheriff and Willis didn't pursue further investigation into a possible homicide. It was plain as day. How many other cases like that, either by sheer obliviousness or shoddy police work, went undetected? Maybe it wasn't Kittering. Maybe it was the wife or some other abused student who had had enough and sought revenge for his sexual advances? Yet if Kittering knew of his firing than she certainly would have had the impetus to poison Johnson. Maybe he should have stayed a little longer at Chapman and pried further? Maybe he should have asked Turbinado's secretary or whatever she was. She was one good-looking babe. Might have even been friends with Kittering. Birds of a feather and all.

Chapter Sixty-One

Cooz drove by Marty's family house in Lake Oswego, Oregon, where her mother still lived. The same mother who would occasionally have to visit the nearby private psych resort to treat her bouts of schizophrenia and the bipolar disorder she and Marty shared and whatever else reared its ugly head. Cooz just wanted to get a feel of Kittering's upbringing and have a chat with her. He drove up the driveway, parked, walked towards the door and rang the bell. As he waited for the door to be answered, he got a good sense, especially with the drive into the neighborhood, that it was a high rent area. A few moments later a house servant dressed in a black dress trimmed in white lace, who also doubled as a caretaker for Louissa "Lu" Remy-Kittering when needed, which was often, answered the door. She asked, "Yes, may I help you?"

"I'm looking for Louissa Kittering. I'm with the Los Feliz Police Department, and I have some questions I'd like to ask her about her daughter," Cooz said.

"I'll see if Ms. Remy-Kittering is available," the servant said in a professional manner without a hint of emotion about Martha Kittering. She shut the door as Cooz stood outside. The name Remy ran through his mind. He realized that while driving from the airport, he had passed a modern glass multi-level building that was the Remy Pharmaceutical Company headquarters. He just naturally assumed that Louissa Remy-Kittering was the same Remy based on the locale of the building and Martha's education in chemistry from Golden State. "Shit," he said to himself. "Not that you'd have to be a genius to know about arsenic, but two of the killings were by poisoning. And a chemistry education sure gave Kittering the knowledge. How could I have missed that," he chastised himself.

The servant re-appeared at the door and said, "Ms. Remy-Kittering is unavailable. But if you would like to leave your card, she'll have her lawyer contact you."

"Okay," Cooz said and then reached for a business card and handed it to the servant. She closed the door practically in his face. Cooz just stood there for a second, he was so stunned, not just by how the servant was so unexpectedly curt, but also by the words, "She'll have her lawyer contact you." Had the mother known or expected trouble with her daughter? As he walked to his rental, he noticed an elderly woman, close to eighty, wearing a canvas garden hat with a sheer white kerchief around her neck. She had on a pair of gardening gloves while she tended to her roses that bordered her property and the Kittering property. Cooz walked towards her because at this point in the investigation he was hungry for something they could use, so he didn't mind hitting up a mature woman who might shed some insight into Kittering. When he got closer, she saw him and awaited his arrival.

Cooz introduced himself, and she said, "I'm Nanine, but everybody calls me Nana."

Cooz asked her, "Can you tell me about Martha Kittering? What type of person is she?"

Nana said, "Oh, Marty. She was such a lovely girl. She always brought Harold and me cookies. They weren't the greatest, but she was so kind. Nothing happened to her, I hope?"

Cooz said, "No, just doing a background check. Is Harold your husband? I'd like to also get his opinion of Martha. If you don't mind?"

A melancholy sadness came over Nana as she responded to Cooz's question. "When I was visiting my sister in Nebraska, as I do every year during the end of the summer because it's so darn hot otherwise, Harold left me after almost fifty years for his hairdresser. Well, actually his barber."

Cooz said, "I'm sorry to hear that. How about your husband? You ever hear from him at all?"

Nana said, "Oh no, never. The last time I heard from him was right before he left. He called to tell me Rex, our dog, had been run over. He buried him in the back," as she pointed towards a marshy land area near the lake. "It was a terrible summer that year."

Cooz asked, "Yes. How long ago was that?"

Nana said, "Seven, maybe eight years now."

Cooz asked, "How about your children, they hear from him ever?"

Nana said, "No. They think he was just embarrassed because he fell in love with his barber."

Cooz said, "A man, I see. How did you know that he left with the barber?"

Nana said, "He typed me a note."

Cooz said, "Do you still have the note?"

Nana said, "Oh no, I threw it away after I showed it to the kids. It was a terrible reminder."

Cooz said, "I'm very sorry for you. You mind if I take a walk back towards the lake?"

Nana said, "Please go right ahead."

Cooz stepped through the reeds that ran deep behind Nana's property until he got to the edge of the lake and looked out through the tall trees that stood in front of him. He took in a deep breath and pondered silently to clear his mind. He looked down towards the edge of the lake that had receded some ten feet or so as it did that time of the year and then walked back through the reeds. He thanked Nana, wished her well, got in his rental car and drove off.

What no one knew was that during the summer that Harold supposedly left for some exotic island, as his children and others speculated, Marty, upon seeing the abuse Harold gave poor Rex for so many years—

until he finally went too far and wound up killing Rex with a stick—had had enough. She was home that night, her mother in her barbiturate haze and her father on a business trip to Europe when she heard Rex whimper for the last time. It hit her deeply. She watched from her bedroom window as Harold dragged pour Rex to the edge of the lake and buried him.

Marty prepared some of her butter cookies and dusted them with powdered sugar and brewed a pot of Earl Grey tea with a good helping of a terpene indole alkaloid, strychnine, which is a neurotoxin that affects the central nervous system when ingested and causes convulsions and death in larger doses. It's quite lethal. In fact, Alexander the Great was supposedly poisoned with wine tainted with strychnine. Marty then sauntered over to the Persimmon's, knocked on their door and handed Harold the plate of cookies she made. He invited her in, and she poured the tea for him. He wanted her to stay and have tea with him, but she insisted she had to get back to her mother. He thanked her and smiled.

Marty went back to her house and waited. Later that night she rang the Persimmon's bell. No answer. She went to their back patio and looked inside and saw Harold the Terrible through a window. He was passed out in front of the television set. She opened the screen door and then the back door as it was always unlocked and entered the house. She called out, "Harold. Harold. Are you awake?" No answer. She gingerly stepped towards him, shook his shoulder, and he just slumped over. She checked his breathing under his nose and checked his pulse. As far as she knew, he was dead. She gathered up the empty plate of cookies and teacup and scurried to the kitchen and rinsed the cup out with soapy, warm water, dried it off and replaced in the cupboard. She then grabbed the pot of tea and the plate and made her way back to her house.

Twenty minutes later, with a rain shower in full effect, Marty returned wearing a pair of her father's fly fishing bib overalls complete with booties and carrying a plastic tarpaulin over her head. She laid down the tarpaulin on the floor next to Harold's still body and rolled him off the chair and onto the tarpaulin. She then cleared the path out towards the back door and slowly dragged his body down the hallway and in through the kitchen and out the back door. Marty, ever so quickly, slid Harold's body across the rain-slick reeds towards the lake. When she arrived, she dropped the tarpaulin and then ran back to her house, grabbed a shovel, a flashlight, a can of oven cleaner, and rubber dish gloves and ran back to the lake. She then jumped over the crest of the lake into the muddy bottom and started to dig. It was soft and easy to make a hole deep enough to place Harold's body in. She then began to think of Rex and tears streamed from her eyes as they co-mingled with the rain.

When she had dug the hole about four feet deep and two and a half feet wide, she undid his clothing and slippers and rolled the limp Harold over the crest and straight into the hole. She then repositioned his naked body face down, draped him with the tarpaulin, donned the dish gloves, shook the can of oven cleaner and then sprayed the cleaner all over his body while she perched over the grave underneath the tarpaulin. She hacked and coughed and started to get dizzy from the lye and other pernicious chemicals. When she had emptied the contents of the can she tossed it in the grave and then peeled her gloves off and threw them next to Harold and then started to cover up the grave with dirt as the rain continued to pour. She found a fallen tree that had sat and rotted for a period not too far away and dragged it towards the lake and then rolled it over the crest right on top of the grave. She then put the flashlight on the grave and hoped the lake would start filling up soon.

Marty then ran back to the Persimmon's with her flashlight, hosed the mud off herself, took the fly-fishing bib off and ran inside. She grabbed every bit of clothing of Harold's she could find except for his winter apparel, a few suits, and a few sweaters, found some plastic lawn bags in the garage and then filled the clothing in the bags, six in all. She then went through his jewelry and stuffed them in a Crown Royal bag she found mixed in with his underwear that housed some gold and silver coins. And then gathered his toiletries, including his cologne and hemorrhoid cream, which Marty felt he would probably need on his long trip, and gingerly tossed it and the other items into a smaller plastic bag that she would later toss away. She then trudged back to her car dragging the six bags of clothes, holding the toiletries and the Crown Royal bag in her mouth, opened her trunk and tossed everything in her trunk. From a distance she could hear her mother yell out in her sluggish voice, "Martha, where are you?" And then the mother's bedroom light went on. Marty could see her figure at the window, but she knew her mother wouldn't remember a thing even if the circus ran through the house with a team of elephants.

She then went back inside the Persimmon's house, found a pair of dish gloves under their kitchen sink and went into their den. Marty typed a farewell letter to Harold's wife on an old typewriter that the Persimmons still used explaining how he had found his true love. He was sorry, but a man must be true to his heart. She then taped the letter to one of the kitchen cabinet doors, grabbed some paper towels, sprayed a wad of towels with some window cleaner and rubbed clean the front door bell and every spot she could think of that she touched, including Harold's chest of drawers, the closet door, the garage door the kitchen sink and cabinets. She then damp-mopped the kitchen floor on her knees with some paper towels and stepped outside and wiped down the back door.

She could still hear her mother calling her from the distance, but knew she would pass out soon enough from her Xanax and whiskey sour cocktails. She then hosed down the patio of any dirt accumulated from her disposal activity and went back to her house barefoot with her hair, bra and panties soaking wet and her knees red. When she got inside her house, she discarded the dish gloves and then toweled herself off. She went upstairs and peeked through her mother's bedroom door. The light was off, and the mother groggily asked, "What were you doing in the backyard, Martha?"

Marty said, "Just cleaning up some things."

The mother said, "You know, Martha, you need to be careful, especially having your grandfather's blood in you. You know why he had to leave France, don't you?"

Marty said, "Yes, Mom. But, why don't you go back to bed?"

The mother continued with her concern as she slowly faded off, "Did you get everything cleaned up?"

"Yes," Marty said and then closed her mother's door.

The following day she drove to several local secondhand stores and donated Harold's clothing. She found a few homeless people and handed them some of Harold's jewelry, including his retirement watch from some aeronautical firm where he was an aerospace engineer, his Navy ring, several tie clips, sterling silver cufflinks, a solid gold Streamliner pen and a variety of rings. One had a ruby, which she liked, but she knew it was best not to keep it. She went to a coin shop and sold Harold's coins for a hundred and seventy-eight dollars and sixty-two cents, which she spent on a new bra and panties to replace the ones she'd tossed out the night before, a massage and facial and light lunch of warm vichyssoise and grilled Alaskan salmon served with citrus-infused crème fraiche and some fresh sliced chilled radishes. She had change to spare.

Chapter Sixty-Two

Cooz met Detective Harris of the San Francisco Police Department in front of the children's daycare center, which was where Dominika the dominatrix operated and lived and died some eight years prior. Harris was tall as ever, still precocious, nearing his mid-forties, with light brown curly hair that had grayed slightly. They shook hands as they greeted each other warmly. They were a part of the same fraternity where a fellow officer would lay down his life for his partner without question. But Detective Harris, although he was a little wily, was a by-the-book kind of guy when Cooz asked him about Martha Kittering.

"Like I said over the phone, the case was sealed, and any particulars pertaining to her are confidential," Harris said.

Cooz responded, "I completely understand," as his hope for some useful information faded. It was like a door being slammed in his face. He was going nowhere with Kittering as a suspect. "What about the lover? Is she still in prison?"

Harris said, "She died last year of lung cancer."

Harris saw the bleakness on Cooz's face and said, "I'll give you one thing. Just as we were about to sign a warrant for Kittering's arrest, the D.A. at the time, Idaho Florez, stepped in and had us re-arrest the ex-lover, who was later convicted. And that case was closed."

Cooz said, "Are you talking about Spuds Florez, the State Attorney General?"

Harris said, "That same one. And you know how that higher stratosphere works?"

Cooz said, "Yeah, a jingle here and a gratuity there and you have all the favors in the world at your doorstep."

Harris said, "Is she your primary suspect in the barbecue killing?"

Cooz responded, "That and two others."

Harris said, "She still pretty?"

Cooz said, "Are you kidding? You should see this woman."

Harris said, "Play Misty for me." Cooz affirmed with his eyes and then Harris continued, "I really wish I could have been more of a help. You know how it is? Everything you do nowadays has to be by some legal standard. So, are you headed back to Los Feliz?"

Cooz said, "Yeah, I know what you mean, but I was thinking about going to Oh's."

Harris grinned and then said, "Oh's, some of the best damn breasts in town. And you know how those Asian women are, but might I recommend the Imperial roll. Lobster, king crab and jade rice wrapped with this wafer-thin white tuna that they top with a creamy roe sauce and toasted sesame seeds. It's great!"

Cooz said, "Nice. You want to join me?"

Harris said, "Love to, it's half day at school. Have to play taxi."

Cooz nodded and shook Harris' hand and said, "Hey, thanks. Nice meeting you."

Harris said, "My pleasure."

And then Cooz's cell phone rang. He flipped it on, nodded at Harris and then said into his phone, "Okay." He immediately hopped into his rental and sped off to the airport.

Chapter Sixty-Three

Marty finally listened to the voice message from her mother on her cell phone. It was only a day, but she just wasn't in the mood; too much was happening. It was the cold wench who took care of her who left the message, but when she heard that Cooz had been up at the house wanting to ask her mother questions about her, she went into a tailspin because the perfect storm was brewing. Not only was she starting to peak with her bipolar condition, her menstrual cycle was kicking in. The stress from the police and now Cooz sniffing around her hometown and at Chapman was too much for her to handle. Even her father's strong, comforting words in her head could not set her mind at peace. She needed to take care of one more thing she felt, and then everything would be all right.

John was busy with Jim and Janet preparing for the new show when Marty interrupted him and said she would be back in an hour or so. He excused himself with Jim and Janet and took Marty into his office. Marty sensed that he was upset. "What is going on? That detective said you promised Evie Ann Pierce that she was going to be on the show? And now they think you two might have had something to do with the killings. What is this?"

Marty said, "They're desperate, John, and they're pulling straws out of a hat."

"Marty, you're killing me," he said despondently.

"I would never do that," she said.

John shot back, "Never do what?"

"Just that I would never want to see you harmed," Marty said.

"I don't know what to think. They even speculated that you two were lovers," he said.

"They're making up lies to confuse everybody because they don't know the truth about anything," she said.

John asked, "What is the truth, Marty?"

"I don't know. I'm sorry I said some things to Evie Ann. I thought she would make the show more interesting with her looks and all," she said while John shook his head in disgust. Marty continued, "You mind if I just step out for a few? I need a little time."

John showed genuine concern but was perplexed and threw up his hands. He said, "Okay, just call me later, then." And then he went back into the meeting.

As Marty scurried into the parking lot and headed towards her car, she saw Fajida and Jonesy in one car and an L.F.P.D. squad car pulling into the studio parking lot, flashing their badges at the security guard at the entrance gate. Marty ducked, not wanting to be seen since she figured they were there for her. And she was right; they were there to arrest her for the murders of Bubba Arnet and Matt Cumatos based on probable cause, motive and M.O., although they didn't have a shred of evidence. But that didn't matter for Marty at that point. She got in her car, slowly crept towards the exit gate, unknowingly waved at Pablano, the security guard, and sped away. Marty immediately shut her cell phone off since she had to make sure she was not traced by any means, especially the GPS tracker in her phone.

Marty quickly made her way back home to the Marina Del Rey apartment, turned on the oven, took all her clothes off because she was feeling constrained by all the pressure coming down on her and needed to be creative to ease her mind. She started to whip up a quick batch of brownies with fresh eggs, melted butter, premium Belgian cocoa, coarsely ground walnuts and the key ingredient, a good helping of LSD powder she had brewed up when John was in New York.

It was a two-day process to cook up the LSD, an acronym for lysergic acid diethylamide. Marty managed to make enough for at least six trips. A trip being slang for the mind-altering experience that LSD produces when ingested, including hallucinations, perceptual distortions, a changed experience of time, and an expansion of personality and cognition, which in some cases leads to a spiritual experience some find extraordinarily illuminating. In what is considered a bad trip, the person is unable to handle the distortions of reality, which cause heightened anxiety to the point of terror and schizophrenic symptoms. Aftereffects can include prolonged depression that can be quite damning, with psychological treatment required. Marty had previously sent away via the internet for some Hawaiian wood rose seeds and started a double batch. She soaked the seeds in a solution and then strained them out, put the solution on cookie trays and slowly evaporated the liquid in a low oven. She then scraped the residue, a mock but potent version of LSD, off the pan and stored it in a vial.

In less than twenty minutes, from start to finish, she had the brownies baked and quickly showered. She then redressed in shorts, a halter top and sandals, grabbed a Royal Crown bag of her jewels and such and the warm brownies and headed off to Highland Park to the east with only a minute or less to spare. As she drove away northward on a side street, she saw in her rear-view mirror Fajida and Jonesy drive by with the other patrol car trailing right behind them. She then slowly eased on the brakes and looked back as the small battery of police pulled up to the curb. Marty continued driving as they all got out of the cars and scurried into her apartment building. She surmised that an all-points bulletin would be immediately broadcast throughout the police communications system once they found she wasn't there.

As she made her trek east of Los Feliz, she kept saying to herself "one more." One more chef, and everything would be ready for the

Ultimate Chef Challenge to proceed. It was time to do the deed. She knew John wouldn't be able to understand her own unique method of accomplishing things, but it was all for the best. He couldn't know that she was the killer under any circumstances; otherwise, he wouldn't have anything to do with her ever again. But what was so amazing to her was that even though John had been preoccupied ever since Chef Bubba was found barbecued, he showed no signs of diminished desire for her, especially in their lovemaking that seemed to blossom to greater heights, much to her delight. And Marty, for some blessed reason, began to feel more pleasure on a consistent basis than she had ever had. Maybe it was the depth of love she had for him or maybe it was the level of peace she had felt because of living together. She had, in any event, had a stasis within her that felt calming and was quite discernable. He was the ballast within the storm of chaos that was all around her. But could end up all for naught because of the trouble she was now in. Yet knowing that didn't dissuade her from her murderous mission.

Chapter Sixty-Four

Marty's GPS led her up a gravel road to a compound in Highland Park that was an orange grove and also a mini pot plantation complete with a chain-link fence that not only bordered but secured five acres of fertile land for prime *cannabis sativa* growth. Marty pulled up to an intercom with a camera system that was perched overhead and hit the buzzer on the speaker. She was at the residence of Childress Peel, aka "Stoner," who was one of the top chef contestants on the World Chef Cook Off Competition and who was supposed to have gone up against Chef Bubba Arnet until the show was canceled. Stoner was an anomaly since he had no formal training but had mastered the art of French cooking.

Stoner had inherited the property from his parents who met their untimely demise on one of their annual quarterly runs to pick up a load of Peruvian pink and Bolivian blue cocaine, some of the finest in the world, which they purchased for distribution. They bought and sold enough to maintain a modest lifestyle as a California orange grower, the perfect front for their waning business that had been much more lucrative during the seventies. In the eighties, cocaine started to lose favor as the drug of choice to the designer-made feel good Ecstasy. Stoner was just an infant at the time and hadn't had a chance to know his parents, given that they hadn't wound up in jail somewhere. He was at the orange grove at the time he lost Timothy and Lucy, as he referred to his parents, and was cared by Tangerine Cream, the young live-in nanny whose parents were remnants from the old Haight-Ashbury days.

Returning in their small prop along coastal Central America, lightning struck their craft, which caused all the power to go out, which resulted in all systems failure. The plane subsequently took a nosedive straight into the Pacific Ocean off the coast of Belize. The bodies of Stoner's parents were never recovered as the plane sunk to the bottom of the sea, but surprisingly the cocaine rose to the surface, stored in floatation devices, which were used not so much for emergencies but in case of pursuit by the law when they might have to ditch the stash from the plane in hopes of retrieving it at some point later via a tracking device.

Being savvy entrepreneurs and concerned parents, the Peels had been insured to the tune of two and a half million dollars. Stoner was the only child and was later adopted by his grandfather David Peel, who was the founder of *Stoner Magazine.* The California court system agreed to this with reluctance, but the senior Peel had such potent lawyers in New York that they had no chance whatsoever and besides he was the only surviving relative who showed any interest in Childress and who also had the means. David Peel lived in Manhattan on the Lower East Side, and that's where Stoner grew up until his grandfather died of a sudden heart attack, whereupon Stoner packed it all up and moved back to the orchard, which had been leased to orange growers for the previous eighteen years. With all that income and the two and a half million, less the debt the grandfather had and of course, the expenses incurred by the grandfather for rearing the child, Childress set himself up in playland with all the toys an aging teenager could handle. Sadly, he didn't have too many friends to play with since he was largely a loner.

David Peel's influence upon his grandson resulted in Childress having such immense knowledge of marijuana that he had his own blog on the *Stoner's Magazine* website and as a result was aptly called Stoner. The magazine was created in the sixties as a resource for marijuana users and growers and according to Childress, it helped make pot a household commodity in the minds of the magazine's readers, if not the world in general. It was also a pioneering advocate for the use of marijuana for medicinal purposes and helped forge legislation, particularly in California. David Peel consulted with the legislative bodies in secret closed hearings.

David Peel's other influence on his grandson was that of fine French cooking. Often they'd spend hours together preparing elaborate seven-course meals after watching recorded episodes of Julia Child and perusing the cookbooks of their idol, the famed French Chef Pierre Cooz, especially *The Brown Derby Elite Cuisine*. At sixteen, Stoner could make duck à l'orange better than any he ever had, according to his grandfather. And David Peel had had some of the best in the world including at the top French restaurants in New York City as well as in Rouen, France, where the dish originated and whose chefs are renowned for their superb preparations. Stoner's little secret was his use of mostly tangerine juice with the addition of blood orange, Meyer lemon and key lime juices, a combination that resulted in an extraordinarily profound glaze on a Peking duckling, a breed that was brought over to America in 1873 from China and is used almost exclusively in the food industry.

When Stoner moved back to the grove, he put in the fencing and security cameras since his plan was to grow various strains of marijuana for personal consumption as well as distribution, in limited quantities as not to draw too much attention to himself; after all he was a seasoned pro in the world of cannabis, knew his stuff and certainly wanted to protect his interests. Some would say he was a little paranoid, but better to be safe than sorry, he'd respond. He also remodeled his kitchen and put in some of the finest equipment, including a Wolf range, a brick oven, a sixty-four-inch cubic refrigerator and freezer, and an ice cream maker. Italian marble counter tops and a walk-in pantry completed the renovation.

Chapter Sixty-Five

Stoner's voice crackled through the speaker, "Can I help you?"

Marty said, "Childress, it's Marty Kittering from the show."

Stoner said, "Ms. Kittering, what are you doing here? Are you lost?"

Marty responded, "No, I've come to see you. I have a little something for you."

A moment passed, and Stoner's voice cleared a little as he said, "Come on through; I'm at the top of the hill." He then electronically opened the gate, and she drove past the gate and up the hill with the gate closing behind her.

When she arrived at the top of the hill, she parked her car and Stoner came out to greet her. At twenty-five, he looked like he was eighteen with long golden-brown hair that ran straight down his back and in front of his face. He was thin with a tan and little facial hair and had olive-green eyes that were permanently glassy. He tended to smile a lot, which gave the impression he was high all the time, which he was. He was wearing a pair of extra-long shorts, a Tommy Bahama print shirt and Hierarchy sandals. Marty grabbed the brownies and handed them to Stoner.

He said, "For me?"

"Especially for you," she said.

Stoner's glassy eyes got watery, and in a quavering voice, he said, "I can't believe it. You drove all the way over here for me? Are they pot brownies?"

"Something better. I added some herbs that make you feel free," she said, plucking at his emotions.

He asked, "You mean like THC? Because I have plenty of that."

"No, something a little more mind-bending, like LSD," she said.

He paused for a second and like a kid in a candy shop, licking his chops, said, "Acid, man. Haven't done that in a while. I didn't know you were that cool?"

"I'm the eighth wonder, Childress," she said.

"I'd say," Stoner said and then asked, "You mind if I try some?"

"Of, course, that's why I brought them," she said.

"Let's go sit on the patio, and we'll have some together," he said as he began to step towards his multi-level house. The patio on the second level overlooked his orange grove with the pot plants towards the back of the grove, so if anyone came to see him, they wouldn't be noticeable unless they were actually looking for them. Besides, the pot-growing area was fenced off and could not be seen from the other part of the grove. When the oranges were picked, the pickers would be curious, but they were paid well and usually never inquired. And from above, to guard against helicopters or surveillance drones, the pot field was shrouded with a huge mesh tarp that was inscribed with, "I heart mom and dad." He would say it was his private garden and so they would likely get the message. And in the seven years he had lived at the grove, the law never bothered him because he hadn't told any of his buyers where he lived, and he was off the beaten track, anyway.

Marty took a seat on the patio where there were several jars of seedless buds of his many strains grown from some of the world's finest seeds, compliments of the far-flung friends whom he had cultivated through *Stoner Magazine,* as well the seeds that he had inherited from his grandfather. She noticed there were a Kona Gold, a Mauie Wauie, California Bud, Blueberry Bud, Purple Haze, a Blessed Shiva and even a Russian River Valley Red. She was taken aback by his collection, which was reminiscent of a fine wine collection, Marty mused. He even had an electronic water bong that triple-filtered the smoke, giving you a clean and potent hit that maximized the marijuana to its fullest potential.

Stoner stepped onto the patio from his kitchen with some plates, napkins, a cake server, a pitcher of iced water with fresh oranges and mint inside and some glasses on a platter. "Voila," he said, "You amaze me, Ms. Kittering."

"Call me Marty," she said.

"Marty, for you to do this for me makes my heart melt," he said with sincerity as he cut up the brownies in eight pieces and served Marty and himself one piece each.

"Well, we want you to be happy. You are one of our star attractions," she said. "So, you're all alone up here?"

"Just you and I and a couple of cats," he said and then forked the brownie and brought it to his mouth, took a whiff, smiled with delight and chewed on the LSD morsel with orgiastic lust. "Oh, my God. What kind of cocoa do you use?"

"Valrhona, of course," she said and then poured Stoner a glass of water. As she poured hers, she accidentally but intentionally spilled it. She quickly got up from her chair as the water dribbled over the table towards her and on her shorts.

"Oops," he said and got up and went into the kitchen for some paper towels. As he did, Marty picked up her brownie and tossed it over the patio into the bushes down below.

Stoner came back out and blotted the water. Marty apologized. He looked over at her and said, "Don't worry about it. You got some water on your shorts."

Marty looked down at her shorts and said, "It's okay." She slipped off her shorts. Stoner was stunned as he glanced at Marty with her wet white cotton panties and her black pubis showing through. She draped her shorts over the railing and wiped off her chair as Stoner watched in dizzy amazement.

Stoner continued to eat the rest of his brownies. Marty served him another piece, and he said, "You know, Marty, if you don't mind me saying so, you're one hot babe. How come you're not in some magazine like *Oui?* Not to sound rude or anything."

"Thank you," Marty said. "I'm a little shy for that. I just can't see myself being ogled by a bunch of guys. Besides, I don't think John would appreciate that."

"John? You mean John Abruzzo? You guys together?" he asked.

"We're lovers, and we live together," she said.

Stoner's eyes widened, and then he gulped. He got very excited at the word "lovers."

"You should eat some more to get the full effect," she said, and he followed her command. She served him another piece as she continued her provocation so he would be under her spell. She said while rubbing her breasts, "He likes to kiss my nipples while he caresses my vagina." Stoner quickly ate that piece and then another and then Marty saw the look go from sexual excitement to a psychedelic daze. He blinked his eyes and then they drifted off into the sky.

He then looked at Marty and said, "Wow."

"Just one more and you won't regret it," she said and got up and started to feed Stoner the brownies with the fork as if she were the mother and he was the baby while he gyrated his lips in eager anticipation for the next bite. She fed him until all the brownies were gone. By that time he was so far into another world that Marty knew he would never return. He got up from his chair in a stupor and scratched his head and then rubbed his hand on his nose as if he had the sniffles. He looked out towards the grove and then the sky while watching his hand twirl about. He looked at Marty and he thought she was totally nude—although she wasn't—and wanted to kiss her. She slowly maneuvered herself to his side while holding on to his arms as he tried to claw her.

She shushed him to be quiet. While he blew her kisses, he said, "I'm in love with you," as he giggled.

"I love you too," she said, trying to placate him until the LSD really kicked in.

Stoner slowly made his way down the patio stairs and walked through the grove, brushing his hands against the orange tree leaves. He then began to lick the leaves, imagining they were candy. While Stoner was off in La-La Land, Marty cleaned up the drinks, wiped down the table and chairs, put back on her shorts, grabbed the brownie pan and brought it to her car. Meanwhile, Stoner started to really hallucinate. He saw a blue giraffe peeking above the orange trees looking down at him. And then saw a plane go by, and he thought it was a giant doob in the sky. And then he saw his parents parachuting from the plane, and they started to pass packets of cocaine into the air for whoever was down below. It had been a plane with some seagulls flying by. And then he began to chase an imaginary pink rabbit that was the size of a mature kangaroo hopping along the ground, and he rolled on his back as the imaginary rabbit played with him.

He looked over at Marty. She appeared to be a jester dressed in red velvet with dangling gold chains hanging off her clothing. Her lips were overly accentuated with ruby lipstick, and she had very large two front teeth, like the rabbit he thought he was playing with a moment ago. And then he heard birds, possibly finches, talking to each other in high chirping voices and one of them said, "I sure like that sugar water, it reminds me of plums." Then his mind slowly started to shift and went into this bizarre alternate universe where nothing appeared quite what it was, all shapes and forms shifted to completely something else. The sky turned a dark steel color that seemed to be lowering towards him. The trees resembled orange odalisques that swayed from right to left and left to right, then every which way.

Stoner somehow managed to remember the hole in the fence towards the back of the grove, and he slipped through it and just took off. He was gone for good, mentally speaking. Two days later he was found hanging off a tree limb near his driveway by a courier delivering a package to his house. Stoner was in a catatonic state with porcupine needles in his face. Apparently, he had tried to pet the porcupine. He was rushed to the hospital and later institutionalized with severe schizophrenia. He perpetually drooled and had a constant stiff penis while mumbling "Marmy." The doctors thought he was saying "Mommy," but what he was saying was "Marty." As for the stiff penis, which some nurse believed, it was a result of the Hawaiian wood rose seeds, which had been used by Hawaiian natives for generations as a male sexual enhancement with great success. It was presumed that he had overdosed on an extraction of some sort from the wood rose seeds they found in the toxicology screen they performed on him. Law enforcement, upon being informed of the overdose, raided his compound, pulled up all his marijuana plants and burnt them on site, less a kilo of the Blueberry Bud one of the officers helped himself to.

Before Marty had left Stoner's compound, right when he slipped through the fence, she helped herself to a couple of hits of Kona Gold off Stoner's electronic bong. She had never tried it before but thoroughly enjoyed it. A brief image of Hawaii popped into her head. She thought she'd like to go there someday. She had paused for a moment on his patio and felt sad in a way for Stoner. He seemed like a nice kid, even though he was as old as she. She sensed that he was very lonely and mostly uninspired with his life, outside of his pot, and even though he was a leading contender on the show, he was mainly a fan favorite for his general persona. Albeit very talented, he had no real ambition. He didn't even ask one question about the show or mention any of the other chefs, Marty said to herself, justifying frying his mind. She realized he wouldn't last long on the Ultimate Chef Challenge and it was best that he be written off.

Chapter Sixty-Six

Marty had left the compound, but not before she erased the surveillance record of her arriving there and then shut the whole system down, just in case Stoner happened to somehow recover from his spaced-out journey or someone got suspicious and started to snoop around like that Detective Cooz. As Marty drove off, she started to feel that feeling again. After all, she was on all her cycles. They were in high gear. She didn't know what to do. She couldn't go back at this point; God only knew what evidence they had on her. Marty had covered all her tracks, and there was no way she could have been framed for any of the killings. She could account for her whereabouts but had no alibi for that Sunday afternoon when she was up in the San Gabriels.

What Marty couldn't understand is why the photos of Raveneitzkya and Chef Bubba that she sent to the D.A.'s office hadn't been used against Raveneitzkya. But what she didn't know was that they were misplaced by the D.A.'s secretary and put on a stack of non-essential material. If they had had those photos, it would have taken the heat right off her. The L.F.P.D. would have their suspect for the killing of Bubba Arnet. As for Matt Cumatos and Larry Fritzimmons, their deaths were just unfortunate accidents. Had Cooz found something up at Chapman? Delilah had told her that Johnson was cremated, leaving no real evidence, she thought, unless Delilah said something to Cooz about her telling Marty about Johnson's firing, but that was unlikely because of their intimate friendship.

Marty drove down the road, about to leave Highland Park when she started to get pangs in her belly. She hadn't eaten since she had her usual banana, yogurt and granola for breakfast and it was almost two. Besides, the pot she smoked had made her a little ravenous. She saw a little

Mexican restaurant and popped in. She ordered a barbacoa taco, carnitas taco and a beef fajita taco with chopped chicharrones. While she waited for her lunch, she helped herself to sliced radishes and marinated carrots and jalapenos and a salsa verde with chopped cilantro and a creamy salsa with roasted tomatoes. After the tacos, she ordered flan. As she paid the tab with cash, she passed by the bar and watched the local news on TV. Her picture was flashed on the screen. She did a double take and then left immediately, not wanting to be noticed.

When she got in her car, she decided not to go back to Los Feliz. What options did she have? She couldn't go up to Portland; they would most certainly be on the lookout for her there. And San Francisco was out of the question. Too many haunting memories, anyway. She thought if she could get down into Baja to their vacation home in La Paz, she could essentially hide out for a while until everything calmed down and hopefully get her father's lawyer to assist in her troubles. Her mind was racing, yet she felt a little groggy from all the food she had eaten. Marty pulled over to the side of the road just outside of Highland Park and closed her eyes. She began to reminisce about all the fun they used to have down in La Paz, her parents getting drunk on shots of agave tequila while singing along with the Mariachi bands. That was a long drive away and too many potholes to maneuver, but it might have to do for the moment, she pondered.

Chapter Sixty-Seven

Marty was chaperoned by a tall, slender man of thirty-five wearing a white lab coat who had dark hair and dark eyes behind a pair of black-framed glasses. They walked through what a seemed like some medieval courtyard, with chain-link fence topped with sharp cylindrical blading surrounding the grounds. But what was so odd to her was that everyone was wearing nondescript white robes with flushed looks on their faces. She turned to the man and asked in Spanish, "Why am I here, sir?"

He said politely in a Spanish accent, "Por favor, call me El Doctoor. But why are you here? Don't you know? While you were preparing for El Presidente's inaugural gala ball you made mini-chimichangas that were served as appetizers."

Marty interrupted him and said, "So?"

"So," he said, questioning her uncertainty, "You had taken the chef, filleted her and then roasted her in pork lard with garlic, onions, oregano and then pulled the meat off the carcass and made the most delicate and *deliscioso* chimichangas El Presidente has ever tasted."

Marty asked, "Was that a problem?"

El Doctoor said, "The chef was El Presidente's mistress. And did he love her dulce de leche. Everything was kept hush-hush. A rapido trial. And here you are. But you already know this."

Marty asked, "So, where am I?"

El Doctoor said, "Oh, I will show you around. Come with me." And then they began to walk the grounds. El Doctoor continued, "This is the finest security facility in all of Chichipapas for the criminally insane."

Marty, shocked, said, "Criminally insane?"

El Doctoor responded, "Why yes. You had the option to plead guilty by insanity or go to jail with half the bureaucrats and academicians in

Chichipapas making Chuckles, that candy-coated bubble gum you get on the streets of Tijuana. And you chose here."

Marty said, "That's hard to believe."

El Doctoor said, "I know, I'd much rather have been there myself."

Marty asked, "You're a prisoner?"

El Doctoor said, "I was the top villain in Juarez and because I missed church one Sunday, they put me in here. I'm on the psychology staff. Could be worse, I suppose. So, are you Catholic?"

Marty said, "I'm not sure."

El Doctoor said, "What did it for me was those angelic girls in the back pew who were ripe for debauching."

Marty said, "Is that so?" And then, looking around, she saw that everyone wore animal costume headpieces. She observed wolves, lions, foxes, coyotes, leopards and others. Marty asked, "Why is everyone wearing a costume on their head?"

El Doctoor said, "You like them? They're my idea. Each animal represents a sin, a crime if you will. The lion is for ambition, the fox is cunning, the leopard is for ferocity and so forth. It's part of their readjustment. It's like when a dog kills a chicken, you put the dead chicken around its neck, so it will learn not to do it again."

Marty asked, "Ambition is a sin?"

El Doctoor said while chuckling, "Which one do you think you should wear? The fox or maybe the leopard perhaps, since you're so finicky?"

Marty said, "How about my own face?"

El Doctoor said, "There are many things you must learn. One is not to ask so many questions. The other is how to make Mexican food without using the liver. We're not fond of the liver. So we are going to have you work in the kitchen."

Marty asked, "You trust me?"

El Doctoor said, "We trust no one, that's why we have cameras everywhere."

Marty saw two young Mexican boys dressed in white cotton clothing with belts around their waists. They wore huarache sandals and were coming their way. One of them had a Chihuahua on a leash with the dog carrying saddlebags on his back. The other boy reached in a saddlebag and grabbed what looked like candy and handed a few pieces to Marty.

El Doctoor said, "Chuckles, *El dopo.*"

Marty said to the boy, "*Gracias.*" And then she tossed the Chuckles over her back and began to mock chew.

The boy responded by saying *da nada* and then, smiling, he showed a gold tooth that sparkled in the sun. He proceeded to blow a bubble with a wad of gum he had in his mouth.

Marty observed a bed that had four wheels like a baby carriage being pushed by three residents who had sparrow masks on their heads. On top of the bed was a naked man performing cunnilingus on a naked woman whose body was completely covered in pink paint and who was performing fellatio on the man. As they neared, she noticed it was John and Evie Ann. John popped up his head and said, "Come join me, Marty. She tastes so good." Marty tried to say something but couldn't. She looked at Evie Ann's vagina; there was a large oyster mushroom emerging from it as the bed slowly strolled away.

Chapter Sixty-Eight

Marty and El Doctoor then went inside the institution's kitchen that looked more like a laundry facility with large round vats everywhere that had a bunch of mushy stews in them. She thought one might have been *menudo,* with tripe and hominy in it and another looked like *pescado* with lots of fish eyes floating around. Each vat of stew was stirred by one of the institution's residents using a canoe paddle. Marty then noticed a tall man wearing nothing but lederhosen and a pair of red woman's lace underwear and bra. He had on vibrant ruby red lipstick. On top of his bald head was a tall hotel chef's hat, and on his feet, he wore stilettos, which made him stand over seven and half feet tall from the bottom of his heels to the brim of his hat. He spoke only German, so none of the residents could understand his instructions as he stuffed chunks of bloody red meat into a grinder with the meat extruding out into sausage casings.

El Doctoor pointed his open hand at the man and said, "That is our chef, Franz Von something or other who likes to wear women's clothes. He's a cross-dresser."

Marty asked, "Was that his crime? Cross-dressing?"

El Doctoor responded, "Certainly not. Actually, we encourage it for those who are excessively angry. It helps get them in touch with their feminine side." El Doctoor continued after thinking about what Marty asked him, "Yes, the reason he's here is similar to why you're here. You should have heard of him. He ground up his townspeople over in Germany and turned them into sausages. Quite gruesome."

Marty queried, "So, why is he here?"

El Doctoor said, "Prisoner exchange."

Marty confused said, "But he's German?"

El Doctoor said. "Of course." And then he squinted his eyes at Marty and continued, "I see you have a long way to go."

Marty then asked, "What's that?" as she pointed to a table with an old washing machine that had a hand-crank roller mechanism to squeeze out excess water from the clothes. A very full woman wearing an apron ran tortillas through the hand crank mechanism and then stacked them in a pile. After each one she made, she sprinkled flour on the rollers.

El Doctoor proudly said, "Gluten-free. We banned wheat flour in all of Chichipapas, you know."

Marty asked, "What do you use, then?"

El Doctoor responded, "Corn flour."

Marty said, "But corn flour has gluten."

Shocked, El Doctoor said, "It does? Then, they'll have to ban that too."

Out of the blue, a trio band stepped into the kitchen. A very thin man played the trumpet; an attractive buxom brunette played the guitar, and a very short diminutive man played a xylophone. They began to play *Guantanamera* and everyone in the kitchen stopped what they were doing, put their hand on their heart and turned to the picture of El Presidente on the wall.

El Doctoor said to Marty, "This is our pledge to El Presidente. Come join in. It's mandatory."

As the female strummed her guitar, she sang the lyrics, *Yo soy un hombre sincero, De donde crecen las palmas, Yo soy un hombre sincero, De donde crecen las palmas, Y antes de morirme quiero, Echar mis versos del alma.*

And then everyone in the kitchen together sang, *Guantanamera, Guajira Guantanamera, Guantanamera, Guajira Guantanamera.*

Then everything went dark, and for a second it was quiet. Marty gathered her thoughts and then she heard a tap, tap, tap. She opened her eyes and looked over to her left. There stood a sheriff. Marty squinted as she collected herself. She realized she had fallen asleep and had been out for a half an hour. She thought she was in a secluded spot and was relatively safe behind an old abandoned building, but she was wrong.

The sheriff said as he sized her up, "We don't recommend anyone, especially women, stop here. We've had some trouble if you know what I mean."

Marty said flatly, "Right."

But there was something in her tone that the sheriff didn't like, especially given the way she was dressed. He thought she might be doing tricks and then he asked, "Can I see your license and registration?"

Marty said, "Okay." She shuffled through her purse for her license and then her glove box for the registration and gave them to the sheriff. He looked at the license and then at Marty as he eyed her. He stepped back towards his car. When he was about halfway there, Marty quickly started her car and sped away leaving a trail of dust behind her. The sheriff darted to his car, got in and followed in hot pursuit.

Chapter Sixty-Nine

Marty trucked it down the road by hitting the gas pedal to the floor, but the sheriff was on her tail with his cherry lights flashing and the car screaming after her on the single-lane highway. She weaved over into the other lane in order to pass the vehicle in front of her and then opened up the engine in her Challenger and gunned it for all it was worth. She was doing about a hundred and ten. Her heart was racing as fast as the super-charged engine she had under the hood. She knew she had to turn off somewhere because there would be another sheriff and who knows if there'd be a helicopter thrown in the mix. Marty hit some hilly terrain, and sparks flew from underneath her carriage as metal hit the pavement. "The fucker is right on my tail," Marty said to herself as she looked in the rearview mirror.

She saw an intersecting street dead ahead and hoped for the best. She hit the brakes to negotiate the turn. It would broadcast her next move, but she would most likely flip her car if she didn't brake. The sheriff was about a hundred yards behind her and almost made up half the distance as she slowed and then made the turn. As she hit the street, a teenage girl was walking her dog across the street on the next block down. Marty cut to the left and went right over a curb and sped across several lawns. The sheriff almost came to a complete stop, just barely missing the teenager and her pet. Marty was relieved that they weren't hurt as she came to a stop and glanced behind her. But, as soon as the teenager scooted across the street, the sheriff gunned it. Marty didn't wait. She found an alley and crept slowly down it, looking for a hideout.

She came upon a garage that opened to the alley with its door lifted. She noticed a man in his late fifties with gray hair wearing faded jeans and a well-worn purple T-shirt tinkering with some old lamp. The garage looked aged and well used and stored all kind of lamp parts, toasters, waffle irons, microwaves and such. There was enough room for her car. She quickly popped her head out her window and said, "Excuse me, sir?"

The man slowly turned towards Marty and then slowly looked up over his glasses that were pushed low on the bridge of his nose. He then put down the pair of pliers he was holding, picked up his lit cigarette from a beanbag ashtray and took a drag as he stepped towards Marty, who was obviously anxious. He then asked, "What can I do for ya?"

Marty said, "I need a place to park my car for a few hours." Marty then peered ahead of her to see if the sheriff was still on her trail and then looked back at the man blowing smoke out of his nose with his shirt that read "Welch's."

He stepped out of the garage and looked both ways down the alley and said, "Well, that depends on watcha got to offer," and then he leaned inside Marty's car. Marty inched back a bit.

Marty quickly said, "Shit," to herself. Her cash was limited since she had forgotten to go to the ATM. She knew that they would have frozen the accounts by now. She was pissed at herself and said as she lifted her right wrist, "I have this bracelet. It has rubies and sapphires. Worth a little money. Can we make this quick?"

The man looked at it and then picked up Marty's left arm and said, "Too delicate. I like this," as he eyed her Rolex watch.

Marty didn't hesitate and said, "All right, but you're getting the better end of the deal. That's for sure." But what could she do? She was in a pickle if there ever was one.

She backed up and then maneuvered her car inside the garage as Welch Man assisted her by navigating his hands to turn a little to the right then left and then forward. He then stepped towards the garage door, peeked out the alley, saw the sheriff drive by down the block and shut the door. Marty turned the car off and stepped outside. Welch Man eyed her from head to toe, furrowed his brow and said, "I think we might have to renegotiate our arrangement."

Marty said, "What do you mean?"

The Welch Man said, "What I mean is that you're the girl they're looking for who barbecued that chef. I can tell, with that pretty black hair of yours and besides, you're like an alley cat being chased by some stray dog the way you look."

Marty said, "What if I am?"

And then the door from the kitchen into the garage crept open ever so slightly, and a female's voice spoke, "Hey, Pops, going over to Munchies and pick up some chicken fried steak. I'll be right back."

Welch Man peered over towards the door while he kept one eye on Marty and said, "Don't forget the extra gravy. And pick up some beer while you're at it, Lollie."

Lollie said, "But you have plenty of beer!"

Welch Man said as he grinned at Marty, "I'm in the mood to party."

Lollie said, "Okay." And then shut the door and left the house.

Marty asked, "Your wife?"

Welch Man said, "Something like that. So, let's get down the business. I'm looking to have some of that fine ribeye I'm looking at."

Marty asked with reservation, "You looking to fuck me?"

Welch Man said, "Sure, I'm looking to fuck ya', but first I want some of that steak sauce."

Marty said, "I'll give you the watch and the bracelet, and we'll call it even."

Welch Man said, "That and the pussy or I call the cops. Your choice."

Marty said, "All right, scumbag. But make it quick and use a rubber."

Welch Man said, "What the fuck would I need a rubber for, Buttercup?"

Marty wanted to say to keep your greasy slime from going inside me but reluctantly held her tongue as not to incite the pig and then she took her Pearl watch and bracelet off and handed them to Welch Man. He just put them in his pants pocket as he watched her pull her shorts off. And then Welch Man unzipped his jeans as Marty slipped off her underwear and dropped them on the floor. Welch Man just eyed her twat and salivated. He stepped towards her and as he went to get down on his knees to partake of the finest pussy he had ever seen, Marty lined up her knee and cocked him in the nose with a hard jerk. Welch Man didn't know what hit him and fell back on the garage floor with his nose bleeding profusely.

Welch Man was barely cognizant as she knelt by him and stuck her hand in his pocket and fished out the watch and bracelet. Welch Man then reached out towards her with his hand and got a piece of the bracelet, which was wrapped around the watch. Marty tried to pull away, but he wouldn't let go. He had a tight grip despite his condition. Marty surrendered her precious jewels, never to be seen or worn by her again. She quickly put her shorts on as Welch Man groggily tried to regain his composure. Marty opened the garage door, jumped in her car, backed out of the garage into the alley and slowly drove away. Welch Man finally sat up as she drove down the alley with blood running down his nose. He saw Marty's underwear, picked them up and dabbed his numb wet nose as he looked down at the watch and bracelet. He then let out an aching smile.

Chapter Seventy

Marty inched her way towards the end of the road. She peered out in both directions, made a right and negotiated her way towards the opposite part of town. It was near dusk, and she had to get somewhere safe out of the way of any highway traffic or people for that matter. She drove on back rural roads for thirty-five miles or so until she came upon a cheap motel that was off the main road. Its sign read the Hideout Motel. The vacancy light was lit, so she pulled up into the parking lot and parked on the side of the motel so as not to be seen from the road. She got out and went inside the lobby.

There was no one there, so she hit the bell. A moment later a handsome man Marty guessed to be in his early twenties, with black wavy hair that hung over his warm gray eyes, stepped in from a back room wiping his hands on a towel. When he saw Marty, he was startled at her beauty and became very shy. He quietly said, "Hello."

Marty said, "I'd like to get a room for the night. I only have cash. Is that all right?"

The Shy Man said, "It's fine. It'll be thirty-five dollars."

Marty took out her money from her purse and paid him. He then hand wrote a receipt and handed her an information card to sign including her driver's license number and license plate number. Everything she wrote was false including her name, Raspberry Truffle. She handed him the card. His eyes widened in disbelief when he read her name, but he was used to that since most people who stayed at the motel were on the run from someplace or someone. He handed her a key and said, "Room six at the far end of the motel," and then continued in an almost apologetic, but obligatory way, "No funny stuff. Okay?"

Marty said, "Certainly not. By the way, is there a liquor store around here?"

The Shy Man said, "About five miles north of here. They're closing soon."

Marty said, "If I paid you twenty bucks, would you go and pick me up some wine and maybe a bag of chips? I'm a little tired."

The Shy Man said, "Sure. I was about to close the office for the night anyway."

Marty paid him and said, "Thanks. A decent bottle of Pinot Noir, if you can, salt and vinegar potato chips and some tasty chocolates. Okay?" Her tone was almost flirting. The Shy Man nodded.

Marty stepped out the motel office and watched the hotel sign turn to "no vacancy" as she walked down past the other rooms towards the other end of the motel. When she got to room six, she noticed a slotted door to her far right. It was probably a storage or boiler room, she thought. She felt a raindrop as she unlocked her door and stepped inside. The ten-by-ten room was sparse with a queen-size bed topped with a white cotton spread that had traveled many miles, a tiny nightstand with a lamp with a tan cloth shade, a small bureau, a cardboard mock painting of a farm scene with a blacksmith shoeing a horse and no TV. What was most odd, she thought, was the mirror on the opposite side of the room that was eight feet long by four feet wide. She immediately felt something strange, a premonition, as if it were a two-way mirror. She tried to look through it at some off angle, maybe to get a glance at the other side, the boiler room perhaps.

Marty then peeked out her window towards the parking lot and saw the Shy Man drive off. She stepped outside her room, took a look around and tried to open the boiler room door. It was locked. She then proceeded to grab a credit card out of her purse, stepped back outside and shimmied the card between the boiler room door and the jam by the lock. She popped it open, found the light switch and flipped it on, proving her suspicion, correct. There was a two-way mirror that opened to her room and to a full-length mirror in the bathroom. There were two camera tripods, one set up for filming the bedroom and the other for the bathroom. She presumed they were triggered by motion. She removed the digital tapes, shut the light and closed the door behind her. A downpour of rain came out of nowhere.

Marty went back in her room and latched the door. She could hear a rhythmic staccato from the rain on her car while she glanced at the mirror and wondered how long the secret filming had been going on. How many unsuspecting and unknowing participants in sex-cam videos from this room were floating around on the internet? Or was the operator, Shy Man, most likely, just some perv seeking pleasure from room six for himself? At least she was one step ahead of them, she thought, as she stepped into the bathroom.

She tossed the tapes into the toilet and flushed them down the drain. She then washed her hands and face, peered at a drinking glass on the vanity that had some murky residue on it, then cupped her hands for some water and drank it. Marty brushed her teeth and wiped her hands and face off. She undid her shorts and realized she had no panties on. She had left them in Welch Man's garage. "Fucking bastard," she blurted out loud. She noticed a small bruise just above her right knee and ran her thumb over it. Marty then spread some toilet paper on the toilet seat and had herself a long overdue pee while feeling for her watch and bracelet on her wrists, but they were long gone. She mouthed, "Damn it" and wiped herself off. She noticed she was still on her cycle and then flushed the toilet and washed her hands several times. She needed to clean the dirt that was brewing in her mind. Marty stepped out of the bathroom and lay down on the bed. She took in a deep breath and tried to close her eyes, but her mind was racing like mad. The gale force within her head was so tumultuous, like that perfect storm that came in from every direction.

Marty got up, grabbed her purse and counted the money in her wallet. Sixty-eight dollars. She couldn't get very far with that, barely into Mexico. The option of going to La Paz was out of the question because she knew she couldn't use her credit cards or debit card to get money, lest she tip off the officials. She thought of calling her father, but would he understand her predicament? Would he care? This was life or death now, and she knew that she would need a potent ally. She needed a lawyer, her father's lawyer who helped her when she was in trouble with Dominika. Marty had an urge to cry but held back because she had to keep sane and not get emotional.

She felt suddenly alone and wondered if she was such an evil woman. Was she so terrible that she would never be loved again by anyone? By John? He'll never want me ever again, she ached. Then she spoke from her soul and prayed, "John, please forgive me if I harmed you, if you are truly there, please forgive me if I have done wrong." She then began to get dizzy and passed out from the anxiety that welled up inside her.

Marty woke to a knock at her door. She slowly lifted her head and then got up and swaggered to the door and opened it. When the Shy Man saw her, he said, "Are you okay?" She fell into his arms. He put down the package on the bureau and then brought her to the bed and laid her head on the pillow. He went into the bathroom, filled the glass that was on the vanity with water and brought it back to Marty. He lifted her head and had her drink the water. He said, "You're probably dehydrated. I'll get you some bottled water. Are you going to be okay?"

Marty nodded and then stroked his arm. He left the room and came back in a flash with several bottles of water. By that time Marty had undressed and slipped under the covers. She said softly, "Turn the light off and make sweet love to me." She lifted the sheets to expose her naked body. He followed her command and shut the light, quickly undressed, slipped in bed with her, and they made passionate love most of the evening while indulging in each other and the chocolates as the rain poured heavily outside. Marty moaned in orgiastic delight, as if this were the first and last time she had ever or would ever have sex.

The Shy Man had experienced this before and wondered if there was enough light from the bathroom to where he could get his sex with Marty on film so it would be distinguishable, but he doubted it and quite frankly didn't care because he was enjoying himself tremendously. He fed Marty some chocolate caramels, and she tenderly chewed on them and then went down on his very long hard penis. She orally brought him to a climax. A bacchanal of seduction was in her mouth with the chocolate caramels and Shy Man's natural cream.

She then got up and began to eat some potato chips while she opened the wine. They both drank from the bottle. Shy Man then poured the water out of the glass he gave to Marty earlier onto the carpet and filled the glass with wine until it overflowed. She leaned into him and the wine spilled on his chest and down his belly. Marty began to suckle the wine off his body right down to his testicles. She then mounted her vagina on his face while she deep-throated his cock. They continued to have sex well into the night and into the morning. She had never had sex like that before, continuously for hours upon hours.

Chapter Seventy-One

That morning, what seemed no more than thirty minutes after she and Shy Man stopped having sex, she woke up alone and utterly lonely. She missed John, but she needed a place to hide somewhere safe away from modern civilization, so she could escape both mentally and physically. Marty wasn't ready to face the music or even a trial of some sort. She remembered a monastery at the northern end of the San Gabriel Mountains. Marty drove towards San Fernando, stopped there and found a local secondhand store. She picked out a nondescript pair of men's khaki pants, a blue checkered flannel shirt, several pair of men's underwear and undershirts, a pair of men's mountain boots, an old California Angels cap, a small knapsack and a bible. She then found a costume store, lucky enough nearby and purchased a black beard and cosmetic glue. She then drove off and cut east towards the San Gabriel Mountain Range.

Marty stopped at a small town at the base of the range and found a storage facility. Paid a month in advance, purchased an over-priced keyed lock and parked her super-charged car inside one of the garage-like storages, shut it off, turned on her headlights and stepped out of the car. She then shut the storage garage door, staying inside, took off all her clothes and stuffed them in the trunk. She proceeded to take out a pair of scissors from her toiletry bag and cut her black hair above her shoulders. Then she took out the black beard she had just purchased, applied some cosmetic glue to the beard and stuck it to her face. She pressed the sideburns and chin, and the moustache on her upper lip, looked at herself in the side view mirror and said, "Charming, as usual."

Marty locked up the storage garage and then hit the road, hiking her way towards the range with the knapsack of her few remaining belongings. She had to leave her possessions behind, less a few valuable jewels she had acquired over the years. As she walked down the road, she realized how physically drained she was, besides having her period. She was also ravenous from the sex.

She saw a burger joint, stopped, went inside and ordered one of those western bacon cheeseburgers with extra bacon and BBQ sauce, some onion rings, zesty horseradish sauce and a bottle of water. She sat down and took a deep breath. She was almost too weak to eat, but once she took a whiff of the food, she found the strength. She unwrapped the burger, took the bun off, topped it with the onion rings, peeled back the cover on the zesty horseradish sauce and squeezed its contents on the burger. She replaced the bun and pressed the burger, letting the sauces commingle, and took one huge bite while the sauce dripped all over her beard.

She looked over at a young teenage kid who was goofing around with his buddies at a table across the way. He was gesturing at Marty like he was smoking a joint and said in a stoner's voice while squinting his eyes, "On the doob, man. Got the munchies, man?"

Marty, in the condition she was, without thinking pointed to her crotch and said, "Period."

The teenage kid, half-embarrassed, said to his buddies, "That guy's weird, let's get out of here." They all got up and left.

Marty sucked down every bit of burger and onion rings, scooping up the last drop of zesty horseradish sauce with her finger. She guzzled half the water, wiped her beard, grabbed her knapsack and headed out the door.

Chapter Seventy-Two

On the way up towards the mountain, an elderly white-haired man, who looked like he had spent a lifetime in the desert and was driving a later model Chevy truck, picked her up on the side of the highway. Marty noticed a sticker on his bumper that read: My other car is a mule. He kept to himself while he hummed underneath his breath, "My Darling, Clementine" all the way up the mountain road to the front entrance of the monastery. She got out, thanked him, and he went on his way. She stopped a second to collect herself and then realized she had her perfume on, the one she wore often with tangerine and citrus essential oils. What could she do?

Two large leather oak trees, like giant stoic monks, stood on either side of the driveway welcoming all visitors. On the right of the oak tree was a large burnished red boulder with a discreet twelve by six-inch brass plate screwed into the boulder that read: Redrock ~ Interfaith Monastery of the Holy ~ Est. 1969.

Marty took a long look up the driveway, took in a deep breath and let out a sigh. And then said out loud with a slight grin, "Do I dare proceed?"

As she made her way up the conifer-lined driveway towards the main building of the monastery, she observed a spectacular pastoral notch that spread over several acres. Bare trees of all sizes stood quietly about the grounds, and along the perimeter of the notch were a host of conifers. Beyond them, craggy red boulders ascended with the mountain landscape. The main building was a two-story stone structure that had a pinkish hue. She knocked on a set of hefty carved oak doors. A moment later, a balding friar with black curly locks on the side of his head greeted her. He was short, round, had a smiley glow on his cherubic face and wore a dark brown habit with a knotted rope around his belly that hung below his waist in Franciscan monk fashion. He said to Marty, "Welcome, brother, what can I do for you?"

Marty, in a deep barreling voice, said, "Hello, brother, I was passing through, making my way to San Francisco, and thought I'd stop in and spend time with my fellow brethren. I'm Brother Thomas."

"Our doors and our hearts are always open, Brother Thomas. I'm Friar Mark, Brother Mark if you will." And then inquisitively asked, "So, what religious order do you serve?"

Taking a shot in the dark at what she remembered from the Spirituality through the Ages course she took at Golden State, Saint Francis of Assisi happened to pop in her head. She hurriedly went through a deduction process trying to figure out what to say. St. Francis…Francisco… She then blurted out, "Franciscan."

Brother Mark's smile got even bigger, and he said warmly, "We are truly brothers, then. So where are you coming from?"

"Back East," Marty quickly shot out.

Brother Mark responded, "Were you in school or at a monastery back there?"

"Yes, I was at Saint Merton," Marty said with complete lack of confidence remembering reading Thomas Merton, who was a Trappist Monk. She was in an unfamiliar world, and maybe she wasn't ready for this, but what options did she have? She tried to remember when she had last been in church. She stopped going after her grandparents died and then it was only occasionally, except on Easter and Christmas. Her father would rather be hunting or even sailing and took Marty along as an excuse not to have to deal with the pomp and circumstance that went along with the obligatory services. She was glad she went with him. "The outdoors is the best church," her father would say. She got that instant feeling about Redrock, like she was in the woods or on the sailboat with her father. It was comforting.

"I didn't know he was canonized." He squinted his eyes in a prying manner. "A learning institution?"

"It's a private college in New York, about a hundred miles north of the city."

"Oh, what did you study?" Brother Mark was well versed in theology, knowing in the back of his mind that Thomas Merton, if that's who she was referring to, had written some interesting literature but was not a saint. Nor had a school been named after him. Nonetheless, he went along with Marty. He felt that the Lord worked in wonderful ways, and each day was a journey to salvation and understanding.

Trying not to fabricate too much she said, "Chemistry and I also took some courses at the culinary academy in Hyde Park."

"Ah, miracles do happen. God knows we can use some help in the food department. You see, our Brother Gregory has a tongue for the word, but not for the cooking. He thinks it's sinful to eat tasty food," Brother Mark said.

"A nourished soul is a happy soul," Marty said, wanting to sound like she had the spirit.

Excited, Brother Mark said, "I can tell we're going to be eating well tonight. I'm sure Brother Gregory won't mind. How long you think you'll be with us?"

Marty responded, "Ahh…a week or two?"

"Stay longer if you like," Brother Mark said.

"Well, thank you, Brother Mark. You sure have some beautiful grounds here," she replied as she looked around in all directions. She saw a variety of religious statues, some that looked like little gnomes and others that were life-sized spread about the grounds, most of them near a bench that was underneath a tree or two or three. It brought her back to the sculpture garden in Portland that overlooked the city. It was her favorite place to go, especially with Roy. It was where she had lost her virginity and where they ate pears off each other's bodies. She wished that she could be there now, a young girl free of all the trouble ahead of her. She drifted off and then heard Brother Mark's voice breaking through her daydreaming.

"Yes, we are gifted through our penance and dedication to the Lord. This used to be all boulders," pointing out across the monastery grounds. "Through the toil of many a layperson, we transformed a pretty inhabitable place into this sanctuary."

Shaking off her own distraction, Marty said, "It's like a heavenly paradise."

"Yes, that it is," Brother Mark looked slightly upward as if he had heard no truer wisdom. He then pointed eastward with his chin and said, "And hell is that way, if you're interested. It's called the Mojave Desert."

Marty could not help but think about the hell she had just been through, but that was her doing. She realized that she had to start mending her ways and make peace with the past. She more than sensed that then. It was not that she feared the law so much as how she began to feel at that moment at Redrock. She was ready for a spiritual cleansing of all her past wrong deeds and deceit as much as she felt justified in the killing she had done. She had a demon inside that needed to be destroyed and maybe by some divine will, it would be. If not, surely, she would perish in hell.

Brother Mark said, "Let's walk the grounds. I'll introduce you to my brethren. Most of us are trained botanists and herbalists."

Marty excitedly said, "Oh!"

"We do grow a fair number of herbs and medicinal plants here. And during the spring and early summer, we gather wildflowers and herbs all along the mountain and down in the desert," Brother Mark remarked.

"Sounds exciting," Marty said, thinking how powerfully aromatic an experience that must be.

"We dry them and also brew various types of herbal elixirs, which we market through our website. Most of our profits go back to our religious communities. Less our operating expenses, of course," Brother Mark said.

Marty got all giddy inside. She loved what she was hearing as if it were music to her ears. She couldn't wait to see the elixirs.

Brother Mark continued, "You probably seen our website, Redrock Herbs?"

"Ah, yes, I believe I have." Marty remembered seeing their site a few times when she did her own elixirs. She had gone out into the desert on occasion herself, though she was more of a novice at it. She drew from some of her books such as *Mastering Herbs, The Herbal Bible* and *The Celestial Herbalist,* which she read religiously. But this was all fascinating to her and excitement welled up inside her.

Chapter Seventy-Three

They stopped at the garden that covered almost a half of an acre of land and butted up close to the main building. Half the garden was for the vegetables and berries that were consumed at Redrock, and the other half was for the herbs and medicinal plants. On the far end of the garden was a twenty-foot-long greenhouse used primarily during the winter months.

Dotted throughout the Redrock grounds were Granny Smith, Pink Lady and Jonagold apple trees, a pear tree, an apricot tree, a peach tree, a plum tree and a lemon tree. Adjacent to the garden running north to west were rows of grape vines.

"The brethren are especially fond of the grape," Brother Mark said and then watched Marty smile.

"And one of our brethren is a beekeeper, and we use the honey to sweeten some of the elixirs, including the cough syrup," Brother Mark offered and then said, "You'll have to come back in the spring when most of the fruit trees are in bloom. It's like you were in heaven, Brother Thomas. It's a heavenly paradise." Then he smiled in chagrin. "I think you said that before."

"From your lips to God's ears," Marty confirmed with a grin.

And then the door to the greenhouse opened and a burly six-foot man wearing the same dark brown habit as Brother Mark, with carrot-orange hair, a red beard and sky-blue eyes, stepped out carrying a basket full of winter greens, a cabbage and a variety of small gold and purple potatoes.

"Ah, Brother Jack, come and meet our new guest," Brother Mark said loudly to Brother Jack. Brother Mark quickly leaned into Marty and out of the side of his mouth whispered, "He's not like us; he's a Benedictine." And then smiled at Brother Jack as he neared. Brother Jack stepped towards them. He had that same smile and glow as Brother Mark. He put down the basket of vegetables, stepped towards Marty and hugged her briefly. Marty was startled.

"Welcome," Brother Jack said in a soft, unassuming voice with a faint French accent.

"Thank you," Marty said in more of her true voice. She was taken by Brother Jack's strength and felt very feminine at that moment. She realized that she had slipped and said in a deeper voice while clearing her throat, "Ah, yeah, I'm Brother Thomas."

Brother Jack shot a look at Brother Mark, reacting to the inflection in Marty's voice.

Brother Mark said, "Brother Thomas is going to cook dinner for us tonight."

Brother Jack picked up the vegetables and said courteously, "I'll put these in the kitchen for you."

Marty replied in a French accent, "*Merci Beaucoup, Frere Jacques.*"

"*Tres Bien*," Jack replied and went his way.

"He was left at our doorstep as a child—we assume by his parents—and he only spoke French. Been with us ever since. Quiet, but a hard worker," Brother Mark spoke with affection.

"Humm…strong like an ox, though," Marty replied.

Brother Mark gently squeezed the back of Marty's arm and then let go and said, "You're a strong fellow, but I can see in your eyes you have a soft and gentle soul."

Brother Mark and Marty walked up the path past the garden that led to a steel door that was the entrance to a hollowed-out tunnel. The door was secured by a lock that opened via a numbered keypad. As he plugged in the numbers, Brother Mark said, "My favorite passage from Corinthians. This way I don't forget."

Marty chuckled more at herself because she was not versed in scripture but had recognized Corinthians.

Chapter Seventy-Four

Once inside, Marty was mesmerized by what she saw. She felt spiritually uplifted. The rocky tunnel was illuminated and sparkled with great intensity. The air she breathed was cool with a taste of mint, oregano, yerba and all kinds of wonderful aromatic herbs. She felt like it was a snowy winter's day underneath the evergreens, as when she spent winter holidays up in Mt. Ranier as a child. On the shelves that ran on either side of the tunnel were a dozen five-gallon glass bottles with spigots at the base, each filled with an elixir. Marty stared at them in wonderment.

"This is called the brew room. Each one of these bottles has its own recipe," Brother Mark stated.

Each bottle had its own distinct color of liquid ranging from a light chlorophyll to a deep licorice and had a large tea bag of herbs inside what Marty thought looked like a bouquet garni. Holding the bags in suspension was a string that ran out through the spout and was wrapped to its neck.

"We do get to share in our own wares, but in little increments. Too much of a good thing can destroy its own essence," Brother Mark said.

"Like too much prayer," Marty said and was surprised at what had just come out of her mouth.

"Indeed, Brother, otherwise we lose sight of our earthly chores. But Redrock is a wonderful place for meditation. I'm sure you'll find that out soon enough," he said.

Further down the tunnel was the wine cellar. There were three fifty-nine-gallon oak barrels on their side that were hoisted about waist high. Brother Mark pointed to each one consecutively, "Pinot, Pinot, Chardonnay."

"No Cabernet?" Marty questioned.

"Why convolute the senses. Keep it simple, keep it pleasantly good and keep it flowing with the finest and most delicate grape," Brother Mark responded with eloquence.

Marty said, "Pinot, I agree. So, where do you do your pressing?"

"We just grow the grapes and then they're trucked to Chateau La Vec over in Santa Clara where they make our wine for us. Brother Gregory oversees the winemaking. It is true that he is a fine herbalist, but sadly most of the wine he made is used on our salads," he said.

"Few are truly gifted in the art of the vine," Marty mused.

On the far wall opposite the entrance next to the wine barrels was an eight-foot-high wrought iron wine trellis that extended the width of the wall. It was two-thirds full of wine bottles marked with their own vintage. Marty smiled with admiration.

"I think the old man is going to charge me a corkage fee when I get upstairs," Brother Mark said and then winked as he pointed his thumb upward. Marty chuckled.

Chapter Seventy-Five

They left the brew room, stepped outside and made a quick left to a modern structure. It was a typical A-frame building with a tin roof. Inside, Marty was immediately introduced to Brother Gregory, a Trappist monk who wore the customary gray habit. He was much more serious than the other brethren, although he did appear to have a glow about him. Leaner and taller than Brother Mark, he had the same curly hair on top of his head, golden brown, almost matching his yellowy-hazel eyes that had flecks of gold in them. When he turned sideways, Marty envisioned a crow. She was taken aback by his looks. She had never seen a person who glowed golden as he did, let alone one who looked like a crow. It was startling.

Marty peered around while Brother Mark and Gregory disappeared to the back room and conversed about her cooking dinner. Brother Gregory was a little territorial but acquiesced. And then the conversation turned to deliveries while she looked around the area where they weighed, packaged and shipped the herbs and elixirs.

Marty became smitten with the mayonnaise jars of various sizes that stored all kinds of herbs, plants and dried flowers mostly labeled in Latin. She recognized names like *Prosopis glandulosa* and *Pectis angustifolia* and *Anemopsis californica*. She immediately thought about how she used to love going to the Chinese herbalist in Portland where she got a kick out of the dried rhinoceros penis. Wondering who the hell would eat or drink a tea made from that?

Brother Samuel, a small-framed African American man of thirty years, stepped in from the back room carrying several boxes that he had prepared for shipping. As a Benedictine monk, he wore a dark brown habit. He saw Marty and nodded and then went back for more. He was fastidious. And then a Browning delivery van pulled up outside. The driver stepped inside and made his presence known with a hello to Brother Samuel, and dropped off and picked up the packages Brother Samuel prepared and left.

On the way from the back room, Brother Gregory glanced over at Marty and said in Latin, "Praepropere, laute, nimis, ardenter, studiose, forente."

Marty tensed up a little since this was the most she had been challenged in the less than an hour she had been at Redrock. From what she could remember from the required Latin courses she took at Golden State, he was saying something about eating too fast and too expensively. Marty nodded to Brother Gregory, and then Brother Mark slipped in from the back room and started towards the door.

Once outside, Brother Mark said to Marty, "He loves to quote Aquinas, especially about gluttony. He's a blessing and a curse at the same time. But we must always love our fellow brethren regardless of their shortcomings." And then let out a sigh.

Brother Mark and Marty began to walk down the pathway towards the main building. Marty felt a surge of happiness. It put a huge smile on her face as she felt a warm glow inside. Redrock was home, at least for a while until it could all be figured out. Her predicament needed ease of mind, contemplation and then a game plan. They passed a life-size statue of Saint Francis of Assisi that was also a birdbath. A finch fluttered in the water and then flew away. Brother Mark felt inspired and said, "You know, Brother Thomas, what we do in life has a ripple effect in other lives."

Marty solemnly nodded and said, "I see what you're saying."

Then Brother Mark quipped, "The Angels made a great acquisition with Pujols."

Marty had no idea what he was talking about and just said, "Yes, I agree."

Chapter Seventy-Six

They stepped onto the back patio just outside the main kitchen. It was tiled in large saltillos and had a massive round wood picnic bench. It had an age and feel as if it were from the biblical era. It was very powerful and masculine, and she knew that all that brethren who sat there must have spoken volumes of passages between courses of food and wine. She wondered if many women had stayed at the monastery over the years. Was she one of only a few? If they knew of her past, they would certainly need to spiritually cleanse the place. She began to rub her hand over the table.

Brother Mark said, "Israeli olivewood. It's about two hundred years old, maybe older."

"Wow, what a patina. It's a beautiful piece," Marty excitedly said.

"From the land of the holy. Never had so much good barbecue in my life as we have had on this table," Brother Mark quipped as he rubbed his round belly.

Brother Mark stepped towards an upright double-stacked smoker that was finished with a rose-colored tile with black cast iron swinging doors. Marty was stunned. She could not believe that monks had it so good—well, at least the ones at Redrock.

"Brother Jack takes care of us pretty nicely. He does plenty of hunting and fishing. I think he uses the mesquite he gets from the desert. It sure makes everything taste good," Brother Mark said.

Brother Mark took her next to a walk-in cooler that was just around back of the patio. He opened the door. Inside was a bevy of hanging carcasses from venison and elk to beef and wild boar.

Brother Mark started to say, "We do our own..."

Marty interrupted him. "Dry aging."

He nodded and showed Marty a chest freezer that was about empty, except for a few packaged cuts of meats like elk shanks, some venison stew meat, a few whole fryers and some rainbow trout that were dated only a week ago. Marty began to creatively come up with ideas for dishes to cook. The Ultimate Chef Show had really exposed her to a lot of innovation as to how to prepare certain foods. She got a grasp of why chefs moved around as much as they do. When she had first started looking at resumes, in her capacity as John's assistant, she couldn't understand it. It seemed unstable, but soon she realized that the more they experienced culinarily, the better chefs they would become.

"There are so many ways to skin a cat," Chef Bubba would say in his Carolinian twang. And that is true, she later realized, with food. For a chef to keep focused on all the different styles and methods of cooking and then devise and prepare a range of foods from appetizers to soups and salads to entrees and desserts on his or her menu is a stunning feat. All your senses must be working in concert, besides having creative ability, skills and knowledge to perform effectively even in the smallest of restaurants where customers are willing to pay for something different or something they could not make at home.

She understood that just because you watch some cooking shows and maybe make some dishes that your friends and family love or even bake the greatest cookies in the world does not mean that you have the breadth or depth to run a five-star restaurant in Hawaii or even some mom and pop café in Cheyenne, Wyoming. Besides having organizational ability, more rather than less, you must have that giddy-up, that everyday strength to want to be able to ride cross-country on a horse so you can deliver the mail, so to speak.

She knew she had some fundamentals in her bag of tricks, especially with her education from Chapman, but she came to the ultimate conclusion that she did not have what it takes to really be a chef. You have to be patient, yet have a sense of urgency, be creative, knowledgeable, organized, efficient with cost control and labor, be an effective leader of staff members and have a tremendous amount of inner strength. You must be able to endure the heat of the kitchen, especially behind the line when it is over a hundred degrees or more at times. She remembered overhearing one of the contestant chefs say one day, "Nothing worse than a hemorrhoid when it's a hundred and ten degrees and a hundred and ten humidity. It's like you have a chili pepper stuck up your ass. You need to walk around with some napkins or corn starch between your cheeks to keep it from chaffing because lotions or creams do no good." She couldn't handle that, as tough as she thought she was.

She could easily cook for the handful or so monks, and they would be pleasantly satisfied, but to do it on a continual basis for countless customers, day-in and day-out with a high degree of satisfaction from them? She knew herself better than that, even with her bipolar disorder that she mostly had a handle on. Anyway, she had more important issues to deal with. *Like, what happens when I must leave Redrock? Certainly, I can't stay here forever. And this beard, I just want to rip it off. I can only imagine what my face will look like with all that glue. But, who am I kidding? I'm not fooling anyone with this get-up. I'd be lucky to last the day without being found out. I bet Brother Mark has me figured already. I wonder if they read the news.*

"Brother Thomas, let's go inside, and I'll show you the kitchen, and then you can have the reins," Brother Mark said.

Chapter Seventy-Seven

They stepped in from the patio and Marty literally freaked out at what captured her attention right away. In the middle of the kitchen and adjacent dining room was a large stone hearth. Oh, the pizza, she smiled, and the flatbreads and French bread and even paella. She held back her excitement, not wanting to seem girlish. Opposite the hearth on the kitchen side was an island with a six-burner range with an oven underneath. Along the wall that butted up against the patio was one continuous row of cabinets with a countertop that had a microwave, a blender, a toaster, a juicer and a five-quart mixer. Above that were more cabinets, and on either side of the cabinets were multi-paned windows looking out at the patio and most of the grounds including the driveway she came up.

"You think this will work for you?" Brother Mark asked.

"It might," Marty said with a wink and a smile.

Off the kitchen next to the massive double-door refrigerator was the walk-in pantry that was loaded to the gills with canned goods, jarred homemade tomato sauce, pickled veggies of all sorts, jarred roasted peppers and various bags of chips, crackers, all types of beverages, including bottled water, beer and a few of the Redrock bottles of wine. And garbage bins on casters filled with all-purpose flour, whole-wheat flour, bread flour, granulated sugar, long-grain rice and pinto beans. Marty thought, they must really like their beans because there must have been at least twenty-five pounds or more. A bunch of men eating beans sure spelled disaster. Maybe in some soup or a cassoulet, but feed them some chili con carne you just might as well go on a drive out of town for the whole day.

Brother Mark then opened the refrigerator and showed Marty all the beverages.

"Brother Jack likes his beer with lunch and dinner. Rabbi likes his fizzy apple juice. Doc needs his tomato juice for his Virgin Marys...hmmm. Brother Samuel prefers the Chardonnay. Brother Gregory takes his tea after his meals, but water will suffice during the meals, and you know what I like," Brother Mark stated.

"Okay," Marty replied. "So, it will just be six of us, then?"

Brother Mark did a quick numbering with his right index counting his left-hand fingers and then sticking up his right thumb and index finger. "There are seven of us, including you. I almost forgot Brother Nui." He looked at his watch and then said, "It's about one-fifteen now. We like to have dinner at four-thirty sharp, so that should give you plenty of time. By the way, do you have your habit with you?"

"No, I had most of my belongings shipped out, so I could travel light," Marty said apologetically.

"Very good idea. You look like we're the same size. Less the belly, of course," Brother Mark said. "Follow me."

Chapter Seventy-Eight

Marty started to go through the kitchen dressed in her brown habit, tasseled at her waist, with her boots on her feet. The first things she did was turn on the oven, find a wine opener and a wine glass, step into the pantry and then open a bottle of the Redrock Pinot Noir. She splashed some in the glass, gave it a swirl, a glance under the light, a sniff and then took a sip of the blessed wine. She swished it in her mouth, held it for a second and then swallowed. Whether or not she had believed in God before, she certainly fell in love with his presence now. She never tasted such divine Pinot in her life. Whether it was the warmth that came up from the desert during the day and then the cool nights or the mineral content of the soil or some blessing from above, all she knew she had just tasted bliss in a bottle. She filled her glass and went outside into the aging room to take out the elk shanks, the venison stew meat and a fryer.

Back in the kitchen she donned an apron, unwrapped the chicken, placed it in the sink and let the water run. She found an onion, a couple of carrots and a bunch of celery. The celery was a little wilted, but she could work with it. She pulled out a small roasting pan, rough-chopped the onion, carrots and celery, the classic *mirepoix,* and tossed it in the pan. She took the chicken from the sink, pulled out the gizzards, split it down the breast and then splayed it out it in the pan with the *mirepoix* and placed it in the oven.

She hunted down a roasting pan large enough to make a combination of braised elk shanks and venison. She peeled another onion and finely chopped it and continued the process with the carrots and celery. She put the roasting pan on top of the range, turned on two burners to medium, added some olive oil and then the finely chopped *mirepoix* and wilted them as she unwrapped the shanks and the stew meat. She seasoned the shanks and stew meat, although they were still a bit frozen, with sea salt and fresh cracked pepper and then dredged them in flour and browned them in the pan over the stove. When that was completed, she poured the remaining Pinot, after she filled her glass again, on top of the meat. She found some boxed chicken stock and added it to the pan and then tossed in a few bay leaves. She hoped there was some fresh thyme in the green-house she could later add to the braising. She put the lid on top, placed it in the oven, and looked at the clock. It was about ten to two. She would be pushing it, but she could pull it off, she felt.

Marty grabbed a beer out of the fridge and her glass of wine, went outside and headed to the greenhouse. She stepped inside the greenhouse. Brother Jack was picking through some greens. She went up to him and handed him the beer. Marty said, "Looks like you could use a cold one."

He looked around, grabbed the beer and toasted Marty's wine glass. "Thanks, cheers." His hands were darkened from the dirt. Marty could see he was in his element.

"I was wondering if you had some fresh thyme. Maybe some cher-vil?" Marty asked.

"I have a little thyme, but no chervil, not till spring," Brother Jack said as he looked Marty in the eyes. He sensed something was different about him. He had a softness, but many of the brethren had that, whether it be compassion or just empathy, but Marty's softness was more gentle, womanly. This new monk even smelled like a woman, Jack thought, as he caught a whiff of her perfume—and such soft hands. What he needs is a few weeks working in the dirt, man him up some. Brother Jack stepped down a row of planters and stopped in front of the herbs. Marty followed.

"Pick what you need," as he pointed at the thyme.

"A few sprigs will do," Marty said and began to pick through the sparse herbs.

He said, "Thank you for the beer," and stepped back over to the greens he was picking through.

"Thank you, Brother Jack," Marty said in response and went back to the kitchen.

Marty made a quick check on the chicken. The skin didn't have much color yet. She was preparing to make chicken stock for the cabbage. The elk and venison needed at least two more hours for the meat to be tender. She decided to bake some biscuits and looked around for a recipe. She thought they had to have a collection of recipes somewhere and shuffled through the drawers. She found a few old index cards that must have been from the 60s, one for shepherd's pie and the other for an ambrosia salad. It called for lime Jello, Cool Whip, walnuts, pineapples and maraschino cherries. How gross, she thought, certainly not the epitome of American cuisine. Try the dry storage. Likely place. She found the *Happy Cook* and a bread-making cookbook, as well as a plastic index card box on one of the shelves. She opened the box, shuffled through the cards and found a buttermilk biscuit recipe. Hopefully, there was some buttermilk.

She got them going, punched out fourteen, two each for all of them, and set aside the raw biscuits on a pan ready to be baked around four o'clock. It was almost three o'clock. Time to add water to the pan of chicken and then boil some water for parslied potatoes. The elk and venison, sautéed cabbage with bacon, parslied potatoes, biscuits and a salad—we need a salad, she reminded herself. And dessert. There was a bag of frozen mixed berries in the freezer. *I'll toss them with some cornstarch, a little sugar and some lemon. Maybe a pinch of cinnamon, put it in a casserole dish and top it with the leftover biscuit dough and sprinkle some cinnamon sugar on top. That'll work. It all has to be timed just right. Everything has to be finished cooking at around four-twenty, so I can get it into the serving bowls. I need salad and dressing. Got to go back out to see Brother Jack for the salad. Who sets the table? Do I set the table? Set the table anyway. Ten minutes, no fifteen minutes for that because I don't know where everything is. And then get the salad. Don't forget the dressing.*

Okay, table is set. It's three-twenty. Okay, boil the potatoes. Cut up bacon, onions and the cabbage. Changed my mind, going to sauté the cabbage. Brown onions in the bacon and then blanch cabbage in the chicken stock and then sauté it with the onions and bacon. Add a teaspoon of sugar and a splash of apple cider vinegar. Season with salt and pepper. We can use the chicken from the stock for chicken salad sandwiches. Bake some fresh homemade bread tomorrow. I wonder if I'll be here long enough to get a sourdough starter going? Now get the salad and don't forget the salad dressing.

Chapter Seventy-Nine

Biscuits go in at four. Need to pull some butter for the biscuits and the potatoes. Need parsley and salad from Jack—it's Brother Jack. He's a nice guy. Quiet, though. Wash salad greens and chop the parsley. Okay everything seems to be working. Drinks, drinks. Who gets the drinks? I guess I do. Need ice and hot water for tea. Tomato juice. Fizzy apple juice for Rabbi. Need to open another bottle of wine. Man, that's some awesome wine. They should turn Redrock into a winery. It would kick ass on 90 percent of all the Pinot out there.

Check the elk and venison. Smells good. Almost tender. I'll season it just before serving. Okay, put in the biscuits. Check the potatoes. Fork tender. Maybe too tender. Take off heat and drain. Reserve the liquid. Add some chopped butter, parsley, salt and pepper. Oops. They're too soft. Turn into mashed potatoes. Find a ricer. Mash away, little sister. Add more butter and some cream. Some more butter, salt and pepper. Tastes good. Ten after four. Almost there. Hope they're a hungry bunch of monks. Hungry Monks and the Hairy Chick. Sounds like some groovy band from the 60s. The beard has to go. Nice idea, Marty. Check biscuits. A few more minutes. Honey would be nice. Didn't Brother Mark say they have a beekeeper? Must have honey. Dry storage. Good, we have some. Put in bowl. Bring to the table with the butter and drinks.

Biscuits are ready. Pull elk and venison. Season. Scoop out potatoes into serving terrine. Add some more butter. Cabbage in serving terrine. Salad ready. Shit! Dressing! A quick vinaigrette. It's four-thirty, they're all coming to the table. Put the braised elk and venison in terrine. Put lids on the serving terrines. Plate biscuits. Ready to go. Oh, pull berry cobbler from oven. Shut off oven. Ready!

Marty removed her apron and then took in a quick breath and stepped into the dining room. Brother Mark wasted no time and introduced Marty to Doc, who was a five-foot-ten man in his early sixties with graying dark hair and brown eyes. He had a face that had seen the world. He looked as if he could have been your family doctor but wore a brown habit.

"Doc was a Doc in his former life," Brother Mark said.

Marty nodded. Then he introduced her to Rabbi, who sat at the table with a walker. He was a slight elderly man, from what she could gather close to eighty, with a full head of short brown hair. He was hunched over a bit but had a pair of lively light blue eyes that were no doubt full of wisdom behind a pair of thick dark-framed glasses. He raised his hand like a Pope would to a crowd and said hello to Marty in a heavy Jewish accent. But what was visibly noticeable was that he wore a gray habit.

"Rabbi spent much time in the abbeys of the Middle East. He was a Rabbi many years ago and then converted to Buddhism and then stumbled upon Jesus. Of course, not literally. He's not quite that old," Brother Mark said casually.

Staring at Brother Mark, Rabbi said, "How do you know who I have met or not met?" And then at Marty, "I hope you enjoy your stay."

"Thank you, Rabbi. And nice to meet you, Doc," Marty responded.

And then Brother Mark introduced her to a very large Hawaiian man who had long black hair that was tasseled and wore a grape-colored habit. "This is Brother Nui; he's from the Islands."

Brother Nui said, "Welcome, Brudder."

Marty nodded and said, "Hello." She figured Brother Nui had an appetite and hoped she had made enough food, but then again Rabbi might not eat as much as everyone else.

Brother Samuel got up and withdrew a gold platter from a cabinet that had a glass carafe accented with gold leaf and eight or so small gold cups while the drinks were poured. Inside the carafe was a translucent liquid with a reddish-brown hue. Brother Samuel passed each brother a small cup and filled it about halfway with the liquid. When everyone was seated, Brother Samuel said a quick, silent prayer to himself while he closed his eyes, and then Brother Gregory started to chant a prayer in Latin while everyone else held up their cup.

Brother Gregory, *"Benedicite."*

And then all the Brothers collectively, *"Benedicite."*

Brother Gregory, *"Edent paupers."*

And then all the Brothers collectively, *"Et saturabuntur, et laudabunt Dominum, qui requirunt eum: vivant corda eorum in saeculum saeculi. Gloria Patri, et Filio, et Spiritui Sancto. Sicut erat in principio, et nunc, et semper, et in saecula saeculorum. Amen."*

All the Brothers made the sign of the cross and then drank the liquid from the gold cups. Marty picked up her cup and then Brother Mark, who sat next to Marty, said to her, "It's our special elixir, *labium diabolus*. Go ahead, I think you'll find it refreshing."

Marty sipped the elixir. She gurgled it a little and observed that it was slightly viscous and initially came off sweet and peppery like a cinnamon candy and then had a sagey menthol nose. It finished bitter, similar to Campari liqueur. And then she drank the rest. "Hmm, very nice," Marty said and felt an instant clarity and uplift in her spirits.

"It also works as an aperitif," Brother Mark said noticing the effect on Marty. "Let's partake of the dinner, shall we?"

The salad was passed around, and then Brother Gregory lifted the lid to the potatoes. He noticed the melted butter and said to Marty in a remonstrative voice, "How much butter did you use?"

"Two sticks," Marty replied.

Brother Gregory sighed, "Oh, my!" And almost passed out in his chair. "That's too much, my goodness," as he gasped for air.

Doc asked, "Are you all right?" He poured a glass of water for Brother Gregory. "Drink it up, you look flush."

"I'm okay, but we must be careful with our intake of butterfat. It's a sin," Brother Gregory said faintly but excitedly.

Marty thought, wait till he eats the biscuits.

Brother Mark said, "We'll go easy next time." And shot a quick glance at Marty.

Marty felt a little embarrassed.

Brother Samuel took the lid off the braised elk and venison and just stared at it.

Brother Nui stood up from his chair and stared at it and said to Marty, "Today is Friday."

"Is it?" Marty responded.

Brother Samuel said, "It's Friday. We're supposed to have fish."

Brother Nui said to Marty, "Do you practice some lesser form of Catholicism?"

"I'm sorry, brothers. Um, we have some chicken I can serve," Marty tried to appease them.

Brother Gregory said, "Friday, we have fish. Don't we have some smoked trout somewhere?"

Brother Jack said quietly, "It's frozen."

"Chicken will have to do. Thank you, Brother Thomas," Brother Mark said to Marty and then looked over at Brother Gregory across the table from him and put a finger up to his lips as to say "Shush." Brother Gregory closed his eyes for a second and said a quick prayer. He was obviously agitated.

"I bet he didn't even make the angel food cake," Brother Samuel added to the insult. Brother Gregory shot Samuel a look of dissatisfaction.

Chapter Eighty

Marty got up and hurried into the kitchen while the brothers ate their salads. She washed her hands at the sink and said to herself, "This is a serious bunch of guys. Fish on Friday. I should have known that. The Remys ate fish on Friday."

As Marty grabbed a bowl out of the cupboard, Doc came into the kitchen and put his hand on Marty's shoulder. He said, "Everything looks good. And ah, Rabbi can't eat cabbage, gives him flatulence. I'll heat up some frozen peas for him." He then went into the freezer.

Marty said, "Could you add a couple of handfuls more. I'm putting together a consommé with the chicken and broth. Little peas will work nicely."

"Sure," Doc said obligingly.

Marty pulled the chicken out of the stock and placed it in the bowl. It was still a little hot as she pulled the meat off the bones. Marty felt bad about causing the brothers grief. But nothing was worse than creating a disruption at mealtime, especially with men; they seem to turn into boys. She remembered all those times she spent with her all-male cousins on vacations and holidays. Not one single female cousin. Seems like old times with the Brothers. Oh well, they'll get over it.

"So, what was in that elixir, Doc?" Marty asked.

"Oh, the *labium diabolus*, the devil's lips. It's more of a liqueur that has everything including the kitchen sink, I believe. It has some *Yerba mansa*, honey, mint, nettles, raspberry leaf, the devil's lips and even some hops. A few other ingredients."

"What's the devil's lips? I never heard of it," Marty asked.

"It's a rare plant that Brother Gregory found down in the desert. It's not even officially classified. But it grows in the most obscure places.

The only way to get to them is to stick your hand between some rocks and feel around. A few of the brothers have been bitten by rattlesnakes. Always need to carry the anti-venom. And you can't go it alone. It's partially why the plant is called devil's lips, besides being shaped similar to lips and having a scarlet red color."

"Why do you say partially?" Marty asked and put some chicken in the soup bowl and added some stock.

"Besides the obvious, it has some addictive qualities. That's why we only drink but a small cup at a time. Most of it is locked up," Doc said.

"Mother Nature is sure interesting," Marty mused.

"God and his funny tricks," Doc retorted.

Marty laughed, "Isn't that the truth?"

"Everything in moderation, you know," Doc said.

"Lead us not into temptation," Marty said coyly.

"But deliver us from evil," Doc said and smiled. "We better get back in there."

They returned to the dining room with the bowls of chicken soup with peas and the peas for Rabbi, and everyone enjoyed the meal. Even Brother Gregory lost himself in delight and had an extra helping of potatoes.

Chapter Eighty-One

As Marty went into the communal bathroom, Brother Samuel walked out carrying some folded magazines.

He said, "These magazines have some nice scenery." And then winked. As he did, he noticed Marty's beard had peeled a little loose from her upper cheek. "Is that a fake beard?" he asked very inquisitively.

"Ah, yeah. I wear it because I have a condition called pseudofolliculitis. I get this really bad rash from shaving. So I wear the beard to cover it up," Marty said.

"Yeah, pseudofolliculitus barbi. I remembered that. They taught us about it in the Army. The brothers get that once in awhile. The bumps from ingrown hairs. You should have Doc take a look at it," Brother Samuel said.

As Marty stepped in towards the bathroom said, "I'll be okay."

"If you ever need some scenery," Brother Samuel said as he lifted the magazines up towards her and then he went on his merry way saying to himself, "Pseudofolliculitus barbi. I haven't heard that term in over twenty years. Hah."

Marty looked at herself in the mirror and then reapplied the beard to her face and said out loud, "Phew, that was a close one. Good thing I remembered." She thought about when Roy had an inflammation on his testicles. The doctor told him he should stop waxing them because that's what caused the problem. Marty thought that's when he figured he was gay since the doctor was probing around his balls and he got an erection. She then caught a whiff of the bowel movement Brother Samuel must have taken. "Jeez, he needs to eat some fruit. Wow, that's bad!"

Chapter Eighty-Two

Marty went into one of the several stalls, closed the door, pulled off the habit, pulled down her underwear and sat on the toilet seat. She took in a deep breath while holding her nose, held it for a second and let it out and then repeated it. She said to herself, "We going to get through this, you crazy girl?" And then urinated like she never had. *Was it that I haven't peed all day or was it that elixir we had? That was actually pretty good stuff. I can see why they limit its intake.* She felt lucid, relaxed and uplifted all at once, recalling the sensation she had at the dinner table. *I wonder if they sell it to their customers? It would be nice to get a supply of it somehow.* She got up off the seat, did her customary wipe and checked the growth of her pubis. Getting a little long, Miss Shaggy, time for a trim, she said to herself. And then she pulled up her underwear and donned her habit.

Marty left the bathroom and went into the library where there were two walls of lined bookshelves. One wall had volumes of books on the major religions ranging from Catholicism to Judaism to Buddhism, as well as various versions of the Bible including the Old and New Testament, the Torah, and others on the Ancient Egyptians and the medieval era. She saw books about Pope Gregory, Thomas Aquinas, Jesus, Mother Teresa and even Thomas Herton's *Houses of the Holy,* which she once read. She eyed an interesting title on one book, *Salvation For A Soul* by W.S. somebody or other. She noticed that in the ones she looked at, inside the jacket cover was a signature and date by all those who had read the book. Some dated back over a hundred years. But to her amazement, on the other wall were books strictly dedicated to cooking, spirit brewing, botany, herbology and a book on stone masonry. She was especially amused by one book entitled *The Official Vatican Cookbook II.* Apparently, there was a version I floating around somewhere. There was even a copy of *Mastering the Art of French Cooking*.

While she sat down and started to read an herbology book, Brother Nui walked in the library carrying a folded massage table. He said to Marty, "Nice dinner, Brudder Thomas. Very tasty. You wouldn't happen to know how to make poi poi, would you?"

"No. What's that?" Marty asked.

"We make it back home in Hawaii. It's like a pudding made from the taro plant," Brother Nui said.

"You like it, then?" Marty asked.

"Ah, it's so good," Brother Nui said with excitement. "But if you ever get bound up, eat plenty of that, and you'll be clean as a whistle." And then he whistled as he set up the massage table.

Marty smirked and then asked, "What do you have going on?"

"I give the brudders their massages. I do one every night. Would you like to have one?"

He rubbed her shoulder and Marty tensed up.

"Nah, that's okay," Marty said with slight annoyance.

"I think you might have what we in Hawaii call lackanookie. Where you get all tensed up. And a massage can't cure it if you know what I mean. I get it from time to time," Brother Nui said coyly.

"What do you do for it?" Marty asked.

"I have a girlfriend down in the Valley I get to see occasionally. A pretty little gal from Guadalajara. She has a friend who's single. I'm going to see her tomorrow. Do you want to come?" Brother Nui asked.

"I'll let you know," Marty sounding a little condescending and then said, "Oh, I get it, lack of nookie. You're not celibate?" Questioning Brother Nui.

"Not if I can help it," Brother Nui grinned from ear to ear.

And then out of the blue Marty heard this incredible sound that seemed to echo throughout the whole monastery.

Brother Nui quickly said, "It must be six o'clock. I forgot. All the brudders stop what they're doing, and we all chant together for a full hour. If you have your own passage, feel free to stay."

Brother Nui knelt on the floor and put his hands together as if to pray and began to chant, *"Ho `o nani ka Makua, mau, Ke Keiki me ka Uhane, no, Ke Akua mau. Ho `o mai ka `I, pu, Ko ke ia ao, ko ke la ao, Amene."*

Brother Nui looked over at Marty and head gestured for her to begin. She quickly knelt on the floor and began to hum in a chanting way, *"Frère Jacques, frère Jacques, Dormez-vous? Dormez-vous? Sonnez les matines! Sonnez les matines! Din, dan, don. Din, dan, don."*

Brother Nui looked over at Marty again and rolled his eyes, thinking he had never heard that chant before, but it sounded familiar.

As Marty got into a rhythm, she heard Brother Mark chanting, "I believe in God, the Father almighty, Creator of heaven and earth, and in Jesus Christ, his only Son, our Lord, who was conceived by the Holy Spirit, born of the Virgin Mary…"

And Brother Gregory chanted in his customary Latin, *"Gloria Patri, Filio, et Spiritui Sancto: Sicut erat in principio, et nunc et semper, et in saecula sæculorum. Amen."*

She vaguely heard Hebrew coming from Doc who must have been with Rabbi and a beautiful classical guitar that reverberated through the monastery halls, which Marty assumed was being played by Brother Samuel. All in all, Marty was in awe. It reminded her of the time when she was at the Newport Jazz Festival listening to several fusion bands. Each player in tune with their own rhythm as they collectively played into one harmonious funky sound. She was tickled with the spiritual twangs of every verse and chord she heard. In that moment in time, she would have given up all of what and who she was for that feeling she had

323

in her soul, regardless of her lack of religion. An hour passed faster than Marty would have imagined. She felt as if she had just finished a two-hour massage with her body and mind in a totally elated yet relaxed state.

Brother Nui slowly stood up and asked Marty, "What was that you were chanting?"

"Oh, something in French I learned a long time ago," she responded aloofly.

"You might want to try the Apostle's Creed. It's easy to remember, anyway. You know it, don't you?"

"I think so?" Marty said, unsure of herself.

"What do you mean? You don't know it? What kind of Franciscan are you?" Brother Nui asked sarcastically.

"Not a very good one, I'm sorry to say," Marty said sheepishly.

Brother Nui grabbed a book off the shelf, opened it up and handed it to Marty and said, "This should help."

Marty pursed her lips in gratitude and said, "Thank you, Brother Nui."

Brother Nui draped a sheet over the massage chair and then said, "No problem, brudder. You sure you don't want a massage?"

Marty said, "Some other time." *All he has to do is get a feel of my breasts and I'm out of here.*

Chapter Eighty-Three

Marty was given the room next to Brother Gregory. There was not much privacy since there was no door. The room was sparse, less an eight-inch wooden cross with a gold and black garnet rosary draped over it, a chair and a bureau. And a bed that was a little firm, but she did not care; it was somewhere to lie her tired head and body. She closed the light and slipped underneath the covers. She thought about taking her habit off, but it was cold, even underneath the covers. She then had a sudden urge to thank God for her respite at the monastery. "Huh, life is sure funny," she said to herself. It's so peaceful she thought as she started to slowly drift into a quiet sleep with the scent of frankincense, myrrh, and cedar beginning to permeate her senses. But, as she did, Brother Gregory began to chant. It seemed like right in Marty's ears since he was in the next room. He kept chanting for what she hoped would be only ten minutes, but it turned into an hour and then two hours and longer. He was naming the virtues: chastity, temperance, charity, diligence, patience, kindness, humility—in Latin, *"Castitas, temperantia, caritas, industria, patientia humanitas, humilitas."*

The sleeplessness reminded her of when she was back in Lake Oswego and Rex the neighbor's dog had been left outside all the time. It would bark all night long. It kept her awake many nights, especially since she was a light sleeper. And it wasn't the dog's fault. It was the owner who should have been aware that the barking most likely would disturb others in the neighborhood, even though there were but a few houses on her block at the time. She questioned, are people just not cognizant of others? *Oh well, poor Harold, hopefully you're resting eternally. But, you should have taken better care of Rex and given him a little more attention. A bone once in a while, a rub on the neck or even a little crunchy treat. But no, you left him alone to be by his neurotic, lonely self. That's why he barked all night and then you took it out on him.*

Why is it that when you most need the sleep, there is something that always keeps you awake? And tonight was no different with Brother Gregory. Maybe he needed a little attention himself. Take that habit off yours, put on some real clothes, go to the grocery store and talk to some fellow shopper. There is nothing more gratifying than having a conversation with a stranger since there is no other obligation than the conversation itself, she wanted to tell him. The chanting was driving her crazy. She could not sleep a wink, nor think too much about anything else other than shutting him up. *God. I'm about to lose it.* She was wide awake now and tired as hell. She wondered what time it was. There were no clocks around. "Oh, how I miss my Pearl," she sighed. It was probably close to one, she figured. *I hope he goes to sleep soon.* "Oh God, please." But he continued.

That's when Marty got up and made her way into the communal bathroom. She looked at her face in the mirror. She felt as if she were looking at a ghost underneath the hood of the habit. The rings that lay heavy under her eyes were the color of port wine, which spooked her a bit. She then looked inside a linen closet and grabbed a towel and a pair of small scissors. She draped the towel on top of one of the sinks and began trimming her beard. She then folded the towel with the trimmings inside, walked over to one of the toilets and flushed the trimmings down the drain. She noticed the chanting had stopped. Okay, Brother Gregory must have gone to sleep by now, as well as the other brothers. They were hard workers, so a good sleep was needed for tomorrow's labor.

Marty sat on a bench listening to a grunge version of *Come Together* on her MP3 with one of the earplugs. In case one of the brothers stepped in out of the blue, she could at least be forewarned. She slipped her manly underwear off, placed them into her habit pocket, and with legs spread apart, trimmed her pubis, catching the trimmings underneath the bench with the towel. It had been a while since she even had a decent wax job. Although her pubic hairs were quite fine, she had felt a little woolly. After she was finished with her pruning, she had an urge to clean the bathroom. She got a little grossed out about the bathroom being used by so many men. She found a bucket, scrub brush, rubber gloves and, much to her chagrin, a bottle of botanical cleanser. But then, why wouldn't they use non-chemical agents? Just made sense with all the herbal activity going on.

They have it pretty good here. Beautiful grounds. It's especially peaceful. They really live well. They get to indulge in elixirs, fine wine, good food, and they're allowed to have a little extra-curricular activity if they want. If I were a man, this wouldn't be a half bad situation, outside of the late-night chanting. Would need to brush up on the bible studies, though. She filled the bucket with warm water, splashed in some cleanser, donned the rubber gloves, pulled up her habit close to her thighs and retied it with her rope. She draped the towel on the floor, knelt on it and began scrubbing the floor.

Marty had finished about half of the bathroom floor when all that she had been through during the day finally caught up with her. She literally passed out on the towel and fell fast asleep. A funny thing happened, though. She had forgotten to put back on her underwear. She was on her side with one knee practically up against her chest, which exposed her freshly coiffed vagina. Moments later Brother Jack slipped into the bathroom to urinate. He had just gotten back from wild boar hunting, which is done at night. He did not even see Marty on the floor.

Brother Jack, wearing a pair of jeans, a blue flannel shirt, an orange vest, wool cap, and a pair of hiking boots, turned from the bathroom stall as he heard Marty groan in her sleep. With his pants down by his knees and penis in his hand, he caught a glimpse of her crotch. Completely taken by surprise, he shimmied closer to her. As he did, Marty awoke slightly. The only thing she saw was Jack's enormous penis in her bird's eye view. His member started to inflate as he looked up at Marty's face and then down again at her vagina where he could see her labia and clitoris popping out. Both became aroused at what they could not believe was occurring.

Jack shimmied towards Marty. She gently put his enormous penis in her hand and then stroked it as if were some precious pet. She then took his monstrous cock into her mouth. Brother Jack began chanting in a low murmur with his eyes closed. Marty was enjoying what had just happened by some miracle. She could have given up, God knows what would have happened. Jack pulled her up from the floor and then led Marty into the showers as if he were some stag and she a doe ripe for the mating. He took her robe off and lifted her t-shirt. He caressed her breasts gently and then kissed her neck while she slipped off his vest and unbuttoned his shirt. He then slipped off his boots and the rest of his clothes as Marty turned on the showers and they began to have intercourse underneath the pulsating water and steam. After a half an hour, the water started to run a little cooler, so they stopped and turned the showers off. Brother Jack kept caressing her fleshy, yet firm backside and then had her turn around so he could take her from behind. He was slow and gentle.

Afterwards, while they dressed, not a word was spoken between them. They kissed each other goodnight and went their way, quietly like church mice scurrying back to their rooms. When Marty lay her head down on the pillow, she realized all the danger she was in. Although exhilarated by the sex she had had with Brother Jack, she felt guilty as sin because she loved John and missed him dearly, but what was she to do? She had to, as the saying goes, give it up or who knows what would have happened, but his penis, my God! She might have been tossed out of the monastery in the middle of the night and where would she have gone then? Tears trickled from her eyes as she lulled herself to sleep thinking of John, his strength, his handsome face and his tender touch.

Chapter Eighty-Four

The following morning, she woke to the aroma of freshly brewed coffee and caught some faint activity from the kitchen with wafts of eggs and bacon. She got up and made her way to the restroom where brother Nui was just coming out of the shower with nothing but a towel wrapped around his waist, a soap on a rope hanging from his neck and a bottle of shampoo in his hand. He said quietly, "Good morning, brudder. How'd you sleep?"

Marty groggily said, "Morning, but why are you so quiet?"

Brother Nui said, "It's the Sabbath. No talking all day."

Marty rolled her eyes and then went into a stall to pee. She sat there and realized she was sore all over, especially her vagina.

Marty washed her hands and face and brushed her teeth and then walked a little bow-legged towards the kitchen where Brother Gregory had a modest meal of scrambled eggs and bacon, oatmeal, dry toast and a scant tumbler of orange juice ready for everyone. She was feeling like she had a hangover between the lack of sleep, the huge pummeling her pussy had taken and her period, which was still lingering. She said to herself, "Boy, I could use some of that *labium diabolus*." Everyone was relatively quiet and somber at the table as they ate their meal. It was their ritual not to speak on Saturdays, nor did they work, other than the meal preparation. Most of the day was for reflections, prayer, and meditation, except for the exercise period at ten o'clock.

All the brothers met on the patio about an hour after breakfast for their daily exercise. The sun shined bright and there was a slight cool breeze coming off the mountaintop. Brother Gregory and Mark wore their habits while Brother Samuel had on a pair of spandex shorts and top with a pair of knee-high cotton socks and some running shoes. Brother

Jack wore a pair of overalls with a t-shirt underneath and a pair of boots. Doc wore a blue warm-up suit and some fashionable track shoes. Rabbi had on a pair of gray sweat pants and top and white gym shoes. And Brother Nui wore just a muumuu around his waist and was barefoot as he led the exercise quietly without music, which he did every other day. Marty wore her habit and boots, joining in as she had the previous day.

But that day was a little different. Brother Nui started the exercise with some basic stretching and then some general calisthenics and then worked up to where everyone used a Hula Hoop, first gyrating the plastic circle around their bellies for a minute and repeating the procedure and then using their hips for a minute and repeating again, except for Rabbi, who lifted some light hand-held weights outward and above his head. And then everyone exercised their arms, which were extended outward. They gyrated the hoop around the right wrist and then the left for about thirty seconds each and repeated it several times. Marty was working up a good sweat, which just happened to ease the soreness in her body. They then lay on their backs and lifted their right legs and gyrated the hula hoop around their ankles. They repeated the procedure once and then switched to their left legs. Brother Nui happened to glance at Marty's smoothly shaven legs as she attempted the exercise. She was having a little difficulty in keeping the hoop gyrating around her ankle. They all took a break. Brother Nui stepped towards Marty and said, "It takes a little getting used to, but you get the knack of it sooner or later."

Marty said, "I remember as a kid having one of these. We just used to spin it around our hips."

Brother Nui stepped closer to Marty and then whispered in her ear, "You're not a man, are you?"

Marty shook her head no and said in a faint voice, "No, I'm not what I appear to be. And I'm afraid I've done wrong."

He whispered back, "Haven't we all done wrong, yet who are we, really?" He then went back in front of everyone and positioned his hula hoop around his belly. Everyone followed suit. He started gyrating the hoop and then extended his right leg forward while continuing to rotate the hoop around. They did that for thirty seconds and repeated it several more times and then switched to the left leg.

After the exercise, Brother Mark brought out some beverages and then Marty had a private conversation with Brother Nui about how she was trying to find herself. That's why she was at Redrock. And then the conversation switched to Brother Nui and how he had found his true calling in the brotherhood after doing time in prison for armed robbery, so he was highly empathetic, although he didn't quite get to know Marty's full story or why she would be in disguise. And then they began talking about herbs and of course the *diabolus labium*. Brother Nui remarked on how they have a similar plant in Hawaii called the king's thistle, which grows underneath the water on the atolls. It has similar properties to the devil's lips. Marty found that not only interesting but very intriguing.

Chapter Eighty-Five

Nighttime arrived slowly, and Marty could not have been more re-lieved. She was very tired and desired much-needed sleep as she lay on the cot she had set up in the monastery kitchen. She was also trying to avoid exposing herself to more risk. She knew Brother Jack would come sniffing for her the way he was giving her the looks all day, without one single word. She began to ruminate about needing a little more time to let things cool down in Los Feliz, so she could figure out what to do, alt-hough she knew what to do. She wasn't quite ready to handle the intensi-ty of her problem. The vagaries of chance had brought her to the monastery looking for a small respite, but now, she was stuck with a horny monk whose massive cock was too much for one woman to handle. Why did she have to be so sexually desirable?

Later that night, roughly at the same time as the previous night, Brother Jack went looking for Marty in the bathroom as expected. He was hoping to repeat the pleasures that he had been thinking about all day long. She was not there. He remembered her saying something earlier to Brother Mark about setting a cot up in the kitchen to sleep. So he silently found his way to the kitchen through the darkness of the monastery. She was fully asleep. He gently nudged her, and she softly awoke, caressing his arm. He wanted to lie next to her, but Marty shook her head and pointed out the window towards the greenhouse. She got up, put her boots on, and they slipped out the kitchen door, across the patio and into the greenhouse.

Once inside, Marty pulled her underwear down towards her knees and lifted her habit and propped herself against the bench. Brother Jack took her and turned her around. She got it. He liked it from behind. She turned around, placed her hands on the edge of the bench, arched her back and stuck her rear end up towards Brother Jack. He took her from behind for what seemed like an hour. Needing desperately to sleep, her head bobbed back and forth until she noticed the St. Francis of Assisi statue. It was odd that his eyes glowed like an owl's, a golden yellow. But then again, she hadn't seen it the night before. Brother Jack finally let out a slight moan and then a sigh. Then he pulled up his long johns and went straight out the greenhouse door without even a kiss or a goodnight.

Marty shook her head and said, "Typical male. Sleep well, my brother."

Marty slowly pulled up her underwear and readjusted her habit and stepped outside. Suddenly, she saw St. Francis of Assisi's eyes start moving towards her. She got spooked and then she heard, "Brother Thomas." Her pace quickened as she tried to make her way back into the kitchen. "Brother Thomas, it's Brother Gregory."

Marty's heart almost exploded from fear, then she stopped and turned around to see Brother Gregory, with his hood over his head and his yellowy-golden eyes beaming brightly. "Beautiful night, isn't it?" he said.

Marty, shaking from fright, "A little cold."

In a suspicious manner, Brother Gregory asked, "So tell me, Brother, what do you find to be the most poignant in Exodus?"

Marty remembered the quick religious quotes on the calendar in the kitchen she had read before she went to sleep and responded, "Thou shall not kill." She was proud of herself.

"Yes, indeed. Exodus 20:13. And why is that?" Starting to grill her at this point.

"Because you would be taking away God's will."

"And why is that not a good thing?"

"Fuck, he is hitting me up hard," she pined. "Because he is the Lord."

Deadly Recipe

"Yes, he is, isn't he? And it's his prerogative," Brother Gregory said, becoming a little snider. "You know what passage in Exodus is important to me?"

"What's that?" Marty sheepishly asked.

"Exodus 20:16." He paused waiting for Marty to respond and since she didn't, he continued, "You shall not give false testimony against your neighbor."

"Yes, I agree."

"Yes. Suppose on a nice suburban street, a mailman drops by a pretty little housewife's place to give her, her mail and makes himself at home, and it happens frequently and often. What do you think the neighbors would say?"

"She's having an affair."

"Precisely, but what if it wasn't the wife, suppose it was the husband who was at home. Maybe he runs a business out of the house. What would the neighbors say then?"

"Yes?" Marty got the feeling it was Brother Gregory who was looking in at the greenhouse only minutes ago. With his golden eyes glaring. She flushed with anxiety.

"But maybe the mailman was giving advice on the Clearinghouse Sweepstakes, but then again he could be having some beverages with a friend watching a women's volleyball tournament. But maybe they were fornicating lustfully."

"That's true," she said, cringing inside. *That's it; I'll tell him the truth about me, so I don't have to hear any more of the preaching and then go on with my life. What life? Hopefully, I can go back to bed and get a good night sleep. Shit, I'd be lucky to get another two hours. Oh God, I need my bed with the down pillows, so I can get at least nine hours of sleep.*

Brother Gregory said, "You see, it's important that one have one's story straight about what one may perceive to be immoral activities before one spills the beans, so to speak. Otherwise?"

"Otherwise, unintended consequences may occur," Marty responded.

"You're wise, Brother Thomas. We wouldn't want to cast a shadow over innocent victims. That's sinful. And that's why Exodus 20:16 should be understood for all its nuances, beyond its simplistic message."

"Sage words to be heeded, Brother Gregory," Marty said.

Brother Gregory took in a deep breath of the cool night air and then looked up to the starry sky. He said, "Enough of the lessons."

"Excuse me, brother, but I think I'll go back inside. It's a little chilly."

"Such a divine sight. Good night, Brother Thomas," as he continued to look upward and proudly smiled at his dutiful accomplishment with Marty.

Marty was relieved that she got away relatively unscathed. She quickly brushed her teeth in the kitchen sink and lay down on her makeshift cot. It was cold in that part of the kitchen, and she huddled herself and let out a little shiver. She knew he knew; that's why the sermon on Exodus. He must think that Brother Jack was gay, then. "For God's sake," she whispered. So he must think that I am too, she thought as she continued to ponder the situation. *This is not how this was supposed to have worked out. I'm making my situation worse.* If she hadn't given in to Brother Jack, maybe she wouldn't be in this dilemma, but his penis was so...enormous! Brother Jack could have told on her. And now she had to contend with Brother Gregory. No more meeting with Big Jack, she thought as she giggled from the sensation in her crotch. "Damn he's big," she blurted out and then fell fast asleep, smiling.

That following night while Marty was asleep, Brother Gregory came to visit her. He nudged her ever so slightly. She awoke, "Brother Gregory, what is it?"

"Let's you and I go into the greenhouse," he said delicately.

Fully awakened now, Marty said in a questioning tone, "No?"

Brother Gregory pressed closer to her and gingerly spoke. "A mortal man has needs. I have a palate of desire for you and must have your flesh upon my flesh. My loins ache for your tender rump."

"It's not what you think, Brother Gregory." And in her true voice, she quickly said, "I'm a woman."

Brother Gregory was thoroughly confused, looked upward and said, "Lord, forgive me, for I know not what I have done."

"I'll leave tomorrow. I'm sorry," Marty said apologetically.

"But you and Brother Jack?"

"Yes, Brother Jack and I," nodding her head.

"Then? But your warm glowing eyes when they looked into mine. And your lips, so soft. I wanted you from the first time I saw you. I knew in my mind it was sinful, but my heart desired you. Every bit of you. I don't care if it is love perverse, or why you are here, just that you are here."

Trying to snap him out of it, she said, "Hey, Brother Gregory, it will be okay." This cloistered life sure had gotten to this boy. He was sex-starved and needs a cold shower, she thought. A long one.

What they did not know was Brother Jack was watching from the other side of the kitchen, behind a wall under darkness. He stood there motionless. He so desired Marty. He had fallen in love with her. No matter his faith in God and the vow of celibacy he took, it could not compare with all the emotions he had for Marty just then. It took all his might not to run over to Brother Gregory and beat him to the ground, maybe even kill him. That's how much rage he felt. He was red hot angry. If he had a leek, he would have violated him mercilessly.

And then Brother Gregory got very serious, "I don't know who you are and what you are doing here, but you will have to leave in the morning. Stay for breakfast and then go. You understand?"

"Yes, and I'm truly sorry," Marty said.

"Oh, you pernicious whore, may you be damned to purgatory," Brother Gregory spoke with vehemence as he seethed. Then he composed himself the best he could and went back towards his room. Marty just sat on the side of her cot doubled over with gut-wrenching anxiety.

Chapter Eighty-Six

The following morning after breakfast Marty was in the kitchen peeling the potatoes she wanted to leave for their evening meal. She thought it funny that Brother Gregory was not at breakfast; perhaps he was embarrassed by what had happened the night before. So she pondered her stay at Redrock. Although brief, it had been an odd and a most peculiar experience.

She stared at Brother Jack in the garden toiling away and preparing it for the spring planting. He was such a strong, strapping man with his curly carrot hair and red beard that shown bright in that morning sunlight. She thought it funny that she and Jack had been lovers. He was so different from any of the other men, and of course, Dominika and all the others she had ever been involved with. It was so spontaneous, that night she saw his blessed penis, so large and fleshy. And then he took her from behind as he had every night, except the one time when they both made love facing each other. He had looked her in the eyes and told her that he loved her. She was not expecting that. His forlorn feelings would go unrequited.

Suddenly Marty felt a bit uneasy and was flushed. She quickly bent over the wastebasket and heaved up right on top of the potato peels. Stood up straight and then heaved again. She washed her mouth off in the sink and then took a drink of water. She thought it best to empty the trash and pulled the half-full trash bag out of the wastebasket, twirled the neck of the bag tight and then tied it into a knot. Marty made her way outside towards the trash bin and tossed it, and then walked towards Jack who was standing there with a wicker basket of spinach he had been picking.

Jack said, "Baby spinach," as he handed the basket to her and gave Marty a grimace.

She slipped him a short note saying that she would miss him and was so thankful to have met him, and that he would be forever in her heart. She signed it "Love, Marty." And then she said, "I'm leaving," and curtly smiled as she made her way back to the kitchen in the brief warm glow of the sun.

Looking at her from behind, Brother Jack solemnly said, "I know," and slipped the note in his pocket.

Back at the sink, Marty grabbed a strainer and began to rinse the baby spinach. She suddenly blurted out, "Baby!" She had come to the sharp and concise realization that she was pregnant. She was elated and then asked, "What am I to do, now?" She had been on the lam for killing Chef Bubba and who knows if they were after her for Chef Johnson, Chef Matt Cumatos, Stoner maybe and what if they re-opened Dominika's case—but they had their killer locked up for that murder, fortunately for her. It was time to leave. Certainly, she could not stay at the monastery.

Hopefully, one day she could right the wrongs she did in the past. That would come in time, *but I just need a chance,* she whispered to herself. Her heart felt purer in ways, cleaner, but she would have to work on her mind, on those little neuroses that would pop up and cause havoc and destruction from time to time. She hoped the elixir she shared with the brothers would help that, keep her somewhat whole. She just needed to get the devil's lips some way, somehow, so she could brew her own. Taking some from them was not an option.

Marty truly loved it at Redrock. Though it was not her preferred way of life, she appreciated the natural things that the monastery had to offer—the solitude, the peace and harmony, the garden, the herbs, the wine and now her baby to be and all the love she had experienced, and the love that Brother Jack gave so much of. She'd take everything she had experienced from the brothers. Although brief, this sojourn was a blessing. How gentle and kind they were, and the spiritual lessons she learned, and even Brother Gregory with all his chanting and didactic sermons. She would begin anew more virtuous, more giving, and never again take another life out of lust or greed or jealousy or anger unless necessary for self-preservation, she promised.

After she peeled the last potato, she cleaned up and went into the bathroom. She took the habit off and put on her khakis, flannel shirt, boots, and coat. She looked herself in the bathroom mirror and then peeled off the beard and picked off the glue from her face. It was a little red, but she was happy to take it off. She donned the Angels cap and then went back inside the kitchen and looked out the window. Brother Jack was not around, and she thought it best to not make a scene. Who knows what the others might be thinking.

She stopped in Brother Mark's office. When he saw her, he said, "There's the pretty woman I assumed you were." Marty humbly smiled and thanked him. He offered to give her a ride down the mountain, but Brother Gregory had taken one of the vehicles down into the desert to go gather herbs and Doc had taken Rabbi to the clinic in town for his monthly checkup. She started to get choked up but held back the tears as she said her goodbye. Brother Mark gave her a small going away gift, a little package. As he handed it to her, he said with some sadness and great sincerity, "This is something that was given to me by my wife, many, many lives ago, when I was in medical sales. I think you may find it useful given your nose for things."

"Thank you," Marty said and then asked with keen interest, "What happened to her?"

He sullenly said, "She died from ovarian cancer."

"I'm sorry," Marty responded with sadness in her voice and a sudden ache in her heart. She wondered if he had any children.

"You remind me of her," he said reminiscently. "I think it was the perfume you had on when you arrived. I thought it odd, a man having a scent of a woman, yet it threw me back in time some thirty years ago, well before I entered the monastic life. Bit of a swinger then, even after I got married. I was a real charmer, too, if you can believe it."

Marty got a sense that he quickly changed the subject from his wife to himself. Maybe what he just gave her was a last reminder of someone he truly loved and needed to let go forever because the pain was too deep. "You still are a charmer," Marty responded with a wink and got a feeling that he had become a monk out of guilt or remorse, maybe even blaming himself for her death. She had grown to really like Brother Mark. He was so warm-hearted and had a funny sense of humor; besides, he liked his Pinot. She thanked him, and the feeling was reciprocated. They hugged, and she went on her way. Marty felt a sadness come from him that she had not sensed before.

She took one last look at the monastery as she walked down the driveway and said, "*Adios, hermanos.*" She came to Redrock in fear of being sent to jail, imprisoned for the rest of her life. A woman out of control. She had felt alone, distraught and dispirited. No more than three days later, she was leaving, oddly enough a much fuller person than she had ever been in her entire life. She was prepared for what lay ahead, she felt, and then started to cry, for real this time. She questioned why she was so emotional and then assumed that it was because she was pregnant. When she reached the road, the sun crested over the mountain range, and she started her trek down to town to pick up her car.

Several vehicles passed her along the way. A few offered her a ride, but she waved them all on. She needed the solitude to contemplate her next course of action. When she neared the base of the mountain, she saw a helicopter fly overhead making its way towards the eastside of the San Gabriels, towards the desert, and then a siren off in the distance, possibly heading in the same direction as the helicopter. What she did not know was that it was for Brother Gregory who had been bitten by a rattlesnake in an attempt to collect the sparse devil's lips. In a poison stupor, he must have stumbled, hit his head on a rock and passed out. A few dirt bikers, hitting the same road as Brother Gregory, had stopped to urinate and just happened to find him lying on the ground. They tried using their cell phones but could not get reception. One of them headed into town, while the other stayed with Brother Gregory, but by the time the EMT arrived, he was already dead.

Chapter Eighty-Seven

Marty arrived at the storage facility. When she tried to key the lock to her space, it did not fit. She thought at first she was at the wrong space but, remembered seeing a Lusty Monk Mustard label on the door, so she was at the correct one. She then went inside the storage facility office and was greeted by the manager. He then handed her a wanted poster of her that some local sheriff had dropped off. He realized who she was and felt compelled to change the lock. He stated, "I'm supposed to call the cops if I happened to see you."

Marty said, "So, what can I do for you to look the other way?"

The manager said, "I don't know, but I was surprised to see you again knowing what kind of trouble you're in."

"Well, at least they didn't take my car," she said.

"I told the sheriff I hadn't seen you," he said.

Marty then reached into her knapsack and pulled out her Royal Crown bag, untied the drawstrings and pulled out the pear-shaped emerald belly button ring she had. She then handed the emerald towards the manager and said, "I'll give you this if you open up the storage for me."

He asked, "What is it?"

Marty responded, "It's a four-carat emerald that is worth a good deal of money. Several thousand."

His eyes and ears perked up. She placed it in his hand. He just looked at it and then looked her in the eyes and asked, "Why are you giving me this?"

Marty said solemnly, "Because you were kind to me."

The manager said, "Okay, so what are you going to do now?"

Marty said, "I guess, I'll have to turn myself in."

The manager said, "You know best." And he said as he handed the emerald back to Marty, "Just keep it. I'll open the storage for you."

She took the emerald back. They both walked to the storage, and the manager opened the lock. He then looked Marty in the eyes and said, "Best of luck to you."

Marty said, "Thank you." And then she handed him the emerald again. She insisted, "Take it and do something good with it." The manager reluctantly accepted the emerald, nodded his head as he thanked Marty and let her be.

Marty opened her car door and turned on her headlights and then closed the storage door while she stayed inside. She changed back into her own clothes, spritzed some of her perfume on and opened the storage door. She stepped into her car, turned the ignition, pulled out, got out of the car and shut the storage door. She got back in her car and realized the gas tank was almost empty. Went through her wallet and counted seventeen dollars and some change. She sped away to find the nearest gas station.

Marty pulled up to the gas pump, got out of her car and went inside the station. She first tried using her debit card in the ATM and as expected, her account was closed. She paid for twelve dollars worth of gas, some gum and a bottled water and was left with about two dollars and a handful of change to her name. While she filled her tank with gas, she stepped into the car and happened to look up at her visor. She saw the lottery ticket that John bought for her when they first met. Marty chuckled and said, "What the hell."

When the gas pump stopped, she replaced the nozzle and went back inside the station. She handed the clerk the lottery ticket and asked him to check it for her. When he did check the ticket, he looked at Marty in complete amazement and said with extreme excitement, "Do you realize what you have here?"

Marty shrugged and said, "No."

He said, "You've won the grand prize!"

Since Marty had never played or gambled in her life and, in fact, never paid attention to the lottery, she said, "So, what does that mean?"

The clerk handed Marty the lottery ticket and said, "That means that ticket is worth sixty-seven million dollars. You probably will clear twenty million or more."

Marty immediately thought that he was bullshitting her and said, "Are you kidding?"

He then handed her a ticket that showed the winning six numbers and the topper number, and it had clear as day the word "winner" printed across the bottom. He said, "Take a look."

Marty looked at the ticket and then looked at her ticket; the numbers all matched.

He said, "You better put that in a safe place somewhere until you cash it in."

Marty in utter disbelief said, "I can't believe it." And then in a daze, she stepped towards the door.

The clerk yelled out towards her, "Don't forget about me."

In her car again, she looked at the lottery ticket and just shook her head. It was unreal what had just occurred, winning that kind of money, yet she was grappling with turning herself in. She then opened the gift she had received from Brother Mark. It was wrapped in plain brown paper and she assumed there was a small book inside. She delicately broke the tape seals and peeled opened the package. She found a remarkable edition of *The Essence: A Guide to Botanical Perfumery* bound in a dark brown cloth with gold lettering. It was in very fine condition. She opened it up and noticed it had been barely read. It had been published in 1946 in London, England. It was first written by a Claude Henri Grasse in French in 1886 and then translated into English. It had a scent of cedar.

He must have had it stored away somewhere, she surmised, like his heart that he cloistered when his wife died.

Inside the book was a recipe and a small packet of the devil's lips. They were roughly three-quarters of an inch long by one-eighth of an inch wide, scarlet in color and were shaped like a pointed knife blade. She was not sure, since she had never seen them before, but had a sneaky suspicion they were. In any event, there was a small note that read:

Dear Marty,

Inserted is the recipe for our *diabolus labium* elixir. Remember that the devil's lips is optional. Well, it is a little story we made up. We found that it adds to the mystique, sort of an ironic parable. As if to say, in order to be happy you have to taste or drink of the devil's lips. Meaning, do we need to indulge ourselves in deadly sins or be tempted by the devil to feel some sort of rapture in our lives? On the contrary, but the devil's lips do have some very powerful immune agents. Use them in good health.

Here at Redrock, we achieve happiness and contentment not through some magic tonic, but through our dedication and devotion to God and humanity. That is why we have that smile on our faces, just in case you were wondering.

You are always welcome at Redrock.

Eternally yours,
Brother Mark

P.S. Remember to go easy on the butter. You don't want to ruin your girlish figure.

Her heart was warm with the love she felt from Brother Mark, but it was heavy with grief. Her eyes welled up, and then she heard a horn blow behind her. Someone wanted her to move so they could fill their car. She quickly started her car and wiped the tears from her eyes. She pulled out of the gas station and headed towards an intersection. Her thoughts and emotions were clouded as well as her eyes. She then glanced down at the lottery ticket and slipped it in the book, then looked at Brother Gregory's letter, and as she did, the intersection light turned red. Coming towards the intersection perpendicular to her was a semi-truck carrying livestock. Marty continued through the intersection and was immediately struck by the semi-truck, whereby Marty's car was crushed. The truck driver tried to brake, but Marty's car was quickly sandwiched between the frontend of the truck and another vehicle coming from the opposite direction as the truck. As that occurred, the backend of the semi swung out towards his right, breaking free from its mounts, and slammed against the traffic light pole. The backend of the semi opened, and almost immediately the cattle inside began to exit. The startled cattle scattered every which way as the traffic came to a halt.

Chapter Eighty-Eight

While Marty lay in a coma in a hospital with trauma to her head, several broken ribs, a fractured left hip and her right arm in a sling she was, nonetheless, under house arrest with a police officer out front of her private room. Inside the room was Marty's mother. She sat in a chair and was lucid. Then Marty's father entered. He stared at Marty for a moment and then turned to his ex-wife and acknowledged her by saying, "Lu."

She said softly, "You know she's pregnant."

He responded, "Yes, the doctor told me."

She asked, "Are you going to help her or be some Nero and watch her life burn up in flames? Because they're going to try to send her away for life."

He said, "Let's hope she recovers. That's the most important thing right now."

The mother said, "She wouldn't have been this way if you hadn't run off with that woman and sold the company."

The father agitatedly said, "Been what way? You really think she killed those chefs?"

The mother said, "You killed my brother, didn't you? She has your blood."

"And what about your family's blood? You haven't always been the model of sanity, you know. And let's not forget about Poppa Remy," he said.

During their debate over Marty's sanity, Cooz and Fajida stepped inside the room. Marty's father turned to Cooz and said, "Can I help you?"

"We just wanted to check in to see how she was doing. We're with the Los Feliz Police Department handling the case," Cooz said.

Marty's father interrupted him and said with raised ire, "What, you're here to see if she's able to stand trial?"

Cooz said, "Yes."

"I'll tell you this right here and now, this case will never see a courtroom with my daughter in it," Marty's father said confidently.

Cooz shot back, "Well, we'll try her in absentia if we have to."

Fajida said, "And we have plenty of motive and opportunity."

Marty's father said with a slight chuckle, "And the rest you'll let fate decide?"

And as he spoke, Marty regained some consciousness and said faintly, "Daddy, is that you?"

Her father quickly moved closer to Marty. He turned to her mother and said, "Go get the nurse." The mother got up and left the room while Cooz and Fajida peered in at Marty. The father stroked Marty's hair, pushing it away from her face and said, "Are you all right, baby?"

Marty asked, "What happened?"

Her father responded, "You were in an accident."

Marty said, "I was?" And then she peered out towards Cooz and Fajida and asked, "Who are they?"

He said, "They're detectives handling your case,"

Marty said, "What case?"

What had happened with Marty is that she lost all memory of the murders she committed, including Dominika and Harold the neighbor. And as later tests revealed, due to the injuries to her head, she most likely had lost other parts of her memory. And as the doctors would explain, it's like a computer's memory chip that crashes—some information gets purged or lost forever, some may float around in limbo, and some or most may be easily retrieved. Marty would come to realize—or not, depending on her memory—that she now had a dramatically increased sense of smell and a decrease in her appetite to kill. Yet she would not remember John, their love for each other and the sex they had.

Without a response from her father, she continued, "I'm hungry for pickled pig's feet and warm milky chai."

Fajida shot a glance at Cooz once she heard pickled pig's feet, thinking about Boo, and then a nurse, a doctor and Marty's mother entered the room. The nurse gently asked Cooz and Fajida to leave. And they did.

As Cooz and Fajida walked down the hospital corridor, Fajida said, mimicking Marty, "Who are they?" And then she continued, "What a performance that was. I thought she was Angela Jordan for a minute."

Cooz responded, "I wonder how many silver spoons can be measured in her life?"

"The father sounded pretty serious, though. Like he's prepared to do anything to protect his little girl," Fajida said, a little concerned.

"Well, he ran a multi-million-dollar pharmaceutical company with great success. I'd say that's serious enough," Cooz said. "And as much as I hate to admit it, he's got a lot of firepower behind him. You know our Attorney General, Spuds Florez?"

Fajida intently listening, "Yeah?"

"Well, they're connected. And I'll lay five-to-one odds that he shuts down this case by tomorrow," Cooz said.

Fajida asked, "So, how come you didn't tell us this before?"

"Just doing my job," Cooz said with a pinch of complacency because he knew that's how politics worked, no matter what his own beliefs were. Besides, the case was a little flimsy.

But Cooz was right. Two days later the Captain got a call. Since they only had circumstantial evidence against Martha Kittering, all charges against her were to be dropped immediately. Of course, it cost Marty to the tune of $650,000. Five hundred went into an undisclosed offshore account, $125,000 thousand went to her father's attorney who just made a phone call to his old schoolmate, and the remaining $25,000 went to Delilah Dish for her friendship and for good measure as a gift from Raspberry Truffle. But Marty had plenty of money and was left with a little more than $22 million from the grand prize lottery earnings.

As Cooz and Fajida stepped towards the elevator, the doors swung open, and both John Abruzzo and Evie Ann stepped out. They practically bumped into each other. It was an uncomfortable moment for each of them. Luckily, the day Evie Ann was visited by Marty and Fajida, she went home and cleaned her apartment inside and out, including throwing away the contents of the basket, since it was the day she set aside to perform the chore, and besides, she was highly upset, and cleaning always felt cathartic. She subsequently tossed the cloth napkin inside the basket into the wash with her other clothes, leaving no trace of poisonous mushrooms. When the police went to her house later that day with a search warrant, found nothing except a variety of herbs that were tested and found benign.

And when Cooz received Evie Ann's and Marty's phone records, they showed that communications were made to each other via text message, but they were all circumspect since Marty was nowhere near the San Gabriel Mountains the day that Cooz and Evie Ann were there, nor did any of the messages suggest foul play other than a mention of the day's events by Evie Ann. Needless to say, Evie Ann didn't want anything to do with Cooz after she felt violated by the police in her home and during the interrogation she received from Fajida and Jonesy while Cooz hid behind the glass encasement. As a result, Marty, Cooz and the District Attorney surmised, acted alone and was then charged with the murder of Bubba Arnet.

A curious thing happened only days after the charges against Marty were dropped. A secretary in the Los Feliz District Attorney's Office was going through a stack of misplaced files and found the photos of Raveneitzkya and Chef Bubba that Marty had sent, including the one where she was pricking him with a knife. Subsequently, Raveneiztkya was charged with the murder of Chef Bubba, extradited from New York, tried and convicted. When she was sentenced to death by lethal injection at Lenore State Prison by the judge, she stripped naked and flashed her bushy red bush at the judge to seduce him into a lesser sentence, to the shock of the courtroom. But it was to no avail and she was remanded for mental evaluation where she was found to be completely insane. Yet the judge eventually commuted her sentence to a private mental health facility and spa where he visited Raveneitzkya from time to time as a gesture of empathy, concern and personal interest.

Chapter Eighty-Nine

A couple of years after the chef murders took place and caused a stir in the culinary world and after the Ultimate Chef Challenge had a brief run and then was canceled by the Food Channel, Cooz and Janet Fink, to the surprise and dismay of many, after dating on and off for a period, decided to marry and went on their honeymoon to Maui in the Hawaiian Islands. Sadly, Boo could not make the trip, since Janet one day drove her down the road from their home in Laurel Canyon and tossed her out of the car to fend for herself after a one-sided argument over privacy, which Janet won. Boo would never be seen again; presumably, she was eaten by a coyote. As Cooz and Janet were in Maui, they perused the various gifts shops in the downtown area. They went into one shop that specialized in macadamia nuts—aptly called The Macadamia Nut—that offered all types of candies, oils, creams and packaged staples of the Hawaiian culture. They purchased some turtle candies, a body and face cream set and some individual packets of the nut for their flight back home. Cooz thought they were gifts for their family and friends back home, but Janet said, "Hell, no."

Then Janet wanted to go inside a perfume boutique called The Pearl Perfumery next door to The Macadamia Nut. In the display windows outside the boutique was a photo of Marty with her hair pulled back, lying on her belly in a sleek black dress, wearing a pair of diamond earrings and a string of pearls draped over her neck. Her legs were bent up and crossed, and she had a pair of stilettos on. She held a crystal cut-glass bottle of Dominika perfume and her steel, blue eyes were illuminated, matching the tint of the photo. Cooz and Janet paused for a moment to look at the photo with curiosity and then went inside.

They were greeted by one of the boutique's associates, an attractive local gal with long straight dark hair who was well tanned and dressed in a Hawaiian print dress, black heels and a string of pearls around her neck. As Marty, dressed in a black dress and diamond earrings, was about to step inside the boutique from the back room, she saw Cooz and Janet, stopped dead in her tracks and closed the black curtain that hung from the doorway. Marty's nanny, a twenty-two-year-old French gal with long blond hair named Monique, sung "Ma Cheri Amore" and fed lunch to Little Jackie, Marty's infant son, who had cherry-red hair and big brown eyes. Monique noticed that Marty was startled and asked, "What is it, *ma cherie?*"

Marty said, "Ghosts from the past," as she peered through the curtain.

Monique responded, "They didn't come to haunt you, did they?"

"Maybe," Marty said.

"You know what they say? Better to face the demons head on than let them control you and your thoughts," Monique mused.

"Hum, I most certainly agree," Marty said and stepped back inside the boutique towards Cooz and Janet, who were being given samples on their wrists of Dominika and the male version of the perfume, which was called Brother, by the associate.

Marty said to Cooz and Janet, "You like either of them?"

Both Cooz and Janet were dismayed by the presence of Marty. Janet looked Marty in the eyes and said, "Not really." And then she grabbed Cooz's arm and fled out the door.

The associate had a stunned look on her face as Marty ironically said, "I must have scared them. I have that affect on some people."

Moments later, Marty left the shop with Monique and Little Jackie. They walked down the row of shops and made their way towards the marina nearby. Monique pushed the stroller with Little Jackie inside and sang *Frere Jacques* to him in a soft tone. Marty said to Little Jackie,

"We're going to see Daddy." Little Jackie got excited as they stopped off at a café named Keahilani, which was half owned by Marty, the other half by none other than Roy, which served up an array of local fare with a Thai/Asian influence. Enrique and he had long split over a disagreement on the type of inn they wanted to open up, but not before Enrique had taken the interior furnishings they were going to use in their new place for a bed and breakfast inn he opened with his new life-mate, a pretty-faced lawyer named Raul Pimento.

Marty, Monique and Little Jackie met John, Marty's husband for the past two years. Even though Marty had lost all memory of him after her accident, his cologne had triggered her remembrance of him. They also met Fat Freddie who was now lean and just as handsome as his father, though he was still referred to as Fat Freddie, and Christina, who was pregnant. A Catalina Morgan 440 yacht with a length of almost forty-six feet and mainsail of four hundred-fifty square feet and cherry-red hull named *My Cherry II* sat out in the marina. It was a wedding gift from Marty to John. Roy and Evie Ann, Roy's sous chef, brought them some fresh grilled Mahi Mahi with a teriyaki glaze that they prepared with a guava salsa, fried Maui onions, ginger and red chilies and poi poi flan to everyone's enjoyment.

Later that night, the boutique was broken into. It was Cooz. He had been able to disarm the alarm system and get in the back door with ease. He looked around with a flashlight in the dark for any evidence that could implicate Martha Kittering for the murders back in Los Feliz. In the back of his mind, he knew that Raveneitzkya Fukovneyev was not their gal. It had to be Martha. He rummaged through the files and papers on her desk and through a few books she had on a shelf. He went through several of her recipe books. One in particular from Chapman fell from the shelf and opened to a page that had a small folded paper marker inside. On the page was a recipe for peach scones. Instinct took over, and Cooz unfolded the marker. "Walters" was scribbled on it. Cooz paused for a second to recall if that was one of the hardware stores Willis mentioned in their conversation—it was. He then replaced the book. All the while, a surveillance camera recorded every move he made.

Chapter Ninety

The following morning Marty, John, Fat Freddie, Christina, Monique and Little Jackie went sailing off some of the Hawaiian Isles on *My Cherry II*. They all took turns snorkeling in pairs as they soaked in the morning sun. As they dropped anchor near the Pearl and Hermes Atoll, Marty looked out towards the light greenish-blue water and the coral reef below and said, "Oh, look a pair of black-footed albatrosses." They all looked over at the birds as they admired the pristine waters.

John said as he pointed along the perimeter of the atoll, "I believe they named this area the Pearl and Hermes Atoll after two whaling ships that sunk here."

Marty coyly shot, "Lovely. You know how I am with omens." John just smirked.

Christina enthusiastically yelled and pointed out near the boat while she held onto Little Jackie, "There's a sea turtle." Marty briefly thought that a turtle option in addition to the chicken or seafood yellow Thai curry they offered at the restaurant with ginger, coconut milk, lime and red chilies would probably go over well. She reminded herself to tell Roy about it, so they could order turtle from their supplier.

Marty then edged herself to the side of the rail and dropped into the ocean, holding onto the facemask and snorkel. She only had a two-piece bathing suit and a pair of neoprene gloves on, so John, concerned about her swimming around the coral said, "Just be careful out there."

Marty gave John a conciliatory smile and then dropped into the water. She then swam briefly backward and put her facemask on. She went snorkeling above the atoll to gather some king's thistle, which she used to make her elixir. As she swam from one spot to another, she happened to hitch one fin on a small ledge and leaned against the coral with her head barely above the water, so she could pick the thistle that grew on a small plateau. Within an instant the ledge broke off and then her leg slipped down into a crevice while she struck her head against the coral, giving her a good knock. Her snorkel was only inches from the top of the water as her lower limb was lodged in the crevice. She slowly ran out of breath. She sensed tragedy and saw a vision of a woman in a bathtub convulsing.

Marty was just barely in the view of the yacht when she lost consciousness. John looked over where Marty had been only a minute ago. He took notice of the color change in the water and immediately dove in after her. He was able to release her leg and bring her back to the yacht. Fat Freddie hurriedly helped get Marty back onboard with everyone obviously distressed as they saw her unconscious with a bloodied forehead and leg. John furiously took her mask and snorkel off and bellowed, "Marty, Marty." And when he was just about to resuscitate her, she choked the seawater out of her mouth and then looked up at John with her dark blue sparkling eyes and smirked mischievously.

Coming Soon!

A Murder in the Kitchen *series*
Deadly Essence
Book 2
By Randy Shamlian

Deadly Essence a must-read sequel to **Deadly Recipe**, a suspense thriller with food, psycho-sexuality, murder and self-discovery.

After several years where all was quiet on the Hawaiian shores of Maui, Marty our main protagonist who operates a perfumery and a restaurant has a snorkeling accident, which awakens her past inclinations. Several years earlier she had murdered a handful of chefs as a result of her dislike of their personalities and behaviors. This all was forgotten in her mind after a car crash…

For more information
visit: www.SpeakingVolumes.us

On Sale Now!

At night, on a cliff in the Arizona desert, Colonel Sam Sawyer asks Rita Kelly, "Do you love me, Rita?" Once they were engaged to be married, but Native American Johnnie Lonetree, Sam's best friend, shattered that…

For more information
visit: www.SpeakingVolumes.us